*Also available by **Alex Kava***
from MIRA® Books

SPLIT SECOND
THE SOUL CATCHER
AT THE STROKE OF MADNESS
ONE FALSE MOVE

ALEX KAVA

A PERFECT EVIL

MIRA® BOOKS

MIRA is a registered trademark of Harlequin Enterprises Limited,
used under licence.

First published in Great Britain in 2000. This edition 2005.
MIRA Books, Eton House, 18-24 Paradise Road,
Richmond, Surrey, TW9 1SR

© S. M. Kava 2000

ISBN 0 7783 0078 1

58-0505

Printed and bound in Spain
by Litografia Rosés S.A., Barcelona

In loving memory of
Robert (Bob) Shoemaker
(1922–1998)
whose perfect good continues to inspire.

Author's Note

This is a work of fiction;
however, I'd like to extend my heartfelt
sympathy to any parent who has ever lost a
child to a senseless act of violence.

I owe my deepest gratitude and appreciation
to all those whose support and expertise made
this fantastic journey possible.

Special thanks to:

Philip Spitzer, my agent, who enthusiastically
offered to represent this book, then made it his
personal mission to see it published. Philip, you
are my hero.

Patricia Sierra, fellow author, for generously sharing
her wisdom, her wit and her friendship.

Amy Moore-Benson, my editor, for her tenacity,
her keen insights and her ability to make the editing
process painless and rewarding.

Dianne Moggy and all the professionals at MIRA®
Books for their efforts and resolve to make this book
a success.

Ellen Jacobs for always saying the right thing at just
the right time.

Sharon Car, my writing cohort, for all those lunches
spent commiserating with and encouraging me.

LaDonna Tworek, who helped me keep my
perspective and encouraged me early on to hang
in there.

Jeanie Shoemaker Mezger and John Mezger, who listened over all those free, delicious dinners they fed me.

Bob Kava for patiently answering all my questions about firearms.

Mac Payne, who gave me something to prove.

My parents, Edward and Patricia Kava, especially my mum for lighting all those candles of hope.

Writing, for the most part, is a solitary act, but certainly wouldn't be possible for me without the loving support of my family and friends. Thanks also must go to Patti El-Kachouti, Marlene Haney, Nicole Keller, Kenny and Connie Kava, Natalie Cummings, Sandy Rockwood and Margaret Shoemaker.

Finally, thanks to Bob Shoemaker. This wouldn't have been the type of book Bob would even have read, but that would not have stopped him from being proud of me and telling everyone he met about it.

PROLOGUE

Nebraska State Penitentiary
Lincoln, Nebraska
Wednesday, July 17

"Bless me Father, for I have sinned." Ronald Jeffreys' raspy monotone made the phrase a challenge rather than a confession.

Father Stephen Francis stared at Jeffreys' hands, mesmerized by the large knuckles and stubby fingers, nails bitten to the quick. The fingers twisted—no, strangled—the corner of his blue government-issue shirt. The old priest imagined those same fingers twisting and choking the life out of little Bobby Wilson.

"Is that how we start?"

Jeffreys' voice startled the priest. "That's fine," he answered quickly.

His sweaty palms stuck to the leather Bible. His collar was suddenly too tight. The prison's deathwatch chamber didn't have enough air for both men. The gray concrete walls boxed them in with only one tiny window, black with night. The pungent smell of green pepper and onion nauseated the old priest. He glanced at the remnants of Jeffreys' last supper, scattered bits of pizza crust and puddles of sticky soda. A fly buzzed over crumbs that were once cheesecake.

"What's next?" Jeffreys asked, waiting for instructions.

Father Francis couldn't think, not with Jeffreys' unflinching stare. Not with the noise of the crowd outside the prison, down below in the parking lot. The chants grew louder with the approach of midnight and the full effect of alcohol. It was a raucous celebration, a morbid excuse for an outdoor frat party. "Fry, Jeffreys, fry," over and over again, like a childhood rhyme or a pep-rally song, melodic and contagious, sick and frightening.

Jeffreys, however, appeared immune to the sound. "I'm not sure I remember how this works. What's next?"

Yes, what came next? Father Francis' mind was completely blank. Fifty years of hearing confessions, and his mind was blank. "Your sins," he blurted out over the tightness in his throat. "Tell me your sins."

Now, Jeffreys hesitated. He unraveled the hem of his shirt, wrapping the thread around his index finger, pulling it so tight that the tip bulged red. The priest stole a long glance at the man slumped in the straight-backed chair. This wasn't the same man from the grainy newspaper photos or the quick television shots. With his head and beard shaved, Jeffreys looked exposed, almost impish and younger than his twenty-six years. He had gained bulk in his six years on death row, but he still possessed a boyishness. Suddenly, it struck Father Francis as sad that this boyish face would never wear wrinkles or laugh lines. Until Jeffreys looked up at him. Cold blue eyes held his. Ice-blue like glass—sharp glass—vacant and transparent. Yes, this was what evil looked like. The priest blinked and turned his head.

"Tell me your sins," Father Francis repeated, this time disappointed in the tremor in his voice. He couldn't breathe. Had Jeffreys sucked all the air out of the room on purpose? He cleared his throat, then said, "Those sins for which you are truly sorry."

Jeffreys stared at him. Then without warning, he barked out a laugh. Father Francis jumped, and Jeffreys laughed even louder. The priest gripped his Bible with unsteady fingers while watching Jeffreys' hands. Why had he insisted the guard remove the handcuffs? Even God couldn't rescue the stupid. Drops of perspiration slid down the priest's back. He thought about fleeing, escaping before Jeffreys realized one last murder would cost him nothing more. Then he remembered the door was locked from the outside.

The laughter stopped as suddenly as it had begun. Silence.

"You're just like the rest of them." The low guttural accusation came from somewhere deep and dead. Yet, Jeffreys smiled, revealing small, sharp teeth, the incisors longer than the rest. "You're waiting for me to confess to something I didn't do.'' His hands ripped the bottom of his shirt, thin strips, a slow grating sound.

"I don't understand what you mean." Father Francis reached to loosen his collar, dismayed to find the tremor now in his hands. "I was under the impression you had asked for a priest. That you wanted to offer up your confession."

"Yes...yes, I do." The monotone was back. Jeffreys hesitated but only for a moment. "I killed Bobby Wilson," he said as calmly as if ordering takeout. "I put my hands...my fingers around his throat. At first, he made a sputtering noise, a sort of gagging, and then there was no noise." His voice was hushed and restrained, almost clinical—a well-rehearsed speech.

"He kicked just a little. A jerk, really. I think he knew he was going to die. He didn't fight much. He didn't even fight when I was fucking him." He stopped, checking Father Francis' face, looking for shock and smiling when he found it.

"I waited until he was dead before I cut him. He didn't feel a thing. So I cut him again and again and again. Then, I fucked him one last time." He cocked his head to the side, suddenly distracted. Had he finally noticed the celebration outside?

Father Francis waited. Could it be the massive pounding of his heart that Jeffreys heard? Like something out of Poe, it banged against the old priest's chest, betraying him just like his hands.

"I've already confessed once before," Jeffreys continued. "Right after it happened, but the priest... Let's just say he was a little surprised. Now I'm confessing to God, you understand? I'm confessing that I killed Bobby Wilson." The ripping continued, now in quick, jerky motions. "But I didn't kill those other two boys. Do you hear me?" His voice rose above the monotone. "I didn't kill the Harper or the Paltrow kid."

Silence, then Jeffreys' lips slowly twisted into a smirk. "But then, God already knows that. Right, Father?"

"God does know the truth," Father Francis said, trying to stare into the cold blue eyes but flinching and quickly looking away again. What if his own guilt should somehow reveal itself?

"They want to execute me because they think I'm some serial killer who murders little boys," Jeffreys spat through clenched teeth. "I killed Bobby Wilson, and I enjoyed it. Maybe I even deserve to die for that. But God knows I didn't kill those other boys. Somewhere out there, Father, there's still a monster." Another twisted smile. "And he's even more hideous than me."

Metal clanked against metal down the hall. Father Francis jerked, sending the Bible crashing to the floor. This time Jeffreys didn't laugh. The old priest held Jeffreys' stare, but neither man made an attempt to pick up the holy book. Were they coming to take Jeffreys away? It seemed too soon, although no one expected a stay of execution.

"Are you sorry for your sins?" Father Francis whispered as if back at the confessional window in St. Margaret's.

Yes, there were footsteps coming down the hall, coming toward them. It was time. Jeffreys sat paralyzed, listening to the *click-clack* of heels marching, getting closer and closer.

"Are you sorry for your sins?" Father Francis repeated, this time more insistent, almost a command. Oh, dear God, it was hard to breathe. The chants from the parking lot grew louder and louder, squeezing through the tightly sealed window.

Jeffreys stood up. Again, his eyes held Father Francis'. The locks grunted open, echoing against the concrete walls. Jeffreys flinched at the sound, caught himself, then stood straight with shoulders back. Was he frightened? Father Francis searched Jeffreys' eyes, but couldn't see beyond the steel blue.

"Are you sorry for your sins?" He tried once more, unable to offer absolution without an answer.

The door opened, sucking the remaining air from the room. Square-shouldered guards clogged the doorway.

"It's time," one of the men said.

"It's show time, Father." Jeffreys' lips curled over gritted teeth. The blue eyes were sharp and clear, but vacant. Jeffreys turned to the three uniformed men and offered his wrists.

Father Francis winced as the shackles snapped. Then he listened to the boot heels clicking, accompanied by the pathetic *shuffle-clank, shuffle-clank* all the way down the long hall.

A stale breeze seeped in through the open door. It cooled his wet, clammy skin and sent a shiver down his back. He gulped greedily at the air, limited to short, asthmatic gasps. Finally, the thunder in his chest eased, leaving behind a tight-fisted ache.

"God help Ronald Jeffreys," Father Francis whispered to no one.

At least Jeffreys had told the truth. He had not killed all three boys. And Father Francis knew this, not because Jeffreys had said so. He knew, because three days ago the faceless monster who had murdered Aaron Harper and Eric Paltrow had confessed to him through the black, wire-mesh confessional at St. Margaret's. And because of his holy vows, he wasn't able to tell a single soul.

Not even Ronald Jeffreys.

CHAPTER 1

Five miles outside Platte City, Nebraska
Friday, October 24

Nick Morrelli wished the woman beneath him wore less makeup. He knew it was ridiculous. He listened to her soft moans—purrs really. Like a cat, she slithered against him, rubbing her silky thighs up and down the sides of his torso. She was more than ready for him. And yet, all he could think about was the blue powder smeared on her eyelids. Even with the lights out, it remained etched in his mind like fluorescent, glow-in-the-dark paint.

"Oh, baby, your body is so hard," she purred in his ear as she ran her long fingernails up his arms and over his back.

He slid off her before she discovered that not all of his body was hard. What was wrong with him? He needed to concentrate. He licked her earlobe and nuzzled her neck, then moved down to where he really wanted to be. Instinctively, his mouth found one of her breasts. He ravished it with soft, wet kisses. She moaned even before his tongue flicked at her nipple. He loved those sounds a woman made—the short little gasp, then the low moan. He waited for them, then wrapped his tongue around her nipple and sucked it into his mouth. Her back arched, and she quivered. He leaned into her, absorbing the shiver, her soft, smooth flesh trembling against him. Normally, that reaction alone would immediately give him an erection. Tonight, nothing.

Jesus, was he losing his touch? No, he was too young to be having this problem. After all, he was four years away from forty.

When in the world had he started keeping track of his age by its distance from forty?

"Oooh, lover, don't stop!"

He didn't even realize he *had* stopped. She groaned impatiently and began moving her hips up and down, slowly, with a sensuous rhythm. Yes, she was definitely ready for him. And he was definitely not ready. Just once he wished women would use his name instead of baby, lover, stud muffin, whatever. Did women worry about yelling out the wrong name, too?

Her fingers twisted into his short, thick hair. She yanked hard, the streak of pain surprising him. Then she pulled his face back to her breasts. In the dim light, he noticed that the triangle of tanned skin was crooked. The point overlapped onto the underside of her breast. What was wrong with him? A beautiful blonde wanted him. Why didn't her breathless anticipation arouse him? He needed to focus. It all felt too mechanical, too routine. Nevertheless, he would compensate again using his fingers and tongue. After all, he had a reputation to maintain.

He began the descent down her body, devouring her with kisses and nibbles. Her body squirmed beneath his touch. She was writhing and gasping for breath even before his teeth tugged at her lace panties. He kissed his way to the inside of her thighs. Suddenly, a sound stopped him. He strained to hear from under the bedcovers.

"No, please don't stop," she groaned, pulling him back into her.

There it was again. Pounding. Someone was at the front door.

"I'll be right back." Nick gently pushed her hands away and stumbled out of bed, disentangling himself from the sheets and almost tripping. He pulled on jeans as he checked the clock on the nightstand—10:36.

Even in the dark, he knew every creak in the staircase by heart. Out of habit, he found himself tiptoeing, though his parents hadn't slept in the old farmhouse for over five years.

The knock was louder and more insistent now.

"Hold on a minute," he called out impatiently, yet relieved by the interruption.

When he opened the door, Nick recognized Hank Ashford's

son, though he couldn't recall his name. The boy was sixteen or seventeen, a linebacker on the football team and built like he could move two or three players at a time off the line of scrimmage. Yet, tonight, as he stood on Nick's front porch, the kid slouched with his hands stashed in his pockets, eyes wild and face pale. He shivered despite the sweaty forehead.

"Sheriff Morrelli, you have to come…on Old Church Road…please, you have to…"

"Is someone hurt?" The crisp night air stung Nick's bare skin. It felt good.

"No, it's not…he's not hurt…Oh, God, Sheriff, it's awful." The boy looked back toward his car. It was only then that Nick saw the girl in the front seat. Even looking into the headlights, he could see she was crying.

"What's going on?" he demanded, sending the boy into a speechless, arm-crossing dance, shifting his weight from one leg to the other.

What stupid game had they been playing this time? Last week, the night before homecoming, a group of boys had played chicken with a couple of Jake Turner's tractors. The loser had tipped over into a rain-filled ditch, pinning himself under the water. The boy was lucky he had escaped with only broken ribs and the flimsy punishment of sitting out two football games.

"What the hell happened this time?" Nick found himself yelling at the shivering linebacker.

"We found…down off Old Church Road…in the tall grass. Oh God, we found…we found a body."

"A body?" Nick wasn't sure he believed him. "You mean a dead body?" Was the boy drunk? Was he stoned?

The boy nodded, tears filling his eyes. He scraped the sleeve of his sweatshirt across his face and looked from Nick to his girlfriend, then back to Nick.

"Hang on a minute."

Nick stepped back inside, letting the screen door slam behind him. They had probably imagined it. Or maybe it was an early Halloween prank. They'd been out partying. Both of them were probably stoned. He pulled on his boots, bypassing socks, then grabbed his shirt from the sofa, where it had been taken off him earlier in the evening. He was annoyed to find his fingers shaking as he buttoned the front.

"Nick, what is it?"

The voice from the top of the stairs startled him. He had forgotten about Angie. Roused from bed, her long, blond hair was ruffled and floated around her shoulders. The blue eye makeup was hardly noticeable from this distance. She wore one of his T-shirts. It was transparent in the hallway's soft light. Now, looking up at her, he couldn't imagine why he had been relieved to leave her.

"I've got to check something out."

"Is someone hurt?"

She sounded more curious than concerned. Was she only looking for a bit of gossip? Something to share with the morning coffee drinkers at Wanda's Diner?

"I don't know."

"Did someone find the Alverez boy?"

Jesus, he hadn't even thought of that. The boy had been missing since Sunday, gone, taken before he began his newspaper route.

"No, I don't think so," Nick told her. Even the FBI was certain the boy had more than likely been taken by his father, who they were still trying to locate. It was a simple custody battle. And this was simply teenage kids playing tricks on each other.

"I might be a while, but you're welcome to stay."

He grabbed the keys to his Jeep and found Ashford sitting on the front steps, his face buried in his hands.

"Let's go." Nick gently yanked a handful of sweatshirt and pulled the boy to his feet. "Why don't the two of you get in with me."

Nick wished he had taken time to put on underwear. Now, in the cramped Jeep, the stiff denim scraped against him every time he put the clutch in and shifted. To make matters worse, Old Church Road was filled with ruts from the rains of the week before. The gravel popped against the Jeep as he weaved from side to side, avoiding the deep gashes in the road.

"What exactly were you two doing out on this washboard?" As soon as he said it, he realized the obvious. He didn't need to be seventeen to remember all the benefits of an old deserted gravel road. "Never mind," he added before either of them had time to answer. "Just tell me where I'm going."

"It's about another mile, just past the bridge. There's a pasture road that runs along the river."

"Sure, okay."

He noticed Ashford wasn't stuttering anymore. Perhaps he was sobering up. The girl, however, who sat between Nick and the boy, hadn't said a word.

Nick slowed down as the Jeep bumped across the wood-slatted bridge. He found the pasture road even before Ashford pointed it out. They bounced and slid over the dirt road that consisted of rutted tire tracks filled with muddy water.

"All the way down to the trees?" Nick glanced at Ashford, who only nodded and stared straight ahead. As they approached the shelter belt, the girl hid her face in the boy's sweatshirt.

Nick stopped, killed the engine, but left on the headlights. He reached across the two of them and pulled a flashlight from the glove compartment.

"That door sticks," he said to Ashford. He watched the two exchange a glance. Neither made any attempt to leave the Jeep.

"You never said we'd have to look at it again," the girl whispered to Ashford as she clung to his arm.

Nick slammed the car door. Its echo sliced through the silence. There was nothing around for miles. No traffic, no farm lights. Even the night animals seemed to be asleep. He stood outside the Jeep, waiting. The boy's eyes met his, but still he made no motion to leave the Jeep. Instead of insisting, Nick pointed the flashlight toward an area down by the riverbank. The stream of light shot through thick grass, catching just a glimpse of rolling water. Ashford's eyes followed. He hesitated, looked back at Nick and nodded.

The tall grass swished around Nick's knees, camouflaging the mud that sucked at his boots. Jesus, it was dark out. Even the orange moon hid behind a gauze of clouds. Leaves rustled behind him. He spun around and shot a stream of light from tree to tree. Was there movement? There, in the brush? He could have sworn a shadow ducked from the light. Or was it just his imagination?

Nick strained to see beyond the thick branches. He held his breath and listened. Nothing. Probably just the wind. He listened again and realized there was no wind. A shiver caught him off guard, and he wished he had brought a jacket. This was crazy. He refused to be suckered by some high-school prank. The sooner he checked it out, the sooner he could be back in his warm bed.

The squashing sound grew louder the closer he got to the river. It was an effort to walk, pulling each foot out and carefully placing it to avoid slipping. His new boots would be ruined. He could already feel his feet getting wet. No socks, no underwear, no jacket.

"Damn it," he muttered. "This better be good." He was going to be mad as hell if he found a group of teenagers playing hide-and-seek.

The flashlight caught something glittering in the mud, close to the water. He locked his eyes on the spot and quickened his pace. He was almost there, almost out of the tall grass. Suddenly, he tripped. He lost his balance and crashed down hard, with his elbows breaking his fall. The flashlight flew out of his hand and into the black water, a tunnel of light spiraling to the bottom.

He ignored the sting shooting up his arms. The sucking mud pulled at him as he pushed himself to his hands and knees. A rancid smell clung to him, more than just the stench of the river. The silvery object lay almost within reach, and now he could tell it was a cross-shaped medallion. The chain was broken and scattered in the mud.

He glanced back to see what had caused his fall. Something solid. He expected to see a fallen tree. But not more than a yard away was a small, white body nestled in the mud and leaves.

Nick scrambled to his feet, his knees weak, his stomach in his throat. The smell was more noticeable now, and it filled the air, stinging his nostrils. He approached the body slowly as if not wanting to wake the boy, who looked asleep despite those wide eyes staring up at the stars. Then he saw the boy's slashed throat and mangled chest, the skin ripped open and peeled back. That's when his stomach lurched and his knees caved in.

CHAPTER 2

"All it takes is one bad apple," Christine Hamilton pounded out on the keyboard. Then she hit the delete key and watched the words disappear. She'd never finish the article. She leaned back to steal a glance at the hall clock—the lighted beacon in the tunnel of darkness. Almost eleven o'clock. Thank God, Timmy had a sleepover.

Janitorial services had shut off the hall light again. Just another reminder of how important the "Living Today" section was. At the end of the dark hall, she saw the newsroom's light glowing under the door that segregated the departments. Even at this distance, she could hear the wire services and fax machines buzzing. On the other side of that door, a half-dozen reporters and editors guzzled coffee and churned out last-minute articles and revisions. Just on the other side of that door, news was being made while she fussed over apple pie.

She whipped open a file folder and flipped through the notes and recipes. Over a hundred ways to slice, dice, puree and bake apples, and she couldn't care less. Perhaps her clever wit had run dry, used up on last week's hot little tomato dishes and a dozen ways to sneak fresh vegetables into your family's diet. She knew her journalism degree was rusty, thanks to Bruce's pigheadedness and his insistence that he wear the pants in the family. Too bad the asshole couldn't keep his pants on.

She slammed the folder shut and tossed it across her desk, watching it slide off and scatter clippings all over the cracked linoleum floor. How long would she remain bitter? No, the real question was, how long would it hurt? Why did it still have to hurt like hell? After all, it had been over a year.

She shoved away from the computer terminal and raked her fingers through her thick mass of blond hair. It needed to be trimmed, and she tried to remember how much time she had before the roots would start darkening. The dye job was a new touch, a divorce present to herself. The initial results had been rewarding. Turning heads was a new experience. If only she could remember to schedule the hairstylist like everything else in her life.

She ignored the building's no smoking rule and slapped a cigarette out of the pack she kept in her handbag. Quickly, she lit it and sucked in, waiting for the nicotine to calm her. Before she exhaled, she heard a door slam. She smashed the cigarette into a dessert plate that bulged with too many lipstick-covered butts for a person trying to quit. The footsteps echoed down the hall in quick bursts. She grabbed the plate and searched for a hiding place while swatting away the smoke. In a mad panic, she dumped the plate into the trash can under her desk. The stoneware shattered against the metal side just as Pete Dunlap entered the room.

"Hamilton. Good, you're still here." He swiped a hand over his weathered face in an unsuccessful attempt to remove the exhaustion. Pete had been with the *Omaha Journal* for almost fifty years, starting as a carrier. Despite the white hair, bifocals and arthritic hands, he was one of the few who could single-handedly put out the paper, having worked in every department.

"Major writer's block." Christine smiled, trying to explain why anyone would be working late in the "Living Today" section. She was relieved to see Pete instead of Charles Schneider, the usual night editor, who commandeered the place like a Nazi storm trooper.

"Bailey called in sick. Russell's still finishing up on Congressman Neale's sex scandal, and I just sent Sanchez to cover a three-car smashup on Highway 50. There's some ruckus out by the river on Old Church Road in Sarpy County. Ernie can't make out too much from the radio dispatch, but a whole slew of patrol cars are on their way. Now, it could just be some drunk kids playing with their daddies' tractors again. I know you're not part of the news team, Hamilton, but would you mind checking it out?''

Christine tried to contain her excitement. She hid her grin by turning back to the half-baked article on her computer screen. Finally, a chance at real news, even if it was a bunch of drunk teenagers.

''I'll cover your ass with Whitman on whatever you're working on,'' Pete said, misreading her hesitation.

''Okay. I suppose I can check it out for you.'' She chose her words carefully to emphasize that she was doing him a favor. Although she had been on the staff for only a year, she knew that journalists were promoted more quickly due to favors than talent.

''Take the interstate since Highway 50's probably tied up with that accident. Take exit 372 to Highway 66. Old Church Road is about six miles south on 66.''

She almost interrupted him. As a teenager she had made out on Old Church Road many times. However, one slip-up could dismantle all her work to shed her country roots. So, instead, she jotted down some directions.

''Get back here before one so we can get a couple paragraphs in the morning edition.''

''Will do.'' She slung her handbag over her shoulder and tried not to skip down the hall.

''Now, if I could just get Russell to write half as fast as he talks, I'd be a happy man,'' she heard Pete grumble as the door closed behind her.

Safe in the dark parking lot, she twirled once and shouted, ''Yes!'' to the concrete wall. This was her chance to get on the other side of the door, to go from recipes and household anecdotes to real news. Whatever was happening out at the river, she planned to capture all the nitty-gritty drama. And if there was no story...well, surely a good reporter could dig something up.

CHAPTER 3

He smashed through the branches, the cracking wood exploding in the dark silence. Were they following? Were they close behind? He didn't dare look back. Suddenly, he skidded on the mud, lost his balance and slid down the riverbank. He crashed knee-deep into ice-cold water. His arms and legs flayed in a panic, splashing water like claps of thunder. He dropped to his knees, burying his sweat-drenched body, sinking into the silt until he was up to his chin in the rolling river. The current sloshed against him, jerking him, threatening to sweep him back to where he had just escaped.

The cold water numbed the convulsions. Now, if only he could breathe. The gasps racked his chest and stabbed at his side. Breathe, he commanded himself as his lungs strangled for air. He hiccuped and swallowed a stomachful of the river, choking and gagging most of it back up.

He couldn't see the spotlights anymore. Perhaps he had run far enough. He listened, straining over his own gasps.

There were no running footsteps, no yelping bloodhounds, no racing engines. It had been a close call—the guy with the flashlight. Was it possible the intruder hadn't seen him crouched in the grass? Yes, he was sure no one had followed him.

He shouldn't have come tonight. It had become a stupid habit, a dangerous risk, a wonderful addiction, a spiritual hard-on. The shame spread through him, liquid and hot despite the cold water. No, he shouldn't have come. But no one had seen him. No one had followed him. He was safe. And now, finally, the boy was safe, too.

CHAPTER 4

The rancid smell clung to Nick. He wanted to crawl out of his clothes, but the scent of river and blood was already soaked deep into his pores. He peeled off his shirt and thanked Bob Weston for the FBI windbreaker. The sleeves stopped six inches above his wrists, and the fabric stretched tight across his chest. The zipper stuck halfway up. He knew he must look and smell like a putz. His suspicions were confirmed when he saw Eddie Gillick, one of his deputies, elbow his way through the crowd of FBI agents, uniformed cops and other deputies just to hand Nick a damp towel.

The scene looked pre-Halloween. Blinding searchlights teetered from branches. Yellow tape flapped around trees. The sizzle and smoke of night flares mixed with that awful smell of death. And in the middle of the macabre scene lay the little, white ghost of a boy, asleep in the grass.

In his two years as sheriff, Nick Morrelli had pulled three victims from car crashes. The adrenaline had erased the sight of tangled metal and flesh. He had witnessed one gunshot wound—a minor scrape, someone cleaning his gun while drinking a pint of whiskey. He had broken up numerous fistfights, sustaining his own cuts and bruises. Nothing, however, had prepared him for this.

"Channel Nine is here." Gillick pointed at the new set of headlights bumping down the path. The bright orange nine emblazoned on the top of the van glowed in the dark.

"Shit. How did they find out?"

"Police scanner. Probably have no idea what's going on, just that something is."

"Get Lloyd and Adam to keep them as far from that line of trees as possible. No cameras, no interviews, no sneak peeks. That goes for the rest of the bloodsuckers when they get here." That was all he needed—a stint on the morning news in his clown jacket and muddy jeans revealing his incompetence to the entire state.

"Oh, good. Another fuckin' set of tire tracks," Weston said to the agents who were on their knees working in the mud, but looked at Nick to make sure he knew the comment was meant for him.

Nick's face grew hot, but he swallowed his response and walked away. Weston made it no secret he thought Nick was a small-town hick of a sheriff. They had been at each other's throats since Sunday when Danny Alverez had disappeared into thin air, leaving behind a brand-new bike and a bagful of unde-livered newspapers. Nick had wanted to call in the masses to search fields and parks, while Weston had insisted they wait for a ransom note that never arrived. Nick had succumbed to Wes-ton's twenty-five years of FBI experience instead of listening to his gut.

Why didn't he buy Weston's suspicions that the boy had sim-ply been taken by his disgruntled father? A father who had been enraged with his ex-wife for keeping him away from his only child. Hell, the paper was full of similar cases. When they couldn't locate Major Alverez, it only made even more sense. So why wouldn't Nick listen to Special Agent Bob Weston, despite his irrational dislike of the man?

From the very beginning, Nick resented Weston's arrogance. At five feet six inches, he reminded Nick of a little Napoleon, always using his wiseass mouth to compensate for his small frame. Weston was a good six inches shorter than Nick and a skinny bit of a man compared to Nick's athletic build. Yet to-night, anything Weston said made Nick feel small. He knew he had screwed up, from contaminating a crime scene to not secur-ing a large enough area to bringing in too goddamn many offi-cers. So, he deserved Weston's put-downs. Now he wondered if Weston had even given him the too-small jacket on purpose.

Nick saw George Tillie making his way through the crowd,

and he was relieved to see the familiar face. George looked as if he had come straight out of bed. His sport jacket was crumpled and misbuttoned over a pink nightshirt. His gray hair stuck up everywhere. His face sagged with deep lines and gray fuzz. He carried his little black bag, hugging it to his chest as he stepped carefully through the thick mud in fuzzy slippers. If Nick wasn't mistaken, the slippers had little ears and dog snouts. He smiled and wondered how George had ever made it past the FBI sentries.

"George," Nick called and almost laughed when George raised his eyebrows at Nick's shoddy appearance. "The boy's over here." He took George's elbow and let the old coroner lean on him as they plodded through the mud and the crowd.

An officer with a Polaroid camera flashed one last picture of the scene, then made room for them. One look at the boy, and George froze. His slumped shoulders straightened, and his face went white.

"Oh, dear God. Not again."

CHAPTER 5

From a mile away, the pasture was lit up like a football stadium on game night. Christine stomped on the accelerator, weaving her car through the gravel.

Something big was definitely happening. The excitement fluttered in her stomach. Her heart pounded rapidly. Even her palms were sweaty. This was better than sex, or what she could remember of sex.

The police dispatch gave little information. "Officer requests immediate assistance and backup."

It could mean anything. As she skidded into the pasture road, her excitement only grew. Rescue vehicles, two TV vans, five sheriff cruisers and a slew of other unmarked vehicles were scattered at haphazard angles in the mud. Three sheriff deputies guarded the scene, which was cordoned off with yellow crime-scene tape. Crime-scene tape—this was serious. Definitely not some drunk teenagers.

Then she remembered the kidnapping—the paperboy whose face had been plastered over every newscast and newspaper since the beginning of the week. Had a ransom drop been made? There were rescue units. Perhaps a rescue was in progress.

She jumped from the car, noticed it still sliding in the mud and hopped back in behind the wheel.

"Don't be stupid, Christine," she whispered and slammed the car into Park, shoving the emergency brake into place. "Be calm. Be cool," she lectured herself, grabbing her notepad.

Immediately the mud swallowed her leather pumps, refusing

to surrender them. She kicked out of her shoes, threw them into the back of the car and padded her way in stockinged feet to the crowd of news media.

The deputies stood straight and unflinching despite the questions being hurled at them. Beyond the trees, searchlights illuminated an area close to the river. Tall grass and a mass of uniformed bodies blocked any view of what was going on.

Channel Five had sent one of their evening anchors. Darcy McManus looked impeccable and ready for the camera, her red suit well pressed, her silky black hair and makeup all in place. Yes, she even had on her shoes. It was, however, too late at night for a live report, and the camera remained off.

Christine recognized Deputy Eddie Gillick in the line. She approached slowly, making certain he saw her, knowing one wrong move could get her throttled.

"Deputy Gillick? Hi, it's Christine Hamilton. Remember me?"

He stared at her like a toy soldier unwilling to give in to any distraction. Then his eyes softened, and there was a hint of a smile before he controlled the impulse.

"Mrs. Hamilton. Sure, I remember. You're Tony's daughter. What brings you out here?"

"I work for the *Omaha Journal* now."

"Oh." The soldier face returned.

She needed to think fast or she'd lose him. She noticed Gillick's slicked-back hair, not a strand out of place, the overpowering smell of aftershave lotion. Even the pencil-thin mustache was meticulously trimmed. His uniform looked wrinkle-free. His tie was cinched tightly at his neck and tacked down with a gold tie tack. A quick glance showed no wedding band. She'd take a chance that he considered himself a bit of a lady's man.

"I can't believe how muddy it is out here. Silly me. I even lost my shoes." She pointed to her mud-caked feet and the red-painted toenails peeking through her stockings. Gillick checked out the feet, and she was pleased when his eyes ran the length of her long legs. The uncomfortably short skirt would finally pay for its discomfort.

"Yes, ma'am, it sure is a mess." He crossed his arms over his chest and shifted his weight, visibly uncomfortable. "You should be careful you don't catch cold." One more look, this time his eyes took in more than just her legs. She felt them stop at her breasts and found herself arching her back to split the blazer open just a little more to accommodate him.

"This whole situation is a mess, isn't it, Eddie? It is Eddie, isn't it?"

"Yes, ma'am." He looked pleased that she remembered. "Although I'm not allowed to discuss the situation at hand."

"Oh, sure. I understand." She leaned in close to him, despite the smell of Brylcream. Even without shoes she was almost his height. "I know you're not allowed to discuss anything about the Alverez boy," she whispered, her lips close to his ear.

His glance registered surprise. An eyebrow raised, and his eyes softened again. "How did you know?" He turned to see if anyone was listening.

Bingo. She'd hit the jackpot. Careful now. Cool and calm. Don't blow it.

"Oh, you know I can't say who my sources are, Eddie." Would he recognize the low hushed voice as seductive or as a line of bull? She had never been very good at seduction, or at least that was what Bruce had told her.

"Sure, of course." He nodded, taking the hook.

"You probably didn't even get a chance to look at the scene. You know, being stuck out here doing the real dirty work."

"Oh, no. I got more than an eyeful." He puffed out his chest as if he dealt with this sort of thing on a daily basis.

"The boy's in pretty bad shape, huh?"

"Yeah, looks like the son of a bitch gutted him," he whispered without a hint of emotion.

She felt the blood rush from her head. Her knees went weak. The boy was dead.

"Hey!" Gillick yelled, and she thought for a second he had discovered the deception. "Shut that camera off! Excuse me, Mrs. Hamilton."

As Gillick snatched at Channel Nine's camera, Christine retreated to her car. She sat with the door open, fanning herself with the empty notepad and taking in long breaths of the cool night air. Despite the chill, her blouse stuck to her.

Danny Alverez was dead, murdered. To quote Deputy Gillick, "gutted."

She had her first big story, yet in the pit of her stomach the butterflies had turned into cockroaches.

CHAPTER 6

Saturday, October 25

Nick gritted his teeth, then swallowed the mouthful of thick, cold coffee. Why was he surprised to find it tasted just as bitter cold as it did hot? It reminded him how much he hated the stuff, but he poured another cup, anyway.

Maybe it wasn't the taste he hated as much as the memories. Coffee reminded him of all-nighters studying for the LSAT. It reminded him of that excruciating road trip to watch his grandfather die. A trip made after his grandmother had pleaded, and necessary because Nick's father, Antonio, had refused to be at the old man's bedside. Even back then, Nick saw the trip as some kind of omen of his own relationship with his father. And he wondered if his father would see the irony if and when the great Antonio Morrelli's time came due, and his own son would refuse to be at his bedside?

Once in a while the association still disarmed Nick—how he could smell the stout aroma of coffee and automatically think of his grandfather's wrinkled gray flesh and those urine-stained sheets. But now, the scent of coffee would forever remind him of the sad, painful screams of a mother identifying her only son's mangled body. It certainly was not much of a replacement.

Nick remembered the first time he had met Laura Alverez last Sunday night—Jesus, less than a week ago. Danny had been missing for almost twelve hours when Nick cut short a weekend fishing trip to question her himself. At first he, too, had been convinced it was one of those custody fights. Another woman using her son to either punish or retrieve her husband. Then he met Laura Alverez.

She was a tall woman, a bit overweight but with a voluptuous figure. The long, dark hair and smoky eyes made her look younger than her forty-five years. There was something statuesque about her that brought to mind the term "tower of strength."

Graceful despite her size, Laura Alverez had glided that evening from her kitchen sink to the cupboard and back to the sink, over and over. She had answered his questions calmly and quietly. Much too calmly. In fact, it had taken him ten, maybe even fifteen minutes before he had realized that, for every cup or plate she had washed and stacked in the cupboard, she removed a clean one, taking it back to the sink with her. Then he noticed the tag sticking out of the collar of her inside-out sweater and the two mismatched shoes. She had been in a state of shock, disguised by a calm Nick found more spooky than reassuring.

Her calm remained throughout the week. She had portrayed an unflinching rock of strength, pouring coffee and baking rolls for the men who had filled her small house each day. Had she displayed some form of emotion, perhaps it wouldn't have been so difficult, moments ago, when he had watched this same stately woman bend in two and crumple to the cold, hard floor of the hospital morgue. Her cries had sliced through the sterilized halls. Nick recognized that sound. It was the low-pitched scream of a wounded animal. No woman should have to face what Laura Alverez faced alone. Now he wished they had located her ex-husband, just so he could beat the crap out of him.

"Morrelli." Bob Weston came into Nick's office without knocking or waiting for an invitation. He plopped down in the chair across from Nick. "You should go home. Shower, change clothes. You stink."

He watched Weston dig the exhaustion out of his eyes and decided he was only stating facts, instead of hurling more insults.

"What about the ex-husband?"

Weston looked up at him and shook his head. "I'm a father, Nick. I don't care how pissed off he might be with his wife—I just don't think a father could do that to his kid."

"So where do we begin?" He must be tired, Nick realized. He was actually asking for Weston's advice.

"I'd start with a list of known sex offenders, pedophiles and child pornographers."

"That could be a long list."

"Excuse me, Nick," Lucy Burton interrupted from the doorway. "Just wanted to let you know that all four Omaha TV stations and both Lincoln stations are downstairs with camera crews. There's also a hallful of newspaper and radio people. They're asking about a statement or press conference."

"Shit," Nick muttered. "Thanks, Lucy." He watched Weston twist in his chair to follow Lucy's long legs down the hall. Maybe he should talk to her about the short skirts and stiletto heels now that they would be making the news. What a shame. She had lovely legs and a walk trained to show them off.

"We've avoided the press all week," Nick said, returning his gaze to Weston. "We're gonna have to talk to them."

"I agree. You need to talk to them."

"Me? Why me? I thought you were the hotshot expert."

"That was when it was a kidnapping. Now it's a homicide, Morrelli. Sorry, this is your ball game."

Nick slumped back in his chair, leaning his head into the leather and swiveling from side to side. This couldn't be happening. Soon he'd wake up in bed with Angie Clark beside him. God, last night seemed like a lifetime ago.

"Look, Morrelli." Weston's voice was soft, sympathetic, and Nick eyed him suspiciously without lifting his head. "I've been thinking. This being a kid and all, maybe I could request someone to help you put together a profile."

"What do you mean?"

"It may be too early for people to start noticing the similarities to Jeffreys, but when they do, you're going to have a frenzy on your hands."

"A frenzy?" Frenzies weren't part of his training. Nick swallowed the sour taste in his mouth. Suddenly, he was nauseated again. He could still smell Danny Alverez's blood soaked into his jeans.

"We have experts who can put together a psychological profile of this guy. Narrow things down for you. Give you a fuckin' idea of who this asshole is."

"Yeah, that would help. That would be good." Nick kept the desperation out of his voice. Now was not the time to reveal his weakness, despite Weston's sudden compassion.

"I've been reading about this Special Agent O'Dell, an expert in profiling murderers practically right down to their shoe size. I could call Quantico."

"How soon do you think they could get someone here?"

"Don't let Tillie cut up the boy yet. I'll call right now and see if we can get someone here Monday morning. Maybe even O'Dell." Weston stood up suddenly with new energy.

Nick untangled his legs and stood, too, surprised that his knees were strong enough to hold him.

Deputy Hal Langston met Weston at the door. "Thought you guys might be interested in this morning's edition of the *Omaha Journal*." Hal unfolded the paper and held it up. The headline screamed in tall, bold letters, Boy's Murder Echoes Jeffreys' Style.

"What the fuck?" Weston ripped the paper from Hal and began reading out loud. "Last night, a boy's body was found along the Platte River, off Old Church Road. Early reports suggest the still-unidentified boy was stabbed to death. A deputy at the scene, who will remain anonymous, said, 'It looked like the bastard gutted him.' Gaping chest wounds were a trademark of serial killer Ronald Jeffreys, who was executed in July of this year. Police have yet to make a statement concerning the boy's identity and the cause of death."

"Jesus," Nick spat as the nausea infected his insides.

"Goddamn it, Morrelli. You're gonna need to put a gag order on your men."

"It gets worse," Hal said, looking at Nick. "The byline is Christine Hamilton."

"Who the fuck is Christine Hamilton?" Weston looked from Hal to Nick. "Oh, please don't tell me she's one of the little harem you're bopping?"

Nick slid back into his chair. How could she do this to him? Had she even tried to warn him, to contact him? Both men stared at him, Weston waiting for an explanation.

"No," Nick said slowly. "Christine Hamilton is my sister."

CHAPTER 7

Maggie O'Dell kicked off her muddy running shoes in the foyer before her husband, Greg, reminded her to do so. She missed their tiny, cluttered apartment in Richmond, despite surrendering to the much-needed convenience of living between Quantico and Washington. But ever since they had bought the pricey condo in the expensive Crest Ridge area, Greg had developed an absurd obsession with image. He liked their condo spotless, an easy task since both their jobs kept them away. Yet, she resented coming home to a place that swallowed her monthly paycheck but felt like one of the hotels to which she had grown accustomed.

She peeled off the damp sweatshirt and immediately felt a pleasant chill. Though it was a crisp fall day, she had managed to work up a sweat after another night of tossing and turning. She balled up the sweatshirt and shot it into the laundry room as she passed on her way to the kitchen. How careless of her to miss the laundry basket.

She stood in front of the open refrigerator. A look inside revealed a pathetic view of their lack of domestic talents—a box of leftover Chinese food, half a bagel twisted in plastic wrap, a foam take-out container with unidentified gooey stuff. She grabbed a bottle of water and slammed the door, now shivering in only running shorts, a sweat-drenched T-shirt and sports bra that stuck to her like an extra layer of skin.

The phone rang. She searched the spotless counters and grabbed it off the unused microwave before the fourth ring.

"Hello."

"O'Dell, it's Cunningham."

She ran her fingers through her wet mass of short, dark hair and stood up straight, his voice setting her at attention.

"Hi. What's up?"

"I just received a phone call from the Omaha field office. They have a murder victim, a little boy. Some of the wounds are characteristic of a serial killer in the same area about six years ago."

"He's on the prowl again?" She began pacing.

"No, the serial killer was Ronald Jeffreys. I don't know if you remember the case. He murdered three boys—"

"Yes, I remember," she interrupted him, knowing he hated long explanations. "Wasn't he executed in June or July?"

"Yes...yes, in July, I believe." His voice sounded tired.

Though it was Saturday afternoon, Maggie imagined him in his office behind the stacks on his desk. She could hear him rustling through papers. Knowing Director Kyle Cunningham, he already had Jeffreys' entire file spread out in front of him. Long before Maggie started working under him in the Behavioral Science Unit, he had been affectionately nicknamed the Hawk because nothing got past him. Lately, however, it looked as though the sharp vision came at the expense of puffy eyes, swollen from too little sleep.

"So this might be a copycat." She stopped and opened several drawers looking for a pen and paper to jot down notes, only to find carefully folded kitchen towels, sterile utensils lined up in annoyingly neat rows. Even the odd utensils, a corkscrew and can opener, lay flat in their respective corners, not touching or overlapping. She picked up a shiny serving spoon and turned it in the wrong direction, making sure it crossed over several others. Satisfied, she closed the drawer and began pacing again.

"It could be a copycat," Cunningham said in a distracted tone. She knew he was reading the file while he talked, that worried indent between his brows, his glasses low on his nose. "It could be a one-time thing. The point is, they requested a profiler. Matter of fact, Bob Weston requested you specifically."

"So I'm a celebrity even in Nebraska?" She ignored the annoyance in his voice. A month ago, it wouldn't have been there. A month ago, he would have been proud that a protégé of his had been requested. "When do I leave?"

"Not so fast, O'Dell." She clutched the phone and waited for the lecture. "I'm sure Weston's pile of glowing reports about you didn't include the last case file."

Maggie stopped and leaned against the counter. She pressed the palm of her hand against her stomach, waiting, preparing for the nausea. "I certainly hope you're not going to hold the Stucky case over my head every time I go out into the field." The quiver in her voice sounded angry. That was good—anger was good, better than weakness.

"You know that's not what I'm doing, Maggie."

Oh, God. He had used her first name. This would be a serious lecture. She stayed put and dug her nails into a nearby hand towel.

"I'm simply concerned," he continued. "You never took a break after Stucky. You didn't even see the bureau psychologist."

"Kyle, I'm okay," she lied, irritated with the sudden tremor invading her hand. "It's not like it was the first time. I've seen plenty of blood and guts in the past eight years. There's not much that shocks me anymore."

"That's exactly what I'm worried about. Maggie, you were in the middle of that bloodbath. It's a miracle you weren't killed. I don't care how tough you think you are, when the blood and guts get sprayed all over you, it's a little different than walking in on it."

She didn't need the reminder. Fact was, it didn't take much to conjure up the image of Albert Stucky hacking those women to death—his bloody death play performed just for Maggie. His voice still came to her in the middle of the night: "I want you to watch. If you close your eyes, I'll just kill another one and another and another."

She had a degree in psychology. She didn't need a psychologist to tell her why she couldn't sleep at night, why the images still haunted her. She hadn't even been able to tell Greg about that night; how could she tell a complete stranger?

Of course, Greg hadn't been around when she had staggered back to her hotel room. He'd been miles away when she tore pieces of Lydia Barnett's brain out of her hair and scrubbed Melissa Stonekey's blood and skin out of her pores. When she had dressed her own wound, an unsightly slit across her abdomen. And it wasn't the kind of thing you talked about over the phone.

"How was your day, dear? Mine? Oh, nothing too exciting. I just watched two women get gutted and bludgeoned to death."

No, the real reason she hadn't told Greg was that he would have gone nuts. He would have insisted she quit, or worse, promise to work only in the lab, examining the blood and guts safely under a microscope and not under her fingernails. He had ranted and raved once before when she had confided in him. It had been the last time she had talked about her work. He didn't seem to mind the lack of communication. He didn't even notice her absence beside him in bed at night, when she paced the floor to avoid the images, to quiet the screams that still echoed in her head. The lack of intimacy with her husband allowed her to keep her scars—physical and mental—to herself.

"Maggie?"

"I need to keep working, Kyle. Please don't take that away from me." She kept her voice strong, grateful the tremor was confined to her hands and stomach. Would he detect the vulnerability, anyway? He tracked criminals by reading between the lines. How could she expect to fool him?

There was silence, and she covered the mouthpiece of the phone, so he couldn't hear her staggered breathing.

"I'll fax over the details," he finally said. "Your flight leaves in the morning at six o'clock. Call me after you get the fax if you have any questions."

She listened to the click and waited for the dial tone. With the phone still pressed against her ear, she sighed, then breathed deeply. The front door slammed and she jumped.

"Maggie?"

"I'm in the kitchen." She hung up the phone and gulped some water, hoping to shake the queasiness from the pit of her stomach. She needed this case. She needed to prove to Cunningham that, although Albert Stucky had assaulted and toyed with her mental state, he had not stolen her professional edge.

"Hey, babe." Greg came around the counter. He started to hug her, but stopped when he noticed the perspiration. He manufactured a smile to disguise his disgust. When had he started using his lawyer acting talents on her?

"We have reservations for six-thirty. Are you sure you have time to get ready?"

She glanced at the wall clock. It was only four. How bad did he think she looked?

"No problem," she said, guzzling more water and purposely letting it dribble down her chin.

She caught him wincing at her, his perfectly chiseled jaw taut with disapproval. He worked out at the law firm's gym, where he sweated, grunted and dribbled in the appropriate setting. Then he showered and changed, not a shiny golden hair out of place by the time he stepped out into public again. He expected the same from her, had even told her how much he hated her running in the neighborhood. At first, she had thought it was out of concern for her safety.

"I'm a black belt, Greg. I can handle myself," she had lovingly reassured him.

"I'm not talking about that. Christ, Maggie, you look like hell when you run. Don't you want to make a good impression on our neighbors?"

The phone rang, and Greg reached for it.

"Let it ring," she blurted with a mouthful of water. "It's a fax from Director Cunningham." Without looking at him she could feel his annoyance. She raced to the den, checked the caller ID, then flipped on the fax.

"Why is he faxing you on a Saturday?"

He startled her. She didn't realize he had followed. He stood in the doorway with hands on his hips, looking as stern as possible in khakis and a crew-neck sweater.

"He's faxing some details on a case I've been asked to profile." She avoided looking at him, dreading the pouty lip and brooding eyes. Usually, he was the one interrupting their Saturdays together, but she convinced herself it was childish to remind him. Instead, she ripped off the fax and began transferring details from paper to memory.

"Tonight was supposed to be a nice quiet dinner—just the two of us."

"And it will be," she said calmly, still not looking at him. "It may just need to be an early night. I have a six o'clock flight in the morning."

Silence. One, two, three...

"Damn it, Maggie. It's our anniversary. This was supposed to be our weekend together."

"No, that was last weekend, only you forgot and played in the golf tournament."

"Oh, I see," he snorted. "So this is payback."

"No, it's not payback." She maintained her calm though she was tired of these little tantrums. It was fine for him to ruin their plans with only half an apology and that charming, smug "I'll make it up to you, babe."

"If it's not payback, what do you call it?"

"Work."

"Work, right. That's convenient. Call it what you want. It's payback."

"A little boy has been murdered, and I might be able to help find the psycho who did it." The anger bubbled close to the surface, but her voice remained amazingly calm. "Sorry, I'll make it up to you." The sarcasm slipped out, but he didn't seem to notice. She took the fax and started past him to the door. He grabbed her wrist and spun her toward him.

"Tell them to send someone else, Maggie. We need this weekend together," he pleaded, his voice now soft.

She looked into his gray eyes and wondered when they had lost their color. She searched for a flicker of the intelligent, compassionate man she had married nine years ago when they were both college seniors ready to make their marks on the world. She would track down the criminals, and he would defend the helpless victims. Then he took the job in Washington at Brackman, Harvey and Lowe, and his helpless victims became billion-dollar corporations. Still, in just a moment of silence, she thought she recognized a flicker of sincerity. She was on the verge of giving in to him when his grip tightened and his teeth clenched.

"Tell them to send someone else, or we're finished."

She wrenched her wrist free. He grabbed for it again, and she slammed a fist into his chest. His eyes widened in surprise.

"Don't you ever grab me like that again. And if this one trip means we're finished, then maybe we've been finished for a long time."

She brushed past him and headed for the bedroom, hoping her knees would carry her and the sting behind her eyes would wait.

CHAPTER 8

And so it begins, he thought as he sipped the scalding-hot tea.

The front-page headline belonged on the *National Enquirer* and not a newspaper as respectable as the *Omaha Journal*. From the Grave, Serial Killer Still Grips Community with Boy's Recent Murder. It was almost as hysterical as yesterday's headline, but, of course, today's large Sunday edition would attract more readers.

The byline was Christine Hamilton again. He recognized the name from the "Living Today" section. Why would they give the story to a newcomer, a rookie?

Quickly, he turned the pages, searching for the rest of the story which continued on page ten, column one. The entire page was filled with connecting articles. There was a school photo of the boy. Beside it ran an in-depth saga of the boy's sudden disappearance during his early-morning paper route just a week ago. The article told how the FBI and the boy's mother had waited for a ransom note that never came. Then, finally, Sheriff Morrelli had found the body in a pasture along the river.

He glanced back at the paragraph. Morrelli? No, this was Nicholas Morrelli, not Antonio. How nice, he thought, for father and son to share the same experience.

The article went on to point out the similarities to the murders of three boys in the same small community over six years ago.

And how the bodies, strangled and stabbed to death, had each been discovered days later in different wooded, isolated areas.

The article, however, made no mention of details, no description of the elaborate chest carving. Did the police hope to withhold that evidence again? He shook his head and continued to read.

He used the fillet knife to scoop jelly and spread it on his burnt English muffin. The stupid toaster hadn't worked right for weeks, but it was better than going down to the kitchen and having breakfast with the others. At least here in his room he could have the solitude of breakfast and the morning paper without the burden of making polite conversation.

The room was very plain, white walls and hardwood floors. The small twin-size bed barely accommodated his six-foot frame. Some nights he found his feet dangling over the end. He had added the small Formica-topped table and two chairs, though he allowed no one to join him. The utility cart in the corner housed the secondhand toaster, a gift from one of the parishioners. There was also a hot plate and kettle that he used for his tea.

On the nightstand stood the most elaborate of his furnishings, an ornate lamp, the base a detailed relief of cherubs and nymphs tastefully arranged. It was one of the few things he had splurged on and purchased for himself with his meager paycheck. That and the three paintings. Of course, he could only afford framed reproductions. They hung on the wall opposite his bed so he could look at them while he drifted off to sleep, though sleep didn't come easy these days. It never did when the throbbing began, invading his otherwise quiet life, crashing in with all those foul memories. Even though his room was simple and plain, it brought short periods of comfort, control and solitude to a life that was no longer his own.

He checked his watch and ran his hand over his jaw. He wouldn't need to shave today, his boyish face still smooth from yesterday's shave. He had time to finish reading, though he refused to so much as look at the ridiculous articles about Ronald Jeffreys. Jeffreys had never deserved the attention he had garnered, and here he was, still in the limelight even after death.

He finished his breakfast and meticulously cleaned the table, no crumb escaping his quick swipes with the damp rag. From his small, brown-stained bathroom sink he removed the pair of

Nikes, now scrubbed clean, not a hint of mud left. Still, he wished he had taken them off sooner. He patted them dry and set them aside to wash the one plate he called his own, a fragile, hand-painted Noritake he had borrowed long ago from the community china cabinet. His matching teacup and saucer, also borrowed, he filled to the brim with more scalding-hot water. Delicately, he dunked the once-used tea bag, waiting for the water to turn the appropriate amber color, then quickly removed and strangled the tea bag as if making it surrender every last drop.

His morning ritual complete, he got down on his hands and knees and pulled a wooden box from under the bed. He laid the box on the small table and ran his fingers over the lid's intricate carving. Carefully, he cut out the newspaper articles, bypassing those on Ronald Jeffreys. He opened the box and put the folded articles inside on top of the other newspaper clippings, some of which were just beginning to yellow. He checked the other contents: a bright white linen cloth, two candles and a small container of oil. Then he licked the remnants of jelly off the fillet knife and returned it to the box, laying it gently on the soft cotton of a pair of boy's underpants.

CHAPTER 9

Timmy Hamilton pushed his mom's fingers away from his face as the two of them hesitated on the steps of St. Margaret's. It was bad enough that he was late. He didn't need his mom fussing over him in front of his friends.

"Come on, Mom. Everybody can see."

"Is this a new bruise?" She held his chin and gently tilted his head.

"I ran into Chad at soccer practice. It's no big deal." He put his hand on his hip as if to conceal the even bigger bruise hidden there.

"You need to be more careful, Timmy. You bruise so easily. I must have been out of my mind when I agreed to let you play."

She opened her handbag and began digging.

"I'm gonna be late. Church starts in fifteen minutes."

"I thought I had your registration form and check for the camp out."

"Mom, I'm late already."

"Okay, okay." She snapped the bag shut. "Just tell Father Keller I'll put it in the mail tomorrow."

"Can I go now?"

"Yes."

"You sure you don't want to check the tags on my underwear or something?"

"Smart-ass." She laughed and swatted him on the butt.

He liked it when she laughed, something she didn't do much of since his dad had left. When she laughed, the lines in her face softened, denting her cheeks with dimples. She became the most beautiful woman he knew, especially now with her new silky, blond hair. She was almost prettier than Miss Roberts, his fourth-grade teacher. But Miss Roberts was last year. This year was Mr. Stedman and, though it was only October, Timmy hated the fifth grade. He lived for soccer practice—soccer practice and serving mass with Father Keller.

In July, when his mom had interrupted his summer and sent him to church camp, he had been furious with her. But Father Keller had made camp fun. It ended up being a great summer, and he'd hardly missed his dad. Then, to top it off, Father Keller had asked him to be one of his altar boys. Though he and his mom had been members of St. Margaret's since spring, Timmy knew Father Keller's altar boys were an elite group, handpicked and given special rewards. Rewards like the upcoming camping trip.

Timmy knocked on the ornate door to the church vestibule. When no one answered, he opened it slowly and peeked in before entering. He found a cassock in his size among those hanging in the closet, and he ripped it from the hanger, trying to make up for lost time. He threw his jacket to a chair across the room, then jumped, startled by the priest kneeling quietly next to the chair. His rod-straight back was to Timmy, but he recognized Father Keller's dark hair curling over his collar. His thin frame towered over the chair, though he was on his knees. Despite Timmy's jacket almost hitting him, the priest remained still and quiet.

Timmy stared, holding his breath, waiting for the priest to flinch, to move, to breathe. Finally, his elbow lifted to make the sign of the cross. He stood without effort and turned to Timmy, taking the jacket and draping it carefully over the chair's arm.

"Does your mom know you throw around your Sunday clothes?" He smiled with white, even teeth and bright blue eyes.

"Sorry, Father. I didn't see you when I came in. I was afraid I was late."

"No problem. We have plenty of time." He tousled Timmy's hair, his hand lingering on his head. It was something Timmy's dad used to do.

At first, Timmy had been uncomfortable when Father Keller touched him. Now, instead of tensing up, he found himself feeling safe. Though he couldn't admit it out loud, he liked Father

Keller way better than he liked his dad. Father Keller never yelled; instead, his voice was soft and soothing, low and powerful. His large hands patted and caressed—never hit. When Father Keller talked to him, Timmy felt as if he was the most important person in Father Keller's life. He made Timmy feel special, and in return, Timmy wanted to please him, though he still messed up some of the mass stuff. Last Sunday, Timmy brought the water to the altar but forgot the wine. Father Keller had just smiled, whispered to him and waited patiently. No one else even suspected his mistake.

No, Father Keller was nothing like his dad, who had spent most of his time at work, even when the three of them had been a family. Father Keller seemed like a best friend instead of a priest. Sometimes on Saturdays, he played football with the boys down at the park, allowing himself to be tackled and getting just as muddy as the rest of them. At camp, he told gory ghost stories—the kind parents forbid. Sometimes after mass, Father Keller traded baseball cards. He had some of the best ones, really old ones like Jackie Robinson and Joe DiMaggio. No, Father Keller was too cool to be like his dad.

Timmy finished and waited for Father Keller to put on the last of his garments. The priest checked his image in the floor-length mirror, then turned to Timmy.

"Ready?"

"Yes, Father," he said and followed the priest through the small hallway to the altar.

Timmy couldn't help smiling at the bright white Nikes peeking out from under the priest's long, black cassock.

CHAPTER 10

Platte City reminded Maggie of the fictional Mayberry R.F.D. She'd never understood the appeal of small towns. Quaint and friendly usually meant boring and nosy. Assignments in small towns made her cranky and edgy. She hated the presumed intimacy that found its way into "how are you?" and "good morning." Immediately, she missed the irritating but familiar sounds of honking taxis and six-lane traffic. Worse yet was settling for Chinese takeout from places called Big Fred's and watered-down cappuccino from convenience-store vending machines.

She had to admit, though, the drive from Omaha had been a scenic one. The foliage along the Platte River put on a show of spectacular colors: bright oranges and flaming reds mixed with green and gold. The overpowering scent of evergreens and impending rain filled the air with an annoyingly pleasant aroma. She kept the car window cracked, despite the chill.

A jet thundered overhead, and Maggie skidded to a stop at the intersection. The sudden burst of sound shook the car and left an echo rumbling through the quiet streets. She remembered that Strategic Air Command was only ten, maybe fifteen miles away. Okay, so perhaps Platte City possessed some familiar sounds, after all.

She purposely took a wrong turn away from downtown. The detour would only take a few minutes and would hopefully give her some insight into the community. A Pizza Hut took up one corner. Across the street was the obligatory convenience store and a shiny new McDonald's. Its golden arches stood taller than anything else for miles, competing only with a grain elevator and a church steeple.

The church's spiky iron cross stabbed at the thick clouds that had begun rolling in only moments ago. Its parking lot was beginning to empty with a line of snail-crawling churchgoers, putting Maggie in the middle of the traffic jam. She sat patiently watching as each car allowed the one in front to back out and get in line. No, it was much too organized. They even ruined a good traffic jam.

Maggie waited for room in front, then flipped the rented Ford around in one quick squeal of tires. Heads turned, the line of snails stopped and watched as she spun out in the opposite direction. She checked the rearview mirror. No flashing lights followed, though she wouldn't have been surprised if they had.

The information she had accessed from the Nebraska Tourism Web site described Platte City (population 3,500) as a growing bedroom community for many who worked in Omaha (twenty miles to the northeast) and Lincoln (thirty miles to the southwest). That explained the beautiful, well-manicured homes and neighborhoods—many recently built—despite the nonexistence of any nearby industry.

Small shops lined the downtown square: a post office, Wanda's Diner, a movie theater, something called Paintin' Place, a small grocery store and, yes, even a drugstore/soda fountain. Bright red awnings hung over some of the shops. Others had window boxes with geraniums still in bloom. In the center of the square, the red brick courthouse towered over the other buildings. Built during an era when pride overrode expense, its facade included a detailed relief of Nebraska's past—covered wagons and plow horses separated by the scales of justice.

The entire block was ornately fenced in with freshly painted, black wrought iron. The courthouse took up only half the space. Cobblestone walkways, bronze statues, a marble fountain, benches and old-fashioned lampposts made the rest of the area a quiet garden-like retreat. What impressed Maggie most as she made her way over the twists of cobblestone was the absence of trash. Not one single hamburger wrapper or foam cup dared to litter the hallowed ground. Instead, huge maple and sycamore leaves decorated the path with gold and red.

Inside the lobby of the courthouse, Maggie's heels clicked on the marble floor, sending an echo all the way to the vaulted cathedral ceiling. There was no security guard, not even a desk clerk. She scanned the wall directory. The county sheriff's department, along with several courtrooms and the county jail, resided on the third floor.

She bypassed the elevator and took the stairs, an open spiral that allowed a bird's-eye view of the atrium. Lavish white and gray marble lined the stairwells and the floor. Solid oak and shiny brass trimmed the banisters and doorways. She found herself tiptoeing.

The sheriff's department appeared empty, though the smell of freshly brewed coffee and the hum of a copy machine seeped in from one of the back rooms. The wall clock showed eleven-thirty. Maggie checked her watch. She was still on eastern time. She reset it as she walked to the windows facing south. The thick, gray clouds now blocked any hint of sun or blue sky. Below, the streets remained quiet. A few customers, dressed in their Sunday best, left Wanda's Diner. Behind the theater a small, gray-haired man heaved trash into a huge Dumpster.

It wasn't noon, and she was already exhausted. She was drained from her battle with Greg and another sleepless night avoiding visions of Albert Stucky. Then, this morning, the turbulent flight had jerked and jolted her thousands of feet above control. She hated flying, and it never got any easier.

It was the control, her mother reminded her whenever possible. "You need to let it go, Mag-pie. You can't expect to be in control twenty-four hours a day."

This from a woman who, after twenty years of therapy, still struggled with the meaning of self-control. A woman who buried her grief for her dead husband by drinking herself into a stupor every Friday night and bringing home whatever stranger had supplied her with the drinks. It wasn't until one of her men friends suggested a threesome—daughter, mother and himself—that she stopped bringing the men home and insisted on motel rooms. Her mother hadn't seemed disgusted by the idea of sharing her twelve-year-old daughter, as much as intimidated by it.

Maggie rubbed the back of her neck, the muscles tight with tension—tension easily brought on by thoughts of her mother. She wished she had checked into a hotel first and eaten some lunch instead of coming directly here. But she was ready to dig in, having spent the hours in the air preoccupying herself with details of Ronald Jeffreys. The recent murder resembled Jeffreys' style, right down to the jagged X carved into the boy's chest. Copycats were often meticulous, duplicating every last detail to amplify the thrill. Sometimes that made them even more dangerous than the original killer. It removed the passion and thus the tendency to make mistakes.

"Can I help you?"

The voice startled Maggie, and she spun around. The young woman who appeared out of nowhere was far from what Maggie had expected of someone working in a sheriff's office. Her long hair was too tall and stiff, her knit skirt too short and tight. She looked more like a teenager ready for a date.

"I'm here to see Sheriff Nicholas Morrelli."

The woman eyed Maggie suspiciously, keeping her post in the doorway as though guarding the back offices. Maggie knew her navy blazer and trousers made her look official, hiding the slender figure that sometimes betrayed her authority. Early in her career she had developed an abrupt and sometimes abrasive manner that demanded attention and compensated for her slight stature. At five foot five and a hundred and fifteen pounds, she had barely met the physical requirements of the agency.

"Nick's not here right now," the woman said in a voice that told Maggie she wasn't about to reveal any additional information. "Was he expecting you?" The woman crossed her arms and stood up straight in an attempt to emphasize her authority.

Maggie looked around the office again, ignoring the question and showing the woman she wasn't impressed. "Can he be reached?" She pretended to be interested in the bulletin board that contained a wanted poster from the early eighties, a flyer announcing a Halloween dance and a notice advertising a 1990 Ford pickup for sale.

"Look, lady. I don't mean to be rude," the young woman said, suddenly a bit unsure of herself. "What exactly is it that you need to talk to Nick...to Sheriff Morrelli about?"

Maggie glanced back at the woman, who looked older now, the lines evident around her mouth and eyes. She teetered on the two-inch spiked heels and was biting her lower lip.

Maggie reached into her jacket pocket, ready to flip out her badge when two men came noisily in the front door. The older man wore a brown deputy's uniform, the pants impeccably pressed, the tie cinched tight at his neck. His black hair was slicked back, tucked behind his ears and curled over his collar, not a strand out of place. In contrast, the younger man was wearing a gray T-shirt drenched in sweat, shorts and running shoes. His dark brown hair, though short, was tousled, strands wet against his forehead. Despite his disheveled look, he was handsome and definitely in good shape, with long muscular legs, slender waist and broad shoulders. Immediately, Maggie was annoyed with herself for noticing these details.

Both men stopped talking as soon as they saw Maggie. There was silence as they looked from Maggie to the frazzled young woman still at her post in the doorway.

"Hi, Lucy. Is everything okay?" the younger man said as his eyes scanned the length of Maggie's body. When his eyes finally met hers, he smiled as if she had met his approval.

"I was just trying to find out what this lady—"

"I'm here to see Sheriff Morrelli," Maggie interrupted. She was getting impatient with being treated like a tax auditor.

"What did you need to see him about?" It was the deputy's turn to interrogate her, his forehead creased with concern, his stance straightening as though on alert.

Maggie ran her fingers through her hair, waiting for the impatience to settle before it turned to anger. She brought out her badge and flipped it open to them. "I'm with the FBI."

"You're Special Agent O'Dell?" the younger man said, now looking more embarrassed than surprised.

"Yes, that's right."

"Sorry about the third degree." He wiped his hand on his T-shirt and extended it to her. "I'm Nick Morrelli."

She was sure the surprise registered on her face, because he smiled at her reaction. Maggie had worked with enough small-town sheriffs to know that they didn't look like Nick Morrelli. He looked more like a professional athlete, the kind whose good looks and charm forgave his arrogance. The eyes were sky blue and hard to ignore against the tanned skin and dark hair. His grip was firm, no gentle graze reserved for women; however, his eyes held hers, giving her all their attention as if she were the only one in the room. A look he reserved for women, no doubt.

"This is Deputy Eddie Gillick, and I guess you already met

Lucy Burton. I am really sorry. We're all just a little on edge around here. We've had a couple of really long nights, and there's been a lot of reporters snooping around.''

"Well, you've certainly come up with an interesting disguise.'' This time Maggie let her eyes slowly scan the length of Morrelli's body, just as he had done to her. When her eyes finally met his, a flicker of embarrassment had replaced his arrogance.

"Actually, I just got back from Omaha. I ran in the Corporate Cup Run.'' He seemed eager to explain, almost uncomfortable, as though he had been caught at something he shouldn't be doing. He shifted from one foot to another. "It's a fund-raiser for the American Lung Association...or maybe it's the American Heart Association. I can't remember. Anyway, it's for a good cause.''

"You don't owe me an explanation, Sheriff Morrelli,'' she said, although she was pleased that her presence seemed to demand one.

There was an awkward silence. Finally Deputy Gillick cleared his throat. "I've got to get back on the road.'' This time he smiled at Maggie. "It was a pleasure meeting you, Miss O'Dell.''

"Agent O'Dell,'' Morrelli corrected him.

"Right, sorry.'' Flustered by the correction, the deputy was now anxious to make his exit.

"I'm sure I'll be seeing you again,'' Maggie added to his misery.

"Lucy, do I smell fresh coffee?'' Morrelli asked with a boyish smile.

"I just made a fresh pot. I'll get you some.'' Lucy's voice was now syrupy and a feminine octave higher.

Maggie smiled to herself as she watched the young woman's rigid, authoritarian stature give way to a soft sway as she started to fetch coffee for the handsome sheriff.

"Would you mind getting a cup for Agent O'Dell, too?'' He smiled at Maggie while Lucy turned and shot her an irritated glare.

"Cream or sugar?''

"None for me, thank you.''

"How about a Pepsi, instead?'' he asked, eager to please her.

"Yes, that sounds good.'' Perhaps the sugar would help fill her empty stomach.

"Forget the coffee, Lucy. Two cans of Pepsi, please."

Lucy stared at Maggie, all the excitement drained from her face and replaced by contempt. She spun around and left, the clicking of her heels echoing all the way down the hallway.

It was just the two of them. Morrelli rubbed his arms as if to ward off a chill. He looked uncomfortable, and Maggie knew she was the cause of his discomfort. Perhaps she should have called. She wasn't good at that etiquette stuff, and it was probably expected in Platte City, Nebraska.

"After almost forty-eight straight hours, we decided to take a break today." Again, he seemed eager to explain away his appearance and the silent department. "I really didn't think you'd be here until tomorrow. You know, it being Sunday."

Maggie found herself wondering if he had been appointed or elected. In either case, his boyish charm had probably outweighed his competence.

"My superiors gave me the impression that time may be important in this case. You are still holding the body for my examination, aren't you?"

"Yes, of course. He's..." Morrelli rubbed a hand across his bristled face. Maggie noticed a small scar, a puckered white line that blemished his otherwise perfect jaw. "We're using the hospital morgue." He dug his fingers into his eyes. Maggie wondered if it was simple exhaustion or an attempt to block out the image that probably haunted his sleep. The report indicated that Morrelli was the one who had found the boy.

"If you'd like, I can take you there," he added.

"Thanks. Yes, I will need to do that. But first, there's someplace else I'd like you to take me."

"Sure. You probably want to unpack. Are you staying here in town?"

"Actually, that's not what I meant. I'd like to see the scene of the crime." She watched Morrelli's face grow pale. "I'd like you to show me where you found the body."

CHAPTER 11

The pasture road dissolved into torn grass and jagged ruts. Tire tracks crisscrossed each other, stamped into the mud. Nick shifted the Jeep into second gear and the vehicle strained forward, the tires cutting still more deeply into the mud.

"I don't suppose anyone realized all this traffic in and out of here may have destroyed evidence?"

Nick shot Agent O'Dell a frustrated look. He was getting tired of being reminded of his mistakes.

"By the time we discovered the body, at least two vehicles had been through here. Yeah, we realized we may have messed up the killer's tracks."

He glanced at her again as he tried to keep the Jeep from sliding into the worst parts of the mud. Though she acted older, he guessed she was only in her late twenties, maybe earlier thirties—much too young to be an expert. Her age wasn't the only thing that disarmed him. Despite her cool, abrupt manner she was very attractive. And even the conservative-style suit couldn't hide what he suspected was a knockout body. Under ordinary circumstances he'd be preparing a full-throttled charm assault. But, Jesus, there was something about her that sent him into a tailspin. She carried herself with such poise, such confidence and self-assurance. She acted as though she knew what she was doing, which only made him more aware of his own lack of expertise. It was annoying as hell.

The Jeep jerked to a stop in front of the shelterbelt of trees, and immediately the nausea of that night struck Nick. The lightheadedness surprised him. It was getting to be embarrassing. He heard O'Dell struggle with the door handle, the familiar click of metal against metal.

"Wait, that door sticks. Here, let me." Without thinking he reached across the seat, leaning against her. His hand was on the door handle before he realized his body hovered over her, his face dangerously close to hers. She pressed herself into her seat to avoid touching him, and he immediately jerked his hand away, returning to his own side.

"I'll get it from the outside."

"Good idea."

Outside the Jeep, Nick berated himself. What a stupid thing to do. Not very professional. He was certainly living up to his reputation as the incompetent playboy sheriff.

He sloshed around to the other side of the Jeep. Back at the office he had taken a quick shower, put on jeans and traded the running shoes for the same boots he had worn that night. Dry mud still clung to the expensive leather. They were instantly devoured again by the sticky ooze. The gray clouds rolled in, threatening to burst at any moment and guaranteeing the ooze would stay for days ahead.

The Jeep's door opened easily from the outside. Would O'Dell think his stupid move in the car was a cheap excuse just to get close to her? It didn't matter. Something told Nick this woman was immune to his charm, what little he seemed to have left.

"Hold on." He stopped her again. "I think I have some boots back here." He climbed inside the doorway, stopping in midair as he realized the inappropriateness of his actions, again. He avoided her eyes and waited until she slid to the other side and was a safe distance away. Then he stretched over the seat. Thankfully, the rubber work boots were within arm's reach.

"Are you sure those are necessary?" She looked at the black boots as though they were shackles.

"You'll never get anywhere in this mud. It's worse by the riverbank."

He had already begun undoing the laces. He handed her a boot and began on the other, distracted when she slipped off her expensive leather flats. Clothed only in sheer socks, her feet were small, slender and delicate. He watched her slide her foot into the oversize boot. It swallowed her foot, and even her attempt at tucking in her pant leg wouldn't guarantee that the huge rubber boot would stay attached.

As they began their hike through the mud, he was impressed that she kept up with him despite her clumsy footwear and her shorter stride. The area was still cordoned off by yellow tape strung from trees. Sections were torn, flapping in the breeze, a breeze that grew stronger as the fast-moving clouds rolled overhead. Nick pulled up the collar of his jacket. His hair was still damp. A shiver slipped down his back. He glanced at O'Dell, who wore only a wool suit jacket and matching trousers. She buttoned the jacket but showed no other sign of feeling the cutting cold.

He watched her step carefully around the impression of the small body that still remained pressed into the grass. She crouched down, examined the blades of grass, scooped up a fingerful of mud and sniffed it. Nick winced, remembering the rancid smell. His skin still felt raw from scrubbing the stench from his body.

O'Dell stood and looked out at the river. The bank was only three or four feet away. The unusually high waters churned, slapping at the banks.

"Where did you find the medallion?" she asked, without looking at him.

He walked to the spot and found the white stake one of his deputies had placed there. "Here," he said, pointing to the plastic marker sunk into the mud, barely visible.

She looked at the spot, then back at the boy's resting place. It was only a couple feet away.

"It was the boy's. His mother identified it," Nick explained, still regretting that he couldn't give it back to Laura Alverez when she had pleaded. "The chain was broken. It must have gotten pulled off in the struggle."

"Except there was no struggle."

"Excuse me?" He looked back at her for an explanation, but she was on her knees again with a small tape measure stretched between the marker and the pressed grass.

"There wasn't a struggle," she repeated calmly, getting to her feet and wiping at the leaves and mud she had gotten on her trousers.

"What makes you say that?" He was annoyed by her matter-of-fact attitude. She had been here only minutes and seemed to have it all figured out.

"You fell here when you tripped, right?" she said, pointing to the torn grass and the indent in the mud.

Nick winced again. Even his report made him look like a putz. "That's right," he admitted.

"The trampling around the perimeter is obviously from your deputies."

"And the FBI," Nick added defensively, though he knew she wasn't concerned with those details. "They were in charge until we ruled out a kidnapping."

"Other than this spot and where the body lay, there is no torn grass or any beaten down. The victim's hands and feet were bound when you found him?"

"Yeah, back behind him."

"My guess is that he was like that when they arrived here. Does the coroner have an approximate time and place of death yet?" She brought out a small notebook and jotted down details.

"He was killed out here, probably less than twenty-four hours before I found him." The nausea was back. He wondered if he would ever be able to get the image of the dead boy out of his mind. Those wide, innocent eyes staring up at the sky.

"When did the victim disappear?"

"Early last Sunday morning. We found his bike and bag of newspapers against a fence. He hadn't even started his route yet."

"So the killer had him for at least three whole days."

"Jesus," Nick mumbled and shook his head. He hadn't thought about the time between the abduction and the murder. They had all been so sure the boy had been kidnapped by his father or someone who would demand a ransom. Nick had believed the boy was being well cared for.

"So how did the chain get broken?" Nick wanted to think of something other than the torture the boy may have endured.

"I don't know for sure. Maybe the killer pulled it off. It was a silver cross, right?" She looked to him for assurance. He only nodded, impressed that she had equipped herself with so many details from his report. She continued as if thinking out loud. "Maybe the killer didn't like staring at it. Maybe he wasn't able to do what he wanted to do as long as the victim was wearing it. Its religious significance is some sort of protection. Perhaps the killer is religious enough to have known that and have been uncomfortable.''

''A religious killer? Great.''

''What other trace do you have?''

''Trace?''

''Other evidence—other objects, torn pieces of fabric or rope? Was the FBI able to pull any tire tracks at all?''

The tire tracks again. How many times would he need to be reminded of his screwup.

''We did find a footprint.''

She stared at him, and he saw a flicker of impatience.

''A footprint? Excuse me, Sheriff, I don't mean to sound skeptical, but how were you able to isolate a footprint? From what I can tell, there must have been over a dozen pairs of feet out here.'' She waved her hand at the shoe impressions trampled in the mud. ''How do you know that the prints you found weren't one of your men or the FBI?''

''Because none of us were barefoot.'' He didn't wait for her reaction but moved closer to the river. He grabbed on to a tree branch just as his boots slid partway down the bank. When he looked up, O'Dell was standing over him.

''Right here.'' He pointed to the set of toes imprinted in the mud and highlighted with remnants of casting powder.

''There's no guarantee those are the killer's.''

''Who else would be nuts enough to be out here without shoes?''

She grabbed the same branch and slid down next to him.

''You mind giving me a hand?'' She extended a hand to him and he took it, allowing her to hang on while she bent down and stretched over the impression without sliding into the water.

Her hand was soft and small in his, but her grip was strong. Her jacket swung open, and he made himself look away. Jesus, she certainly didn't look like an FBI agent.

After a few seconds she pulled herself up and immediately released his hand. Back on solid ground, she started writing in the notebook. Nick stared up at the thick, gray clouds. Suddenly, he wished he was anywhere else. The last forty-eight hours had drained him. His calf muscles ached from the 10K race he had pushed himself to run that morning. And now, here he was feeling incompetent and nauseated again, remembering Danny Alverez's white body, those wide eyes staring up at the stars. A flock of snow geese honked as they passed overhead. Nick caught himself wondering what had been the last thing Danny had looked up at. He hoped it had been some geese, something tranquil and familiar.

"The puncture marks and the carving in the boy's chest were exactly like the Jeffreys murders," he said, forcing his attention back to O'Dell. "How could anyone have that information?"

"His execution was recent. July, wasn't it?"

"Yes."

"Oftentimes, local news media run stories about the murders when an execution occurs. A person could get plenty of information from those accounts."

"The good ole media," Nick said, remembering the sting from Christine's articles.

"Or someone could get detailed information from the court transcripts. They're usually public record after the trial is over."

"So you think this is a copycat killer?"

"Yes. It would be too much of a coincidence to duplicate this many details."

"Why would anyone copycat a murder like this? For kicks?"

"I'm afraid I can't tell you that," O'Dell told him, finally looking up from the notebook and meeting his eyes. "What I can tell you is this guy is going to do it again. And probably soon."

CHAPTER 12

The hospital's morgue was in the basement where every sound echoed off the white brick walls. Water pipes thumped and a fan wheezed in motion. Behind them, the elevator door squeezed shut. There was a whirl and a scrape as cables strained and pulled the car back up.

Sheriff Morrelli seemed to be walking on tiptoe to avoid the clicking of his freshly cleaned boot heels against the tile floor. Maggie glanced up at him as they walked side by side. He was pretending that all of this was routine for him, but it was easy to see through the disguise. Back by the river, she had caught him wincing once or twice, betraying his calm, cool exterior.

Still, he had insisted on accompanying her here after discovering that the coroner had gone hunting for the day and couldn't be reached. Even the idea seemed ironic to Maggie—a coroner spending the day hunting. After all the dead bodies she had examined, she couldn't imagine spending a relaxing Sunday afternoon participating in more death.

She stood back while Morrelli fumbled with a tangle of keys, then discovered the door to the morgue unlocked. He held it open for her, pressing his body against its weight and requiring her to squeeze past him. She wasn't sure whether it was intentional or not, but this was the second or third time he had arranged for their bodies to be within touching distance.

Usually her cool, authoritarian manner quickly put a stop to any unwanted advances. But Morrelli didn't seem to notice. Somehow, she imagined he treated every woman he met as a potential one-night stand. She knew his type and also knew that his flirting and flattery, along with the boyish charm and athletic good looks, probably got him as far as he wanted to go. It was annoying, but in Morrelli's case it seemed harmless.

She had dealt with much worse. She was used to lewd comments from men who were uncomfortable working with a woman. Her experiences included plenty of sexual harassment, from mild flirtation to violent gropes. If anything, at least, it had taught her to take care of herself, protect herself with a shield of indifference.

Morrelli found the light switch, and like dominoes falling, the rows of fluorescent lights blinked on, one after another. The room was larger than Maggie had expected. Immediately, the smell of ammonia hit her nostrils and burned her lungs. Everything was immaculately scrubbed. A stainless-steel table occupied the middle of the tiled floor. On one wall was a large double sink and a counter that held various tools, including a Stryker saw, several microscopes, vials and test tubes ready for use. The opposite wall contained five refrigerated vaults. Maggie couldn't help wondering if the small hospital had ever had use for all five at one time.

She took off her jacket, laid it carefully over a stool and started rolling up the sleeves of her blouse. She stopped and looked around for a lab gown or utility apron. She looked down at the expensive silk blouse, a gift from Greg, a gift he would certainly notice if she never wore again because of unremovable stains. He would accuse her of being thoughtless and irresponsible, just as she had been with her wedding ring, which now sat somewhere on the murky bottom of the Charles River. Oh, well. She rolled up the sleeves.

She had brought with her a small, black bag that contained everything she would need. She opened it and began laying its contents on the counter, first taking out the small jar of Vicks VapoRub and dabbing a bit around her nostrils. She had learned long ago that even refrigerated dead bodies gave off a smell that was worth avoiding. She started to close the lid, then stopped and turned to Morrelli, who watched from the door. She tossed him the jar.

"If you're going to stay, you might want to use some of this."

He stared at the jar, then reluctantly opened it, following her example.

Next, she took out plastic surgical gloves. She handed him a pair, but he shook his head.

"You really don't have to stay," she told him. He was beginning to look pale again, and they hadn't even rolled out the body.

"No, I'll stay. I'll just...I don't want to be in your way."

She wasn't sure if it was out of a sense of duty, or if he simply felt it was required for his macho reputation. She preferred to do the examination alone but reminded herself this was Morrelli's territory and his case. Whether he assumed the role or not, he would technically be the head of this investigation.

She continued as though he weren't there. She pulled out a recorder, checked the tape inside and set it for voice activation. She took out a Polaroid camera and made sure it was loaded with film.

"Which drawer?" she asked, turning to the vaults, ready to begin, her hands on her hips. She glanced back at Morrelli, who stared at the wall of drawers as if he hadn't realized they would actually have to take the body out.

He moved slowly, hesitantly, then unlatched the middle drawer and pulled. The metal rollers squealed then clicked as the drawer filled the room.

Maggie kicked the brake off the wheels of the steel table and rolled it under the drawer. It fit perfectly. Together they unhitched the drawer tray with the small body bag, so that it lay flat on the table. Then they pushed the table back to the middle of the room under the suspended lighting unit. Maggie kicked the brakes back into place, while Morrelli closed the drawer's door. As soon as she began unzipping the bag, Morrelli retreated to the corner.

The boy's body seemed so small and frail, which made the wounds even more pronounced. He had been a good-looking kid, Maggie found herself thinking. His reddish-blond hair was closely cropped. The freckles around his nose and cheeks stood out against the white, pasty skin. He was bruised badly under the neck, the strands of rope leaving indents just above the gaping slash.

She began by taking photos, close-ups of the puncture marks and the jagged X on the chest, then the blue and purple marks on the wrists and the slashed neck. She waited for each Polaroid to develop, making sure she had enough light and the right angle.

With the recorder close by, she began documenting what she saw.

"The victim has bruise marks under and around his neck made by what looks to be a rope. It may have been tied. There appears to be an abrasion just under the left ear, perhaps from the knot."

She gently lifted the boy's head to look at the back of his neck. He felt so light, so weightless. "Yes, the marks are all the way around the neck. This would indicate that the victim was strangled, then his throat slashed. The throat wound is deep and long, extending just below the ear to the other ear. Bruises on the wrists and ankles are similar to the neck. The same rope may have been used."

His hands were so small in hers. Maggie held them carefully, reverently, as she examined the palms. "There are deep fingernail marks on the inside of his palms. This would indicate that the victim was alive while some of the wounds were inflicted. The fingernails themselves appear to be clean...very clean."

She rested the small hands at the boy's sides and began examining the wounds. "The victim has eight—no, nine—puncture marks in the chest cavity." She carefully poked the wounds, watching her gloved index finger disappear into several. "They appear to have been made by a single-edged knife. Three are shallow. At least six are very deep, possibly hitting bone. One may have gone through the heart. Yet, there is very little...actually, there is no blood. Sheriff Morrelli, did it rain while the body was in the open?"

She looked up at him when he didn't answer. He was leaning against the wall, hypnotized by the small body on the table. "Sheriff Morrelli?"

This time he realized she was talking to him. He pushed off the wall and stood straight, almost at attention. "I'm sorry, what did you say?" His voice was hushed. He whispered as if not to wake the boy.

"Do you remember if it rained while the body was out in the open?"

"No, not at all. We had plenty of rain the week before."

"Did the coroner clean the body?"

"We asked George to hold off doing anything until you got here. Why?"

Maggie looked over the body again. She stripped off a glove

and pushed her hair back out of her face, tucking it behind her ear. There was something very wrong. "Some of these wounds are deep. Even if they were made after the victim was dead, there would still be blood. If I remember correctly, there was plenty of blood at the crime scene in the grass and dirt."

"Lots of it. It took forever to get it off my clothes."

She lifted the small hand again. The nails were clean, no dirt, no blood or skin, even though he had dug them into the palm of his hand at one point. The feet, also, showed no sign of dirt, not a trace of the river mud. Though he couldn't have struggled much with his wrists and ankles bound, there still should have been enough movement to warrant some dirt.

"It's almost as if his body has been cleaned," she said to herself. When she looked up, Morrelli was standing beside her.

"Are you saying the killer washed the body after he was finished?"

"Look at the carving in the chest." She pulled the glove back on and gently poked her finger under the edge of the skin. "He used a different knife for this—one with a serrated edge. It ripped and tore the skin in some places. See here?" She ran her fingertip over the jagged skin.

"There would be blood. There *should* be blood, at least initially. And these puncture wounds are deep." She stuck her finger into one to show him. "When you make a hole this size, this deep, it's going to bleed profusely until you plug it up. This one, I'm almost certain, went into the heart. We're talking major artery, major gusher. And the throat...Sheriff Morrelli?"

Morrelli was leaning against the table, his weight jerking the stainless steel and sending out a high-pitched screech of metal against tile. Maggie looked up at him. His face was white. Before she realized it, he slumped against her. She caught him by the waist, but he was too heavy, and she slipped to the floor with him, her knees crumpling under her. The weight of him crushed against her chest.

"Morrelli, hey, are you okay?"

She squeezed out from under him and propped him against a table leg. He was conscious, but his eyes were glazed over. She climbed to her feet and looked for a towel to wet. Despite the well-equipped lab, there were no linens—no gowns or towels to be found. She remembered seeing a pop machine next to the elevators. Fumbling for the correct change, she was there and back before Morrelli moved.

His legs were twisted underneath him. His head rested against the table. Now, at least, his eyes were more focused when she knelt next to him with the Pepsi can.

"Here," she said, handing it to him.

"Thanks, but I'm not thirsty."

"No, for your neck. Here…" She reached over and put a hand at the back of his neck, gently pushing his head forward and down. Then she laid the cold Pepsi can against the back of his neck. He leaned into her. A few more inches, and his head would rest between her breasts. But now, dealing with his own vulnerability, he seemed completely unaware. Perhaps the macho ego did come with a sensitive side. She started to pull her hand away just as Morrelli reached up and caught it, gently encircling it with his large, strong fingers. He looked into her eyes, the crystal blue finally focused.

"Thanks." He sounded embarrassed, but his steady gaze held hers. A bit shook up and yet, if she wasn't mistaken, he was still flirting with her.

In response, she jerked her hand away, too quickly and much more abruptly than necessary. Just as abruptly, she handed him the Pepsi, then sat back on her knees, putting more distance between them.

"I can't believe I did that," he said. "I'm a little embarrassed."

"Don't be. I spent a lot of time on the floor before I got used to this stuff."

"How *do* you get used to it?" He looked back into her eyes, as if searching for the answer.

"I'm not sure. You just sort of disconnect, try not to think about it." She looked away and quickly got to her feet. She hated how his eyes seemed to look deep inside her. She realized it as a simple device, a cunning tool of his charm. Still, she was afraid he might actually see some weakness she had carefully hidden. Months ago there wouldn't have been anything to hide. Albert Stucky had supplied her with her own vulnerability, and she hated that it stayed so close to the surface where others might see it.

Before she could offer him a hand, Morrelli slowly stretched his long legs from the twisted knot and got to his feet without staggering or assistance. Other than his almost fainting, Maggie noticed that Sheriff Morrelli moved very smoothly, very confidently.

He smiled at her and rubbed the cold condensation of the can against his forehead, leaving a wet streak. Several strands of hair slipped across his forehead and stuck to the wetness. "Do you mind meeting me up in the cafeteria when you're finished?"

"No, of course not. I won't be much longer."

"I think I'll take a Pepsi break." He lifted the can to her as if in a toast. He started to leave, glanced back at the boy's body, then walked out.

Maggie's stomach churned, and she regretted not eating the breakfast offered during her roller-coaster flight. The room was cool, but her shuffle with Morrelli had left her hot and perspiring. She pulled off a glove and wiped her hand across her forehead, not surprised to find it damp. As she did so, she glanced at the boy's forehead. From this angle she could see something smeared on his brow.

She bent over the table, looking closely at the transparent smudge in the middle of his forehead. She wiped a finger across the area and rubbed her fingers together under her nose. If the body had been washed clean, that meant the oily liquid had been applied after. Instinctively, Maggie checked the boy's blue lips and found a smear of the oil. Before she even looked, she knew she'd find more of the oil on the boy's chest, just above his heart. Perhaps all those years of catechism had finally paid off. Otherwise, she may have never recognized that someone, perhaps the killer, had given this boy last rites.

CHAPTER 13

Christine Hamilton tried to edit the article she had scribbled in her notebook while pretending to know the score of the soccer game being played on the field down below her. The wooden bleachers were terribly uncomfortable no matter how she shifted her weight. She wanted a cigarette, but chewed the cap of her pen instead.

A sudden burst of applause, hoots and whistles made her look up just in time to see the team of red-clad, ten-year-old boys high-fiving each other. She had missed another point, but when the small, red-haired boy looked up from the huddle, she gave him a smile and thumbs-up as if she had seen the whole thing.

He was so much smaller than his teammates, yet to her he seemed to be growing too quickly. It didn't help matters that he was looking more and more like his father every day.

She pushed her sunglasses on top of her windblown hair. The sun was disappearing behind the line of trees that bordered the park. Thankfully, most of the clouds had passed over without dumping more rain. It was bad enough they were playing a make-up game on a Sunday evening.

She had isolated herself on the top bleacher away from the other soccer moms and dads. She didn't care to know these obsessive parents who wore team jerseys and screamed profanities at the coach. Later, they would slap the coach on the back and congratulate him on yet another win.

She flipped a page and was about to return to her editing when she noticed three of the other divorced soccer moms whispering to each other. Instead of watching the game, they were pointing to the sidelines. Christine turned to follow their gaze and immediately saw what had distracted them. The man striding up the sidelines typified the cliché—"tall, dark and handsome." He wore tight jeans and a sweatshirt with Nebraska Cornhuskers emblazoned across the chest. He looked like an older version of the college quarterback he used to be. He watched the game as he walked—no, glided—up the sidelines. But Christine knew he was well aware of the attention he was drawing from the bleachers. When he finally looked over, she waved to him, enjoying the look of envy on the women's faces when he smiled at her and made his way up the bleachers to join her.

"What's the score?" Nick asked, sliding in beside her.

"I think it's five to three. You realize, don't you, that you just made me the envy of every drooling, divorced soccer mom here?"

"See, the things I do for you, and you repay me with such abuse."

"Abuse? I never hit you a day of your life," she told her younger brother. "Well, not hard."

"That's not what I meant, and you know it." He wasn't joking.

She sat up straight, preparing to defend herself despite the guilt gnawing at her stomach. Yes, she should have called him before she turned in the story. But what if he had asked her not to run it? That story had put her on the other side of the door. Rather than being stuck writing helpful household hints, she had two front-page articles in two days with her byline. And tomorrow she'd be sitting at her own desk in the city room.

"How about I make it up to you? Dinner tomorrow night? I'll fix spaghetti and meatballs with Mom's secret sauce."

He looked over at her, glanced at the notebook. "You just don't get it, do you?"

"Oh, come on, Nicky. You know how long I've been waiting to get out of the "Living Today" section? If I hadn't filed that story, someone else would have."

"Really? And would they have quoted an officer who told them something off the record?"

"He never once said it was off the record. If Gillick told you otherwise, he's lying."

"Actually, I didn't know it was Eddie. Gee, Christine, you just gave away an anonymous source."

Her face grew hot, and she knew the red was quickly replacing her fair complexion. "Damn you, Nicky. You know how hard I'm trying. I'm a little rusty, but I can be a damn good reporter."

"Really? So far I think your reporting has been irresponsible."

"Oh, for crying out loud, Nicky. Just because you didn't like what I wrote doesn't make it irresponsible journalism."

"What about the headlines?" Nick spoke through gritted teeth. She couldn't remember the last time he'd been this upset with her. He avoided looking at her and watched the boys running up the field. "Where do you get off comparing this murder to Jeffreys'?"

"There are basic similarities."

"Jeffreys is dead," he whispered, looking around to make sure no one was listening. He clasped his hands together over a knee and tapped his foot on the empty bench in front of them, a nervous habit Christine recognized from childhood.

"Grow up, Nicky. Anyone with half a brain is going to compare this murder to Jeffreys'. I just wrote what everyone else is thinking. Are you saying I'm off target?"

"I'm saying we don't need another panic in a community that just started to feel like maybe their kids were safe again." He crossed his arms, looking unsure of what to do with his clenched fists. "You made me look like a goddamn idiot, Christine."

"Oh, I see. That's what this is really about. You don't care about a panic in the community. You're just worried about how you look. Why am I not surprised?"

He glared at her. For a moment, he looked as though he would defend himself, but instead he looked back out at the field. She hated when he absorbed her cheap shots without fighting back. Even as a kid, he never knew how to combat the insults—her secret weapons. She must be getting old, because suddenly she regretted hurting his feelings.

At the same time, though, she grew impatient with the way her brother approached things. He constantly took the easy way out, but then, why not? Everything seemed to be handed to Nick, from job opportunities to women. And he floated from one to the next without much effort, remorse or thought. When their father retired and insisted that Nick run for sheriff, Nick had left his professorship at the university without any hesitation. At least, none Christine had witnessed, though she knew he loved being on campus, being a walking legend and having coeds drool over him. Without a hitch—and quite predictably, in fact—he had been elected to the post of county sheriff. Though Nick would be the first to admit it was only because of their father's name and reputation. But he didn't seem to mind. He just took things as they came.

Christine, on the other hand, had to scrape and claw for everything she wanted, especially since Bruce's departure. Well, this time she deserved the break she was getting. She refused to apologize for capitalizing on her sudden streak of good fortune.

"If it is a copycat, don't you think people deserve a warning?" She kept her voice sincere, though she didn't want or need to justify herself. This was news. She knew what she was doing. The public had a right to know all the grisly details.

Nick didn't answer. Instead, he brought his feet up on the bench in front so he could lean forward, elbows on his knees, chin resting on clenched fists. They sat silently in the middle of whoops and howls. There was something different, something unfamiliar about him, and the change was disconcerting.

After what seemed like a long time, Nick said quietly, calmly, "Danny Alverez was just a year older than Timmy." His eyes were focused straight ahead.

Christine looked out at Timmy bouncing down the field, weaving in between the boys that towered over him. He was fast and agile, using his smallness to his advantage. And, yes, she had noticed the resemblance. Timmy looked very much like the school photo they had used in the newspaper of Danny. They both had reddish-blond hair, blue eyes and a sprinkle of freckles. Like Timmy, Danny also was small for his age.

"I just spent the afternoon at the morgue." His voice startled her back to reality.

"Why?" she asked, pretending not to be interested. She stared at the game, but watched Nick out of the corner of her eye. She had never seen him so serious before.

"Bob Weston called in an expert to help us come up with a profile—Special Agent Maggie O'Dell from Quantico. She got in this morning and was raring to get to work." He glanced over at Christine, then did a double take when he noticed her scratching down something in her notebook. "Jesus, Christine!" he spat out so suddenly it made her jump. "Isn't anything off the record with you?"

"If you wanted it off the record, you should have said so." She watched him rub his hand across his jaw as if she had sucker punched him. "Besides, by tomorrow everyone will know about Agent O'Dell when she starts asking questions. What are you worried about, Nicky? Calling in an expert is a good thing."

"Is it? Or will it just make me look like I don't know what the hell I'm doing?" He shot her another look. "Don't you dare print that."

"Relax. I'm not the enemy, Nicky." She noticed the boys doing their victory dance between the required handshakes. The game was over, and it was beginning to get dark. The park lights slowly turned on one by one. "You know, Dad wasn't afraid to work with the news media."

"Yeah, well, I'm not Dad." Now she had made him angry. She knew to stay away from the comparison, but she hated him treating her like an ambulance chaser. Besides, if he didn't like the comparisons, perhaps he shouldn't have followed in their father's footsteps. As usual, she simply sidestepped the subject.

"I'm just saying that Dad knew how to use the media to help."

"To help?" Nick asked incredulously, his voice rising above the cheering in front of them. He quickly looked around, realizing he was too loud. He lowered his voice again and leaned toward her. "Dad used the news media because he loved being in the limelight. There were so many leaks, it's amazing they ever caught Jeffreys."

"What leaks? What are you talking about?"

"Never mind," he said, glancing at her notebook.

Christine rolled her eyes at him, wondering if he was just baiting her now.

"But they did catch Jeffreys, and Dad solved the case," she reminded him.

"Yeah, they did catch Jeffreys, and good ole Dad took all the credit."

"Nicky, no one's asking you to fill Dad's shoes. You always take that on yourself." Okay, there it was. A slip, an innocent slip. She watched his face, waiting.

Instead, he simply shook his head. A frustrated smile caught at the corner of his mouth as if he thought she couldn't possibly understand.

"Haven't you ever wondered..." He hesitated, looking out at the field, his thoughts far away. "Didn't you ever think it happened all too quickly...too neat and convenient?"

"What are you talking about?"

This wasn't the response she expected. The night air was chilly, and Christine felt a shiver down her back. She rubbed her arms and tried to look into her brother's eyes. He was starting to scare her with his anger and his hushed manner. Normally, he joked around and never took anything too seriously, even their sibling banter. Had the mention of their father brought all this on? No, it was something else. What did he know? What was it that had her arrogant, confident little brother so spooked?

"Nicky, what do you mean?" she tried again.

"Forget it," he said, standing up and stretching, closing the subject.

"Uncle Nick, Uncle Nick! Did you see me score?" Timmy yelled as he ran up the bleachers, carefully watching his small feet the whole way up.

"You bet I did," Nick lied.

She watched as Nick's entire face changed, relaxing into a smile as he snatched her small son up into his long arms, wrestling him in close for a hug.

Christine knew her brother was hiding something, and she was going to find out what it was.

CHAPTER 14

He drove around the park again, this time slowly. The game was finally over. He pulled into a parking space far from the other cars, alone in the corner of the lot. He turned off the headlights and sat watching, listening to the music and waiting for the jerky strings of Vivaldi to smooth out and silence the throbbing in his temples.

It was happening again and so soon. He couldn't stop it, couldn't control it. And worse, he didn't want to. He was so tired. He tried to remember when he had last slept through an entire night, instead of pacing or wandering the streets. He rubbed his eyes, wiping at the exhaustion, then stopped suddenly. His fingers were trembling beyond his control.

"Dear God, make it stop," he whispered as he tore at the hair at his temples. Why wouldn't it stop? The throbbing, the pounding made his head ache.

He watched the group of boys in grass-stained uniforms. They looked so happy, fresh from their victory, arms crossing around one another, hands patting each other on the back. They touched so carelessly, so casually. Their singsong voices grew loud as they approached, drowning out Vivaldi with lyrics of gibberish.

The memory came flooding back to him, paralyzing him and pinning him to the stiff leather of the car seat. He was eleven years old and his stepfather had made him join the Little League team, bargaining with the coach to get him out of the house on Saturday mornings. He knew it was only because his stepfather wanted to fuck his mother all morning.

He had accidentally walked in on them the Saturday before, only because they were out of milk. The memory washed over him—powerful despite the years. So clear, so vivid he grabbed the steering wheel to brace himself.

He stood in the doorway of his mother's bedroom, paralyzed by the sight of his mother's skin, white and naked with the silver cross swinging between her big breasts. Her breasts wagged back and forth. She held herself up on her hands and knees while his stepfather rode her like a dog in heat.

It was his stepfather who saw him first. He yelled at him, panting and jerking, while his mother's eyes grew wide in horror. She twisted out from under his stepfather, falling and tumbling off the bed, grabbing for the sheet. It was then that he turned to run. He stumbled down the hall, tripping and falling only once before he got to his room. Just as he began to slam the door, his stepfather crashed through it.

His stepfather was still naked. It was the first time he had seen a grown man's penis, and it was horrible: huge, stiff and erect, protruding through the thick black hair. His stepfather grabbed him by the neck and shoved his face to the wall.

"You interested in watching or maybe you want some of this." He could still hear the man's graveled voice, out of breath and panting in his ear.

He stood perfectly still. He couldn't breathe. His stepfather's fingers strangled his neck with one hand while he ripped his pajama pants with the other. His mother screamed and pounded her fists against his locked door. Then he felt it. The intense pressure, the pain so stifling he thought his insides would explode. He kept quiet and still, though he wanted to scream. His cheek scraped against the rough texture of the bedroom wall. All he could do was stare at the crucifix hanging next to his face, while he waited for his stepfather to stop slamming into his small body.

A car's horn blasted. He jumped and clutched the steering wheel even harder. His palms were sweaty, his fingers still trembling. He watched the boys getting into the cars and vans with their parents. How many of them were hiding secrets like his own? How many of them hid their bruises and scars? How many waited for some sort of relief, some sort of salvation from their misery? From their torture?

Then he saw the small boy waving to the others as he started up the sidewalk. He watched to see if anyone would join the boy tonight, or if he would walk home alone as he usually did.

It was starting to get dark. Several street lights blinked on. He listened to the gravel grind beneath the cars as they pulled out and drove off. Headlights flicked on and blinded him as they turned to leave. No one noticed him. No one took extra time to look his way. Those who recognized him smiled and waved, for there was nothing unusual about him taking in a neighborhood soccer game.

Half a block away, the boy still walked alone, tossing the soccer ball from one hand to the other. He looked thin and small in his baggy uniform, so very vulnerable. The boy practically skipped, regardless of no one showing up to watch him play. Perhaps he had grown accustomed to his loneliness.

The last car left the parking lot. He silenced Vivaldi in the middle of *The Four Seasons: Autumn.* Without looking, his fingers found the small, glass vial from inside the glove compartment. Expertly, he cracked the vial and let it dampen the brilliant white handkerchief. He wished the extra precautions were not necessary, but he had been reckless with Danny. He grabbed the black ski mask and got out of the car, gently closing the door. Immediately, he noticed that his hands were no longer trembling. Yes, he was finally feeling back in control. Then he followed quietly up the sidewalk.

CHAPTER 15

Monday, October 27

Maggie poured the rest of the Scotch from the small bottle to the plastic cup. The ice cubes cracked and tinkled against each other. She took a sip, closed her eyes and welcomed the lovely sting sliding down her throat. Lately, she worried that she had acquired her mother's taste for alcohol, or worse, her addiction to the pleasant numbness promised by the sacred liquid.

She rubbed her eyes and glanced at the cheap clock radio across the room on the nightstand. It was after two in the morning, and she couldn't sleep. The dim table lamp gave her a headache. It was probably the Scotch, but she made a note to ask the hotel clerk for a brighter light.

The small tabletop was covered with the Polaroid photos she had taken earlier. She attempted to put them in chronological order—hands tied, neck strangled then slashed, puncture wounds. This madman was methodical. He took his time. He cut, sliced and peeled back skin with frightening precision. Even the jagged X followed a specific diagonal from shoulder blade to belly button.

She scattered two file folders full of police reports and newspaper clippings. There were enough gory details to provide nightmares for a lifetime. Except it was impossible to have nightmares if you couldn't sleep.

She pulled her bare legs up, tucking her feet underneath her in an attempt to make herself comfortable in the hard chair. Her

Green Bay Packers jersey had stretched and become misshapen from too many washes. It barely covered her thighs, yet it was still the softest nightshirt she owned. It had become a sort of security blanket that made her feel at home no matter how many miles away. She refused to get rid of it despite Greg's constant complaints.

She looked at the clock again. She should have called Greg when she had gotten back to the hotel. Now it was too late. Perhaps it was just as well. They both needed some cooling-down time.

She sifted through the scattered papers and examined her notes, several pages of details, small observations, some that would probably seem insignificant to anyone else. Eventually, she would pull them all together and create a profile of the killer. She had done it many times before. Sometimes she could describe the killer right down to height, hair color and, in one case, even his aftershave lotion. This time, though, it was more difficult. Partly because the obvious suspect had already been executed. And partly because it was always difficult to crawl inside the sick, disgusting mind of a child killer.

She picked up the silver medallion and chain from the corner of the desk. It resembled the one Danny Alverez had worn. Though this one had been given to Maggie by her father for her first Holy Communion.

"As long as you wear this, God will protect you from any harm," her father had told her. Though his own, identical medallion had not saved him. She wondered if he had gone into the burning building that night believing it would.

Until a month ago she had worn the medallion faithfully, perhaps out of routine and remembrance of her father rather than out of any sense of spirituality. She had stopped praying the day she watched her father's casket lowered into the cold, hard earth. At twelve, none of her catechism teachings could explain why God had needed to take her father away.

In fact, she had put aside Catholicism until she joined the forensic lab at Quantico eight years ago. Suddenly, those crude drawings in her Baltimore Catechism of demons with horns and glowing red eyes had made sense. Evil did exist. She had seen it in the eyes of killers. She had seen it in the eyes of Albert Stucky. Ironically, it was that evil that had brought her closer to believing in God again. But it was Albert Stucky who made her wonder whether God simply didn't care anymore. The night she watched Stucky slaughter two women, Maggie had gone home and removed the medallion from around her neck. And although she couldn't bring herself to wear it anymore, she still carried it with her.

She ran her fingers over the smooth surface of the medal and wondered what Danny Alverez must have felt. What must he have thought when the madman ripped away what the small boy may have seen as his last protection? Like her father, had Danny Alverez put his final breath of faith in a silly metal object?

She clutched the medallion tightly in her fist, pulled back her arm and was ready to fling the worthless charm across the room when a soft tap on the door stopped her. The knock was barely audible. Instinctively, Maggie got to her feet and slipped out her Smith & Wesson .38 revolver from its holster. She padded quietly to the door in bare feet, feeling vulnerable in only the night-shirt and underpants. She gripped the revolver, waiting for its power to remove her sense of vulnerability. Through the peephole she could see Sheriff Morrelli, and the tension slid away from her shoulders. She opened the door, but just enough to look out at him.

"What's going on, Sheriff?"

"Sorry. I tried to call, but the night desk clerk has been on the phone for over an hour."

He looked exhausted, his blue eyes swollen and red, his short hair sticking up out of place and his face still unshaved. His shirt was untucked, the tails hanging out over his jeans and peeking out from under his denim jacket. She noticed that several of the top buttons were missing, and his twisted collar was open, exposing wisps of dark curly hair. Immediately, she looked away, annoyed with herself for noticing this last detail.

"Is something wrong?" she asked.

"Another boy's missing," he said, swallowing hard as if it was difficult to get the words out.

"That's impossible," she said, but knew, in fact, that it wasn't. Albert Stucky had taken his fourth victim less than an hour after his third victim was discovered. The beautiful, blond coed had been sliced in pieces, some of which were stuffed in takeout boxes and discarded in the Dumpster behind a restaurant Stucky had eaten at earlier that evening.

"I've got men going door-to-door in the neighborhood and searching alleys, parks, fields." He rubbed his hand over his exhausted face and scratched his bristled jaw. His eyes were a watery blue. "The kid was walking home from a soccer game. He only had five blocks to walk." His eyes darted down the hall, avoiding Maggie's gaze while pretending to make sure no one else was in the deserted hallway.

"Maybe you should come in."

Maggie held the door open for him. He hesitated, then walked in slowly, staying in the entrance as he glanced around the room. He turned back to Maggie, and his eyes dropped to her legs. She had forgotten about the short nightshirt. He looked up quickly, met her eyes and looked away. He was embarrassed. The charming, flirtatious Morrelli was embarrassed.

"Sorry. Did I wake you?" Another glance, and this time when his eyes found hers, she felt her face grow hot. As nonchalantly as possible, she squeezed past him and went to the dresser.

"No, I was still up."

She slid her gun back into its holster, opened one of the dresser drawers and started digging for a pair of jeans. Finally, she found a pair and pulled them on while she watched Morrelli pace the small space between the bed and table.

"Did I mention that I tried to call first?"

She looked up in the mirror and caught him watching her. Their eyes met again, this time in the mirror.

"Yes, you did. It's okay," she said, struggling with the zipper. "Actually, I was going over my notes."

"I was at that game," he said softly, quietly.

"What game?"

"The soccer game. The one the boy was walking home from. My nephew played. Jesus, Timmy probably knows this kid." He continued to pace the room, making the space seem even smaller with his long strides.

"Are you sure the boy didn't go home with a friend?"

"We called other parents. His friends remember seeing him start walking up the sidewalk toward home. And we found his soccer ball. It's autographed by some famous soccer player. His mom says it's one of his most prized possessions. She insists he wouldn't have just left it.''

He scraped a sleeve across his face. Maggie recognized the panic in his eyes. He wasn't prepared to handle a situation like this. She wondered what experience he had in crisis management. She sighed and raked her fingers through her tangled hair. Already she regretted that it would be up to her to keep him focused.

"Sheriff, maybe you should sit down."

"Bob Weston suggested I compile a list of pedophiles and known sex offenders. Do I start hauling them in for questioning? Can you give me any idea who I should be looking for?" He glanced over the papers spread out on the table in one of his passes.

"Sheriff Morrelli, why don't you sit down?"

"No, I'm fine."

"No, I insist." She reached up and grabbed him by the shoulders, gently shoving him into a chair behind the table. He looked as though he'd stand up again, thought better of it, then stretched out his long legs.

"Did you have any suspects at all when the Alverez boy was taken?" Maggie asked.

"Just one. His father. His parents are divorced. The father was refused custody and visitation because of his drinking and abusiveness. We were never able to track him down. Hell, the air force can't even find him. He was a major at the base, but went AWOL two months ago. He ran off with a sixteen-year-old girl he met over the Internet."

She found herself pacing as she listened. Perhaps it had been a mistake to make him sit. Now that he gave her his full attention it dismantled her thought process. She rubbed her eyes, realizing how exhausted she was. How long could a person function without sufficient sleep?

"Have you made any progress in tracking him down?"

"We stopped."

"What do you mean you stopped?"

"After we found Danny's body, Weston said it couldn't be the father. That a father wouldn't be able to do that to his own son."

"I've seen what fathers can do to their sons. I remember a

case three, no, four years ago where a father buried his six-year-old son in a box. He dug a hole in the backyard and left just a small airhole with a piece of rubber hose. It was punishment for something stupid. I can't even remember now what the kid had done. After several days of rain, he couldn't find the air hole. Instead of digging up his entire backyard, he tried to make it look like a kidnapping. The wife went along with his crazy scheme. She probably didn't want to end up in a box of her own. Maybe you should continue searching for Mr. Alverez. Didn't you say he was abusive?''

"Yeah, the guy's a real asshole. Beat up regularly on his wife and Danny, even after the divorce. She's had a half-dozen restraining orders out on him. But what possible connection could there be with this boy? I don't think Matthew Tanner even knew Danny Alverez.''

"There may not be a connection. We don't know for sure that this boy was taken. He could still show up at a friend's house. Or he may have run away.''

"Okay." He sighed, not looking convinced. He slid down farther in the chair to rest his head against the back. "But you don't really believe he ran away, do you?''

Her eyes searched his. Despite his confusion and panic, he wanted the truth. She decided to level with him.

"No. Probably not," she said. "I knew the killer would strike again. I just didn't think it would be *this* soon.''

"So tell me where to begin. Have you had time to figure out anything about this guy?''

She came around the table and stared at the montage of photos, notes and reports.

"He's meticulous, in control. He takes his time, not only with the murder, but in cleaning up after himself. Though the cleaning isn't to hide evidence—it's part of his ritual. I think he may have done this before." She fingered through her notes. "He's definitely not young and immature," she continued. "There was no sign of struggle at the site, so the victim was tied beforehand. That means he has to be strong enough to carry a seventy-to-eighty-pound boy at least three hundred to five hundred yards. I'm guessing he's in his thirties, about six feet tall, two hundred pounds. He's white. He's educated and he's intelligent.''

At some point during her description, Morrelli sat up, suddenly alert and interested in the mess she poked through.

"Remember at the hospital after I examined the Alverez boy, I told you he may have given the boy last rites? That would mean the killer's Catholic, maybe not practicing, but his Catholic guilt is still strong. Strong enough that he's bothered by a medallion in the shape of a cross, so he rips it off. He performs extreme unction, perhaps to atone for his sin. You might check to see whether this boy, Matthew Tanner," she said, looking at Nick to make certain she had the name right. When he nodded, she continued, "if he belonged to the same church as the Alverez boy."

"Right offhand, I'd say it's unlikely," Nick said. "Danny went to school and church out by the base. The Tanner house is only a few blocks from St. Margaret's, unless the Tanners aren't Catholic."

"Chances are, the killer doesn't even know the boys." Maggie started pacing again. "It could be he simply looks for easy targets, boys out alone, with no one else around. I do think he may still be connected somehow to a Catholic church, and quite possibly in this area. Odd as it might seem, these guys don't often stray too far from their own familiar territory."

"He sounds like a real sicko. You said he may have done this before. Is it possible he may have a record? Maybe child abuse or sexual molestation? Maybe even beating up a gay lover?"

"You're assuming he's gay or that he's a pedophile?"

"An adult male who does this to little boys—isn't that a safe assumption?"

"No, not at all. He may be worried that he is, or he may have homosexual tendencies, but no, I don't think he's gay, nor do I believe he's a pedophile."

"And you can tell all that just from the evidence we've found?"

"No. I'm guessing that from the evidence we haven't found. The victim didn't appear to be sexually abused. There were no traces of semen in the mouth or rectum, though he may have washed it off. There were no signs of any penetration, no indication of sexual stimulation. Even with Jeffreys' victims, only one—Bobby Wilson," she said, checking her notes. "Only the

Wilson boy showed signs of sexual abuse and those seemed very obvious. Multiple penetration, lots of tearing and bruising.''

"Wait a minute. If this guy is only copying Jeffreys, how can we be sure any of what he does is an indication of who he is?''

"Copycats choose murders that often play out their own fantasies. Sometimes they add their individual touches. I can't find any indications that Jeffreys gave his victims last rites, though it could easily have been overlooked.''

"I do know he asked for a priest to hear his confession before he was executed.''

"How do you know that?'' She looked down at him, only then realizing she was half sitting on the chair's armrest. Her thigh rubbed against Morrelli's arm. She stood up. Perhaps a bit too suddenly. He didn't seem to notice.

"You probably know that my dad was the sheriff who brought in Jeffreys. Well, he had a front-row seat at the execution.''

"Is it possible to ask him some questions?''

"He and my mom bought an RV a few years ago. They travel year-round. They check in from time to time, but I don't know how to get ahold of them. I'm sure once they hear about this, he'll be in touch, but it may take a while.''

"I wonder if it's possible to track down the priest?''

"No problem. Father Francis is still here at St. Margaret's. Though I don't know what help he could be. It's not likely he'll share Jeffreys' confession.''

"I'd still like to talk to him. Then we better talk to the Tanners. You've obviously met them already?''

"His mom. Matthew's parents are divorced.''

Maggie stared at him, then began digging through her files.

"What is it?'' Nick leaned forward, almost touching her side.

She found what she was looking for, flipped through the pages, then stopped. "All three of Jeffreys' victims came from single-parent households. Mothers raising their sons alone.''

"What does that mean?''

"It means there may be nothing random about how he picks his victims. I was wrong about him waiting to simply find a boy alone. He chooses each one very carefully. You said the Alverez boy left his bike and newspapers against a fence somewhere?''

"Right. He hadn't even started his route yet.''

"And there was no sign of a struggle?''

"None. It looked like he carefully parked his bike and got in with this guy. That's why we thought it might be someone he knew. These kids are small-town kids, but they still know the drill. I just don't think Danny would get into a stranger's vehicle."

"Unless he thought it was someone he could trust."

Maggie could see Morrelli growing more and more concerned. She recognized the panic, that look on people's faces when they realized the killer could be someone in their community.

"What do mean? Like someone who pretended to know him or his mom?"

"Perhaps. Or someone who looked official, maybe even wearing a uniform." Maggie had seen it dozens of times before. No one seemed to question whether a person in uniform actually belonged in the uniform.

"Maybe a military uniform like his dad's?" Nick asked.

"Or a white lab coat, or even a police officer's uniform."

CHAPTER 16

Timmy slid against the wall until he was sitting on the floor, watching the bathroom door. He had to pee but knew better than to interrupt his mom. If he knocked, she would insist he come in and take care of business while she finished her makeup. He was getting too old to pee with his mom in the same room.

He listened to her singing and decided to retie his tennis shoes. The crack in the sole had spread. Soon he'd need to ask for new ones, even though his mom couldn't afford them. He had overheard her on the phone with his dad and knew his dad hadn't sent them any of the money the court had said he was supposed to send each month.

It was something from *The Little Mermaid*—that's what his mom was singing. Her Jamaican accent needed help, even though she had watched that movie almost as many times as he had watched *Star Wars*. The phone started ringing. She would never be able to hear it down "under the sea." He scrambled to his feet to answer it.

"Hello?"

"Timmy? This is Mrs. Calloway—Chad's mom. Is your mom there?"

He almost blurted out that Chad had hit him first. If Chad said it was the other way around, he was lying. Instead, he said, "Just a minute. I'll get her."

Chad Calloway was a bully, but if Timmy had told his mom that Chad had purposely inflicted the bruises, she would have most definitely made him quit soccer. And now the bully had probably lied about his own bruises.

Timmy knocked softly on the bathroom door. If she didn't answer, he'd have to tell Mrs. Calloway that his mom couldn't come to the phone right now. The door, however, clicked and opened. His heart sank down to his cracked shoes.

"Was that the phone?" She came out smelling good and bringing a trail of perfume with her.

"It's Mrs. Calloway."

"Who?"

"Mrs. Calloway, Chad's mom."

She squinted at him, her eyebrows raised as she waited for more.

"I don't know what she wants." He shrugged and followed her to the phone even though he still had to pee, more than ever now.

"This is Christine Hamilton. Yes, of course." She spun around to Timmy and mouthed, "Calloway?"

"She's Chad's mom," he whispered. She never listened to him.

"Yes, you're Chad's mom."

He couldn't tell what Mrs. Calloway was telling his mom. She paced as she normally did while on the phone, nodding though the other person couldn't see her. Her answers were short. A couple of "uh-huhs" and one "oh, sure."

Then suddenly, she stopped and gripped the phone. Here it was. He needed to prepare his story. Wait a minute. He didn't need a story. The truth was, Chad had picked on him. No, beat the shit out of him was more accurate. And for no real reason, other than he liked it.

"Thank you for calling, Mrs. Calloway."

His mom hung up the phone and stared out the window. He couldn't tell whether she was angry. She couldn't make him quit soccer. He was ready to spit out his defense when she turned and beat him to it.

"Timmy, one of your teammates is missing."

"What?"

"Matthew Tanner never came home last night after the soccer game."

So it had nothing to do with Chad?

"Some of the other soccer parents are meeting at the Tanner house this morning to help out."

"Is Matthew in trouble? Why didn't he go home?" He hoped he didn't sound relieved, but in fact, he was.

"Now, I don't want you to worry, Timmy, but do you remember my articles about that boy, Danny Alverez?"

He nodded. How could he not remember? She had sent him out yesterday morning to buy five extra copies of the newspaper, even though she could have had as many copies as she wanted from work.

"Well, we don't know for sure yet, so I don't want you to get scared, but the man who took Danny may have taken Matthew."

His mom looked worried. Those lines around her mouth showed up every time she frowned.

"Go use the bathroom, and I'll take you to school. I don't want you walking today."

"Okay." He raced back to the bathroom. Poor Matthew, he found himself thinking. Too bad Chad couldn't have been the one taken, instead.

CHAPTER 17

Christine couldn't believe her luck, though she tried to contain her excitement. While Timmy had been in the bathroom, she had called Taylor Corby, the news editor, her new boss. They had talked several times over the weekend by phone, and, although they had never met, Christine knew exactly who he was. Her co-workers in the "Living Today" section called Corby a news nerd. He wore funky wire-rimmed glasses and seemed to own only black trousers and white oxford shirts, which he decorated with different Looney Tunes ties. To make matters worse, he rode a bicycle even in the winter—and not because he couldn't afford a car, but simply because he wanted to.

This morning when she told him about Matthew Tanner, Corby quietly listened.

"Christine, you know what that means?"

It was easy to understand why he had chosen print instead of broadcast journalism. His voice never changed, showed no emotion. And regardless of his choice of words, it was sometimes difficult to tell whether he was excited, bored or simply disinterested. "If you have copy for this evening's paper, we will have scooped the other media three days in a row."

"I still need to convince Mrs. Tanner to let me interview her."

"Interview or not, you already have enough for a great story. Just make sure you substantiate your facts."

"Of course."

Now, Christine looked over at her son, knowing he must be worried about his friend. He had made no fuss about her driving him to school and had sat most of the trip in silence. She turned the corner to the school and immediately slammed on the brakes. A line of cars extended to the corner as parents pulled in front of the school to drop off their children. On the sidewalks, parents walked alongside their kids. Every intersection in view had adult crossing guards accompanying their smaller charges.

A horn behind them blasted, making both Christine and Timmy jump. She inched the car forward, getting in line.

"What's going on, Mom?" Timmy snapped out of his seat belt so he could sit on his feet, allowing a view over the dash.

"Parents are just making sure their kids get to school okay." Some of the parents looked frantic, scurrying along with one hand on a shoulder, an arm, a back, as though the extra contact would add protection.

"Because of Matthew?"

"We don't know what's happened to Matthew yet. He may have just gotten upset and run away from home. You shouldn't say anything about Matthew." She shouldn't have told Timmy about Matthew. Though she had promised to be open and honest with her son after Bruce left, this was not something she should have shared with him. Besides, very few people even knew about Matthew. This panic was in response to her articles. Just the mention of Ronald Jeffreys invoked a protectiveness in parents. This was the same panic parents had displayed when Jeffreys had been on the prowl.

Christine recognized Richard Melzer from KRAP radio. He hurried up the sidewalk in his trench coat, carrying his briefcase and holding the hand of a small blond girl, his daughter no doubt. Christine needed to get to Michelle Tanner's as soon as possible. It wouldn't be long before others found out about Matthew.

The line moved along at a crawl, and she searched for an opening. Perhaps she could just let Timmy out here. She knew he wouldn't mind, except everyone would notice.

"Mom?"

"Timmy, we're moving as fast as possible."

"Mom, I'm pretty sure Matthew wouldn't just run away from home."

She glanced at her small son perched on his feet, watching the unusual parade outside his window. His hair stuck up where he had plastered down the cowlick. The sprinkle of freckles only made his skin more pale. When had this little boy grown so wise? She should have felt proud, yet this morning it made her a little sad that she could no longer preserve his innocence.

CHAPTER 18

Brightly colored stained-glass figures stared down from their heavenly perch. The scent of burning incense and candle wax filled Maggie's nostrils. Why was it that being inside of a Catholic church always made her feel as if she was twelve again? Immediately, she thought of the black bra and panties she wore—too much lace, an inappropriate color. The butt of her gun stabbed into her side. She reached inside her jacket and readjusted the shoulder strap. Should she even be carrying a gun inside a church? Of course, she was being ridiculous.

She glanced over her shoulder as if expecting to see a casket being rolled up the aisle behind them. She could still hear the *click-clack* of rollers, the soft tap of a dozen leather shoes marching in unison along with her father's casket. When she looked up, Morrelli was watching her, waiting for her at the altar.

"Everything okay?"

He had left her hotel room at five o'clock to go home, shower, shave and change clothes. When he arrived two hours later to pick her up, she hardly recognized him. His short hair was neatly combed back. His face was clean-shaven, and the white scar on his chin—even more pronounced—added a rugged edge to his good looks. Underneath his denim jacket he wore a white shirt and black tie with crisp blue jeans and shiny black cowboy boots. It was a stretch from the customary brown uniforms the rest of his department wore, but he still looked official. Perhaps it was simply the way he carried himself, straight and tall, self-assured with long, confident strides.

"O'Dell, are you okay?" he asked again.

She looked around the church. It seemed large for a town of Platte City's size, with rows and rows of wooden pews. She couldn't imagine all of them being filled.

"I'm fine," she finally answered, then regretted taking so long because he truly did look concerned. His eyes betrayed his fresh appearance, still puffy from too little sleep. She had tried to hide her own signs of fatigue with a bit of makeup.

"It seems so big," she said, trying to explain her distraction.

"It's relatively new. The old church was a small country parish about five miles south of town," he told her. "Platte City's grown, practically doubled in the last ten years. Mostly people tired of living in the city. They still commute to work either in Omaha or Lincoln. Kind of ironic, huh? People moving out here to get away from big-city crime, thinking they'll raise their kids someplace quiet and safe." He shoved his hands into his pockets and stared off over her head.

"You folks need some help?" A man appeared from a curtain behind the altar.

"We're looking for Father Francis," Morrelli said without offering any more explanation.

The man eyed them suspiciously. Though he carried a broom, he was dressed in dress slacks, a crisply pressed shirt, tie and long, brown cardigan. He looked young despite his dark hair peppered with gray. When he approached them, Maggie noticed he had a slight limp and wore bright white tennis shoes.

"What do you want with Father Francis?"

Morrelli glanced at Maggie as if asking how much to reveal. Before he had a chance to say anything, the man seemed to recognize Morrelli.

"Wait a minute. I know who you are." He said it as if it were an accusation. "Didn't you play quarterback for the Nebraska Cornhuskers? You're Morrelli, Nick Morrelli, 1982 to 1983."

"You're a Cornhuskers fan?" Morrelli grinned, obviously pleased by the recognition. Maggie noticed dimples. A quarterback—why wasn't she surprised?

"Big-time fan. My name's Ray...Ray Howard. I just moved back here last spring. They didn't televise very many games back East. It was horrible, just horrible. Actually, I played a bit." His excitement rambled on in quick bursts. "In high school. At

Omaha Central. Even had Dr. Tom come check me out. Then I boogered up my knee. Our final game. Against Creighton Prep, of all the sissy teams. I twisted it up pretty good. Never played again.''

''Sorry to hear that,'' Nick said.

''Yeah, the Lord moves in mysterious ways. So, is this here your wife?'' He finally acknowledged Maggie. She felt his eyes slide over her body, and she resisted the urge to button her jacket.

''No, we're not married.'' Morrelli seemed embarrassed.

''Your fiancée then. That's probably what you want to see Father Francis about, huh? He's married hundreds.''

''No, we're not—''

''It's an official matter,'' Maggie interrupted, relieving Morrelli. The man stared at her, waiting for an explanation. Now she crossed her arms over her chest, emphasizing her authority and stifling his wandering eyes. ''Is Father Francis here?''

Howard looked at Morrelli, then back at Maggie when he realized neither was willing to say more.

''I think he's in back changing. He said mass this morning.'' He made no effort to leave.

''Would you mind getting him for us, Ray?'' Morrelli asked much more politely than Maggie would have.

''Oh, sure.'' He turned to leave, then stopped. ''Who should I say wants to see him?'' He looked at Maggie, waiting for an introduction.

Maggie sighed and shifted her weight impatiently. Morrelli shot her a look, then said, ''Just tell him Nick Morrelli, okay?''

''Oh, sure.''

Howard disappeared behind the curtain. This time Maggie rolled her eyes at Morrelli, and he smiled. ''A quarterback, huh?'' she said.

''That was a long time ago. Actually, it seems like a lifetime ago.''

''Were you any good?''

''I had a chance to go on and play for the Dolphins, but my dad insisted on law school.''

''Do you always do everything your dad tells you to do?''

She meant it as a joke, but he bristled, and his eyes told her it was a touchy subject. Then he smiled, and said, ''Apparently, I do.''

"Nicholas." A small gray-haired priest glided onto the altar in his black, floor-length cassock. "Mr. Howard said you had official business to talk to me about."

"Hello, Father Francis. Sorry I didn't call before we dropped in on you."

"That's perfectly all right. You're always welcome here."

"Father, this is Special Agent Maggie O'Dell. She's with the FBI and is here to help me on the Alverez case."

Maggie offered her hand. The old priest took it in both of his and held it tightly. Thick blue veins protruded from the thin, brown-spotted skin. A slight tremor jiggled her hand. He looked deep into her eyes, and suddenly she felt exposed, as though he could see clear into her soul. A slight shiver slid down her back as she held his gaze.

"It's a pleasure to meet you." When he let go, he grasped the nearby podium, depending on it for strength. "Christine's son, Timmy, reminds me of you, Nicholas. He's one of Father Keller's altar boys." Then to Maggie, he said, "Nicholas was an altar boy for me years ago at the old St. Margaret's."

"Really?" Maggie glanced at Morrelli, anxious to witness his discomfort. Something behind him caught her eye. The altar curtain moved. There was no breeze, no draft. Then she saw the toes of two white tennis shoes poking out from underneath. Instead of drawing attention to the intruder, she smiled at Morrelli, who now seemed flustered by the priest's attention.

"Father Francis." He was anxious to change the subject. "We wondered if you could answer a few questions."

"Certainly. What can I do to help?" He looked at Maggie.

"I understand you heard Ronald Jeffreys' last confession," Nick continued.

"Yes, but I cannot share any of that with you. I hope you understand." His voice was suddenly frail, as though the subject drained the energy from him.

Maggie wondered whether he was sick, something terminal that would explain the gray pallor to his skin. Even his breathing came in thick, short gasps when he talked. When he was silent, a soft wheeze lifted his bony shoulders in an odd rhythm.

"Of course, we understand," she lied. The fact was, she didn't understand, but she prevented the impatience from creeping into her tone. "However, if there is anything that would shed light on the Alverez case, I would hope you'd share it with us."

"O'Dell, that's Irish Catholic, yes?"

Maggie was startled and annoyed by his distraction. "Yes, it is." Now she allowed a bit of the impatience to slip out. He didn't seem to notice.

"And Maggie, named for our very own St. Margaret."

"Yes, I suppose so. Father Francis, you do understand that if Ronald Jeffreys confessed anything that would lead us to Danny Alverez's murderer, you must tell us?"

"The sanctity of confession is to be preserved even for condemned murderers, Agent O'Dell."

Maggie sighed and glanced back at Morrelli, who also looked as though he was becoming impatient with the old priest.

"Father," Morrelli said. "There's something else you might be able to help us with. Who, other than a priest, can or is allowed to administer last rites?"

Father Francis looked confused by the change of subject. "The sacrament of extreme unction should be administered by a priest, but in extreme circumstances, it's not necessary."

"Who else would know how?"

"Before Vatican II, it was taught in the Baltimore Catechism. The two of you may be too young to remember. Today, I believe, it is taught only in the seminary, although it may still be a part of some deacon training."

"And what are the requirements for becoming a deacon?" Maggie asked, frustrated that this might add to their list of suspects.

"There are rigorous standards. Of course, one must be in good standing with the church. And unfortunately, only men can be deacons. I'm not sure I understand what any of this has to do with Ronald Jeffreys."

"I'm afraid we can't share that with you, Father." Morrelli smiled. "No disrespect intended." Morrelli glanced at Maggie, waiting to see if she had anything more. Then he said, "Thanks for your help, Father Francis."

He motioned to her for them to leave, but she stared at Father Francis, hoping to see something in the hooded eyes that held hers. It was almost as though they were waiting for her to see what they revealed. Yet, the priest only nodded at her and smiled.

Morrelli touched her shoulder. She turned on her heels and marched out alongside him. Outside on the church steps she stopped suddenly. Morrelli was down on the sidewalk before he realized she wasn't beside him. He looked up at her and shrugged.

"What's wrong?"

"He knows something. There's something about Jeffreys that he's not telling us."

"That he *can't* tell us."

She spun around and ran back up the steps.

"O'Dell, what are you doing?"

She heard Morrelli behind her as she threw open the heavy front door and walked quickly up the aisle. Father Francis was just leaving the altar, disappearing behind the thick curtains.

"Father Francis," Maggie yelled to him. The echo instantly made her feel as though she had broken some rule, committed some sin. It did, however, stop Father Francis. He came back to the middle of the altar where he watched her hurry up the aisle. Morrelli was close behind.

"If you know something... If Jeffreys told you something that could prevent another murder... Father, isn't saving the life of an innocent little boy worth breaking the confidence of a confessed serial killer?"

She didn't realize until now that she was breathless. She waited, staring into those eyes that knew so much more than they were willing or able to reveal.

"What I can tell you is that Ronald Jeffreys told nothing but the truth."

"Excuse me?" Her impatience was rapidly changing to anger.

"From the day he confessed to the crime to the day he was executed, Ronald Jeffreys told only the truth." His eyes lingered on Maggie's. But if there was something more they were saying, she couldn't see it. "Now, if you'll excuse me."

Morrelli was at her side. They stood quietly, watching the priest disappear behind the flowing fabric of the curtains.

"Jesus," Morrelli finally whispered. "What the hell does that mean?"

"It means we need to take a look at Jeffreys' original confession," she said, pretending to know what she was talking about. Then she turned and walked out, this time carefully keeping her heels from clicking noisily on the marble floor.

CHAPTER 19

He skidded out of the church parking lot. The bag of groceries tumbled across the seat and spilled onto the floor. Oranges rolled underneath his feet as he pressed down on the accelerator.

He needed to calm down. He searched the rearview mirror. No one followed. They had come to the church asking questions. Questions about Jeffreys. He was safe. They knew nothing. Even that newspaper reporter had insinuated that Danny's murder was a copycat. Someone copycatting Jeffreys. Why hadn't it occurred to any of them that Jeffreys was the copycat? The fact that Jeffreys had also been a cold-blooded murderer had simply made him the perfect patsy.

Within blocks of the school, parents scurried like frightened rats leading their children, huddling at intersections. They carted them to the curb. They watched them skip up the steps of the school until they were safely inside. Until now, they hardly noticed their children, left them alone for hours, pretending that "latchkey" was a term of endearment. Leaving them with bruises and scars that, if not stopped, would last a lifetime. And now those same parents were learning. He was actually doing them a favor, providing a precious service.

The wind hinted at snow, biting and whipping at jackets and skirts that would be quickly out of season. It reminded him of the blanket in the trunk. Did it still have blood on it? He tried to remember, tried to think while he watched the rats cover the sidewalks and clog the intersections. He stopped at a stop sign.

Waited for the crossing guards. A stream of rats crossed. One recognized him and waved. He smiled and waved back.

No, he had washed the blanket. There was no blood. The bleach had worked miracles. And it would be warm, should the weather turn cold.

As he drove out of town, he noticed a flock of geese overhead getting into formation like fighter pilots from the base. He rolled down his window and listened. The squawks and honks cut through the crisp morning air. Yes, this time the thick, bulging clouds would bring snow, not rain. He could feel it in his bones.

He hated the cold, hated snow. It reminded him of too many Christmases, quietly unwrapping the few presents his mother had secretly put under the tree for him. Following his mother's instructions, he would get up early Christmas morning and unwrap his gifts by himself. Quiet enough to hear his mother keeping his stepfather preoccupied in their bedroom, just several feet away.

His stepfather never suspected a thing, grateful for his own early-morning present. Had he found out, he and his mother would have both received beatings for their frivolous waste of his stepfather's hard-earned money. For it was that first Christmas beating that had initiated their secret tradition.

He turned onto Old Church Road and drove along the river. The riverbank was on fire with brilliant reds, oranges and yellows. Thousands of cattails waved at him, poking up out of the tall, honey-colored grass. The snow would ruin all of this. It would cover the vivid colors of life and leave its shroud of white death.

It wasn't much farther. Suddenly, he remembered the baseball cards. In a mad panic, he patted himself down, checking all his jacket pockets while he steered with one hand. The car veered sharply to the right. The tire slammed into a deep rut before he twisted the steering wheel and gained control. Finally, he felt the bulge in the back pocket of his jeans.

He pulled off the road into a grove of plum trees. The canopy of branches and leaves hid the car. He stuffed the spilled groceries back into the sack and shoved it under his arm. He popped the trunk. The thick wool blanket was rolled neatly and tied with rope. He grabbed it and slung it over his shoulder. He slammed the trunk, its echo bouncing off the trees and water. It was quiet and peaceful despite the wind whispering through the branches, threatening to bring cold. It swept up the smell of river water, a wonderful musty mixture of silt, fish and decay. He stopped to watch the water rolling in ripples and waves, moving quickly and carrying with it driftwood and other debris. It was alive and dangerous with powers of destruction. It was alive and redemptive with powers of healing and cleansing.

The muddy leaves hid the wooden door so well that even he had to search for its exact location. He cleared it of all debris, then, with both hands, yanked and pulled until it creaked open. A haze of light dimly lit the steps as he descended into the earth. Immediately, the smell of wet dirt, moist with mold, filled his lungs. As soon as he reached the bottom, he put down the sack and blanket.

From his jacket pocket he pulled the rubber mask. It was better than the ski mask, less frightening and more appropriate for this time of year. Although he hated the damn thing. But even more, he hated remembering the look in Danny's eyes, recognizing him, trusting him and then looking at him as though betrayed. If only Danny had understood. But that look and that damn cross around the boy's neck had almost unraveled him. No, he couldn't take any more chances. He yanked on the mask. In seconds, his face began to perspire.

Like a zombie, with hands and arms outstretched, he took small steps until he bumped into the wooden shelf. His fingers found the lantern and matches. Fur brushed against his skin. He jerked his hand away, hitting the lantern and catching it without seeing it before it slid off the shelf.

"Damn rats," he muttered.

His fingers lifted the rusty metal. He struck the match and lit the wick on the first try. The dark came to life in the yellow glow. Pieces of dirt wall crumbled and filtered down on him. He avoided looking up at the scratchy skitters of night creatures escaping. He waited. In a few seconds they would find new darkness and all would be safe and quiet again.

He shoved his weight against the thick wooden shelf, using his shoulder to push. The heavy structure groaned, wobbled and began to move. It scraped against the floor, taking clumps of dirt with it. Sweat rolled down his back. The mask was excruciatingly hot—his face crushed by a vapor lock. Finally, the secret passage revealed itself. He crawled through the small hole, reaching back to grab the sack and drag the blanket.

He hoped Matthew enjoyed the baseball cards.

CHAPTER 20

The Tanner house sat on the corner of its block at the edge of town. Behind it stretched an open field where huge, yellow construction equipment chomped at the landscape like hungry monsters removing trees in one gulp. It was one of the sights Nick hated most about Platte City's rapid growth. Countryside covered with pink wild roses, blazing goldenrod and waving prairie grass suddenly turned into perfect sections of bluegrass and gray pavement sprinkled with plastic swing sets and Big Wheels.

"Jesus," he muttered at the line of vehicles parked in front of the Tanner house.

"You have someone here to contain things?" O'Dell asked.

Nick glanced at her next to him in his Jeep.

"I'm only asking, Morrelli. There's no need to get defensive."

She was right. There was no accusation in her tone. He needed to remember that she was on his side. So he filled her in on what he had done so far, details they hadn't had time to discuss in the early hours of the morning.

Last night, almost near panic, he and Hal Langston had set up a mini-command post in Michelle Tanner's living room. Grudgingly, he had relied on lessons Bob Weston had taught him during the Alverez case. Within minutes of Michelle Tanner's desperate phone call, Nick had sent Phillip Van Dorn to tap her phones and set up a surveillance around her house. Before midnight Lucy Burton had begun converting the sheriff's office conference room into a strategy briefing room with maps and enlarged photos of Matthew tacked up and a hot line ready.

This time Nick had immediately called in the county police chiefs from neighboring Richfield, Staton and Bennet for extra feet to scour the alleys, surrounding fields and even the riverbank. His own men had gone door-to-door, instructed to politely ask questions without stirring panic. If that was possible. In fact, he wondered if it may already be too late. Especially after this morning's drive and witnessing the panic of parents accompanying their children to school. The frenzy had already begun, thanks to his sister. He hated to think what would happen when everyone found out about Matthew. Nick knew he was fooling himself if he thought he could stop the frenzy or even contain it.

The front door of the Tanner house was open. The chatter of voices drifted into the yard. O'Dell knocked on the screen door and waited. Nick would have knocked and entered. Standing so close behind her he noticed she was about six inches shorter than he was. He leaned closer to smell her hair just as a breeze whipped several strands against his chin in a soft caress.

Her fingers brushed her hair back into place, almost grazing his skin. He stepped back and watched her tuck the unruly strand behind her ear, revealing soft, white skin. This morning she wore a dark burgundy suit jacket and matching trousers. The color made her skin seem softer, smoother.

The screen door screeched on old hinges as a man Nick didn't recognize opened it just enough to examine the two of them.

"Who are you?" the man asked suspiciously, wasting no time on good manners as his eyes darted over them.

"It's okay." Hal Langston came up behind him and gently nudged the man to the side. Hal grabbed the screen door and opened it. The man shot Hal a look, but walked away. Hal could be as imposing as hell when he wanted. He and Nick had played football together in high school, and although Hal had added some softness to his bulk, he was still in good shape.

"Married life," he explained when Nick teased him about the extra weight. "You should try it, buddy," he would always add. And to his credit, Hal had snagged one of the best catches in town.

Tess Langston had moved to Platte City ten years before to teach high-school history. As beautiful as she was smart, she had intimidated all the bachelors who drooled in her presence. All but Hal. For almost three weeks, he had called Nick, who'd been tucked away out East in law school, every night, racking up his long-distance bill. Between torts and breaches of contract, Nick had helped plot Hal's next move.

Nick wrote snippets of poetry, recommended what flowers—daisies, not roses—and even advised when and where to touch—gentle flicks to the earlobe when cuddling, no breast groping. He had felt as though he was wooing Tess himself, so much so that, when the calls stopped, Nick had felt a loss. It wasn't until later he realized the loss wasn't of his buddy, but of a woman he had met only once and had come to know so intimately through his friend that he, himself, had fallen in love.

Hal and Tess had married after six short months, and even today Nick felt a closeness to Tess that he could never explain. Didn't want to explain, really. He had no idea whether Hal had shared with her the secrets of their courtship, yet sometimes Tess looked at Nick in a way that told him she knew, and that she was grateful.

The Tanner living room was filled with his deputies and with police officers he didn't recognize. Some were drinking coffee, while others huddled over notes and maps. Nick looked for Michelle Tanner and wondered whether he would recognize her. Last night in her pink chenille robe and red eyes and blotchy face, she had looked drunk and disoriented. Her red hair had fallen partially out of its bun and flew around her head like wild snakes. Her entire small body had seemed to convulse with arms swinging and legs pacing.

The kitchen was clogged with more bodies.

"Who the fuck are all these people, Hal?" He turned and bumped into Hal, who was close behind. O'Dell had wandered over to Phillip Van Dorn, and without any introduction seemed to have Phil revealing all his secrets of the technology he strung around the house.

"It was her idea," Hal whispered in his defense. "She called a few neighbors, her mother, the parents of her kid's soccer team."

"Jesus, Hal. We've got the whole fucking soccer team here!"

"Just a few parents."

Nick elbowed his way through the crowd. Then he began shoving when he recognized the woman sitting at the table, sipping coffee with Michelle Tanner.

"What the hell are you doing here?" he bellowed, and the entire room went silent.

CHAPTER 21

Before Christine could answer, her brother charged through the group, spilling Emily Fulton's coffee and almost knocking Paul Calloway to the floor. Everyone stared as Nick pointed his finger at her and said to Michelle Tanner, "Mrs. Tanner, do you realize this woman is a reporter?"

Michelle Tanner was a petite woman, slender to the point of being frail and, from what Christine had already learned, easily intimidated. Michelle's small face went pale, the large hazel eyes widened. She looked at Christine, fumbled with her coffee cup, then stared at it as though surprised by its *click-clack* rattle amplified in the silence. Finally, she looked up at Nick.

"Yes, Sheriff Morrelli. I'm well aware that Christine is a reporter." She folded her hands together, apparently noticed a slight tremor and tucked them under the table, safely into her lap. With her eyes now on her coffee, she continued, "We think it would be beneficial to have something in tonight's paper... about Matthew." The tremor was now in her voice.

Christine saw Nick softening. If there was one thing her macho brother couldn't handle, it was a tearful woman. She had used them herself, though there was nothing manipulative about Michelle Tanner's tears.

"Mrs. Tanner, I'm sorry, but I don't think that's a good idea."

"Actually, it's a very good idea."

Christine shifted in her chair, so she could see the woman who appeared from behind Nick. She could have been a model, with flawless skin, lovely high cheekbones, full pouty lips and silky, short dark hair. Her suit draped over a slender, athletic figure with enough curves to hold every man's attention in the room. However, her voice and stance showed she was unaware of the effect of her femininity. She carried herself confidently and with an air of authority. This woman was not easily intimidated by anything or anyone, let alone a roomful of people who had no idea who she was. Already, Christine liked her.

"Excuse me?" Nick seemed irritated with the woman.

"I think it would be a good idea to involve the media right away."

Nick glanced around the room. He looked uncomfortable and flustered.

"Can I talk to you a minute? Alone." He took the woman's arm, but she immediately jerked it away. Still, she turned to leave the room with him. The crowd opened for her exit. Nick followed.

"Excuse me." Christine patted Michelle's hand. She grabbed her notebook. Despite Nick's fury, she wanted to meet the woman who had just put him in his place. This had to be the FBI expert from Quantico, Special Agent Maggie O'Dell. She wondered what information Agent O'Dell might be willing to supply. Information Nick would keep in a vise grip if it meant protecting his precious reputation.

Nick and Agent O'Dell huddled in a corner of the living room next to the bay window that overlooked the front yard. Several of the police officers stared. Nick's men knew better and pretended to be occupied with their work.

"I told you he wouldn't like you being here," said a voice behind her.

Christine glanced over her shoulder at Hal. "Well, it looks like someone might be changing his mind."

"Yeah, he's definitely met his match with that one. I'm going outside for a smoke. Why don't you join me?"

"Thanks, no. I'm trying to quit."

"Suit yourself."

He headed out the front door. The screen whined, then slammed. Nick and Agent O'Dell didn't even notice. Nick spoke in a hushed tone, confining his anger with clenched teeth. Agent O'Dell looked unscathed by any of it, her voice calm and even.

"Excuse me for interrupting." As she approached Christine

felt Nick's glare like a slap in the face. She avoided his eyes. "You must be Special Agent O'Dell. I'm Christine Hamilton." She offered her hand, and O'Dell took it without hesitation.

"Ms. Hamilton."

The grip was strong and steady.

"In his fury I'm sure Nicky failed to tell you that I'm his sister."

O'Dell glanced up at Nick, and Christine thought she saw a hint of a smile on the otherwise stoic face.

"I wondered if there was a personal connection."

"He's obviously pissed at me, so it's hard for him to see that I'm really here to help."

"I'm sure you are."

"So, you won't mind answering some questions?"

"I'm sorry, Ms. Hamilton..."

"Christine."

"Of course, Christine. Despite my opinions, this isn't my investigation. I'm here strictly to profile this case."

Christine knew without looking at him that Nick was smiling now. It only made her angry. "So what does that mean? Another press blackout like in the Alverez case? Nicky, that's only going to make matters worse."

"Actually, Christine, I think Sheriff Morrelli has changed his mind," O'Dell said, watching Nick, whose smile transformed into a grimace.

He pushed his hair from his forehead. O'Dell folded her arms over her chest and waited. Christine looked from one to the other. The tension filled the corner, and she found herself taking a step backward.

Finally, Nick cleared his throat as though his discomfort was lodged somewhere between his larynx and tongue. "There'll be a press conference in the courthouse lobby tomorrow morning at eight-thirty."

"Can I print that in tonight's article?" She looked from Nick to O'Dell and back to Nick.

"Sure," he grudgingly answered.

"Anything else I can use in tonight's article?"

"No."

"Sheriff Morrelli, didn't you say you already have copies of the boy's photo?" Again, O'Dell said this very matter-of-factly, no underlying edge. "It may jog some memories if Christine included one with her piece."

He shoved his hands into his pockets, and Christine wondered whether it was so he wouldn't strangle both her and O'Dell.

"Stop by the courthouse and pick one up. I'll instruct Lucy to leave it at the front desk. The front desk, Christine. I don't want you in my office snooping around."

"Relax, Nicky. I keep telling you I'm not the enemy." She started to leave, but turned back at the door. "You're still coming over for dinner tonight, aren't you?"

"I may be too busy."

"Agent O'Dell, would you like to join us? Nothing fancy. I'm fixing spaghetti. There'll be plenty of Chianti."

"Thanks, that sounds nice."

Christine almost burst out laughing at the surprise on Nick's face.

"I'll see the two of you about seven. Nicky knows the address."

CHAPTER 22

The sheriff's department bristled with nervous energy. Nick could feel it as soon as he and O'Dell walked in the door. Here he was, worried about a frenzy taking over the community, and he had one in his own department.

Phones rang incessantly. Machines beeped. Keyboards clicked. Faxes hummed. Radios squawked. Voices yelled out to each other from room to room. Bodies dashed and scurried, amazingly not bumping into one another.

Again, there were police officers he didn't recognize and equipment he couldn't identify. He was depending on people he barely knew to handle things he hardly understood. It made him as uncomfortable as hell.

Lucy looked relieved to see him. She smiled and waved from across the room. There was a quick glance of contempt in O'Dell's direction. O'Dell didn't seem to notice.

"Nick, we've checked every inch of this city," Lloyd Benjamin's voice rasped with exhaustion. He removed his glasses and wiped his eyes. The deep worry lines in his forehead were pronounced, like permanent indents. The oldest member of Nick's team, Lloyd was also the most reliable next to Hal. "Richfield's men are still checking the river where we found the Alverez kid. I've got Staton's men on the north side of town. They're going to check that gravel pit and Northton Lake."

"Good. That's good, Lloyd." Nick patted him on the back. There was something else. Lloyd rubbed his jaw, glanced at O'Dell.

"Some of us were talking," Lloyd continued in a low voice, almost a whisper. "Stan Lubrick thought he remembered Jeffreys having a partner...you know...sort of a...well, a lover, at the time he was arrested. I do kind of remember us bringing a guy in for questioning, but I don't think he ever testified. A Mark Rydell," he said, scanning a notepad with illegible scratches. "We were wondering if we should try and check the guy out. See if he's anywhere around."

They both looked at O'Dell, who was distracted by the chaos. Nick wasn't even sure she had heard Lloyd. Her hands were shoved deep into her jacket pockets. Her eyes darted back and forth, watching the commotion. Then suddenly, she seemed flustered when she realized they were waiting for her to answer.

"I didn't realize Jeffreys was gay. How do know this guy was his lover?" Again, her tone was matter-of-fact. No hint of condescension, though Nick knew she was capable of turning stubborn speculation into ridiculous trivia.

Lloyd loosened his tie and collar. The subject obviously made him uncomfortable.

"Well, they were living together at the time."

"Wouldn't that make them roommates?"

O'Dell was as tough and unflinching as she was beautiful. Nick found himself relieved that this time he wasn't on the other side of her questions. Lloyd looked to him for help. Nick only shrugged.

"Is it possible to check if Rydell kept in touch with Jeffreys after he was sentenced?" O'Dell asked Lloyd, instead of dismissing his hunch.

"They may have some information at the penitentiary."

"You might check out what other visitors Jeffreys had or who else he may have kept in touch with. See if there were any prisoners or even guards he befriended. On death row they don't have much contact with other prisoners, but there may have been someone."

Nick liked the way her mind processed information quickly, refusing to disregard even the slightest details. A lead that Nick had believed far-fetched materialized into something substantial. Even Lloyd, who proudly came from a generation of keeping women in their place, seemed satisfied. He had added more scratches to his notes while O'Dell had been talking. Now he nodded at both of them and wandered off to find a phone.

Nick was impressed once again. O'Dell caught him watching her, and he simply smiled.

"Hey, Nick. That woman called again," Eddie Gillick called out from behind his desk, a phone cradled under his chin.

"Agent O'Dell, here's a fax from Quantico for you." Adam Preston handed her a roll of paper.

"What woman?" Nick asked Eddie.

"Sophie Krichek. Remember, she was the one who said she saw an old blue pickup in the area when the Alverez kid was snatched."

"Let me guess. She saw the pickup again. This time with another little boy who happens to look like Matthew Tanner."

"Wait a minute," O'Dell interrupted, looking up from the trail of fax paper that stretched to the floor. "What makes you think she's not serious?"

"She calls all the time," Nick explained.

"Nick, here's your messages." Lucy handed over a stack of pink "while you were out" slips and waited in front of him. She was dressed in the usual tight sweater and tight skirt. It would be so much easier to stop her if she didn't have such a voluptuous figure.

"Let me get this straight. You're not going to check out this lead because this woman has surpassed her quota of phone calls?" O'Dell had that look in her eyes that told Nick she thought he was bordering on incompetent. He wondered whether it had anything to do with his slight distraction over Lucy's stretched blue-and-green-knit stripes.

"Three weeks ago she called to tell us she saw Jesus in her backyard pushing a little girl on a swing set. She doesn't even have a backyard. She lives in an apartment complex with a concrete parking lot. Lucy, are the transcripts from Jeffreys' confession and trial here yet?"

"Max said she'd bring them over herself as soon as possible." Lucy swayed on the spike heels, and he knew it was strictly for his benefit. "They need to make copies of everything. Max won't let the originals out of the clerk's office. Oh, Agent O'Dell, a Gregory Stewart called for you like three or four times. He said it was important and that you have his number."

"Your boss checking up on you?" Nick smiled at O'Dell, who suddenly looked distraught.

"No, my husband. Is there a phone I can use?"

Nick's smile disappeared. He glanced at her hand. No wedding ring. Yes, he was sure he had checked before, simply out of habit. She was waiting for an answer.

"You can use my office," he said, trying to sound disinterested and shuffling through the stack of messages. "Down the hall, last door on the right."

"Thanks."

As soon as she disappeared around the corner, Eddie Gillick stopped beside Nick on his way to the fax machine. "Why do you look so surprised, Nick? She's quite a catch. Why wouldn't she be married?"

It was ridiculous. This morning at Michelle Tanner's he had been ready to strangle her. But now he suddenly felt as if someone had punched him in the stomach.

CHAPTER 23

The office was simple and small with a gray metal desk and matching credenza. Shelves displayed a variety of trophies—all football championships of some sort. Several pictures hung on the wall behind the desk. Maggie sank into the soft leather chair, the only extravagance in the otherwise plain office. She picked up the phone while she got a better look at the wall of honor.

There were several photos of young men clad in red and white football jerseys. One photo was obviously a young Morrelli under the sweat and dirt. He stood proudly next to an older gentleman, who, from the scratched autograph, was a Coach Osborne.

In the corner, almost hidden behind a file cabinet, hung two framed degrees collecting dust. One was from the University of Nebraska. The other was a law degree from... Maggie almost dropped the phone. The other was a law degree from Harvard University. She stood up to examine it more closely, then sat back down, embarrassed that she even, for one fleeting moment, thought it a fake, a practical joke. It was, in fact, very real.

She looked back at the football photo. Sheriff Nicholas Morrelli was certainly full of surprises. The more she learned, the more curious she became. It didn't help matters that they seemed to spark off each other with an unhealthy amount of electricity. It was a part of Nick Morrelli's personality. It was not, however, a part of her own, and she found it annoying.

She and Greg had always had a comfortable relationship. Even in the beginning it wasn't so much heat or chemistry that had brought them together, but friendship and common goals. Goals that had changed over the years. And a friendship that had turned to complacency. They didn't even extend each other the common courtesies of friendship anymore. Lately, she wondered if they had drifted apart, or if they had ever been close.

It didn't matter. Marriage was something a person worked at, despite the changes. She believed that. She wouldn't have made it this far if she didn't. Now, at least, Greg had called her, made the first move toward reconciliation. That had to be a good sign.

She dialed his office and waited patiently through four, five, six rings.

"Brackman, Harvey and Lowe. How may I help you?"

"Greg Stewart, please."

"Mr. Stewart is in a meeting, may I take a message?"

"Could you please see if you can interrupt him. This is his wife. He's been trying to reach me all morning."

There was a pause while the receptionist decided how unreasonable a request it was. "One moment, please."

One moment turned into two, then three. Finally, after five minutes, Greg's voice said, "Maggie, thank God, I got ahold of you." His voice sounded urgent, but not remorseful. She was immediately disappointed instead of alarmed. "Why isn't your cellular phone turned on?" Even in his urgency he had to get in a scolding.

"I forgot to recharge it. I'll have it by this evening."

"Well, never mind." He sounded irritated, as if she were the one who had brought it up. "It's your mother." His tone automatically changed to that sympathetic one he used with clients who had just lost their case. She dug her fingernails into the leather armrest and waited for him to continue. "She's in the hospital."

Maggie leaned her head back, closed her eyes and swallowed hard. "What was it this time?"

"I think she might be getting serious, Maggie. She used a razor blade this time."

CHAPTER 24

Maggie hung up the phone and massaged her temples. A throbbing invaded her head, reaching down into her neck and shoulder blades. She had spent the last twenty minutes arguing with the doctor assigned to her mother's case. He had graduated at the top of his class, the arrogant, little bastard had reassured her. Fresh out of medical school and he thought he knew it all. Well, he didn't know her mother. He hadn't even looked at her history yet. When Maggie recommended he call her mother's therapist, he sounded relieved, even grateful when she gave him the name and phone number. She wondered how many people kept the name and phone number of their mother's therapist in their memory bank.

They *did* agree that Maggie shouldn't hop on the next plane to Richmond. Her mother was screaming for attention, but Maggie dropping everything and rushing to her side only seemed to reinforce the behavior. Or at least it had the last five times. Dear God, Maggie thought, one of these times her mother would succeed, if only by sheer accident. And although she agreed with Greg that razor blades were a serious advancement, the cuts—according to Dr. Boy Wonder—were horizontal, not vertical.

Maggie sank her throbbing head into the soft leather back of the chair and closed her eyes. She had been taking care of her mother since she was twelve. And what did a twelve-year-old girl, who had just lost her father, know about taking care of anyone? Sometimes she felt as though she had let her mother down, until she remembered that it was her mother who had abandoned her with her drunken stupors.

There was a soft tap on the frosted glass of the office door. Without prompting, the door eased open just enough for Morrelli to peek in.

"O'Dell, you okay in here?"

She remained paralyzed, her body scrunched down in the chair. Suddenly, legs, arms, everything seemed too heavy to move. "I'm fine," she managed to say, but knew immediately that she didn't sound or look very convincing.

His brow furrowed, and soft blue eyes showed concern. He hesitated, then came into the office slowly, cautiously. He set a can of Diet Pepsi in front of her. The cold condensation dripped down the side, and she wondered how long he had stood outside his own office before getting the nerve to come in.

"Thanks." She still made no effort to move, and it obviously made Morrelli uncomfortable. He stood with arms crossed, then shoved his hands into his pockets.

"You look like hell," he finally said.

"Thanks a lot, Morrelli." But she smiled.

"Listen, could you do me a favor? Call me Nick. Every time you call me Morrelli or Sheriff Morrelli, I start looking around for my dad."

"Okay, I'll try." Even her eyelids felt heavy. If she closed her eyes right this minute, would she finally sleep?

"Lucy is ordering lunch up from Wanda's. What can I get for you? Blue plate special on Monday is meat loaf, but I'd recommend the chicken-fried steak sandwich."

"I'm really not very hungry."

"I've been with you since two this morning, and you haven't eaten a thing. You need to eat, O'Dell. I'm not going to be responsible for you whittling away that cute little…" He caught himself, but it was too late. The embarrassment washed over his face. He wiped a hand across his jaw as if to erase it. "I'm ordering a ham and cheese sandwich for you." He turned to leave.

"On rye?"

He glanced at her over his shoulder. "Okay."

"And with hot mustard?"

Now he smiled, and there were definitely dimples. "You're a pain in the ass, you know that, O'Dell?"

"Hey, Nick." She stopped him again.

"What now?"

"Call me Maggie."

CHAPTER 25

"Do you like the baseball cards?" The mask muffled his voice. He sounded as though he were underwater. With all the dripping perspiration, he felt like it, too.

Matthew stared at him from the small bed in the corner. He sat on top of tangled bedcovers and hugged a pillow to his chest. His eyes were red and puffy. His hair stuck up in places. His soccer uniform was wrinkled. He hadn't even taken off his shoes to sleep last night.

Light filtered in through cracks in the boarded-up window. Pieces of broken glass rattled as the wind crept in through the rotted slats. It whistled and howled, creating a ghostly moan and licking at the corners of the posters hiding the cracked walls. It was the only sound in the room. The boy hadn't said a word all morning.

"Are you comfortable?" he asked.

When he approached, the boy skittered into the corner, smashing his small body against the crumbling plaster. The chain that connected his ankle to the steel bedpost clanked. There was enough length for the boy to reach the middle of the room. Yet, the cheeseburger and fries he had left last night sat untouched on the metal tray table. Even the triple-chocolate shake was still filled to the brim.

"Didn't you like your dinner, or do you prefer hot dogs? Maybe even chili dogs? You can have anything you want."

"I wanna go home," Matthew whispered, squeezing the pillow, one hand twisted so he could bite his fingernails. Several were chewed down to the quick and had bled during the night. Dried blood spotted the white cotton pillowcase. It would be hell to wash out.

"Maybe you'd enjoy comic books more than baseball cards. I have some old Flash Gordons I bet you'd like. I'll bring them with me next time."

He finished unpacking the contents of the grocery sack: three oranges, a bag of Cheetos, two Snickers bars, a six-pack of Hires root beer, two cans of SpaghettiOs and a snack pack of Jell-O chocolate pudding. He laid each item on the old wine crate he had found in what must have been a supply room. He had gone to great lengths to get all of Matthew's favorites.

"It may get chilly tonight," he said as he unrolled the thick wool blanket and draped it over the bed. "I'm sorry I can't leave a light. Is there anything else I can get for you?"

"I wanna go home," the boy whispered again.

"Your mom doesn't have the time to take care of you, Matthew."

"I want my mom."

"She's never home. And I bet she brings strange men home at night, doesn't she? Ever since she threw your dad out." He kept his voice calm and soothing.

"Please let me go home."

"She leaves you alone all the time. She works late. She even works on weekends."

"I just wanna go home." The boy began to cry, quiet sniffles he muffled with the pillow.

"And you can't stay with your dad." Calm and cool. He must remain calm, though already he could feel the anger starting in his gut. "Your dad beats you, doesn't he, Matthew?"

"I just wanna go home," the boy whined, no longer keeping quiet.

"I'm going to help you, Matthew. I'm going to save you. But you must be patient. Look, I brought all your favorite things."

But still, the boy cried, a high-pitched whine that made him grimace. He felt the explosion racing up from his stomach. He must control it. Calm, why couldn't he just remain calm? Yes, cool and calm.

"I wanna go home." The wail grated.

"Goddamn it! Shut up, you fucking crybaby."

CHAPTER 26

Christine's article in the evening edition hit downtown Omaha's newsstands at three-thirty. By four o'clock, newspaper carriers tossed the rolled-up *Omaha Journal* onto porches and lawns in Platte City. By four-ten, phones started ringing nonstop in the sheriff's department.

Nick assigned Phillip Van Dorn the task of adding more phones and phone lines, even suggesting to go as far as commandeering the county clerk's office down the hall. This was exactly what he had hoped to avoid. The frenzy had officially begun, and already Nick could feel it churning up his insides.

Angry citizens demanded to know what was being done. City Hall wanted to know how much the extra personnel and equipment would cost the city. Reporters badgered for an interview of their own, not wanting to wait for the morning press conference. Some were already camped out in the courthouse lobby, restrained by manpower better used on the street.

Of course, there were also leads. Maggie was right. Matthew's photo jogged plenty of memories. The problem was sorting the real leads from the crackpot ones—although Maggie insisted the crackpot leads could not be thrown out entirely. Tomorrow Nick would even send someone to check on Sophie Krichek's story about an old blue pickup. He still believed it would be a waste of time. Krichek was just some lonely old woman looking for attention. But he didn't want anyone thinking he hadn't checked every lead, especially Maggie.

"Nick, Angie Clark has called for you four times." Lucy

caught up with him in the hallway, obviously irritated with being the messenger for his love life.

"Next time tell her I'm sorry, but I just don't have time to talk."

She seemed pleased and started to walk away, but spun back. "Oh, I almost forgot. Max is on her way down the hall with those transcripts from Jeffreys' confession and trial."

"Great. Tell Agent O'Dell, would you please?"

"Where do you want me to put them?" She skipped alongside him as he made his way to his office.

"Can't you just give them to Agent O'Dell?"

"All five boxes?"

He stopped so suddenly she bumped into him. He grabbed her by the elbows as she teetered on her two-inch spiked heels.

"There's five boxes?"

"You know Max. She's pretty thorough, so everything's labeled and cataloged. She said to tell you she also included copies of all the evidence that was entered and logged, as well as affidavits from witnesses who didn't testify."

"Five boxes?" He shook his head. "Put them in my office."

"Okay." She turned to leave, then stopped again. "Do you still want me to tell Agent O'Dell?"

"Yes, please." Her distrust, contempt—whatever it was—for Maggie was beginning to wear thin.

"Oh, and the mayor's holding on line three for you."

"Lucy, we can't afford to hold up any of those lines."

"I know, but he insisted. I couldn't just hang up on him."

Yes, he was sure Brian Rutledge would have insisted. He was a royal pain in the ass.

Nick retreated to his office. Behind closed doors he plopped into his leather chair and uncinched his tie. He wrestled with the collar button, almost ripping it off. He dug a thumb and forefinger into his eyes, trying to remember how much sleep he had gotten since Friday. Finally, he grabbed the phone and punched line three.

"Hi, Brian. It's Nick."

"Nick, what the hell's going on over there? I've been on hold for goddamn near twenty minutes."

"Don't mean to inconvenience you, Brian. We're a little busy."

"I've got a crisis of my own, Nick. City council thinks I should cancel Halloween. Goddamn it, Nick, I cancel Halloween and I look like the goddamn Grinch."

"I think the Grinch is Christmas, Brian."

"Goddamn it, Nick. This isn't funny."

"I'm not laughing, Brian. But you know what? I have a few more serious things to worry about than Halloween."

Lucy peeked in from behind his door. He waved her in. She opened the door and motioned for the four men following her to set the boxes in the corner under the window.

"Halloween is serious, Nick. What if this nut ends up pulling something when all those kids are out running around in the dark?"

Rutledge's whiny, tin voice grated on Nick's nerves. He smiled and mouthed "thank you," to Maxine Cramer, who had hauled in the final box. Even at the end of the day and after hauling a box halfway down the hall, her royal-blue suit held its sharply pressed seams. Her blue-gray, salon-permed hair matched her suit, not a strand out of place. She smiled back at Nick and nodded, then made her way out the door.

"Brian, what do you want from me?"

"I want to know how goddamn serious this thing is. Do you have any suspects? Are you making any arrests in the near future? What the hell are you doing over there?"

"One boy is dead and another is missing. How goddamn serious do you think this is, Brian? As far as how I handle the investigation, it's none of your fucking business. We need this phone line open for more useful things than reassuring your sorry ass, so don't call again." He slammed the phone down and noticed O'Dell standing in the doorway, watching him.

"Sorry." She seemed embarrassed to have witnessed his fury. Twice in one day. She must think he was a madman, a raving lunatic, or worse, simply incompetent. "Lucy told me the transcripts were in here."

"They are. Come on in. Close the door behind you."

She hesitated as though assessing whether it was safe to be behind closed doors with him.

"That was the mayor," Nick explained. "He wanted to know if I'm going to have an arrest made by Friday, so he won't have to cancel Halloween."

"What did you tell him?"

"Pretty much what you just heard. The boxes are here under the window." He rolled his chair around to point to them, then kept it there to stare out the window. He was tired of cloudy weather. Sick of rain. He couldn't remember the last time there'd been a full day of sunshine. It was as though all of Sarpy County were trapped under one of those glass globes. The kind you shake and it snows. Only here, you shake it and the clouds rolled in, over and over again—the same clouds, rounding the globe and passing over again.

O'Dell was on her knees. She had several box lids off and files scattered on the floor around her.

"Can I get you a chair?" he offered, but made no motion to leave his own.

"No, thanks. It'll be easier this way."

She looked as though she had found what she was looking for. She opened the file and began scanning the contents, flipping pages, then settling on one. Suddenly, her entire face went serious. Her eyes darted over the page. She sat back on her feet.

"What is it?" Nick leaned forward, trying to see what had grabbed hold of her so intensely.

"It's Jeffreys' original confession, right after his arrest. It's very detailed, from the kind of tape he used to bind the hands and feet to the carvings on the hunting knife he used." She spoke slowly, continuing to scan the document.

"Okay, and Father Francis said Jeffreys hadn't lied. That means the details are true. So what?"

"Did you realize that Jeffreys confessed to murdering only Bobby Wilson? In fact," she said, flipping through several more pages, "in fact, he was adamant about having nothing to do with the other two boys' murders."

"I don't remember hearing any of that. They probably thought he was lying."

"But if he wasn't?" She looked up at him, her brown eyes haunted by something more than the file she held.

"Okay, if he wasn't lying, and he did kill only Bobby Wilson..." Nick didn't finish. Suddenly, he felt sick to his stomach, even before Maggie finished his sentence.

"Then the real serial killer got away, and he's back."

CHAPTER 27

Christine hoped Nick didn't detect the relief in her voice when he called to cancel dinner. If this new lead panned out, she'd be working late to claim yet another front page on tomorrow morning's paper.

"Can we do it tomorrow night?" he asked, almost apologetic.

"Sure, no problem. Is something big going down tonight?" she added, just to push his buttons.

"This newfound success of yours is ugly on you, Christine." He sounded tired, drained of energy.

"Ugly or not, it feels wonderful."

"So this number the paper gave me, it sounds like a cellular?"

"Yep, just one of the perks of my new, ugly success. Look, Nick." She needed to change the subject before he asked where she was or where she was headed. "Can you please bring your sleeping bag tomorrow night when you come over? Remember, Timmy asked if he could borrow it for his camping trip?"

"They're going camping on Halloween?"

"They'll be back Friday night. Father Keller has mass. Remember, for All Saints' Day? Will you remember the sleeping bag?"

"Yes, I will."

"And don't forget Agent O'Dell."

"Right."

She turned the corner into the parking lot as she flipped her cellular phone closed and shoved it into her purse. Nick would be furious if he knew where she was.

The four-story apartment building looked run-down. The bricks were weathered and chipped. Rusted air conditioners hung out windows, clinging to rickety brackets. The building looked out of place in an old neighborhood of small, wooden-framed houses. Despite being old, the houses were well kept. Their backyards were filled with sandboxes, swing sets and huge old maples perfect for tree houses and hammocks.

The air filled with the smell of burning wood from someone's fireplace. A dog barked down the street, and she heard the tinkling of a wind chime. This was Danny Alverez's neighborhood. Danny's shiny, red bike had been found leaning against the chain-link fence that separated the apartment's parking lot from the rest of the neighborhood. It was right here that the horrors of his last days began. Here in a place he had come to take for granted as safe.

Inside the main entrance a heavy metal trash can held open the security door. It overflowed with cigarette butts falling onto the floor. Christine stepped carefully.

The elevator smelled of stale cigarettes and dog urine, and she eyed the stained carpet. She pushed the button for the fourth floor, stabbing it two, then three times before it lit up and the doors whined shut. The elevator rattled, shook and wheezed. She started to push the open-door button when the elevator finally started up slowly. Pulleys ground and whined.

She hated elevators. Hated small places. She should have taken the stairs. Her eyes searched for the emergency phone. There wasn't one. Seconds flew by and the light above showed only that she had reached the second floor. She punched three, hoping to cut short her trip, but the button crumbled into pieces. Frantically, she picked up the bigger pieces and began replacing them into the frame like a puzzle. Two stayed, one fell down into the hole, the others fell back to the floor. The elevator jolted to a stop, and finally its doors screeched open. Christine squeezed through before they were completely open.

She stopped in the hallway, leaning against the dirty wall, waiting to catch her breath. The light was dim, the carpeting filled with more stains. Again, the smell of dog urine mixed with the scent of old, musty newspapers and someone's burnt dinner. How could anyone live in a hole like this?

Apartment 410 was at the end of the hallway. A hand-braided

welcome mat lay outside the scratched and battered door. The mat was clean, spotless.

Christine knocked and held her breath to avoid the hallway's suffocating odors. Several locks clicked inside, then the door opened just a crack. A pair of hooded and wrinkled blue eyes peered at her through thick glasses.

"Mrs. Krichek?" she asked as politely as possible while holding her breath.

"Are you that reporter?"

"Yes. Yes, I am. My name is Christine Hamilton."

The door opened, and she waited for the woman to back out of the way with her walker.

"Any relation to Ned Hamilton, owns the Quick Mart on the corner?"

"No, I don't think so. Hamilton is my ex-husband's name, and he isn't from around here."

"I see." The woman shuffled away.

Once inside, Christine was accosted by three large yellow and gray cats rubbing against her legs.

"I just fixed a pot of hot chocolate. Would you like some?"

She almost said yes, then saw the steaming pot on the coffee table where another large cat helped itself to several licks off the top.

"No, thank you." She hoped her voice disguised her disgust.

Other than the cats, the apartment smelled much cleaner than the hallway. The ammonia of a hidden litter box was obvious but bearable. Colorful afghans and quilts were draped over the couch and a rocker. Green plants hung above the windows, and crocheted doilies dotted an antique buffet and secretary's desk. Both tops were filled with black-and-white photos of servicemen, a young couple in front of an old Buick and three colored photos of a little girl at various stages of her life.

"Sit," the old woman instructed, backing herself into the rocker. "Oh, the pain in this shoulder," she said, rubbing the bony knob sticking up through her sweater. "Such pain I wouldn't wish on my worst enemy."

"I'm sorry to hear that."

Her bones did look brittle. Knobby knees stuck out from under her plain cotton housedress. Her round face twisted into a permanent scowl. Her brilliant blue eyes were magnified and distorted by the thick wire-rimmed glasses. Her white hair was twisted neatly into a bun, clasped by beautiful turquoise hair combs.

"It's hell getting old. If it wasn't for my cats, I think I'd call it quits."

Christine sat and watched her navy skirt fill with cat hair. Two of the cats still circled her legs while one jumped onto the back of the couch to take a closer look.

"Rummy, get down from there," the woman scolded, waving a bony finger at the cat. He ignored her.

"It's okay, Mrs. Krichek. I don't mind," she lied. "I'd like to get right to what you saw the morning Danny Alverez disappeared. You don't mind, do you?"

"No. Not at all. I'm glad somebody's finally interested."

"The sheriff's office has never come here to question you?"

"I called them twice. In fact, just this morning before I seen your article. They hemmed and hawed like they think I'm making it up or something. So, then I called you. I don't care what anybody says, I seen what I seen."

"And just what did you see, Mrs. Krichek?"

"I seen that boy park his bike and get in an old blue pickup."

"Are you sure it was the Alverez boy?"

"Seen him dozens of times. He was a good little paperboy. Brought my newspaper all the way to my door and laid it on my mat. Not like the kid we have now. He steps off the elevator and tosses it down here. Sometimes it makes it. Sometimes it doesn't. It's not easy getting this walker through that doorway. I think your paper should make sure those kids do a better job."

"I'll let them know. Mrs. Krichek, tell me about the pickup. Could you see the driver?"

"No. It was still dark out. I stood right at that there window. Sun was barely coming up. He pulled into the parking lot so that the passenger's side was all I could see. He must've said something to the boy, 'cause Danny leaned his bike against the fence, came around and got up into the pickup."

"Danny got into the pickup? Are you sure the man didn't grab him and pull him in?"

"No, no. It was all quite friendly—otherwise, I would have called the sheriff sooner. It wasn't until I heard Danny was missing that I put two and two together and called."

Christine couldn't believe no one had checked out this woman's story. Was she missing something? The woman was old, but her story seemed believable. She stood and went to the window the woman had pointed to. Below was a perfect view of the parking lot and the chain-link fence. Even someone with poor vision could make out the events Mrs. Krichek had described.

"What kind of pickup?"

"I know little about cars and trucks." The woman hoisted herself back into the walker and shuffled her way over to join Christine. "It was old, royal blue with paint chipped and some rust. You know, on the bottom part. It had running boards. I remember 'cause Danny stepped up on it to climb in. And it had wooden stockracks, homemade ones on the back. The kind farmers put on when they're hauling something. Oh, and one of the headlights wasn't working."

If the woman was senile, she had a creative imagination. Christine jotted down the details. "Were you able to see any of the license plate?"

"No, my eyes aren't that good."

A screen door slammed below, and a little girl raced out into a backyard on the other side of the fence. She jumped onto a swing and called out to the man who followed. He had long hair and a beard and wore blue jeans with a long tunic-like shirt.

"They just moved in last month." Mrs. Krichek nodded down at the pair as the man pushed the little girl, and she squealed with delight. "The first day I saw him, I tell you I thought I was looking down at the Lord himself. Don't you think he looks like Jesus?"

Christine smiled and nodded.

CHAPTER 28

Maggie watched Nick step carefully around the piles she had scattered all over the floor of his office. He cleared a spot and set down the steaming pizza and cold Pepsis. Then he joined her on the floor, his long legs stretching out next to her. A foot almost brushed her thigh. All day she had found herself acutely aware of his presence. She thought she was too tired to feel, but then her body surprised her every time his elbow accidentally brushed her arm or his hand grazed her thigh while he shifted the Jeep into gear.

She had removed her shoes hours ago and had sat on her feet until they fell asleep. Now she massaged them one at a time while she read the coroner's reports on Aaron Harper and Eric Paltrow, the two dead, little boys whom Jeffreys may have erroneously been convicted of killing.

The pizza smelled good despite the gruesome details she read. She glanced up to find Nick watching her rub her feet. Immediately, he looked away as though she had caught him at something. He popped open a can of Pepsi and handed it to her.

"Thanks." This time she was actually hungry. The ham and cheese sandwich from Wanda's had sat on a plate with only two bites removed when young Deputy Preston had finally volunteered to take it off her hands. That was hours ago. Now it was black outside the window. Phones down the hall had quieted. Staff had thinned out. Some had been sent home to rest while others were sent back out to search for a little boy who seemed to have disappeared off the face of the earth.

Nick lifted a thick slice of pizza, pulling it expertly away so he didn't lose the cheese. He plopped it down onto a paper plate and handed it to Maggie. She could smell green peppers, Italian sausage and Romano cheese. He had done good. She bit off more than she should have, dripping cheese and sauce down her chin.

"Jesus, O'Dell. You've got sauce all over your face."

She licked the side of her mouth while he watched.

"Other side." He pointed. "And on your chin."

Her hands were full of pizza and coroner reports. She licked at the other side while she fumbled for a safe spot to set something down.

"No, higher," he still instructed. "Here, let me."

As soon as his thumb touched the corner of her mouth, her eyes met his. His fingers wiped at her chin. His thumb rolled over her lower lip where she was certain there was no sauce or cheese. In his eyes she saw that he felt the unexpected surge of electricity, too. His fingertips lingered longer than necessary on her chin, moved up, caressed her cheek. His thumb took its time to leave her lip and wipe the corner of her mouth. Completely surprised by her body's reaction, she shifted away, just out of his reach.

"Thanks," she managed to say, now avoiding his eyes. She practically flung the plate with pizza to the side, grabbed a napkin and finished the job, rubbing harder than necessary in an attempt to wipe away the electrical current.

"I think we might need more napkins and Pepsis." Nick scrambled to his feet.

Maggie looked up at him, and he seemed flustered. From the small refrigerator in the corner of his office, he pulled two more cans and added napkins to the pile already on the floor. This time when he sat down, he kept more distance between them. She noticed his charm had been put on hold, his flirting almost nonexistent since he had discovered she had a husband. So the touch, the caress had caught him off guard, too.

"There are so many discrepancies," she said, trying to get her mind back on the coroner's reports. "I don't know why anyone believed Jeffreys killed all three boys."

"But don't serial killers change the way they do things?"

"They may add things. They may experiment. Jeffrey Dahmer experimented with different ways to keep his victims alive. He'd drill holes in their skulls that would incapacitate them but keep them alive.''

"So maybe Jeffreys liked to experiment, too."

"What's unusual here is that the Harper and Paltrow murders were almost identical. Both were bound, hands behind their backs, with rope. They were strangled and their throats slashed. The chest wounds resembled each other almost exactly down to the number of puncture wounds. The same knife was used to carve the X's. Neither boy appeared to have been sexually molested. Their bodies were found in different remote areas near the river.''

She referred to several documents laid out in front of her, leaning carefully so she wouldn't soil them. In the last hour she had started to feel the full impact of her exhaustion. Her eyes blurred as she looked over the coroner's scratchy notes. George Tillie had not been as precise as he should have been. The Paltrow report was the only one to mention the body being clean with little residue found. None of the reports indicated a smudge of oil on the forehead or anywhere else on the body.

Maggie glanced at Nick, who slumped against the hard credenza and rubbed at his eyes. His hair was tousled from too many reckless run-throughs with his fingers. His sleeves were rolled up to the elbows, revealing muscular forearms. He had gotten rid of the tie and had undone several buttons on his wrinkled shirt, exposing enough of his chest to distract her. She shook her head, grabbed a report off the floor and tried to stay focused.

"The Wilson boy, on the other hand—"

"I know," Nick interrupted, sitting forward. "His hands were bound in front with duct tape, no rope. He was stabbed to death— no signs of strangulation. His throat wasn't slashed. A hunting knife was used. Though there were plenty of puncture wounds..."

"Twenty-two."

"Twenty-two puncture wounds, but no carving."

"The Wilson boy was also sodomized, repeatedly."

"And his body was found in a park Dumpster, instead of by the river. Jesus, this stuff makes me sick to my stomach." He shoved the pizza aside, grabbed his Pepsi and emptied the can, wiping his mouth with the back of his hand. "Okay, there's a lot of differences, but couldn't Jeffreys have changed things?

Even the sodomy, couldn't that be seen as...I don't know...an escalation?''

"Yes, it could. But remember the sequence was Harper, Wilson, Paltrow. It would be very unusual for a killer to change, to experiment, to escalate and then go back to the exact format. He uses one knife—something with a small blade—perhaps a fillet knife. Then he changes to a hunting knife, then back to the other knife. Even the styles are very different. The Harper and Paltrow murders are meticulous in detail. Both boys were murdered by someone taking his time—someone who enjoys inflicting pain. Very much like Danny Alverez's murder. Bobby Wilson's murder, however, looks like it was done in the heat of the moment with too much emotion and passion to pay any attention to detail.''

"You know, I always thought it seemed too easy," Nick said wearily. "I've been wondering if my dad wasn't so caught up in the media circus that he may have overlooked something.''

"What do you mean?"

"Well, you know how you hear about things getting missed in the excitement, the so-called rush to judgment? My dad's always enjoyed being the center of attention. The year I started as quarterback for UNL, he'd meet me at the locker room, insisted on it, in fact—every single game. My mom said it was because he was so proud of me. Except there were too many times when he greeted the TV cameras before he even acknowledged me.''

Maggie listened patiently, then waited out his silence. Nick and his father obviously had a complex relationship. And though he was uncomfortable discussing it, she knew he was trying to tell her something important, something pertinent to the Jeffreys investigation. Did Nick really believe his father may have mishandled the case?

Finally, he glanced at her as though he'd read her thoughts.

"Don't get me wrong. I'm not saying my dad would purposely jeopardize any case. He's very well respected and has been for years. In fact, I know I would never have been elected if I wasn't Antonio Morrelli's son. I'm just saying that it all seemed a bit too easy—the way my dad caught Jeffreys. One day there was an anonymous tip, and the next day they had Jeffreys babbling out a confession.''

"What kind of anonymous tip?"

"It was a phone call, I think. I don't know for sure. I wasn't living here at the time. I was teaching down at UNL, so I got most of this stuff secondhand. Isn't there anything in the reports?"

Maggie searched through several file folders. She had read most of them and couldn't remember any phone calls being mentioned. But she also had seen no phone logs of any kind, even for a hot line.

"I haven't seen anything at all about an anonymous tip," she said, handing him the file labeled Jeffreys' Arrest. "What do you remember?"

He seemed flustered, and she wasn't sure if it was his memory he questioned or his father. She watched him look over the reports filed and signed by Antonio Morrelli.

"Your father's reports are very detailed, including a blow-by-blow of the actual arrest. He even includes the evidence they found in the trunk of Jeffreys' Chevy Impala." She checked her own notes and read the list. "They found a roll of duct tape, a hunting knife, some rope...wait a minute."

She stopped to check that she had copied the list correctly. "A pair of boy's underpants, which were later identified as belonging to..." She looked up at Nick, who had found the list in the report and was reading the same items she had in front of her. His eyes met hers, revealing he was thinking precisely what she was.

She continued, "A pair of underpants later identified as Eric Paltrow's."

Maggie rifled through the coroner's report to double-check her memory, though she already knew what she would find.

"Eric Paltrow's body was found with his underpants on."

Nick shook his head in disbelief.

"I bet even Jeffreys was surprised to find all that stuff in his trunk."

They stared at each other, neither wanting to acknowledge out loud what they had stumbled upon. Ronald Jeffreys had been framed for two murders he hadn't committed, and there was a good chance the frame-up had been done by someone in the sheriff's department.

CHAPTER 29

Tuesday, October 28

The day had not gone well, and Nick blamed the two hours of sleep in his office chair. Maggie had gone back to her hotel room at three in the morning to rest, shower and change. Instead of driving the five miles to his house in the country, Nick had fallen asleep at his desk. All day his neck and back had reminded him again that he was only four years away from forty.

His body certainly wasn't what it used to be, although his concerns about sexual performance may have diminished thanks to Agent O'Dell. Last night, the touch of her lips against his fingers, the look in her eyes, the electricity. Jesus, he was grateful the county jail's shower blasted only cold water. Even he had rules about married women. Now if only his body didn't talk him into changing the rules.

Unfortunately, his stash of clean clothes at the office had been used up in the last few days. He had resorted to the uniform browns, a more appropriate choice for the morning press conference. Not that it had made a difference. The press conference had quickly turned into a lynch mob within minutes, especially after Christine's morning headline: Sheriff's Department Ignores Leads in Alverez Case.

He thought for sure Eddie had checked out where old lady Krichek lived, a long time ago, after her first call. Why the hell wouldn't he have realized Krichek had a perfect view of the parking lot where Danny had been abducted? Jesus, he wanted to strangle Eddie or worse, offer him up to the media as a scape-goat. Instead, he let him off with a simple and private verbal lashing and a warning.

Hell, right now he needed every officer he had. It was no time to be losing his cool, which he almost did at the press conference when the questions got ugly. But O'Dell, in her calm and authoritative manner, had rapidly put things back in perspective. She had challenged the media to help find the mysterious blue pickup, making them a part of the hunt for the killer instead of hunting for faults in the sheriff's department. He began wondering what he'd do without her and hoped he wouldn't have to find out any time soon.

He turned the Jeep onto Christine's street just as the sun made a rare appearance from a hole in the clouds, then sank slowly and gently behind a line of trees. It had gotten colder with a biting wind promising the temperature would drop even more.

Maggie had spent the entire trip next to him quietly buried in the Alverez file. Photos from the crime scene and her own Polaroids were scattered across her lap. She was obsessed with completing her profile as though it could somehow save Matthew Tanner. After an afternoon of contradictory leads and a string of unimpressive witnesses, Nick worried that it was too late. Since Matthew's disappearance, a hundred and seventy-five deputies, police officers and independent investigators had been searching almost nonstop. Not one shred of evidence brought them closer to finding the boy. It really did seem as though someone had pulled up alongside Matthew and had him willingly get into his vehicle, just as Sophie Krichek had described.

If that was true, then there was a good chance the killer was someone the boys knew and trusted. Jesus, Nick would rather believe the boys were disappearing into thin air than being killed and mutilated by someone they knew. Someone who lived in the community. Maybe someone *he* knew.

Nick absently pulled into the driveway and hit the brakes, sending photos across the seat and onto the floor.

"Sorry." He shoved the Jeep into park, his hand sliding along Maggie's thigh. He jerked his hand away and reached to pick up the photos. Their arms crisscrossed each other. Their foreheads brushed. He handed her the photos he had retrieved, and she thanked him without looking at him. They had been tiptoeing around each other all day. He wasn't sure if it was to avoid talking about their discovery in the Jeffreys case or to avoid touching one another.

At Christine's door, Maggie's cellular phone began ringing.

"Agent Maggie O'Dell."

Christine motioned for them to come in. "I thought for sure you'd cancel," she whispered to Nick and led him to the living room, leaving Maggie to the privacy of the foyer.

"Because of the article?"

She looked surprised, as though she hadn't even thought of the article. "No, because you're swamped. You're not mad about the article, are you?"

"Krichek is nutty as a fruitcake. I doubt she saw anything."

"She's convincing, Nicky. There's nothing wrong with the lady. You should be looking for an old blue pickup."

Nick eyed Maggie. He could see her pacing. He wished he could hear her conversation. Then, suddenly, he got his wish as her angry voice carried into the living room.

"Go to hell, Greg!" She snapped the phone shut and shoved it into her pocket. It began ringing again.

Christine looked at Nick, eyebrows raised.

"Who's Greg?" she whispered.

"Her husband."

"I didn't know she was married."

"Why wouldn't she be?" he snapped, then regretted his abruptness as soon as he saw his sister's smile.

"No wonder you've been on your best behavior with her."

"What the hell is that supposed to mean?"

"In case you haven't noticed, little brother, she's gorgeous."

"She's also an FBI agent. This is strictly professional, Christine."

"Since when has that stopped you? Remember that cute little attorney from the state attorney's office? Wasn't that supposed to be only professional?"

"She wasn't married." Or if he remembered correctly, at least, she was getting a divorce.

Maggie came in, that distraught look invading her face again.

"Sorry about that," she said as she leaned against the door-jamb. "Lately, my husband has had the annoying tendency of pissing me off."

"That's why I got rid of mine," Christine said with a smile. "Nicky, get Maggie some wine. I need to check up on dinner." She patted Maggie on the shoulder on her way out.

The wine and glasses were on the coffee table in front of him. He poured, watching Maggie out of the corner of his eye. She paced, pretending to be interested in Christine's decorating talents, but obviously distracted. She stopped at the window and stared out into the backyard. He picked up the glasses of wine and came alongside her, startling her.

"You okay?" He handed her the wine, hoping for a glimpse of her eyes.

"Have you ever been married, Nick?" She took the glass without looking at him, suddenly interested in the shadows swallowing Christine's garden.

"No, I've done a pretty good job avoiding it."

They stood quietly, side by side. Her elbow brushed his arm when she took a sip. He stood perfectly still, enjoying the surprising rise in his temperature the slight contact generated, and hoping for more. He waited for her to continue, wanting to hear how her marriage was falling apart. Then immediately, the guilt hit him. Perhaps to justify his thoughts, he said, "I couldn't help noticing you don't wear a wedding ring."

She held up her hand as if to remind herself, then tucked it into her jacket pocket. "It's at the bottom of the Charles River."

"Excuse me?" Without seeing her eyes, he wasn't sure if it was a joke or not.

"About a year ago, we were dragging a floater from the river."

"A floater?"

"A body that's been in the water a while. The water was very cold. My ring must have slipped off."

She kept her eyes ahead, and he followed her lead. As twilight set in, he could see her reflection in the glass. She was still thinking about the conversation with her husband. He wondered what he was like—the man who had, at one time, captured the heart of Maggie O'Dell. He wondered if Greg was some intellectual snob. He bet the guy didn't even watch football, let alone like the Packers.

"You never replaced it?"

"No. I think maybe subconsciously I realized all those things it was supposed to symbolize were gone long before it fell to the bottom of the river."

"Uncle Nick," Timmy interrupted, running into the room and jumping up into Nick's arms, giving Nick little time to even turn around. Immediately, he felt the results of his chair nap. His back screamed at him to put the boy down, but he spiraled Timmy around, hugging him close while his little legs threatened to knock down the knickknacks scattered about.

"You guys!" Christine yelled from the doorway. Then to Maggie, "It's like having two kids in the house."

Nick set Timmy down and gritted his teeth into a smile as he straightened out and absorbed the pain that trailed all the way down his spine. Jesus, he hated these physical reminders that he was getting older.

"Maggie, this is my son, Timmy. Timmy, this is Special Agent Maggie O'Dell."

"So you're an FBI agent just like Agent Mulder and Agent Scully on *The X-Files*?"

"Except I don't track aliens. Although some of the people I track down are pretty scary."

Nick was always amazed at the effect children had on women. He wished he could bottle it. Maggie tucked her hair behind her ear, and she was smiling. Her eyes sparkled. Her entire face seemed to relax.

"I have some *X-Files* posters in my bedroom. Would you like to see them?"

"Timmy, we're going to eat soon."

"Do we have time?" Maggie asked Christine.

Timmy waited for his mom's "sure." Then he grabbed Maggie's hand and led her down the hall.

Nick didn't say anything until they were out of earshot. "It's nice to see he's learning from the master. Although I've never thought of using the old line, 'would you like to see my *X-Files* posters.'"

Christine rolled her eyes and threw a dish towel at him. "Come help. Oh, and bring me a glass of wine, too."

CHAPTER 30

Maggie hated to admit that she had never watched *The X-Files*. Her life-style allowed little time for television or movies. Timmy, however, seemed unconcerned. Once in his room, he anxiously showed off everything, from models of the *Starship Enterprise* to his collection of fossils. One, he said with certainty, was a dinosaur tooth.

The small room was wonderfully cluttered. A baseball mitt hung on the bedpost. A *Jurassic Park* bedspread covered lumps she guessed were matching pajamas. On a corner bookshelf, an old microscope propped up copies of *King Arthur, Galaxy of the Stars* and *The Collector's Encyclopedia of Baseball Cards*. The walls were hidden, plastered with an odd assortment of posters including *The X-Files,* the Nebraska Cornhuskers, *Star Trek, Jurassic Park* and *Batman.* She took it all in, not as an observant FBI agent, but as a twelve year old robbed of this part of her childhood.

Then she remembered her conversation with Greg. The tension was hard to shrug off. He had now accused her of ignoring her own mother. She reminded him that she was the one with the degree in psychology. It didn't matter. He was still angry with her for ruining their anniversary and carried that anger like some trophy he had won that he deserved. How did they ever get to this point?

Timmy grabbed her hand again and led her to the dresser. He pointed to the empty hull of a horseshoe crab.

"My grandpa brought this home for me from Florida. He and Grandma travel a lot. You can touch it if you want."

She ran her finger over the smooth shell. She noticed a photo behind the crab. About two dozen boys in matching T-shirts and shorts lined the inside of a canoe and the dock behind it. She recognized the boy at the front of the canoe and leaned in for a closer view. Her pulse quickened. She lifted the photo, careful not to disturb the crab. The boy was Danny Alverez.

"What's this photo, Timmy?"

"Oh, that's church camp. My mom made me go. I thought it'd ruin my summer, but it was fun."

"Isn't this boy Danny Alverez?" She pointed, and Timmy took a closer look.

"Yeah, that's him."

"So you knew him?"

"Not really. He was down in the Red Robin cabins. I was in the Goldenrod."

"Didn't he go to your church?" She examined the other faces.

"No, I think he went to school and church out by the air force base. Do you want to see my baseball card collection?" He was already digging through the drawers of his nightstand.

Maggie wanted to know more about church camp. "How many boys were there at camp?"

"I don't know. Lots." He set a wooden box on the bed and began taking out cards. "They come from all over, different churches around the county."

"Is it just for boys?"

"No, there's girls, too, but their camp's on the other side of the lake. Somewhere in here I've got a rookie Darryl Strawberry." He sorted through piles he had scattered on the bed.

There were two adults in the photo. One was Ray Howard, the janitor from St. Margaret's. The other was a tall, handsome man with dark curly hair and a boyish face. Both he and Howard wore gray T-shirts with St. Margaret's written across the front.

"Timmy, who's this guy in the photo?"

"Oh, that's Father Keller. He's really cool. I'm one of his altar boys this year. Not many boys get to be his altar boy. He's really choosy."

"How is he choosy?" She made sure that she sounded only interested, not alarmed.

"I don't know. Just by making sure they're reliable and stuff. He treats us special, sort of like our reward for being good altar boys."

"How does he treat you special?"

"He's taking us camping this Thursday and Friday. And sometimes he plays football with us. Oh, and he trades baseball cards. Once I traded him a Bob Gibson for a Joe DiMaggio."

She started to put the photo back. Another face caught her eye. This time she almost dropped the frame. Her heart began to pound. Up on the dock, partially hidden behind a bigger boy, peered the small, freckled face of Matthew Tanner.

"Timmy, do you mind if I borrow this photo for a few days? I promise I'll get it back to you."

"Okay. Do you carry a gun?"

"Yes, I do." She kept the frantic tone from her voice. Carefully, she tugged the photo out of its frame, noticing a slight tremor in her fingers from the sudden rush of adrenaline.

"Are you wearing one now?"

"Yes, I am."

"Can I see it?"

"Timmy," Christine interrupted them. "It's time for dinner. You need to wash up." She held the door open and swatted him with a kitchen towel on his way out.

Maggie slipped the photo into her jacket pocket without Christine noticing.

CHAPTER 31

After dinner Nick insisted he and Timmy do the dishes. Christine knew it was all for Maggie's benefit, but she decided to take advantage of her little brother's temporary generosity.

The two women retreated to the living room where they heard only the muffled discussion of Nebraska football. Christine set the coffee cups and saucers on the glass tabletop and wished Maggie would sit down and relax. Stop being Agent O'Dell for a few minutes. She'd seemed restless throughout dinner and was now pacing. Her body seemed wired with energy, though she looked exhausted. The puffy eyes were poorly concealed with makeup. She was easily distracted.

"Come, sit," Christine finally said, patting the spot on the sofa next to her. "I thought I couldn't keep still, but I think you've got me beaten."

"Sorry. Maybe I've been spending too much time with killers and dead bodies. My manners seem to have disappeared."

"Nonsense. You've just been spending too much time with Nicky."

Maggie smiled. "Dinner was delicious. It's been a long time since I've had a home-cooked meal."

"Thanks, but I've had lots of practice. I was a stay-at-home mom until my husband decided he liked twenty-three-year-old receptionists." Immediately, Christine realized she had revealed too much and made Maggie uncomfortable. She certainly hadn't intended for this to be some sort of tit-for-tat girl talk.

When Maggie crossed the room to sit down, she chose the

recliner instead of sitting next to her. Christine wanted to tell Maggie she knew it wasn't a lack of manners as much as an avoidance of intimacy on any level. It was easy to recognize. Christine did it herself. Since Bruce's departure, she had kept plenty of distance from everyone, with the exception of her son.

"How long will you stay in Platte City?"

"For as long as necessary."

No wonder her marriage was in trouble. As if reading Christine's mind, Maggie explained, "Developing a killer's profile, unfortunately, is something that takes time. It helps to be in his surroundings, his environment."

"I did some research on you. I hope you don't mind. You have an impressive background—a B.S. in criminal psychology and premed, with a master's in behavioral psychology, a forensic fellowship at Quantico. Eight short years with the FBI and already you're one of their top profilers of serial killers. If I calculated right, you're only thirty-two. That's got to feel good—to have accomplished so much."

She expected Maggie might be a bit flustered with the attention. Instead, her vacant stare seemed haunted. From her research, Christine also knew about some of the psychos Maggie had helped put away. Perhaps her success had come with a hefty price tag.

"I suppose it should feel good," Maggie finally said.

Christine waited for more, then realized there would be no more. "Nicky will never admit it, but I know he's grateful to have you here. This is all pretty new to him. I'm certain he didn't expect something like this when my dad talked him into running for sheriff."

"Your father talked him into it?"

"Dad was getting ready to retire. He'd been sheriff for so long, I think he couldn't stand to not have a Morrelli take his place."

"But what about Nick?"

"Oh, he was teaching in the law school down at the university. I think he actually liked it." Christine stopped herself. She wasn't quite sure she understood the complexities of her father and Nick's relationship, let alone explain them to an outsider.

"Your father must be a remarkable man," Maggie said quite simply, without surprise or accusation.

"Why do you say that?" Christine eyed her suspiciously, wondering what Nick may have told her.

"For one thing, he practically captured Ronald Jeffreys singlehandedly."

"Yes, he was quite a hero."

"Also, he seems to have a lot of influence over Nick's decisions."

She did know something more. Now Christine was uncomfortable. She poured herself more coffee, taking time with the cream.

"I think our dad just wants Nicky to have all the opportunities he never had. You know, do the things he didn't have a chance to do."

"What about you?"

"What do you mean?"

"Doesn't he want those same opportunities, those same things for you?"

Christine had to admit, the woman was good. Maggie O'Dell sat in Christine's recliner, sipping coffee and very coolly and calmly probing her.

"I love my dad, knowing full well that he's a bit of a male chauvinist. No, whatever I did was fine with him. I was a girl. Anything out of the ordinary that I did impressed him. Nicky, on the other hand, had it tougher. It's a little more...complex. Nick's constantly had to prove himself, whether he wanted to or not. I suppose that's one of the reasons why he gets so pissed at me."

"No, usually it's because of your big mouth." Nick startled them from the doorway. Timmy stood beside his uncle, smiling as though he was about to get in on something Christine would normally censor.

The phone rang, saving her from a lecture. Christine jumped up, almost knocking her coffee cup off its saucer. She crossed the room and picked up the phone before its third ring.

"Hello?"

"Christine, it's Hal. Sorry to bother you. Is Nick still there?" His voice crackled. She heard humming, an engine. He was in his car.

"Yes. As a matter of fact, you may have just saved my day."

She glanced back at Nick and stuck out her tongue, making Timmy giggle and Nick fume.

"That would be nice—to save someone's day." The crackle couldn't hide the distress in his voice.

"Hal, are you okay? What's going on?"

"Could I just talk to Nick, please?"

Before she could say anything more, Nick was at her side, reaching for the phone. She surrendered it and loitered by the desk until Nick shot her a look.

"Hal, what is it?" He turned his back to them and listened. "Don't let anyone touch anything." The panic in his voice exploded, laced with urgency.

Maggie responded, immediately getting to her feet. Christine gently grabbed Timmy by the shoulders.

"Timmy, go get ready for bed."

"Ah, Mom, it's early."

"Timmy, now." Her brother's panic was contagious. The boy grudgingly headed upstairs.

"I mean it, Hal." Now there was anger to camouflage the panic. It didn't fool her. Christine knew her brother all too well. "Secure the area, but don't let anyone touch a thing. O'Dell's here with me. We'll be there in about fifteen to twenty minutes." When he turned, his eyes immediately sought out Maggie's as he hung up the phone.

"My God. They found Matthew's body, didn't they?" Christine said what only seemed obvious.

"Christine, I swear, if you print a word." The angry panic threatened to turn into fury.

"People have the right to know."

"Not before his mother. Will you, at least, please have the decency to wait—for her sake?"

"On one condition…"

"Jesus, Christine, listen to yourself!" he spat out in such anger it forced her to take a step backward.

"Just promise you'll call me when it's okay to go ahead. Is that too much to ask?"

He shook his head in disgust. She looked to Maggie, who waited by the door, no longer willing to come between brother and sister. Then, she looked back at Nick. "Come on, Nicky. You don't want me camped out on Michelle Tanner's front porch, do you?'' She smiled, just enough to let him know she wasn't serious.

"Don't you dare talk to anyone or print a damn thing until you hear from me. And stay the hell away from Michelle Tanner.'' He wagged an angry finger in her face, then stomped out.

Christine waited until the Jeep's taillights turned the corner at the end of the street. She grabbed the phone and punched *69. It rang only once.

"Deputy Langston.''

"Hal, hi, it's Christine.'' Before he could ask any questions she hurried on. "Nicky and Maggie just left. Nicky asked me to keep trying George Tillie. You know, ol' George, he could sleep through World War III.''

"Yeah?'' The one word was filled with suspicion.

"I can't remember the exact location, you know to tell George.''

Silence. Damn, he was onto her.

She took a stab. "It's off Old Church Road...''

"Right.'' He sounded relieved. "Tell George to go a mile past the state-park marker. He can leave his car in Ron Woodson's pasture, up on top of the hill. He'll see the spotlights down in the woods. We'll be close to the river.''

"Thanks, Hal. I know it probably sounds insensitive and unlikely, but I keep hoping it's some runaway and not Matthew, for Michelle's sake.''

"I know what you mean. But there's no doubt. It's Matthew. I gotta go. Tell George to be careful walking down here.''

She waited for the click, then dialed Taylor Corby's home number.

CHAPTER 32

Light snow glittered in the Jeep's headlights. They parked on an incline that overlooked the river. Bright spotlights illuminated the grove of trees below, creating eerie shadows, ghosts with spindly arms that waved in the breeze.

It reminded Maggie of a similar night, years ago, searching for a killer in the dark woods of Vermont. She wondered how much of her memory bank was filled with horror stories where other normal people stored things like Christmas traditions and family events.

The temperature had plunged in the last two hours. The cold cut through her wool jacket, sharp slashes like tiny knives. She hadn't thought to pack a coat. Even Morrelli shivered in his denim jacket. Within seconds, snowflakes clung to her eyelashes, her hair and her clothes, adding wetness to the biting cold. To make matters worse, they had over a quarter of a mile to walk. After contaminating the last crime scene, Morrelli was now over-compensating, instructing his officers and deputies to create a wide perimeter. A perimeter they guarded like military sentries.

The underbrush was thick—like walking through knee-deep water. What was once mud had begun to freeze, leaving a crunchy film. A narrow path twisted through the trees. Nick led the way, snapping branches and twigs. Those that escaped his grasp whipped Maggie's face. She could no longer feel the sting of some where the cold had left her skin numb.

Tree roots jutted up out of the earth, tripping her once. The final descent to the riverbank was steep, forcing them to hang on to branches, tree roots, vines, anything strong enough. The snow had accumulated just enough to add a slick finish to the rugged terrain. Nick lost his footing, slipped and slammed down hard on his butt. He scrambled back to his feet more embarrassed than hurt, waving off her help.

The path ended at the river's bank, where a line of cattails and tall grass separated the woods from the water. Hal met them. Maggie noticed that a pasty white had replaced his normal ruddy complexion. His eyes were watery, his demeanor quiet. She had witnessed it before—the murder of a child momentarily reducing men to speechless shells. He led the way while Nick threw questions at him, receiving only nods as answers.

"Bob Weston is sending an FBI forensic team to collect evidence. Nobody else gets through. Nobody. You got that, Hal?"

Suddenly, Hal stopped and pointed. At first, Maggie saw nothing. It was peaceful and quiet despite the presence of over two dozen officers scattered throughout the woods. In the distance, a train whistle cut through the thick silence. Snowflakes danced like fireflies in the harsh light of the massive spotlights. Then she saw him, the little, white body with a necklace of blood, naked in the snow-laced grass. His chest was so small, the jagged X slashed from his neck to his waist. His arms lay by his sides, his fists clenched. There had been no need to tie this boy who was much too small to present any threat to his killer.

She left both men and approached slowly, reverently. Yes, the body had been washed clean. Of that, she was already certain. She knelt beside him and carefully brushed the snow from his forehead. Without leaning forward, she saw the smudge of oily liquid. It smeared his blue lips and left another smudge between the X over his heart.

He seemed so fragile, so vulnerable, she wanted to cover him, protect him from the snow that glittered on his gray skin, covering the nasty red-raw slashes and gaping wounds.

He had been out here for a while. Even the sudden cold couldn't disguise the smell. She noticed small puncture marks on the inside of his left thigh, deep but leaving no trace of blood. They had been made after the boy was dead. Perhaps an animal, she thought as she dug out a small flashlight. The punctures were definitely teeth, but human teeth, she realized, overlapping several times as though bitten in a madness or purposely to disguise the imprint. They were close to the groin, but she couldn't see any marks on the penis. He hadn't done this before. The killer was adding to his routine, getting reckless and accelerating. He had only taken the boy two days ago. Something had changed. Maybe the news reports were making him nervous. Something was different. Something was wrong.

She sat back on her feet, suddenly dizzy and a bit nauseated. She never got sick at crime scenes anymore. In fact, years ago when she stopped vomiting at the sight and smell of dead bodies, she had seen it as an initiation passage. Had Albert Stucky dismantled her defense system, punctured her armor? Or had his evil simply made her human again? Retaught her to feel?

She started to crawl back to her feet when she noticed it. A torn piece of paper peeked from between the tiny fingers. Matthew Tanner had something clutched tightly in his fist. She glanced over her shoulder. Nick and Hal stood where she had left them. Their backs were turned to her as they watched five men in FBI windbreakers descend the wooded ridge.

As gently as possible, she twisted the fingers, now stiff and unbending in the advance stages of rigor mortis. She dislodged the crumpled piece of paper. It was thicker than paper and no more than a torn corner. Without even examining it closely, she recognized what it was. Just hours ago she had seen dozens spread out on Timmy Hamilton's bed. Twisted tightly in Matthew Tanner's fist was the corner of a baseball card, and Maggie was pretty sure she knew whom it belonged to.

CHAPTER 33

The forensic team worked quickly, now threatened by a new enemy. Snow fell more heavily and in large, wet flakes, covering leaves and branches, sticking to grass and burying valuable evidence.

Maggie and Nick were huddled near the tree line, out of the wind's merciless path. Maggie couldn't believe how cold it had become. She dug her hands deep into her jacket pockets, trying not to wrinkle the photo she had borrowed from Timmy. She and Nick watched in silence as they waited for Hal to bring a blanket, extra jackets, anything to warm them. They stood so close Nick's shoulder brushed against her. She felt his breath against her neck, reassuring her that she could still feel despite the numbness.

"Maybe we should just head back." It was cold enough to see his breath. "There's nothing more we can do here." Nick rubbed his arms, shifted his weight from one foot to the other. She could hear the soft chatter of his teeth.

"Do you want me to go with you to Michelle Tanner's?" She pulled her jacket collar up. It didn't help. The cold had invaded every inch of her body.

"Tell me if you think this is a cop-out." He hesitated, gathering his thoughts. "I'd like to wait until morning, not just because I'd be waking her up in the middle of the night. She probably hasn't slept since Sunday. But it might be a while before they get him to the morgue. And no matter how painful it is, she'll want to see him. Laura Alverez insisted on identifying Danny. She wouldn't believe me until she saw him herself." His eyes were watery blue from the wind and the memory. He wiped a sleeve across his face.

"It's not a cop-out. It certainly makes sense. In the morning she may have more people there to lean on. And you're right. By the time they get finished here, it will be morning."

"I'll let these guys know we're leaving."

He started for the forensic team when Maggie saw something and grabbed his arm. Not more than fifteen feet behind Nick was a set of footprints—bare footprints, freshly stamped in the snow.

"Nick, wait," she whispered. "He's here." Her heart started pounding in her ears. Why hadn't she thought of it before? Of course, it made perfect sense.

"What are you talking about?"

"The killer. He's here." She held his arm, digging her nails into the denim jacket to immobilize him and to steady her nerves. Her eyes surveyed the area while she tried to keep her body from twisting and turning, from tipping off the killer who she knew was watching them.

"Do you see him?"

"No, but he's here," she said, carefully glancing around now, making sure he wasn't within earshot. "Try to stay calm and keep your voice down. He could be watching us."

"O'Dell, I think the cold has frozen your brain." Nick looked at her as though he thought she was nuts, but he obeyed her instructions and spoke softly. "There's over two dozen deputies and police officers surrounding this area."

"Directly behind you, next to that tree with the huge knot. There's a set of footprints, bare footprints made in the snow."

She loosened her grip, allowing him to look.

"Jesus." His eyes darted around before they made their way back to hers. "With the snow falling as heavy as it is, those were made recently, very recently. Like, say, minutes ago. The son of a bitch may have been right behind us. What the hell do we do?"

"You stay here. Wait for Hal. I'll head up the path like I'm going back to the cars. He must still be inside the perimeter of your people. He shouldn't be able to get out without going past one of them. From up above I might be able to see him."

"I'll come with you."

"No, he'll notice if he's watching. Wait for Hal. I'll need the two of you as backup. Stay calm and try not to look around."

"How will we know where you are?"

"I'll let you know somehow." She kept her voice calm and even, while the adrenaline began to surge. "I'll fire my gun into the air. Just don't let any of your men shoot me."

"Like I can control that."

"I'm not joking, Morrelli."

"Neither am I."

She glanced up at him. He wasn't joking, and for a moment she realized how stupid it might be to sneak around in a woods filled with armed police. But if the killer was still here, she couldn't hesitate. And he *was* here. He was watching. She could feel it. This was part of his ritual.

She started up the path. Her leather flats were caked with snow, making the climb even more slippery. She grabbed at branches, tree roots and vines. Within minutes she was out of breath. The adrenaline pumped through her veins, propelling her numb body.

A branch snapped off in her hands, sending her skidding. She slammed to a stop, ramming her hip into a tree. Her hands were raw with cold, but she crawled back to her feet, digging her fingers into the bark. She was almost to the perimeter. She could hear the crime-scene tape flapping in the wind. Just above her, she heard voices.

The ground finally leveled enough for her to stand without assistance. She veered off the path and headed into the thick brush. From above she could see Nick at the bottom of the tree line. Hal was just joining him. Between the trees and the river, the forensic team worked quickly, hunching over the small body and filling little plastic bags of evidence. They were bringing out special equipment from their backpacks to deal with the accumulating snow. Behind them, beyond the cattails and tall grass, she could see the black waters of the river churning with motion.

Down below something moved in the trees. Maggie froze. She listened, trying to hear over the pounding in her ears and her rapid breathing. It was hard to breathe in the cold air. Had she imagined seeing movement?

A twig snapped not more than a hundred feet below her. Then she saw him. He was pressed against a tree. In the shadows of the spotlights he looked like an extension of the bark. He blended in, tall, thin and black from head to bare feet. She had been right.

He was watching, twisting and leaning to see the forensic team below. He started moving from tree to tree, a low crouched-over motion, smooth and sleek like an animal sneaking up on its prey. He slithered his way down the ridge and around the murder site. He was leaving.

Maggie crept through the thicket. In her urgency, snow and leaves crunched beneath her. Branches snapped and creaked in what seemed like explosions of sounds. But no one heard, including the shadow who was quickly and silently moving toward the riverbank.

Her heart pounded against her rib cage, and her hand shook when she pulled out her gun. It was only the cold, she convinced herself. She was in control. She could do this.

She followed, never letting him out of her sight. Twigs scratched her face and grabbed her hair. Branches stabbed at her legs. She fell and smashed her thigh against a rock. Each time he stopped, she skidded to a halt and slammed her body against a tree, hoping to be hidden in the shadows.

They were on level ground, just on the edge of the woods. The forensic team was behind them. She heard them call to each other. Their equipment whined in the wind. He was making his way to the perimeter, using the trees to camouflage himself. Suddenly, he stopped again and looked back in her direction. She scrambled behind a tree, pressing herself into the cold, rough bark. She held her breath. Had he seen her? She hoped the pounding of her heart didn't betray her. The wind whirled around her, a ghostly moan. The river was close enough for her to hear its rolling water and smell the musty decay it carried with it.

She peered out from behind the tree. She couldn't see him. He was gone. She listened but only heard voices behind her. There was only silence ahead. Silence and darkness, well beyond the spotlight's reach now.

It had only been seconds. He couldn't be gone. She slid around the tree and strained to see into the darkness. There was movement in the dark, and she aimed her gun, arms stretched out in front of her. It was only a branch, swaying in the wind. But was something, or someone, hiding behind it? Despite the cold, her palms were sweaty. She walked slowly and carefully, keeping close to the trees. The river ran close to the tree line. As she walked into the darkness, she noticed that even the cattails and grass disappeared. There was nothing separating the woods from the steep riverbank, a ridge of three to four feet that the water had carved. Below, the water was black and fast-moving, dotted with eerie shapes and shadows that rode the waves.

Suddenly, she heard a twig snap. She heard him running—legs swishing through grass—before she could see him. She spun to her right where branches cracked. An explosion of sound came at her. She turned and fired a warning shot into the air just as he emerged from the thicket, a huge, black shadow, charging straight for her. She aimed, but before she had time to squeeze the trigger, he knocked into her, sending her backward, flying through the air and plunging the two of them into the river.

The cold water stung her body like thousands of snakebites. She clung to her gun and raised her arm to fire at the floating black mass only feet away from her. Pain shot through her shoulder. She twisted and tried again. This time she felt metal stabbing into her flesh. It was only then she realized she had crashed into a pile of debris. It held her from being washed away by the current. And something was ripping into her shoulder. She tried to break free, but it only stabbed deeper and tore into her flesh. Then she noticed blood dripping out the bottom of her sleeve, covering her hand and gun.

She heard the voices above yelling to each other. The stampede of footsteps ground to a halt, and a half-dozen flashlights came over the edge, blinding her. In the new light she twisted again, despite the pain, just enough to find the floating shadow. But there was nothing on the river's surface for as far as she could see.

He was gone.

CHAPTER 34

The frigid water paralyzed his body. His skin burned. His muscles screamed with pain. His lungs threatened to burst. He held his breath and kept his body submerged just under the surface. The river carried him in a violent rocking motion. He didn't fight its power, its rapid force. Instead, he allowed it to cradle him, to accept him as its own. To rescue him once again.

They were close. So close he could see the flitters of flashlights dance across the surface. To his right. To his left. Just above his head. Voices yelled to each other. Voices filled with panic and confusion.

No one dived in after him. No one attempted the black water. No one except for Special Agent O'Dell, who wasn't going anywhere. She had entangled herself neatly into the little present he had found for her. It served her right for thinking she could outsmart him, sneak up on him and trap him. The bitch had gotten what she deserved.

The flashlights found her. And soon the people on the riverbank would no longer search for him. He sneaked to the surface for air. The wet ski mask clung to his face like a spiderweb. But he didn't dare remove it.

The river carried him downstream. He watched men scramble down the riverbank, silly, slip-sliding shadows dancing in the light. He smiled, pleased with himself. Special Agent O'Dell would hate being rescued. First being incapacitated and helpless and now being rescued. Would it shock her to discover how much he knew about her? This she-devil who claimed to be his nemesis. Did she really expect to dig inside his mind and not have him return the gesture? Finally, a worthy adversary to keep him on his toes, unlike these other small-town hicks.

Something floated next to him, small and black. A trace of panic fluttered inside his gut until he realized it wasn't alive. He grabbed the hard plastic. It flipped open and a light flashed on, startling him. It was a cellular phone. What a shame to see it go to waste. He stuffed it deep into the pocket of his pants.

He maneuvered himself closer to the riverbank. In seconds, he found his marker. He grabbed the crooked branch that hung over the water. It creaked under his weight, but didn't break.

The current pushed and slapped against his body. The water possessed a strength, a power that demanded respect. He understood that, welcomed it and used it to his advantage.

His fingers stung with cold as he clawed at the branch. Bark flaked off and threatened to send him downstream. His arms ached. Only another foot, a few more inches. His feet struck land, ice-cold, snow-covered land, but his feet were already numb. The soles, heavily callused, expert navigators. He ran through the ice-coated sea of grass. It clinked and tinkled like breaking glass as hundreds of clinging icicles shattered. He gasped for breath but didn't slow his pace. The silvery snow floated through the pitch-black night—small angels dancing alongside him, running with him.

He found his hiding spot. The grove of plum trees sagged with snow-covered branches, adding a cavelike effect to the already thick canopy. Just then, a sudden ringing sent him into another frenzy. Quickly, he realized it was the phone vibrating inside his pants. He dug it out, held it for two, three rings, staring at it. Finally, he flipped it open. It lit up again. The ringing stopped. Someone was yelling,

"Hello!"

"Hello?"

"Is this Maggie O'Dell's phone?" the voice demanded. The man sounded angry, and for a second he thought about hanging up.

"Yes, it is. She dropped it."

"Can I talk to her?"

"She's kind of tied up right now," he said, almost laughing out loud.

"Well, tell her that her husband, Greg, called, and that her mother is in serious shape. She needs to call the hospital. You got that?"

"Sure."

"Don't forget," the man snapped at him and hung up.

He smiled, still holding the phone to his ear and listening to the dial tone. But it was too cold to take much pleasure in his new toy. Instead, he peeled off the black sweat pants, sweatshirt and ski mask. He threw them into the plastic garbage bag without even wringing them dry. The wet hairs on his arms and legs developed ice crystals before he wiped himself down and pulled on dry jeans and a thick wool sweater.

He sat on the running board to tie his tennis shoes. If it continued to snow, he might have to resort to wearing shoes. No, shoes would make it impossible to maneuver the river. They only acted as anchors. Besides, he hated getting them dirty.

If only he could be crawling into the nice, warm Lexus, but someone would have noticed it missing tonight. So, he climbed up into the old pickup, instead. The engine sputtered to life, and he drove home, shivering and squinting as the one headlight cut through the black night and white snow.

CHAPTER 35

It had seemed like a good idea at the time. His house was less than a mile away. She had been soaked to the bone and bleeding. Now Nick wasn't so sure he should have brought her here. As he strung up Maggie's clothes to dry in the utility room, he fingered the soft lace of her bra, and he couldn't help imagining what it would look like filled. It was ridiculous, especially after all that had happened in the last several hours. Yet, the soft scent of her perfume calmed him, soothed him, not to mention turned him on.

He had left her in the master bathroom upstairs. He had taken a shower downstairs, lit a fire in the fireplace and hung her clothes to dry. From the sound of running water in the pipes above him, he knew she was still in the shower. He wondered whether he should check on her. Despite that irritating calm, she had been shaken up, even if she wouldn't admit it. And in pain. The bastard had managed to shove her into a tangle of old splintered fence posts and rusted barbed wire.

The water shut off above him. He grabbed a fresh shirt from the dryer and fumbled with the buttons. He felt like a high-school kid unable to control his body's responses. It was crazy. After all, it wasn't as though a naked woman had never been in his house before. Fact was, there had been plenty—more than plenty.

The medicine cabinet was well stocked, remnants of his mother's paranoia. He filled his arms with cotton balls, rubbing alcohol, gauze, washcloths, hydrogen peroxide and a tin of salve probably as old as his mother. He set up his nursing station by the fire, adding pillows and blankets. The furnace was making that thumping sound again. He should have had it checked. He stuffed huge logs on the fire, filling the fireplace and warming the room with a glowing yellow heat. Of course, it couldn't possibly match the one already roaring inside him. For once he'd ignore his raging hormones and do the right thing. It was as simple as that.

He turned to find her coming down the long, open staircase. She wore his old terry-cloth robe. It parted with every step, just enough to reveal well-shaped calves, sometimes a glimpse of a firm, smooth thigh. No, there would be absolutely nothing simple about this.

Her wet hair glistened. Her cheeks were ruddy from too much hot water. Her pace was slow, almost hesitant. The water had washed away her defenses. A hidden vulnerability exposed itself in those luscious, brown eyes.

As soon as she saw his arsenal of healing tools, she shook her head and dismissed them with a wave of her hand.

"I think I washed everything out. None of that is necessary."

"It's either this or I take you to the hospital."

She frowned at him.

"Humor me, okay? That wire was full of rust. When was your last tetanus shot?"

"I'm sure it's up-to-date. The Bureau hauls us in every three years, whether we need it or not. Look, Morrelli, I appreciate the gesture, but I really am fine."

He uncapped the alcohol and peroxide, lined up cotton balls and pointed to the ottoman in front of him. "Sit."

He thought she would refuse again, but perhaps she was too tired to argue. She sat down, loosened the robe's cinch, hesitated, then let the robe drop off her shoulder while she held it tightly at her breasts.

Immediately, he found himself distracted by her smooth, creamy skin, the beginning swell of her breasts, the curve of her neck, the fresh scent of her hair and skin. He felt light-headed, and already he was hard. How could he touch her and not want to do more? It was stupid. He needed to concentrate and ignore his erection for once in his life.

About a half-dozen bloody, triangular marks marred her beautiful skin, starting on top of her shoulder and trailing down her shoulder blade and arm. Several were deep and bleeding. In one place, the skin had ripped open, leaving a gash of torn skin.

He dabbed an alcohol-soaked cotton ball against the first puncture, and she jerked from the sting. However, she made no sound.

"Are you okay?"

"Fine. Let's just get this over with."

He tried to be gentle with dabs and soft wipes. Still, she winced and grimaced beneath his touch. He cleaned each wound, hoping the alcohol would sterilize as much as it stung. Then he applied gauze and tape to those that kept bleeding.

Finally finished, he ran his open palm over the top of her shoulder and continued the slow caress down her arm, letting his hand make the journey he wished his mouth could. He felt her tremble, just slightly. Her back straightened, alerting her body to danger or responding to the electricity. His hand lingered, enjoying the sensation of silky skin. Then gently, reluctantly, he lifted the robe up over her shoulder, covering the beautiful and battered skin. She hesitated, as if surprised, as if expecting something more. Then she gathered the robe together and tightened the cinch.

"Thanks," she said without looking back at him.

"We have several hours before morning. I thought we could rest here, by the fire. Can I get you anything...hot chocolate, brandy?"

"Brandy would be nice." She left the ottoman and sat on the rug in front of the fireplace, leaning against a pile of pillows and tucking the robe in around her shapely legs.

"Can I get you anything to eat?"

"No, thanks."

"You sure? I could fix some soup, maybe a sandwich."

She smiled up at him. "Why is it that you're always trying to feed me, Morrelli?"

"Probably because I'm not allowed to do the things I'd really like to do with you."

Her smile disappeared while he looked into her eyes and held her gaze. The color rose in her cheeks. He was bordering on totally inappropriate behavior. Yet, all he could think about was whether she felt as hot as he did. Finally, she looked away, and he retreated to the kitchen while he was still able to move.

CHAPTER 36

The photo Maggie had retrieved from her jacket pocket was creased and wrinkled. The corners curled as it dried. Lint from the robe's pocket stuck to the glossy finish. She owed Timmy a replacement, though she didn't know how she'd accomplish that. At least the photo hadn't disappeared into the dark water like her cell phone. She seemed destined to lose things at the bottoms of rivers and lakes.

Nick was taking a long time in the kitchen. She wondered whether he had decided on a sandwich, after all. His last remark left her with an unsettled feeling, nothing she could even describe without using an annoying reference to butterflies. He was being a perfect gentleman. She had absolutely no reason to be concerned, even though she leaned against pillows scented with just a hint of his aftershave lotion. Even though she sat in front of his fireplace wearing nothing but his robe.

The entire time he dressed her wounds, she welcomed the sting of pain. It was the only thing that kept her mind from relishing his touch. When he finished by running his hand over her shoulder and down her arm, she was shocked to find herself waiting breathlessly, hoping for the caress to continue. Now, she wondered what it would feel like to have his big, steady hands caressing her neck, sliding gently over her shoulders and slowly down to her breasts.

She heard Nick come into the room and her hand flew to her face. Her skin was flushed again, but the fire would account for that. It would not, however, account for her shortness of breath.

She steadied herself and avoided looking up at him as he approached.

He handed her a glass of brandy, then sat next to her. He pulled his long, bare feet up underneath himself, leaning so close he brushed her shoulder.

"So, that's the photo you told me about?" He nodded in its direction as he grabbed a handmade quilt off the sofa. He began wrapping it around their legs. He did this as though it was natural for the two of them to be curling up next to each other. The intimacy of the act immediately sent the heat from her face down to other parts of her body.

Perhaps he recognized it. Maybe he felt it. Suddenly, he looked embarrassed as he explained, "The furnace isn't working quite right. I need to have it checked. I just didn't expect it to get this cold in October."

She handed him the photo. With both hands now cupped around the globe of brandy, she swirled the liquid in the glass, breathed in its sweet, stout aroma, then took a sip. She closed her eyes, tilted her head back against the soft pillows and enjoyed the lovely sting sliding down her throat. Several more sips would release her from that unsettled feeling. It was during these initial light-headed moments that she understood her mother's escape. Alcohol possessed the power to level tension and dissolve unwanted feelings. There was no pain if she couldn't feel it. Grief didn't exist if she was too numb to recognize it.

"I agree," Nick said, interrupting her pleasant descent into numbness. "It is too much of a coincidence. But I can't just haul Ray Howard in for questioning, can I?"

Her eyes flew open, and she sat up. "Not Howard. Father Keller."

"What? Are you nuts? I can't haul in a priest. You really can't believe a Catholic priest could kill little boys."

"He fits the profile. I need to find out more about his background, but yes, I do think a priest is capable."

"I don't. It's crazy." He avoided her eyes and gulped his brandy. "The community would hang me by my thumbs if I hauled in a priest for questioning. Especially this Father Keller. He's like Superman with a collar. Jesus, O'Dell, you're way off target."

"Just listen to me for a minute. You said yourself it looked like Danny Alverez didn't put up a fight. Keller was someone he knew and trusted. Father Francis told us it was unlikely for a layperson post-Vatican II—which would be anyone under the age of thirty-five—to know how to administer last rites, unless that person had some training.''

"But this guy is a hero with kids. How could he do something like this and not slip up?''

"People who knew Ted Bundy never suspected anything. Look, I also found a torn piece of a baseball card in Matthew's hand. Timmy told me earlier tonight that Father Keller trades baseball cards with them.''

Nick wiped at the wet strands on his forehead, and she could smell the same shampoo she had used upstairs. He leaned back against the pillows, set his glass on his chest and watched the last bit swirl around.

"Okay,'' he said finally, "you check him out. But I need something more than a photo and a piece of baseball card before I haul him in for questioning. In the meantime, I want to do some checking on Howard. You have to admit he's a weird character. What kind of guy dresses in a shirt and tie to clean a church?''

"It's not a crime to dress inappropriately for your job. If it were, you would have been arrested long ago.''

He shot her a look, but couldn't hide the smile caught at the corner of his mouth.

"Look, it's late. We're both wiped out. How 'bout we try to get some sleep?'' he said, then emptied his glass and set it aside on the floor. He stretched his legs under the quilt. He grabbed a remote from an end table, pressed a few buttons and the lights dimmed. She smiled at his handy little toy for his romantic romps in front of the fire. Why did she find herself almost disappointed that she didn't need to worry about this being one of them?

"Maybe I should go back to the hotel.''

"Come on, O'Dell. Your clothes are still wet. All your stuff's labeled dry-clean. I couldn't just stick them in the dryer. Look, I'm too tired to make a pass, if that's what you're worried about.'' He made himself comfortable against the pillows, his body close to her.

"No, it's not that,'' she said and wondered why her own body wasn't too tired. Instead, every muscle, every nerve ending seemed attuned to the proximity of his body. Would she even resist if he did make a pass? Did she have no feelings left for Greg? What exactly was going on with her? This was beyond annoying. "I don't usually sleep much. I might just keep you awake," she offered in place of the real reason.

"What do you mean you don't sleep?" He slumped down next to her, his head almost touching her arm. He closed his eyes, and she noticed how long his eyelashes were.

"I haven't been able to sleep for over a month now. If I do, I usually have nightmares."

He looked up at her but kept his head on the pillow. "I imagine with the stuff you see, it's hard not to have nightmares. You probably noticed I didn't spend a lot of time looking at Matthew's body. Did something in particular happen?"

She looked down at him. His body curled under the quilt. Despite the dark bristle on his face, there was something boyish about him. Then he pulled himself up on one elbow, twisting open his half-buttoned shirt in the process and exposing his muscular chest and the curly wisps of dark hair. The boyish image disappeared quickly, and she imagined slipping her hand into his shirt and letting her fingers explore. She needed to stop. This was absolutely ridiculous. Suddenly, she realized he was waiting for an answer, his eyes filled with concern.

"Did something happen?" he asked again.

"Not anything I care to discuss."

He stared at her as though trying to look deep inside her. Then, he sat up.

"Actually, I think I have a remedy for nightmares. It works with Timmy when he sleeps over."

"Well, then, it can't be more brandy."

"No." He smiled. "You hang on to someone else real tight while you fall asleep."

Her eyes met his. "Nick, I don't think that's a good idea."

His face was serious again. "Maggie, this isn't some cheap trick to get close to you. I just want to help. Will you let me do that? What do you have to lose?"

When she didn't answer, he slid closer. Slowly, hesitantly, he put his arm around her as though waiting, giving her plenty of opportunity to protest. When she didn't, he put his hand on her shoulder and gently pulled her into him so that her face rested hot against his chest. She heard his heart pound in her ear. Her own heart beat so noisily it was difficult to distinguish between the two. Her cheek brushed against the opening in his shirt, the coarse, wiry hair wonderfully scratchy and soft against her skin. She resisted the temptation of allowing her fingers access. He rested his chin on the top of her head. His voice vibrated against her.

"Now relax," he said. "Imagine that nothing can get to you without going through me first. Even if you can't sleep, just close your eyes and rest."

How could she possibly sleep with her entire body alive, alert and on fire everywhere it touched his?

CHAPTER 37

Maggie awoke groggy, her arms and legs heavy. She was cold. The fire had gone out. Nick was no longer beside her. She looked around the dark room and saw the back of his head, asleep on the sofa.

A flicker of light outside the window caught her eye. She sat up. There it was again. A dark shadow with a flashlight passed the window. Her heart began to pound. He had followed them from the river.

"Nick," she whispered, but there was no movement. Her mind raced. Where had she left her gun? "Nick," she tried again. No response.

The shadow disappeared. She crawled to the bottom of the staircase, watching the window. The room was lit only by the ghostly glow of the moon. She had taken off her gun when they first came in, on her way upstairs. She had laid it on a stand near the staircase. The stand was gone, moved, but where? Her eyes darted around the room. The pounding of her heart made her chest ache. It was cold without the fire, so cold her hands shook.

Then she heard the twist and click of the doorknob. She searched for a weapon, anything sharp, anything heavy. The metal clicked again and held. The door was locked. She grabbed a small lamp with a heavy metal base and ripped off the shade. She listened. Her breathing came in gasps and gulps. She tried to hold it as she listened again.

She crawled back to the sofa, clutching the lamp close to her. "Nick," she whispered and reached up to poke him. "Nick, wake up.'' She shoved his shoulder, and his body rolled toward her, tumbling onto the floor. Her hand was smeared with blood. She looked down at him. Oh God, oh, dear God. She stuffed her bloody hand into her mouth to prevent the scream, to stop the terror. Nick's blue eyes stared up at her, cold and vacant. Blood covered his shirtfront. His throat was slashed, the gaping wound still bleeding.

Then she saw the flicker of light again. The shadow was at the window, looking in, watching her, smiling. It was a face she recognized. It was Albert Stucky.

This time she awoke with a violent flaying of arms, beating and thrashing at anything nearby. Nick grabbed her wrists, preventing her from pummeling his chest. She tried to breathe, but it only came in rapid gasps. Her body shook, wild convulsions beyond her control.

''Maggie, it's okay.'' His voice was soft and soothing but alarmed and urgent. ''Maggie, you're safe.''

She stopped suddenly, though her body still shook. She stared into Nick's eyes. They were warm blue filled with concern, and they were alive. Her eyes darted around the room. A fire raged, licking at the huge logs Nick had fed it earlier. The room was lit by the fire's warm yellow glow. Outside the window, snow glittered against the glass. There was no flicker of a flashlight. No Albert Stucky.

''Maggie, are you okay?'' He held her fisted hands against his chest, caressing her wrists.

She looked into his eyes again. Her own were suddenly very tired. ''It didn't work,'' she whispered. ''You lied to me.''

''I'm sorry. You were sleeping peacefully for a while. Maybe I wasn't holding you tight enough.'' He smiled.

She relaxed her fists against his chest while his hands continued to caress her arms, moving up over her elbows, up inside the wide sleeves of the robe. They made it all the way to her shoulders before they began their slow descent. Inch by inch, they warmed her. But the chill was deeper, crawling beneath her skin like ice in her veins.

She leaned against him. He radiated heat. Her cheek brushed against his shirt, the warm cotton fibers. It wasn't enough. She lifted herself away, just enough to give her fingers room while she unbuttoned the rest of his shirt. She avoided his eyes, and felt his body stiffen. His own hands stopped. Perhaps his breathing had, also. She opened the shirt, resisted the urge to run her hands over the bulging muscles, her fingers through the coarse hair. Instead, she leaned her face against him, listening to the thunder of his heart and allowing his heat to warm her. She only hoped he understood.

He trembled, though she knew he wasn't cold. Then, finally, she felt his body relax. His breathing began again, a little rapid at first, though it was clear he was trying to steady it. His arms wrapped around her waist, but he allowed them no exploration, no caresses. He simply held her body close to his, and this time, he held her tightly.

CHAPTER 38

Christine held her breath and double-clicked on Send. In minutes her article would spit out from the newsroom's printer, then roll on the presses—presses that were actually stopped and waiting. Never in her wildest dreams had she imagined being in this position.

Despite her exhaustion, the adrenaline had kept her mind racing and her fingers flying over the keyboard. Her palms were still sweaty. She wiped them on her jeans before she shut off the laptop computer, folded it shut and unplugged it from the phone jack. Modern technology—she didn't understand how it worked, but she was grateful. It had allowed her son to sleep soundly down the hall while she pounded out her fifth consecutive front-page article. She wondered what the record was at the *Omaha Journal*.

She glanced at her watch. The newspaper would be an hour late hitting the streets, but Corby seemed content. She gulped down the last of her coffee, avoiding the glob of cream and sugar congealed at the bottom. She couldn't believe she had gotten through it without a cigarette.

She slid the laptop off the desk, knocking a pile of envelopes to the floor. Picking them up put an immediate end to her elation. Several were late notices for bills she couldn't pay. One, from the State Department of Nebraska, remained unopened. It contained more forms in triplicate with old-fashioned blue carbon paper between each copy. How could she trust and believe in a state that still used carbon paper? This was the system that was going to track down her ex-husband and make him pay child support? It was bad enough that Bruce had screwed her. But how could he screw his son? She hated that Timmy couldn't see his own father, that she didn't even have a way to contact Bruce. And all because he didn't want to pay her any child support.

She stuffed the pile of envelopes behind a lamp on the desk, hidden for the time being. Her newfound success had only brought a small raise in pay, and it would be weeks, months, before it made a difference.

She could sell the house. She plopped onto the sofa and looked around the room she had spent hours wallpapering. She had pulled up musty carpeting and sanded the wood floor herself until she saw her reflection in its varnished surface. Outside the window—now black with night—she knew every inch of her backyard. She had replaced scraggly bushes with beautiful pink roses. A brick walkway—bricks she had laid herself—had transformed her garden into a retreat. How could she be asked to give this up? Outside of Timmy, this house was all she had.

Nick didn't understand, *couldn't* understand. Her journalistic success wasn't about hurting him. It was about saving herself. For once, she was doing something all on her own—not as Tony Morrelli's daughter or Bruce Hamilton's wife or Timmy's mom, but as Christine Hamilton. It felt good.

She regretted all those years she had put on a show for her family and friends. She had played the role of supportive wife and good mother. All those years she had obsessed in making Bruce happy. For over a year she had known about the affair. It was hard to miss the credit card bills for hotels she had never stepped foot into and flowers she had never received. It had only made her more obsessed. If her husband was having an affair, it had to be her fault—something she lacked, something she wasn't able to give him.

Now, it embarrassed her to remember the expensive Victoria's Secret teddies she had bought to lure him back to her. Their lovemaking, which had never been fantastic, had become quick, sultry one-act plays. He had slammed into her as if punishing her for his own sins, then rolled over and slept. Too many nights she had snuck out of bed after waiting for his snores. She'd peeled off the sometimes torn and soiled teddies, and then cried in the shower. Even the pulsating, scalding water couldn't make her whole again. And that the love had disappeared from their marriage was surely her fault, as well.

Christine curled up on the sofa and pulled an afghan over her shivering body. She was no longer that weak, obsessive wife. She was a successful journalist. She closed her eyes. That's what she would concentrate on—success. Finally, after so many failures.

CHAPTER 39

Wednesday, October 29

Maggie had offered to go to Michelle Tanner's with Nick, but he insisted on going alone. Instead, he dropped her off at the hotel. Despite their intimacy—or perhaps because of it—she found herself relieved to be away from him. It had been a mistake getting so close. She was angry and disappointed in herself, and this morning during the drive into town, she punished Nick with her silence.

She had to maintain her focus, and in order to do that, she needed to maintain her distance. As an agent, it was stupid to get personally involved, not just with one individual, but with a community. An agent could quickly lose his or her edge and objectivity. She had seen it happen to other agents. And, as a woman, it was dangerous to get involved with Nick Morrelli, a man who rigged his house with romantic booby traps for his one-night stands. Besides, she was married—degrees of happiness didn't count. She told herself all this to justify her sudden aloofness and to absolve herself of her guilt.

Her damp clothes still reeked of muddy river and dried blood. The ripped sleeves of her jacket and blouse exposed her wounded shoulder. As she entered the hotel, the pimple-faced desk clerk looked up, and his expression immediately changed from a "good morning" nod to an "oh, my God" stare.

"Wow, Agent O'Dell, are you okay?"

"I'm fine. Do I have any messages?"

He turned with the gawkiness of a teenager—all arms and legs—almost spilling his cappuccino. The sweet aroma drifted in the steam, and despite being a fast-food imitation of the real thing, it smelled wonderful.

The snow—almost six inches and still falling—clung to her pant legs and dripped inside her shoes. She was cold and tired and sore.

He handed her a half-dozen pink message slips and a small sealed envelope with SPECIAL AGENT O'DELL carefully printed in blue ink.

"What's this?" She held up the envelope.

"I dunno. It came in the mail slot sometime during the night. I found it on the floor with the morning mail."

She pretended it didn't matter. "Is there someplace here in town I can buy a coat and boots?"

"Not really. There's a John Deere implement store about a mile north of town, but they just have men's stuff."

"Would you mind doing me a favor?" She peeled a damp five-dollar bill from the folded emergency bills she kept stuffed in the slot behind her badge. The kid seemed more interested in the badge than the five. "Would you call the store and ask them to deliver a jacket? I don't care what it looks like, as long as it's warm and a size small."

"What about boots?" He jotted down instructions on a desk pad already filled with doodles and notes.

"Yes, see if they have something close to a woman's size six. Again, I don't care about style. I just need to get around in the snow."

"Got it. They probably don't open until eight or nine."

"That's fine. I'll be in my room all morning. Call me when they're here, and I'll take care of the bill."

"Anything else?" Suddenly, he seemed eager to earn his five dollars.

"Do you have room service?"

"No, but I can get you just about anything from Wanda's. They deliver for free, and we can put it on your hotel tab."

"Great. I'd like a real breakfast—scrambled eggs, sausage, toast, orange juice. Oh, and see if they have cappuccino."

"You got it." He was pleased, taking his tasks all very seriously as if she had given him an official FBI assignment.

She started sloshing down the hall, but something made her stop. "Hey, what's your name?"

He looked up, surprised, a bit worried. "Calvin. Calvin Tate."

"Thanks, Calvin."

Back in her room, she kicked off the snow-caked shoes and wrestled out of her trousers. She turned up the thermostat to seventy-five, then peeled off her jacket and blouse. This morning her muscles ached from her neck to her calves. She tried rolling the wounded shoulder, stopped, waited for the streak of pain to pass, then continued.

In the bathroom, she turned on the shower and sat on the edge of the bathtub in her underwear while she waited for hot water. She flipped through the messages recorded in two different handwritings. One was from Director Cunningham at eleven o'clock, no a.m. or p.m., no message. Why hadn't he called her cellular? Damn, she had forgotten. She needed to report it missing and get a replacement.

Three messages were from Darcy McManus at Channel Five. The desk clerk, obviously impressed, had recorded the exact times on all three. Each message had a new set of detailed instructions telling when and where to call McManus back. They included her work, cellular and home numbers and an e-mail address. Two messages were from Dr. Avery, her mother's therapist, both late last night with instructions to call when possible.

She was guessing the sealed envelope was from the persistent Ms. McManus. Steam rolled in over the shower curtain. Usually, hotel showers barely reached lukewarm. She got up to adjust the water, then stopped at her reflection in the mirror. It was quickly disappearing behind the gauze of steam. She wiped an open palm across the surface until she could examine her shoulder. The triangular punctures looked red and raw against her white skin. She yanked off Nick's homemade bandage, revealing a two-to-three-inch gash, puckered and smeared with blood. It would leave a scar. Wonderful. It would match her others.

She turned and twisted, lifting the lower section of her bra. Under her left breast was the beginning of another puckered red scar, recently healed. It trailed four inches down and across her abdomen—a present from Albert Stucky.

"You're lucky I don't gut you," she remembered him telling her as the knife blade sliced through her skin, carefully cutting just the top layer of skin, ensuring a scar. At the time, she hadn't felt anything, too numb and drained. Perhaps she had already resigned herself to die.

"You'll still be alive," he had promised, "when I start eating your intestines."

By then, nothing could shock her. She had just watched him slice and dice two women, cutting off nipples and clitorises despite the women's horrible, ear-piercing screams. Then came the gutting, followed by the smashing of skulls. No, there was nothing more he could have done to shock her. So, instead, he left her with a constant reminder of himself.

She hated that her body was becoming a scrapbook. It was bad enough that her mind had been stamped and tattooed with the images.

She rubbed her hands over her face and up through her hair, watching her reflection. It startled her how small and vulnerable she looked. Yet, nothing had changed. She was still the same determined, gutsy woman she had been when she had entered the Academy eight years ago. Maybe a little battle-fatigued and scarred, but that same restless determination existed in her eyes. She could still see it behind the steam, behind the horrors she had witnessed. Albert Stucky was a temporary setback—a roadblock she needed to plow through or go around, but never retreat from.

She unhooked her bra and let it fall to the floor. She started slipping out of her underpants when she remembered the unopened envelope on top of the other messages spread across the sink's counter. She ripped it open and pulled out the three-by-five index card. It took only one glance at the boxy lettering, and her heart began racing. Her pulse quickened. She grabbed the countertop to steady herself, gave up and slid to the damp, tiled floor. Not again. It couldn't happen again. She wouldn't allow it. She hugged her knees to her chest, trying to silence the panic rising inside her.

Then she read the card again:

WILL YOUR MOTHER BE NEEDING HER LAST RITES SOON?

CHAPTER 40

It was too early for any traffic, so Nick let the Jeep slide and cut through the drifts on its own. Street lamps continued to glow as the thick mass of snow clouds kept the sun from appearing. The windshield iced up again, and he blasted it with hot air, even though he was sweating. He turned up the radio and punched several buttons before leaving it on KRAP—"News every day, all day."

He dreaded telling Michelle Tanner about her son. He wanted those images—no, he *needed* those images of Matthew and Danny out of his mind or he'd be of no use to Mrs. Tanner. So he kept his mind on Maggie. He had never felt so pleasantly uncomfortable in all his vast experiences with women. The woman had managed to turn him inside out. Something he didn't think was possible for any one woman to do. What was worse, Maggie hadn't intended for any of it to be sensual, making him even more hot and bothered. He couldn't erase the image of her cheek pressed against his chest, the feel of her breath on his skin. He didn't want to erase it, so he played it, over and over again, until he could conjure it all up on demand—the smell of her hair, the feel of her skin, the sound of her heart. It seemed ironic—criminal—that the one woman who had revived him was the one woman he couldn't have.

He skidded onto Michelle Tanner's street just as the radio announcer was explaining that Mayor Rutledge was canceling Halloween because of the snow, which was expected to keep falling throughout the day.

"Lucky bastard." Nick smiled and shook his head.

He pulled into the Tanner driveway, almost sliding into the back of a van. It wasn't until he was at the front door that he noticed the KRAP News Radio sign, partially hidden by plastered snow. Panic chewed at his insides. It was awfully early for a simple "how are things going?" interview. He knocked on the screen door. When no one came, he opened it and pounded on the inside door.

Almost immediately it opened. A small, gray-haired woman motioned for him to come into the living room. Then she scurried back into the room and took her seat beside Michelle Tanner on the sofa. A tall, balding man with a tape recorder sat across from them. In the doorway to the kitchen towered a barrel-chested man with a crew cut and thick forearms. He looked familiar, and with a quick glance around the house, Nick realized he must be the ex-husband, Matthew's father. There were still several framed photos with the three of them—taken in happier times.

Nick heard voices and the banging of pots and pans coming from the kitchen. The smell of fresh-brewed coffee mixed with the scent of melting wax. A row of candles burned on the fireplace mantel next to a large photo of Matthew and a small crucifix.

"Is it true?" Michelle Tanner looked up at Nick with red, puffy eyes. "Did you find a body last night?"

All eyes stared at him, waiting. Jesus, it was hot in the house. He reached up and loosened his tie.

"Where did you hear that?"

"Does it fucking matter?" Matthew's father wanted to know.

"Douglas, please," the old woman reprimanded him. "Mr. Melzer, here, from the radio said it was in the *Omaha Journal* this morning."

Melzer held up the paper. Second Body Found was emblazoned across the front. Nick didn't need to see the byline. There was no time for anger. The panic backed up into his throat, leaving an acidy taste in his mouth and a lump obstructing his air. Christine had done it to him again.

"Yes, it's true," he managed to say. "I'm sorry I didn't get here sooner."

"You're always just a few steps behind, aren't you, Sheriff?"

"Douglas," the old woman repeated.

"Is it him?" Michelle looked up at Nick, pleading, hoping.

He thought it had been obvious. But she needed the words. He hated this. He shoved his hands into his jean pockets and forced himself to look into her eyes.

"Yes. It's Matthew."

He expected the wail and yet wasn't prepared for it. Michelle fell into the old woman's arms, and they rocked back and forth. Two women appeared from the kitchen. When they saw Michelle, they broke down into tears and hugged each other. Melzer watched, glanced at Nick, then gathered up his equipment and quietly left. Nick wanted to follow him out. He wasn't sure what to do. Douglas Tanner stared at him, leaning against the wall, his anger red on his face and clenched in his fists.

Then suddenly, in three steps, the man came at him. Nick didn't see the left hook until it slammed into his jaw, knocking him backward into a bookcase. Books flew from the shelves, crashing into him and onto the floor. Before he regained his balance, Douglas Tanner came at him again, pounding a fist into his stomach. Nick gasped for breath and stumbled, slipping to his knees. The old woman was yelling at Douglas. The commotion silenced the painful cries, while the women watched, wide-eyed.

Nick shook his head and started to crawl back to his feet when he saw the blur of another fist coming at him. He grabbed Tanner's arm, but instead of swinging back, Nick simply shoved the man away. He probably deserved this beating.

Then he caught a glimpse of the shiny metal. In one quick burst, Tanner came at him again, and this time stabbed at his side. Nick jumped out of the way, grabbing for his gun and ripping it from its holster. Tanner froze, a hunting knife gripped expertly in his left hand, and a look in his eyes that said he had every intention of using it.

The old woman got up from the sofa and quietly walked over to Douglas Tanner. She pulled the knife out of his fist. Then she surprised all of them and slapped him across the face.

"Damn it, Mom. What the fuck?" But Tanner now stood perfectly still, red-faced and hands silent at his side.

"I'm sick and tired of you beating on people. I've sat back and watched for too long. You just can't treat people like this—

not your family or strangers. Now, apologize to Sheriff Morrelli, Douglas.''

"No fucking way. If he had done his job maybe Matthew would still be alive.''

Nick rubbed his eyes, but the blur stayed. He realized his lip was bleeding, and he wiped it with the back of his hand. He put his gun away but leaned against the bookcase, hoping the ringing in his head would stop.

"Douglas, apologize. Do you want to get arrested for assaulting a law officer?''

"He doesn't need to apologize,'' Nick interrupted. He waited for the room to stop spinning and for his feet to hold him up. "Mrs. Tanner,'' he said, leaving the safety of the bookcase and finding Michelle's eyes, grateful for finding only one pair in the blur. "I'm very sorry for your loss. And I apologize for waiting until this morning to tell you. I really didn't mean any disrespect. I just thought it would be better to tell you when you were surrounded by family and friends than pounding on your door in the middle of the night. I promise you, we'll find the man who did this to Matthew.''

"I'm sure you will, Sheriff,'' Douglas Tanner said from behind him. "But how many more boys will he murder before you get a clue?''

CHAPTER 41

No one had to tell him. Timmy just knew. Matthew was dead, just like Danny Alverez. That's why Uncle Nick and Agent O'Dell left all of a sudden last night. Why his mom sent him to bed early. Why she stayed up almost all night writing for the newspaper on her new laptop computer.

He climbed out of bed early to listen to the school closings on the radio. There had to be at least a half foot of snow, and it was still coming down. It would be excellent tubing snow, though his mom forbade him to use anything but his boring plastic sled. It was bright orange and stuck out like some kind of emergency vehicle in the snow.

He found her asleep on the sofa, curled up in a tight ball and tangled in Grandma Morrelli's afghan. Her hands were balled up in fists and tucked under her chin. She looked totally wiped, and he tiptoed into the kitchen, leaving her to sleep.

He tuned the radio to the news station, away from the sappy elevator music his mom listened to. She called it "soft rock." Sometimes she acted so old. The announcer was already in the middle of the school announcements, and he turned the radio up loud enough to hear over his breakfast fumblings.

Instead of dragging a chair to the counter, he used the bottom two drawers to reach a bowl from the cupboard. He was tired of being short. He was smaller than all the boys in his class and even some of the girls. Uncle Nick told him he'd probably have a growth spurt and pass them all up, but Timmy didn't see it coming anytime soon.

He was surprised to find an unopened box of Cap'n Crunch between the Cheerios and the Grape-Nuts. Either it had been on sale, or his mom hadn't realized what she had bought. She never let him have the good stuff. He grabbed it and opened it before she discovered her mistake, pouring until the bowl overflowed. He munched the excess, making room for milk. As he poured, the radio announcer said, "Platte City Elementary and High School will be closed today."

"Yes," he whispered, containing his excitement so he didn't spill any milk. And since tomorrow and Friday were teachers' convention, that meant they had five days off. Wow, five whole days! Then he remembered the camping trip, and his excitement was short-lived. Would Father Keller call off the trip because of the snow? He hoped not.

"Timmy?" Wrapped in Grandma's afghan, his mom padded into the kitchen. She looked funny with her hair all tangled and sleep crusted in the corners of her eyes. "Did they close school?"

"Yeah. Five days off." He sat down and scooped up a spoonful of cereal before she noticed the Cap'n Crunch. "Do you think we'll still go camping?" he asked over a mouthful, taking advantage of her being too tired to correct his manners.

She filled the coffee machine, shuffling back and forth. She almost tripped on the drawers he had left out and kicked them back in without yelling at him.

"I don't know, Timmy. It's only October. Tomorrow it could be forty degrees and the snow will all be gone. What are they saying about the weather on the radio?"

"So far it's just been school closings. It'd be really cool to camp out in the snow."

"It'd be really cold and stupid to camp out in the snow."

"Ah, Mom, don't you have any sense of adventure?"

"Not when it means you coming down with pneumonia. You get sick and hurt enough without any outside help."

He wanted to remind her that he hadn't been sick since last winter, but then she might bring up the soccer bruises again.

"Is it okay if I go sledding today with some of the guys?"

"You have to dress warm, and you can only use your sled. No inner tubes."

The school closings were finally finished and the news came

on. His mom turned up the volume just as the announcer said, "According to this morning's *Omaha Journal,* another boy's body was found along the Platte River last night. It has now been confirmed by the sheriff's department that the boy is Matthew Tanner, who has been..."

His mom snapped the radio off, filling the room with silence. She stood with her back to him, pretending to be interested in something out the window. The coffee machine hummed, then started its ritual gurgling. Timmy's spoon clicked against the bowl. The coffee smelled good, reminding him that it didn't seem like morning until the kitchen was filled with that smell.

"Timmy." His mom came around to the table and sat across from him. "The man on the radio is right. They did find Matthew last night."

"I know," he said and kept eating, though the cereal didn't taste as good all of a sudden.

"You know? How do you know?"

"I figured that's why Uncle Nick and Agent O'Dell left in such a hurry last night. And why you were up all night working."

She reached across the table and brushed his hair off his forehead. "God, you're growing up fast."

She caressed his cheek. In public he'd have batted her hand away, but it was okay here. He actually kind of liked it.

"Where did you get Cap'n Crunch cereal?"

"You bought it. It was down with the other cereals." He filled his bowl again though it wasn't quite empty, just in case she took the box away.

"I must have grabbed it by mistake."

The coffee was ready. She got up, leaving the afghan draped over the back of the chair and the box of cereal on the table.

"Mom, what does dead feel like?"

She spilled coffee all over the counter and snatched a towel to stop the puddle from running over the edge.

"Sorry," he said, realizing it had been his question that had caused her clumsiness. Adults got so bent out of shape about stuff.

"I really don't know, Timmy. That's probably a good question for Father Keller."

CHAPTER 42

The breakfast Maggie had ordered from Wanda's sat untouched on the small table. It had come bundled in an insulated pack, served on stoneware and encased in stainless-steel covers. Steam had risen from the plate when the desk clerk had proudly unveiled it as though he had prepared it himself.

She was becoming a regular of Wanda's cuisine without ever stepping foot in the diner. And although the golden eggs, butter-slathered toast and glistening sausage links smelled and looked delicious, she had lost her appetite. She had left it somewhere on the bathroom floor while she fought to gain control over her panic. The only thing she touched was the frothy cappuccino. One sip, and she thanked Wanda for having the good sense to invest in a cappuccino maker.

Her laptop occupied the other side of the table, close to the wall where a recently installed phone jack allowed the hotel to advertise itself to business travelers. She paced while her computer slowly connected her to Quantico's general database. She wasn't able to access any classified information. The FBI remained skeptical about the confidentiality of modems, and rightly so. They were constantly a target for hackers.

She had already put in several calls to Dr. Avery. The old-fashioned desktop phone confined her to the bed, so she couldn't do her usual pacing. She stretched out on the hard mattress. After her shower, she had put on jeans and her Packers jersey. The exhaustion was overwhelming. It had taken every last bit of her strength to pull herself together, and that frightened her. How could one simple note provoke such terror? She had received notes from killers before. They were harmless. It was only a part of the sick game. It came with the territory. If she were going to dig into a killer's psyche, she had to be prepared for the killer to dig back.

Albert Stucky's notes had not been harmless. God, she needed to get past Stucky. He was behind bars and would be there until they executed him. She was safe. At least this note hadn't been accompanied by a severed finger or nipple. Besides, the note was now carefully packaged and on its way Express Mail to a lab at Quantico. Maybe the idiot had sent her his own arrest warrant by leaving his fingerprints or his saliva on the envelope's seal.

By this evening, she would be on a plane home, and this bastard wouldn't be able to play his sick, little game. She had done her job, more than what was asked. So why did it feel as if she was running away? Because that's exactly what she was doing. She needed to leave Platte City, Nebraska, before this killer unraveled any more of her already frazzled psyche. She could feel the vulnerable fray already, starting when she had cowered on the cold bathroom floor.

Yes, she needed to leave, and she needed to do it quickly—today—while she still felt in control. She would tie up a few loose ends and then get the hell out. Get out while she was still in one piece. Get out before she started coming apart at the seams.

She decided to make a quick phone call while she waited for her computer to connect on the other line. She found the number in the thin directory and dialed. After several rings, a deep male voice answered, "St. Margaret's rectory."

"Father Francis, please."

"May I tell him who's calling?"

She couldn't tell whether or not the voice belonged to Howard. "This is Special Agent Maggie O'Dell. Is this Mr. Howard?"

There was a brief pause. Instead of answering her question, he said, "One moment, please."

It took several moments. She turned to see the computer screen. Finally, the connection was completed. Quantico's royal-blue logo blinked across the screen.

"Maggie O'Dell, what a pleasure to talk with you again." Father Francis' high-pitched voice was almost singsong.

"Father Francis, I wonder if I might ask you a few more questions."

"Why, certainly." There was a faint *click-click*.

"Father Francis?"

"I'm still here."

And so was someone else. She'd ask the questions, anyway. Make the intruder sweat.

"What can you tell me about the church's summer camp?"

"Summer camp? That's really Father Keller's project. You might speak to him about it."

"Yes, of course. I will. Did he start the project, or was it something St. Margaret's has been doing for years?"

"Father Keller started it when he first came. I believe that was the summer of 1990. It was an instant success. Of course, he had a track record. He had been running one at his previous parish."

"Really? Where was that?"

"Up in Maine. Let's see, I usually have a very good memory. Wood something. Wood River. Yes, Wood River, Maine. We were quite lucky to get him."

"Yes, I'm sure you were. I look forward to talking to him. Thanks for your help, Father."

"Agent O'Dell," he stopped her. "Is that all you needed to ask me?"

"Yes, but you've been very helpful."

"Actually, I was wondering if you found the answers to your other questions. Your inquiries about Ronald Jeffreys?"

She hesitated. She didn't want to sound abrupt, but she didn't want to discuss what she knew with someone listening. "Yes, I think we did find the answers. Thanks again for your help."

"Agent O'Dell." He sounded concerned, the lilt no longer present in his voice. If she wasn't mistaken, he suddenly sounded distressed. "I may have some additional information, though I'm not certain of its importance."

"Father Francis, I can't talk right now. I'm expecting an important phone call," she interrupted before he revealed anything more. "Could I meet you perhaps later?"

"Yes, that would be nice. I have morning confessions and then rounds at the hospital this afternoon, so I won't be free until after four o'clock."

"As a matter of fact, I'll be at the hospital this afternoon. Why don't I meet you in the cafeteria about four-fifteen?"

"I look forward to it. Goodbye, Maggie O'Dell."

She waited for him to hang up, then heard the second set of clicks. There was no mistake. Someone had been listening.

CHAPTER 43

Nick stormed into the sheriff's department, slamming the door so hard the glass rattled. Everyone came to a halt in midsentence and midstride. They stared at him as though he had gone mad. He felt as if perhaps he had.

"Listen up, everybody!" He yelled over the ringing in his ear. He waited for those sauntering in from the conference room with their mugs of coffee and glazed doughnuts. "If we have another breach of confidence from this department, I personally will kick the ass of whoever is responsible and see to it that that person never works in law enforcement ever again."

His jaw hurt like hell, especially when he clenched his teeth. The tip of his tongue found a sharp edge where a tooth had chipped. The corner of his mouth bled again, and he wiped at it with the sleeve of his shirt.

"Lloyd, I want you to get some men together and check every abandoned shack within a ten-mile radius of Old Church Road. He's keeping these boys somewhere. Maybe it's not here in town. Hal, find out everything you can about a Ray Howard. He's a janitor at the church. Not just where he's from and details about his unpleasant childhood. I want to know this guy's shoe size and whether or not he collects baseball cards. Eddie, get over to Sophie Krichek's."

"Nick, you can't be serious. The lady's loony."

"I'm dead serious."

Eddie shrugged, and there was a smirk under the pencil-thin mustache that Nick wanted to knock off.

"Do it this morning, Eddie, and treat it like your job depends on getting the details right."

He waited for any other grumbling, then continued, "Adam, call George Tillie and tell him Agent O'Dell will be assisting him this afternoon with Matthew's autopsy. Then call Agent Weston and get the evidence his forensic team found. I want photos and reports on my desk by one this afternoon.

"Lucy, find out anything you can about a summer church camp that St. Margaret's sponsors. Get together with Max and see if you can connect Aaron Harper and Eric Paltrow to that camp."

"What about Bobby Wilson?" She looked up from her notes.

He paused while he watched their faces, wondering whether he'd be able to pick out the Judas—that is if he was still a part of the department. Six years ago, someone had gone to the trouble of making it look as though Ronald Jeffreys had killed all three boys. Someone had taken Eric Paltrow's underpants from the morgue and planted them in Jeffreys' trunk with other incriminating evidence connecting Jeffreys to all three murders. It could easily have been someone in the sheriff's department, someone who was still here. And if he was, why not make the bastard sweat?

"If I read any of this in tomorrow's paper, I swear I'll fire the whole lot of you. Ronald Jeffreys may have only murdered Bobby Wilson. There's a good chance that the guy who killed Danny and Matthew also killed Eric and Aaron." He watched their faces as it sank in, especially the group that had worked with his father and had celebrated the capture of Jeffreys.

"What are you saying, Nick?" Lloyd Benjamin had been one of them, and now his wrinkled forehead looked angry. "You saying we messed up the first time?"

"No, Lloyd, you didn't mess up. You caught Jeffreys. You caught a murderer. But it looks like Jeffreys may not have murdered all three boys."

"Is that what you think, Nick, or is it Agent O'Dell maybe influencing your way of thinking?" Eddie said, again with the smirk.

Nick felt the anger rising and knew he had to contain it. Now was not the time to defend his relationship with Maggie. He wasn't even sure he could without getting tangled in his own personal feelings. And he certainly didn't want to share any details about Jeffreys, especially since he was beginning to question the loyalty of his own department.

"I'm saying there's a good chance. Whether it's true or not, let's make sure this bastard doesn't get away with it, maybe for a second time." He shoved past Eddie, knocking against his shoulder and dismissing the group. Lloyd caught up with him down the hall at his office door.

"Nick, wait up." Lloyd's short, stubby legs jogged to keep up with Nick. He was breathing hard and loosened his tie. "I didn't mean anything back there. I'm sure Eddie didn't, either. This thing is just taking a toll on all of us. Just like before."

"Don't worry about it, Lloyd."

"About checking old shacks. Nick, there's not much out there that we didn't check the first time. There's an old barn about ready to fall down on Woodson's property. Other than a deserted lean-to or grain bin, there isn't anything else. Except for the old church, but it's boarded up tighter than a virgin on Sunday."

Nick frowned at the reference.

"Sorry," Benjamin apologized though he didn't look sorry. "You're getting awfully touchy, Nick. O'Dell isn't even here."

"Check the church again, Lloyd. Look for broken windows, footprints, any sign of entry in the last several days."

"Hell, we're not gonna find any footprints with this snow coming down."

"Just check, Lloyd."

Nick retreated to his office, already exhausted, and the morning had just begun. Within seconds there was a knock on the door. He slumped into his chair and yelled to come in.

Lucy peeked around the door, assessing his mood. He waved her in. She carried an ice pack and cup of coffee.

"What in the world happened to you, Nick?"

"Don't even ask."

She put aside her initial hesitation and came around the desk. She leaned against the corner and her skirt hiked up over her thighs. She saw him notice and made no effort to pull it down. Instead, she reached for his chin, cupping it in her hand and laying the ice pack against his swollen jaw. He jerked away, using the pain as an excuse to wheel out of her reach.

"Oh, poor Nick. I know it hurts," she said, making baby talk sound sensual.

This morning she wore a rose-colored sweater pulled so tight across her breasts the knitted loops hinted at a black bra underneath. She scooted across the desk toward him, and he jumped out of his chair.

"Look, I don't have time for ice packs. I'll be fine. Thanks for thinking of it."

She looked disappointed. "I'll leave it in your little refrigerator, in case you want it later."

She crossed the room to the small cube on the floor. She bent at the waist, purposely giving him a view of what he was missing, and put the ice pack in the small freezer space. She glanced back at him as if checking to see if he had changed his mind, smiled, then swayed out the door.

"Jesus," he muttered, plopping down into the chair again. What kind of a department had he created? Michelle Tanner's raging ex-husband was right. No wonder he was no closer to finding the killer.

CHAPTER 44

Father Francis gathered the newspaper clippings and slid them into his leather portfolio. He stopped, held up his hands and stared at the brown spots, the bulging blue veins and the trembling that had become commonplace.

It had only been three months since Ronald Jeffreys' execution. Three months since he had listened to the confession of the real killer. He could no longer keep silent. He could no longer preserve the sanctity of a killer's confession. Maybe it wouldn't make a difference, but he had convinced himself that it was the right thing to do.

He shuffled down the hall to the church. His footsteps were the only sound echoing off the majestic walls. No one waited for confession. It would be a quiet morning. Still, he entered the small confessional.

Despite his having seen no one in the church, the door in the black cubicle next to him opened within minutes. Father Francis sat up and laid his elbow on the shelf, allowing himself to lean closer to the wire-mesh window between the two small rooms.

"Bless me, Father, for I have killed again."

Oh, dear God. The panic came crashing against the old priest's chest. It was difficult to breathe. Suddenly, the small, wooden box had only hot and stale air. The throbbing began in his ears. Father Francis strained to see beyond the thick wire mesh that separated them. All he could see, though, was a huddled black shadow.

"I killed Danny Alverez and Matthew Tanner. For these sins, I am truly sorry and ask forgiveness."

The voice was disguised, barely audible, as if forced through a mask. Was there anything, anything at all, that he could recognize?

"What is my penance?" the voice wanted to know.

Could he speak if he could not breathe?

"How can..." It was difficult. His chest ached. "How can I absolve you of your sins...heinous, horrible sins...if you only intend to do them again?"

"No, y-you don't understand. I only bring them peace," the voice sputtered. He obviously hadn't come prepared for a confrontation, Father Francis realized with some degree of satisfaction. He had come only for absolution and to do his penance.

"I cannot absolve you of your sins if you intend to only go out and do it again." Father Francis' strong, unflinching voice surprised him.

"You must...you have to."

"I absolved you once before, and you've made a mockery of the sacrament by committing the sin again, not once but twice."

"I am truly sorry for my sins and ask forgiveness from God," he tried again, mechanically saying the phrase like a child memorizing it for the first time.

"You must prove your remorse," Father Francis said, suddenly feeling powerful. Perhaps he could influence this black shadow, make him face his demons, stop him once and for all. "You must show your repentance."

"Yes. Yes, I will. Just tell me what my penance is."

"Go prove your repentance and come back in a month."

There was a pause.

"You aren't absolving me?"

"If you can prove your worthiness by not killing, I will consider absolving you then."

"You will not give me absolution?"

"Come back in a month."

There was silence, but the shadow made no motion to leave. Father Francis leaned closer to the wire mesh, again straining to see into the pitch-black cube. There was a soft smack, then a hiss as a spray of saliva flew through the wire mesh, hitting him in the face.

"I'll see you in hell, Father." The low guttural tone sent shivers down Father Francis' spine. He clung to the small shelf, gripping the Bible. And though the sticky saliva dripped down his chin, he couldn't move even to wipe at it. When he heard the door open and the shadow exit, his paralyzed body made no attempt to follow or look out after him.

He sat for what seemed like hours. Thankfully, no one else came in. Perhaps the snow had kept other sinners home, he thought absently. Which meant no one had seen the shadowy figure enter or exit the confessional.

Finally, his heart resumed its normal beating. Hc could breathe again. He fumbled for a handkerchief and wiped his face with hands trembling more violently than usual. He held on to the walls of the small confessional as he eased himself out of the hard chair and onto wobbly knees. He gathered his leather portfolio and Bible and peered out. The church was empty and silent. Outside, he heard the laughter of children, probably crossing the parking lot to go sledding on Cutty's Hill. At least they traveled in groups.

He shuffled to the front of the church, hanging on to the backs of pews as he made his way down the aisle. The panic and terror had exhausted him, drained him of energy. He would share this morning's visit with Maggie O'Dell. The decision to do so made him feel stronger. Already the guilt lifted from his soul. Yes, it was the right thing to do. He started down the hallway from the church to the rectory, and even his feet seemed lighter. The ache in his chest eased to a mere annoyance.

On the way to his office he noticed that someone had left the door to the wine cellar open. He stopped in the doorway and peered down the dark steps. He could smell the musty dampness. A draft made him shiver. Was there a shadow? Down in the far corner, was someone huddled in the darkness?

He stepped onto the first step, clinging with a shaky hand to the railing. Was it his imagination, or was someone huddled between the stacked wine crates and the concrete wall?

He leaned forward on weak knees. He never saw the figure behind him. He only felt the violent shove that sent him sailing down the steps headfirst. His frail body crashed against the wall, and he tumbled the rest of the way. He was still conscious when he heard the steps creak, one by one by one. The sound of the slow descent sent terror through his aching body. He opened his mouth to scream but only a moan erupted. He couldn't move, couldn't run. His right leg was on fire and twisted beneath him at an abnormal angle.

The last step creaked just above him. He lifted his head in time to see a blaze of white canvas smash into his face. Then darkness.

CHAPTER 45

Christine treated herself to Wanda's homemade chicken noodle soup and buttercrust rolls. Corby had given her the morning off, but she had brought her notepad and jotted down ideas for tomorrow's article. It was early, and the lunch crowd filtered in slowly, so she had a booth to herself in the far corner of the small diner. She sat next to the window and watched the few pedestrians shuffling through the snow.

Timmy had called and asked whether he and his friends could have lunch at the rectory with Father Keller. The priest had joined them sledding on Cutty's Hill and, to make up for the inevitably canceled camping trip, he had invited the boys for roasted hot dogs and marshmallows by the huge fireplace in the church's rectory.

"Great series of articles, Christine," Angie Clark said as she refilled Christine's cup with more steaming coffee.

Caught off guard, Christine swallowed the bite of warm bread. "Thanks." She smiled and wiped a napkin across her mouth. "Your mom's rolls are still the best around."

"I keep telling her we should package and sell some of her baked goods, but she thinks if people can take home a batch, they won't stay here for lunch or dinner."

Christine knew that Angie was the financial mind behind her mother's business. Not able to build on to the small diner, it was Angie's advice to start a delivery service. After only six short months, they had added an extra cook and were keeping two vans and drivers busy, without jeopardizing their normal crowded breakfast, lunch and dinner rushes.

Sometimes Christine wondered why Angie had stayed in Platte City. She obviously had a mind for business and a body that drew plenty of attention. But after only two years at the university and a rumored affair with a married state senator, she had returned home to her widowed mother.

"How's Nick?" Angie asked while pretending to rearrange the silverware on a nearby table.

"Right now he's probably pissed at me again. He hasn't appreciated my articles." She knew that wasn't what Angie had wanted to hear, but Christine had learned long ago to keep out of her brother's love life.

"Next time you see him, tell him I said hi."

Poor Angie. Nick probably hadn't called her since any of this mess started. And though he denied it, Christine knew his mind was filled with the lovely and unavailable Maggie O'Dell. Perhaps his heart would finally get broken, and he'd get a taste of his own medicine.

She watched Angie greet two burly construction workers who came in and began peeling off their layers of jackets, hats and overalls. Why did women knock themselves out over Nick? It was something Christine had never understood as she had watched him go from one woman to another without any explanation or hesitation. He was a handsome, charming jerk, and even after days—maybe even weeks—of not calling, she knew Angie Clark would still welcome him back with open arms.

She sipped the steaming coffee and jotted down "coroner's report." George Tillie was an old family friend. He and her dad had been hunting buddies for years. Maybe George could supply her with some new information. As far as she could tell, the investigation was at a standstill.

Suddenly, the volume on the corner television blasted the room. She looked up just as Wanda Clark waved at her.

"Christine, listen to this."

Bernard Shaw on CNN had just mentioned Platte City, Nebraska. A graphic behind him showed its location while Shaw talked about the bizarre series of murders. They flashed Christine's Sunday headline, From the Grave, Serial Killer Still Grips

Community With Boy's Recent Murder, as Bernard described the murders and Jeffreys' killing spree six years before.

"A source close to the investigation says the sheriff's department still has no clues, and that the only suspect on their list is one who was executed three months ago."

Christine cringed at Shaw's hint of sarcasm, and for the first time she sympathized with Nick. The rest of the diner broke into applause and waved thumbs-up gestures at her. They'd simply heard that their town had made the national news. The sarcasm and befuddled-country-folk references fell on deaf ears.

The volume went down, and she went back to her notes. Soon her cellular phone began ringing, screaming at her from the bottom of her purse. She dug for it, removing wallet, hairbrush and lipstick and scattering them on the table. She looked up to find all eyes on her again. Finally, she ripped the contraption from the bag and waved it at her audience, who smiled and went back to their meals. The phone rang two more times before she found the On switch.

"Christine Hamilton."

"Ms. Hamilton, hello. This is William Ramsey at KLTV Channel Five. I hope I'm not interrupting anything. Your office gave me this number."

"I am having lunch, Mr. Ramsey. How can I help you?"

The last several nights the television station had depended on her newspaper articles for information on the murders. Other than a few fluff pieces interviewing relatives and neighbors, their newscasts had lacked the hype they counted on for ratings.

"I wonder if we might get together for breakfast or lunch tomorrow?"

"My schedule is very full, Mr. Ramsey."

"Yes, of course it is. Then I guess I'll have to get to the point."

"That would be nice."

"I'd like you to come work for Channel Five as a reporter and weekend co-anchor."

"Excuse me?" She almost choked on her roll.

"Your gutsy reporting on these murders is just the kind of thing we need here at Channel Five."

"Mr. Ramsey, I'm a newspaper reporter. I don't—"

"Your style of writing would lend itself very well to broadcast news. We'd be willing to coach you for the anchor position. And I happen to know you're quite easy on the eyes.''

She wasn't above flattery. Fact was, she craved it, having had so little in the past. But Corby and the *Omaha Journal* had given her a big break. No, she couldn't even entertain the idea.

"I'm flattered, Mr. Ramsey, but I just can't—"

"I'm prepared to offer you sixty thousand dollars a year if you start right away."

Christine dropped her spoon. It catapulted off her bowl, splattering soup onto her lap. She made no motion to wipe it up.

"Excuse me?"

Her surprise must have sounded like another decline, because Ramsey hurriedly said, "Okay, I can go to sixty-five thousand. In fact, I'll throw in a two-thousand-dollar bonus if you start this weekend."

Sixty-five thousand dollars was more than twice the amount Christine made even with her meager pay increase. She could pay off her bills and not worry about hunting down Bruce for child support.

"Can I get back to you, Mr. Ramsey, after I've had some time to think about it?"

"Sure, of course you should think about it. Why don't you sleep on it and give me a call in the morning."

"Thank you. I will." She slapped the phone shut and was still in a daze when Eddie Gillick slid into the booth next to her, shoving her up against the window. "What do you think you're doing?" she demanded.

"It was bad enough when you tricked me into giving you a quote for your newspaper article, but now your little brother is giving me chicken-shit assignments, so I figure you also told him I was your anonymous source."

"Look, Deputy Gillick…"

"No, hey, it's Eddie, remember?"

He helped himself to her coffee, adding a heap of sugar and gulping it without scalding himself. The smell of his aftershave lotion was overpowering.

"I didn't exactly tell Nick. He—"

"No, that's okay, because the way I figure it, now you owe me one."

She felt his hand on her knee, and the look of contempt in his eyes immobilized her. His hand moved up her thigh and under her skirt before she wrestled it away. The corner of his mustache twitched into a smile as she felt the color rise into her face.

"Can I get you anything, Eddie?" Angie Clark stood over the table, obviously well aware that she was interrupting and not about to leave until she had succeeded.

"No, Angie dear," Eddie said, still smiling at Christine. "Unfortunately, I can't stay. I'll just have to catch up with you later, Christine."

He slid out of the booth, ran a hand over his slicked-down black hair and replaced his hat. Then he sauntered back down the aisle and out the door.

"You okay?"

"Of course," Christine answered. She kept her trembling hands out of sight under the table.

CHAPTER 46

The door flung open just in time for Nick to see Maggie race back across the room.

"Come on in," she yelled to him as she poked at the keyboard of her laptop computer. Then, she stood back and watched the screen. "I'm accessing some information from Quantico's database. It's proving to be very interesting."

He came into the small hotel room slowly, passing the bathroom, and was immediately accosted by the scent of her shampoo and perfume. She wore jeans and the same sexy Packers jersey from the other night. Its color was faded. The neckline was stretched and misshapen so that it draped down and exposed a bare shoulder. Knowing she had nothing underneath made him hot, and he tried to divert his attention to something, anything else.

She glanced up at him, then did a double take. "What happened to your face?"

"Christine didn't wait. There was an article in this morning's paper."

"And Michelle Tanner saw it before you got there?"

"Sort of. Someone told her about it."

"She hit you?"

"No," he snapped, then realized there was no need to be so defensive. "Her ex-husband, Matthew's dad, sort of let me have it."

"Jesus, Morrelli, don't you know how to duck?"

The anger must have still been in his eyes, because she quickly added, "Sorry. You should put some ice on it."

Unlike Lucy, Maggie went back to the computer screen, offering no nursing services.

"How's the shoulder?"

She looked up again. Her eyes met his. For a brief moment they softened, remembering. Then she quickly looked away. "It's okay." She rolled it as if to check. "It's still pretty sore."

The Packers jersey slipped further down her shoulder, revealing creamy, soft skin. It easily distracted him. God, he wanted to touch her so bad it hurt. It didn't help matters that her rumpled bed was just feet away.

"So, you're a Packers fan." He filled the silence while she clicked through information on the computer screen.

"Actually, my dad grew up in Green Bay," she said without looking up. The computer screen changed quickly as she scanned its contents. "My husband keeps trying to get me to throw this old thing away. But it's one of the few things I have that reminds me of my dad. It was his. He used to wear it when we watched the games together."

"Used to?"

There was a pause, and he knew it had nothing to do with the information on the screen. He watched her tuck her hair behind her ears and recognized it as a nervous habit.

"He was killed when I was twelve."

"I'm sorry. Was he an FBI agent, too?"

She stopped and stood up straight, pretending to stretch, only he knew it was to buy time. It was easy to see the subject of her father brought back memories.

"No, a firefighter. He died a hero. I guess you and I have that in common." She smiled up at him. "Except your father managed to stay alive."

"Just remember, my father had a lot of help."

She searched his eyes, and this time he quickly looked away before she saw something he wasn't ready to reveal.

"You don't think he had something to do with Jeffreys being framed, do you?"

He felt her watching him. He purposely came up beside her to view the computer screen, making it impossible for her to examine his eyes.

"He gained the most from Jeffreys' capture. I don't know what I believe."

"Here it is," she said, watching the screen fill with what looked like newspaper articles.

"What is this?" He leaned forward. "The *Wood River Gazette,* November 1989. Where is Wood River?"

"Maine." She poked at the scroll button, scanning the headlines. Then she stopped and pointed to one.

"'Boy's Mutilated Body Found Near River.' This sounds familiar." He started reading the article that stretched over three columns of the front page.

"Guess who was a junior pastor at Wood River's St. Mary's Catholic Church?"

He stopped, looked back at her and rubbed his jaw. "You still don't have any evidence. It's all circumstantial. Why didn't this case come up during Jeffreys' trial?"

"There was no need. From what I've been able to find, a transient working at St. Mary's Church took the blame."

"Or maybe he did it." He hated where this was leading. "How did you find out about it?"

"Just a hunch. When I talked to Father Francis this morning, he told me Father Keller had started a similar summer camp at his previous parish in Wood River, Maine."

"So you looked for murdered boys in the area at the time he was there."

"I didn't have to look very hard. This murder matches right down to the X. Circumstantial or not, Father Keller needs to be considered a suspect." She closed down the program and shut off the computer.

"I've got to meet George in about an hour," Maggie said, "then I'm meeting with Father Francis." She started taking clothes out of the closet and laying them on the bed. "I need to leave for Richmond tonight. My mother's in the hospital." She avoided looking at him while she pulled more of her things from drawers.

"Jesus, Maggie, is she okay?"

"Sort of...I guess she will be. I'll have some information for you on disk. Can you access Microsoft Word?"

"Sure...yeah, I think so." Her matter-of-fact attitude flustered him. Was something wrong, or was she simply concerned about her mother?

"I'll leave my notes from this afternoon's autopsy with George. If I find out anything from Father Francis, I'll call you."

"You're not coming back, are you?" The realization struck him like another fist to the jaw. It also stopped her. She turned to face him, though her eyes darted from his to the blank computer screen to his to the mess on the bed. She had never had a tough time meeting his eyes before.

"Technically, I finished what I was asked to do. You have a profile and maybe even a suspect. I'm not even sure that I need to be involved with this second autopsy."

"So that's it?" He shoved his hands into his pockets. Suddenly, he felt nauseated at the thought of never seeing her again.

"I'm sure the Bureau will send someone else to help you."

"But not you?" He caught something in her eyes. Was it a flicker of regret, sadness? Whatever it was, she didn't let him see it. She started filling her suitcase. "Does this have anything to do with what happened this morning?"

"Nothing happened this morning," she snapped, and stopped shoving things into her bag. She kept her back to him. "I'm sorry if I gave you the wrong impression." Then she glanced over her shoulder at him. "Look, Nick, I don't mean to sound ungrateful." She kept her hands busy folding, tucking and shuffling items into her bag.

Of course, she hadn't given him the wrong impression. He had done that all on his own. But what about the heat, the electricity? He certainly hadn't imagined that.

"I'm gonna miss you." The words surprised him. He hadn't meant to say them out loud.

She stopped, straightened and turned slowly, this time meeting his eyes. Those luscious brown eyes made him weak in the knees, like a high-school kid admitting to his first girlfriend that he liked her. Jesus, what was wrong with him?

"You've been a pain in the ass, O'Dell, but I'm going to miss you giving me a hard time." There. He corrected his slip.

She smiled. There was the hair-tuck behind the ears. At least she wasn't totally in control.

"Do you need a lift to the airport?"

"No, I have a rental I need to turn in."

"Well, have a good flight." It sounded cold and pathetic when what he really wanted to do was wrap his arms around her and convince her to stay. He crossed the room to leave in three long strides, hoping his knees didn't buckle.

"Nick."

He stopped at the door, his hand on the handle, and glanced back at her. She paused, and in a brief moment he saw her change her mind from whatever she was going to say.

"Good luck," she said simply.

He nodded and left, feeling lead in his shoes and an ache in his chest that made it hard to breathe.

CHAPTER 47

Maggie watched the door close as her hands strangled and twisted a silk blouse.

Why didn't she just tell Nick about the note, about Albert Stucky? He had understood about the nightmares. Maybe he'd understand about this. Maybe he'd understand that she just couldn't allow herself to be psychologically poked and probed by another madman. Not now. Not when she felt so vulnerable, so damn fragile, like she could shatter into a million tiny pieces, just as she had earlier on the bathroom floor. She couldn't risk it. It would cloud her judgment.

Perhaps it already had. Last night in the woods she hadn't even seen the killer coming at her until it was too late. He could easily have killed her. But like Albert Stucky, this killer wanted her alive, and oddly enough, that terrified her even more. Somehow she knew sharing all that with anyone would make her feel more vulnerable. No, it was best this way—to leave Nick and everyone else thinking her departure was only because of her mother.

She stuffed the garment bag, crushing and wrinkling her dry-cleanables. Director Cunningham had been right. She needed to take some time off. Maybe she and Greg could take a trip. Some-place warm and sunny, where it didn't get dark at six in the evening.

The phone rang, and she jumped as if it were a gunshot. She had already talked to Dr. Avery. Her mother had survived the seventy-two-hour suicide watch and was doing quite well. But this was the part her mother was good at—playing the model patient and devouring all the special attention.

Maggie grabbed the phone. "Special Agent O'Dell."

"Maggie, why are you still there? I thought you were coming home."

She lowered herself to the bed, suddenly exhausted. "Hi, Greg." She waited for a real greeting, heard papers shuffling and knew she had only half his attention. "I'm catching a flight tonight."

"Good, so that dunce actually gave you my message last night?"

"What dunce?"

"The one I talked to last night who picked up your cellular. He said you must have dropped it and couldn't come to the phone."

Her grip tightened. Her pulse raced.

"What time was that?"

"I don't know…late. About midnight here. Why?"

"What did you tell him?"

"Oh, for cryin' out loud. That asshole didn't give you the message, did he?"

"Greg, what did you tell him?" Her heart thumped against her rib cage.

"What kind of incompetent hicks are you working with, Maggie?"

"Greg." She tried to stay calm, to keep the scream from clawing its way out of her throat. "I lost my cellular phone last night when I was chasing the killer. There's a good chance he was the one you talked to."

Silence. Even the paper shuffling had come to a stop.

"For God's sake, Maggie. How was I supposed to know?" His tone was subdued.

"There's no way you could have known. I'm not blaming you, Greg. Just please, try to remember what you told him."

"Nothing really…just to call me and that your mother wasn't doing too well."

She leaned back on the bed, sinking her head into the pillows and closing her eyes.

"Maggie, when you get home we need to talk."

Yes, they would talk on a beach somewhere, sipping fruity

drinks, the ones with little umbrellas stuffed in them. They'd talk about what was really important, rekindle their lost love, rediscover the mutual respect and goals that had brought them together in the first place.

"I want you to quit the Bureau," he said, and then she knew there would never be a sunny beach for them.

CHAPTER 48

The snow exploded into flying white powder as his feet came down with heavy thuds, smashing through drifts. Snow clung to his pant legs and leaked inside his shoes, turning his feet to ice. His body wasn't his own, propelling him through branches and down the side of the hill at a speed that would surely send him tumbling headfirst at any moment.

Then he heard them, squealing and giggling. He slid to a halt, crashing into shrubs and snow-laced prairie grass that prevented him from rolling into the sledders' path. He lay there, pressed into the snow, the white death sucking the heat from his body. He hid, trying to control his rapid breathing, inhaling through his mouth and creating a vapor each time he exhaled.

They should have gone home while the throbbing in his head was silent. Why hadn't they gone home? It would be getting dark soon. Would there be plates set on a dinner table waiting for them or only a note and a microwave dinner? Would their parents be there to make sure they took off their wet clothing? Would anyone be there to tuck them into bed?

He couldn't stop the memories, and he no longer tried. He laid his face into the snow hoping it would stop the pounding. He could see himself at twelve, wearing a green army jacket with little lining to keep out the cold. His patched jeans allowed drafts to assault his body. He hadn't owned a pair of boots. The snowfall had been over ten inches and the entire town ground to a stop, leaving his stepfather with nowhere to go except his mother's bedroom. He had been told to leave the house, to "go play in the snow with his friends.'' Only he had no friends. The kids had only paid attention to him to make fun of his shabby clothes and his scrawny build.

After hours of sitting in the cold backyard watching the other kids sledding, he had gone back to the house only to find the door locked. Through the thin wood and fragile glass, he had listened to his mother's screams and moans—pain and pleasure indistinguishable. Did sex have to hurt? He couldn't imagine growing to enjoy such pain. And he remembered feeling ashamed because he had been relieved. He knew as long as his stepfather slammed into his mother, he wouldn't slam into his small body.

It was while he sat in the bitter white cold that day that he had plotted, a plot so simple it required only a ball of string. The next morning when his stepfather retreated to his basement workshop, he would come back up on a stretcher. He and his mother would never feel ashamed or scared again. How could he have known that his mother would go down to the basement first that morning? That morning when his life had ended; when that horrible wicked, little boy had ended his mother's life.

Suddenly, he felt someone above him, breathing and sniffing. He slowly looked up to find a black dog within inches of his face. The dog bared his teeth, emitting a low growl. Without warning, his hands shot out at the dog's throat and the growl became a quiet whine, a stifled gurgle, then silence.

He watched the boys dressed in thick parkas running and jumping with stiff legs and arms. Finally, they gathered up their sledding contraptions and said their goodbyes. One boy called for the dog several times but gave up easily to catch up with his friends. They separated and headed in different directions, three one way, two another while one crossed the church's parking lot alone.

The sky changed from light gray to slate. Streetlights blinked on one at a time. A jet thundered overhead, the sound amplified by the white, silent town. There wasn't a single vehicle or pedestrian when he climbed into his own car. He pulled the ski mask back on despite the perspiration gathering on his forehead and upper lip. On the seat next to him, he laid out a fresh handkerchief, carefully and meticulously as though it were already a part of the ceremony. He brought a vial out of his coat pocket, cracked it and anointed the white linen. Then he kept the headlights off and the engine soft as he slowly followed the boy who dragged his bright orange plastic sled behind him.

CHAPTER 49

The sheriff's department could afford only five fully equipped squad cars, and four were parked outside the courthouse when Nick returned. Immediately, the fury burned in his stomach. What would it take to get these people to listen to him, to take his orders seriously? Yet, he knew it was his own fault.

He had treated his position as sheriff with the same reckless disregard that had ruled the rest of his life—to simply kick back and take nothing too seriously. That was before. Before he had fallen into Danny Alverez's blood. Now he couldn't help wondering whether a real sheriff could have saved Matthew Tanner. But Platte City had a skirt-chasing college quarterback with a law degree, absolutely no experience and only his father's name and reputation to win him the right to call himself sheriff and to carry a badge and a gun. A gun, by the way, that he hadn't fired since target practice to get the job nearly two years ago.

Michelle Tanner's ex-husband had knocked more than just his jaw out of whack. Too bad it had taken a fist to knock some sense of responsibility into him. And now that Maggie was leaving, it was up to him to take control. He just wished he knew how the hell to do that.

He entered the courthouse and immediately wanted to flee in the other direction. The huge marble lobby echoed with the chatter of reporters. Cords and cables snaked over the floor. Bright lights blinded him and a dozen microphones were shoved into his face while reporters assaulted him with questions.

Darcy McManus—an ex-beauty queen turned TV anchor—

barricaded the staircase with her tall, lean body. It was hard to ignore the long legs she showed off in the short skirts she pretended were part of a suit. She offered him a spot beside her in front of Channel Five's camera. He shoved his way to the staircase but purposely kept his distance. In the past, he would have flirted with her and taken advantage of the attention. Maybe he would have even gotten her phone number. Now he just wanted to get past her and escape to his office.

"Sheriff, do you have any suspects yet?" She looked older than she did on TV. Up close he saw the caked makeup concealing the lines at the corners of her mouth and eyes.

"I have no comment at this time."

"Is it true Matthew Tanner's body was decapitated?" a man in an expensive double-breasted suit wanted to know.

"Jesus. Where the hell did you hear that?"

"Then it's true?"

"No. Absolutely not."

Others joined in, pressing against Nick. He tried to elbow his way through.

"Sheriff, what about the rumor that you've ordered the exhumation of Ronald Jeffreys' grave? Do you believe Jeffreys wasn't the one executed?"

"Was the boy sexually assaulted?"

"Have you found the blue pickup yet?"

"Sheriff Morrelli, can you at least tell us whether this boy was murdered in the same manner? Are we dealing with a serial killer?"

"What shape was Matthew's body in?"

"Stop! Hold it," Nick yelled, raising his hands to ward off any more questions. The shuffle halted. The shoving came to a standstill, and there was silence as the vultures waited. The sudden quiet disarmed him. He glanced around and backed his way to the first step of the open staircase. A trickle of sweat rolled down his back. He raked his fingers through his hair and noticed his fingers trembling. He was used to being confronted with accolades, not criticism and skepticism.

What the hell was he supposed to tell them? Last time, Maggie had bailed him out. Now, in her absence, he felt exposed and vulnerable, and he hated it. He grabbed the handrail to steady himself and pulled himself up beside McManus. She looked pleased and began smoothing her hair and clothing, preparing for the camera. He ignored her and looked out over the crowd, eyes staring back at him, pens, cameras and recording devices ready. His gut told him to turn around and leave them in silence. He could take the stairs three at a time and be in his office before they could follow. After all, he didn't owe them an explanation. None of this would help him catch the murderer. Or would it?

"You all know I can't reveal specific details about the victims' bodies. But for God's sake, for Mrs. Tanner's sake, Matthew's body was not—I repeat—not decapitated. That's not to say that this guy isn't one sick son of a bitch."

"Is this a serial killing, Sheriff? The people deserve to know if they should lock up their children."

"Early indications do show that Matthew was killed by the same person who killed Danny Alverez."

"Any suspects?"

"Is it true you have absolutely no leads?"

Nick backed up another step. He had nothing to satisfy them. The crowd and bright lights made him hot and nauseated. He pulled at his jacket's zipper and tugged at his tie, loosening its strangling hold.

"We do have a couple of suspects. I'm not at liberty to say who they are. Not yet." He turned and a flood of questions assaulted his back as he started up the steps.

"When will you be able to tell us?"

"Are they local men?"

"Will your father be heading the investigation now?"

"Have you tracked down a blue pickup?"

Nick spun around, almost losing his balance. "What about my father?"

Everyone stared at the man in the double-breasted suit. Nick noted the man's shiny, dark hair. It looked professionally manufactured, and his goatee was perfectly trimmed with just a hint of gray. His expensive leather shoes labeled him an outsider—his shoes and the way he cocked his head to one side with the impatience of a man who had better things to do than repeat himself to a small-town sheriff. Nick wanted to grab him by the collar of his monogrammed shirt. Instead, he waited, teetering in snow-caked cowboy boots that were creating puddles and threatening to send him sliding down the smooth, marble steps.

"Why in the world would my father head this investigation?"

"He *did* catch Ronald Jeffreys," Darcy McManus said into her channel's camera, and only then did Nick realize they had been filming this whole fiasco. He avoided looking into the camera and stared at the man, waiting and ignoring his expression of boredom.

"When your father talked to us earlier, he made it sound—"

"He's here?" Nick blurted, and immediately regretted it. His incompetence was showing once more.

"Yes, and he made it sound as though he had returned to help with the investigation. I believe his exact words were..." The man slowly and deliberately flipped through his notes. "'I've done this before. I know what to look for. You can bet this guy's not getting by this old bloodhound.' I'm not familiar with bloodhounds, but I did interpret it to mean he was here in a professional capacity."

Other reporters nodded in agreement. Nick looked from one to another while his insides churned. His collar strangled him, the jacket made him sweat. Another trickle slid down his back. They waited. Every word would be weighed, every gesture measured. He imagined tonight someone would rewind their videotaped version of the news just to see him run down the steps backward. He didn't care. He turned and ran up the staircase, taking two and three steps at a time, silently praying he didn't trip and end up back at the bottom.

He crashed through the sheriff's department doors, smacking the glass against a metal trash can and a wall. A spider crack raced through the bottom of one of the doors, but no one seemed to notice. Instead, all eyes stared at Nick, their heads turned, their attention diverted from the tall gray-haired man in the center of them.

The same group Nick couldn't get to check a lead without a groan or a question was gathered around the distinguished-looking gentleman, an aging prophet with the beginning of a paunch over his belt and the bushy eyebrows that were now raised in indignation.

"Slow down, son. You just damaged government property," Antonio Morrelli said, pointing to the crack in the glass.

Despite the rage and frustration, Nick shoved his hands into his pockets, felt his shoulders slump as his eyes found his boots. Suddenly, he found himself wondering how much it would cost to replace the glass.

CHAPTER 50

Maggie sipped her Scotch and watched from a corner table as she tried to determine which of the airport-lounge customers were business travelers and which were vacationers. The storm had delayed flights, hers included, and had packed the small, poorly lit lounge, which consisted of an L-shaped bar, several small tables and chairs, dozens of model airplanes suspended from the ceiling and an old jukebox filled with songs like "Leaving on a Jet Plane" and "Outbound Plane."

Her green and black John Deere jacket was stretched across the chair opposite her to prevent any unwanted company. She had already checked her luggage, everything except her laptop computer, which was secure underneath the John Deere green. She thought about calling St. Margaret's again. She was beginning to think something dreadful may have happened. Otherwise, why would Father Francis have stood her up at the hospital? And why was there no one at the church rectory to answer the phone?

She wanted to call Nick, had in fact dialed the number but then hung up. He had enough things to handle without checking on her hunches. Besides, she was running out of change for the pay phone and had spent her last ten-dollar bill on this and the two previous Scotches. Not much of a dinner, but after spending the afternoon slicing Matthew Tanner's small body, weighing pieces of him and poking through his tiny organs, she had decided she deserved a dinner of Scotch.

The mark on Matthew's inside thigh had indeed been human bite marks. Poor George Tillie had tried to come up with several other theories before giving in to the realization that the killer had bitten Matthew over and over again in the same spot, making it impossible to register a set of dental prints. What made matters worse and more bizarre—the bites had occurred hours after Matthew was dead.

The killer didn't return to the scene of the crime only to watch the police. He continued his absurd fascination with the victim's body. He was slipping from his carefully planned ritual. Something was causing him to degenerate, to lose control. In his recklessness, he could soon leave incriminating evidence.

Maggie had told George they should look for smudges of semen; that the killer may have masturbated this time, while biting the dead boy, and may have smeared some on the victim. The old coroner's face had turned scarlet as he mumbled something about doing his job in private.

She didn't blame George. It had been obvious her presence made him uncomfortable. His manner and method resembled the reverence of a priest, with his careful and deliberate touches and his hushed speech. It was almost as though he hadn't wanted to disturb the boy's soul.

Maggie, on the other hand, had cut with clinical precision and had spoken loud and clear for her voice-activated recorder. It was a dead body, void of life and warmth. Whatever had resided within the bone-and-flesh cavity had escaped hours ago. Yet, she had to admit there was something wrong, something almost sacrilegious about slicing apart a child's body. The soft, smooth and hairless skin hadn't seen nearly enough scrapes and bruises, nor the bones enough chips and breaks to have really lived. It seemed such a waste, such an injustice. But that was what the Scotch was for—to make sense of it all or, at least, to take her to a place where she wouldn't care, even if only temporarily.

"Excuse me, ma'am." The young bartender stood over her table. "The gentleman at the end of the bar bought you another Scotch." He set the glass in front of her. "And he asked me to give you this."

Maggie recognized the envelope and the boxy handwriting before he handed it to her. Her stomach lurched, her pulse quickened. She stood up so abruptly, her chair teetered on two legs.

"Which man?" She stretched to see over the crowd. The bartender did the same, then shrugged his shoulders.

"He must have left."

"What did he look like?" She patted her side through her blazer, reassured by the feel of the butt on her gun pressing against her just under her breast.

"I don't know...tall, dark hair, maybe twenty-eight, maybe thirty. Look, I didn't pay a whole lot of attention. Is there a problem with—"

She shoved past him and pushed through the crowd, racing out into the bright airport walkway. Frantically, she searched and scanned the passengers coming and going. Her heart pounded against her chest. Her head throbbed, and her vision was a bit blurred from the Scotch.

The long walkway stretched straight in both directions. There was a family with three children, several businessmen carrying laptops and briefcases, an airport employee pushing a handcart, two gray-haired women and a group of black men and women in colorful robes and headdresses. But there was no tall, dark-haired man without luggage.

He couldn't possibly have gotten beyond the walkway. She ran toward the escalator at the far end, bumping into passengers and almost tripping over a deserted luggage gurney. The escalator went up and down. She chose up and twisted over the handrail to see down. Again, the array of passengers didn't include a tall, dark-haired man. He was gone. He had slipped by her again.

She made her way back to the lounge, only now realizing she had left her jacket and laptop along with the envelope. Though the lounge was packed, no one had attempted to take over her small table. Even the envelope leaned against the fresh drink where the bartender had left it.

She eased into the hard chair and stared at the small envelope. She gulped the remainder of Scotch in her glass and set it aside. She started on the fresh drink despite the swirling inside her head. She wanted to be numb.

She took the envelope carefully by a corner. The seal broke easily, and she slipped the index card out onto the table without touching it. Even the Scotch couldn't prevent the nausea and the stab of terror the words inflicted.

In the same boxy lettering, the note said:

SORRY TO SEE YOU LEAVE SO SOON. PERHAPS I CAN STOP BY YOUR CONDO THE NEXT TIME I'M IN THE CREST RIDGE AREA. SAY HI TO GREG FOR ME.

CHAPTER 51

From down on the sidewalk, he could see Maggie O'Dell inside, scrambling up the escalator. He did have to admit she moved quite nicely—definitely a runner. He imagined those strong, athletic legs looked good in a pair of tight shorts, though the image didn't much interest him.

He pushed the handcart aside and removed the cap and jacket he had borrowed from the sleeping airport employee. He rolled them into a ball and shoved them into a trash can.

He had left the Lexus with the radio blaring in the loading zone. With the radio and the jets overhead, no one would ever hear Timmy, should he wake up sooner than expected. Besides, the trunk was tight, almost soundproof, meaning there was also very little air.

He got into the car just as a security guard with a pad of tickets started in his direction. He squealed away from the curb and zipped around the unloading vehicles. It would be pitch-black by the time he got Timmy settled in, but the detour had been worth seeing the look on Special Agent O'Dell's face.

The wind had picked up, creating swirls of snow and promising drifts by morning. The kerosene heater, lantern and sleeping bag in the back seat, originally packed for the camping trip, would come in handy, after all. Perhaps he would drive through McDonald's on the way. Timmy loved Big Macs, and he found himself getting hungry.

He eased into traffic, waving a thank-you to the red-haired lady in the Mazda who let him in front of her. The day had not been a waste. He gunned the engine, ignoring the slip and slide of the tires on icy pavement. He was in control again.

CHAPTER 52

"This guy's making a fuckin' spectacle out of you," Antonio Morrelli lectured Nick while looking quite comfortable behind Nick's desk, twirling back and forth in the leather chair that was once his. It was the only piece of the elaborate furnishings Nick had kept when replacing his father as sheriff.

"You need to spend some time with those TV people," his father continued, "reassure them you know what you're doing. Last night Peter Jennings made you sound like some country hick who couldn't find his own ass with a flashlight. Goddamn it, Nick, Peter fucking Jennings!"

Nick stared out the window, past the snow-covered streets and toward the dark horizon beyond the streetlights. A hint of an orange moon peeked from behind a veil of clouds.

"Did Mom come with you?" he asked from his window perch without looking at his father, ignoring his insults. It was the same old game they played. His father hurled insults and instructions, and Nick kept quiet and pretended to listen. Most of the time he followed the instructions. It was easier. It had come to be expected.

"She stayed with your aunt Minnie and the RV down in Houston," his father answered, but his look told Nick he wouldn't be sidetracked from the real subject. "You need to start hauling in suspects off the street. You know, the usual scumbags. Bring 'em in for questioning. Make it look like you're on top of things."

"I do have a couple of suspects," Nick said suddenly, remembering that he did, indeed.

"Great, let's haul them in. Judge Murphy could probably get a search warrant by morning. Who are your suspects?"

Nick wondered whether it had been that easy with Jeffreys: a late-night search warrant used only after the evidence had been carefully planted.

"Who are your suspects, son?" he repeated.

Perhaps he just wanted to shock his father. Common sense should have kept his mouth shut. Instead, he turned from the window and said, "One of them is Father Michael Keller."

He watched his father stop rocking in the chair. The older man's face registered surprise, then he shook his head and frustration creased the leather-like forehead.

"What the fuck are you trying to pull, Nick? A fucking priest—the media will crucify you. Is this your idea, or that pretty, little FBI agent the guys told me about?"

The guys. His guys. His department. Nick could imagine them laughing and making jokes about Maggie and him.

"Father Keller fits Agent O'Dell's profile."

"Nick, how many times do I have to tell you. You can't go letting your Mr. Johnson make your decisions for you."

"I'm not." Nick's face grew hot. He turned back toward the window, pretending to stare down at the streets, but his vision was blurred by his anger.

"O'Dell makes a good point. And I'm sure she makes a good omelet for breakfast after a night of fucking. Doesn't mean you should listen to her."

Nick rubbed a hand across his jaw and mouth to prevent the rage that formed its own words. He swallowed hard, waited, then turned to face his father again.

"This is my investigation, my decision, and I'm bringing in Father Keller for questioning."

"Fine." His father held up his hands in surrender. "Make a fucking asshole of yourself." He got up and started for the door. "In the meantime, I'll see if Gillick and Benjamin can round up some real suspects."

He waited until his father was out the door and down the hall. Then Nick turned and slammed his fist into the wall. The rough texture ripped open his knuckles and pain shot up his arm. He tried to control his breathing, waiting for the rage to settle, for the frustration and humiliation to be overwhelmed by the pain.

Then, without thinking, he wiped at the blood running down the wall using his white shirtsleeve. He already had to pay for a broken glass door; he couldn't afford to have his office repainted, too.

CHAPTER 53

The house was dark when Christine pulled into the driveway. She loaded the warm pizza box on top of her laptop computer and realized she'd probably be eating the pizza herself if Timmy was still at one of his friends' houses. He'd come home with storybook descriptions of something they called meatloaf and mashed potatoes—food that didn't come from a can, a box or a carton. Surely he remembered the days when she had actually fixed real dinners and had them on the table at the same time every night. She wondered if he missed their life as a family. What had she cost him for the price of her own self-respect?

She fumbled through the dark foyer until she found the light switch. For some reason the quiet sent a chill down her spine. Perhaps it was only the wind. She kicked the front door closed and made her way to the kitchen, stopping by the answering machine. No blinking red light, no messages. How many times did she have to tell Timmy to call and leave a message? There was no excuse, especially now that she had a cellular phone, although even she hadn't memorized that number yet.

She threw her coat over a kitchen chair and piled her computer and handbag onto its seat. The pizza's aroma reminded her how hungry she was. After Eddie Gillick's visit at Wanda's, she had lost her appetite and left most of her lunch unfinished.

She poured herself a glass of wine, tucked a folded newspaper under her arm and scooped up a piece of pizza, using only a napkin as a plate. Hands filled, she kicked off her shoes and padded into the living room, finding refuge on the soft sofa. No food was allowed in the living room, especially on the sofa. She expected Timmy to come in at any moment and catch her in the act.

She set her dinner on the glass coffee table and unfolded the newspaper. This evening's paper carried the same headline from the morning: Second Body Found. Only underneath, she had now confirmed that the body was Matthew Tanner's. Tonight's article also included a quote from George Tillie. She found the paragraph and reread her handiwork, letting George confirm that the murders were the work of a serial killer, since Nick wouldn't.

She had closed the article with a quote she had gotten from Michelle Tanner on Monday, a melodramatic plea for her son's return. Christine followed the quote with, ''A mother's desperate plea has, once again, fallen on deaf ears.'' Now, seeing it in print, it seemed a tad too much; however, Corby had loved it.

She flipped through the rest of the paper and scanned the readers'-comment column to see whether her name was mentioned. Suddenly, she remembered the time, frantically searched for the remote and turned on the TV, flipping to Channel Five.

As usual, Darcy McManus looked impeccable in a deep purple suit and crimson red blouse. Christine examined McManus's silky black hair, large brown eyes, darkened even more by the eyeliner and smudge of highlight on the eyelids. The lipstick was bold, a red to match her blouse. Christine couldn't imagine herself in McManus's place. She'd need a whole new wardrobe, but then she'd be able to afford one with what Ramsey was offering to pay her.

She had to admit the idea of being on TV did excite her. The Omaha ABC affiliate claimed a viewership of almost a million people throughout eastern Nebraska. She'd be a celebrity and maybe even cover national events. Though she had told Ramsey she needed time to decide, she knew her mind was already made up. She couldn't justify turning down the money. Not with bills stacking up and the remote possibility of losing their home. No, she had no room for principles. She would accept the position in the morning, but only after talking to Corby.

She finished her wine. Another piece of pizza sounded good, but suddenly she was too exhausted to move. She decided to lay her head down for just ten or fifteen minutes. She closed her eyes and thought of all the things she and Timmy would spend her new salary on. In minutes, she was fast asleep.

CHAPTER 54

"Why don't you eat some of your Big Mac?" the man in the dead president's mask was saying.

Timmy curled into the corner. The bedsprings squeaked each time he moved. His eyes darted around the small room lit only by a lantern on an old crate. The light created its own creepy shadows on the walls with spiderweb cracks. He was shaking, and he couldn't control it, just like last winter when he got so sick his mom had had to take him to the emergency room. And he did feel sick to his stomach, but it wasn't the same. He was shaking because he was scared, because he didn't know where he was or how he had gotten here.

The tall man in the mask had been nice so far. When he had stopped Timmy by the church to ask for directions, he had been wearing a black ski mask, the kind robbers wore in the movies. But it was cold out, and the man seemed lost and confused but not scary. Even when the man had gotten out of his car to show Timmy a map, Timmy hadn't felt scared. There was something familiar about him. That was when the man had grabbed him and shoved a white cloth against his face. Timmy couldn't remember anything else, except waking up here.

The wind howled through the rotted boards that covered the windows, but the room was warm. Timmy noticed a kerosene heater in the corner, the kind his dad had used when they had gone camping. Only that was ages ago, when his dad still cared about him.

"You really should eat. I know you haven't had anything since lunch."

Timmy stared at the man, who looked more ridiculous than scary dressed in a sweater, jeans and bright white Nikes that looked new except that one shoestring was knotted together. A pair of huge, black, dripping rubber boots sat by the door on a paper sack. It struck Timmy as odd that such new Nikes could already have a broken and knotted shoestring. If *he* had new Nikes, he'd take better care of them than that.

There was something about the muffled voice that Timmy recognized, but he wasn't sure what it was. He tried to think of the president's name—the one the mask resembled. It was the guy with the big nose who had to resign. Why couldn't he think of his name? They had just memorized the presidents last year.

He wished he could stop shivering, but it hurt to try to stop, so he let his teeth chatter.

"Are you cold? Is there anything else I can get you?" the man asked, and Timmy shook his head. "Tomorrow I'll bring you some baseball cards and comic books." The man got up, took the lantern from the crate and started to leave.

"Can I keep the lantern?" Timmy's voice surprised him. It was clear and calm, despite his body shaking beyond his control.

The man looked back at him, and Timmy could see the eyes through the mask's eyeholes. In the light of the lantern, they were sparkling as if the man were smiling.

"Sure, Timmy. I'll leave the lantern."

Timmy didn't remember telling the man his name. Did he know him?

The man set the lantern back down on the crate, pulled on his thick rubber boots and left, locking the door with several clicks and clacks from the outside. Timmy waited, listening over the thumping of his heart. He counted out two minutes, and when he was sure the man wouldn't return, he looked around the room again. The rotted slats over the window were his best bet.

He crawled off the bed and tripped over his sled on the floor. He started for the window when something caught his leg. He looked down to find a silver handcuff around his ankle with a thick metal chain padlocked to the bedpost. He yanked at the chain, but even the metal-framed bed wouldn't budge. He dropped to his knees and tore at the handcuff, pulling and tugging until his fingers were red and his ankle sore. Suddenly, he stopped struggling.

He looked around the room again, and then he knew. This was where Danny and Matthew had been taken. He crawled into his plastic sled and curled up into a tight ball.

"Oh, God," he prayed out loud, the tremble in his voice scaring him even more. "Please don't let me get dead like Danny and Matthew."

Then he tried to think of something, anything else, and he began naming the presidents out loud, starting with, "Washington, Adams, Jefferson..."

CHAPTER 55

After making several phone calls and getting no response, Nick decided to drive over to the rectory. He couldn't go home. Eventually, that would be where his father would go. That was the one disadvantage of living in the family home—the family moved back whenever they wanted. And although the old farmhouse was certainly large enough, Nick didn't want to see or talk to his father for the rest of the evening.

The rectory was actually a ranch-style house connected to the church by an enclosed brick walkway. The church's stain glass hinted at just a flicker of candlelight, but the rectory was lit up inside and outside as if for a party. Yet, Nick waited a long time before anyone answered his knock.

Father Keller opened the door, dressed in a long black robe.

"Sheriff Morrelli, sorry for the delay. I was taking a shower," he said without surprise, as if he had been expecting him.

"I did try calling first."

"Really? I've been here all evening, except I'm afraid I can't hear the phone from my bathroom. Come in."

A freshly fed fire roared in the huge fireplace that was the room's center of attraction. A colorful Oriental rug and several easy chairs sat in front. Books were piled up next to one of the chairs, and at a glance Nick noticed they were art books—Degas, Monet, Renaissance painting. He felt silly expecting them to be on religious and philosophical topics. After all, priests were people. Of course, they had other interests, hobbies, passions, addictions.

"Please sit down." Father Keller pointed to one of the chairs. Though he knew Father Keller only from the few times he'd attended Sunday mass, it was hard not to like the guy. Besides being tall, athletic and handsome, with boyish good looks, Father Keller possessed an ease, a calm that immediately made Nick feel comfortable. He glanced at the young priest's hands. The long fingers were clean and smooth with fingernails well manicured—not a cuticle in sight. They certainly didn't look like the hands of a man who strangled children. Maggie was way off base. There was no way this guy killed little boys. Nick should be questioning Ray Howard, instead.

"Can I get you some coffee?" Father Keller asked, sounding as if he genuinely wanted to please his guest.

"No, thanks. This won't take long." Nick unzipped his jacket and pulled out a notepad and pen. His hand ached. The knuckles bled through his homemade bandage. He tucked it up into the sleeve of his jacket to avoid attention.

"I'm afraid there's not much I can tell you, Sheriff. I think he simply had a heart attack."

"Excuse me?"

"Father Francis. That is why you're here, isn't it?"

"What about Father Francis?"

"Oh dear, God. I'm sorry. I thought that was why you were here. We think he had a heart attack and fell down the basement steps sometime this morning."

"Is he okay?"

"I'm afraid he's dead, God rest his soul." Father Keller picked at a thread on his robe and avoided Nick's eyes.

"Jesus, I'm sorry. I didn't know."

"I'm sure it's a shock. It certainly was for all of us. You served mass for Father Francis, didn't you? At the old St. Margaret's?"

"Seems like ages ago." Nick stared into the fire, remembering how fragile the old priest had looked when he and Maggie questioned him.

"Excuse me, Sheriff, but if you're not here about Father Francis, what is it I can help you with?"

For a moment the reason escaped him. Then Nick remembered Maggie's profile. Father Keller matched the physical characteristics. His bare feet even looked about a size twelve. But like his hands, his feet looked too clean, too smooth to have been out in the cold, trampling through rocks and branches.

"Sheriff Morrelli? Are you okay?"

"I'm fine. Actually, I just had a few questions for you about...about the summer church camp you sponsor."

"The church camp?" Was the look one of confusion or alarm? Nick couldn't be sure.

"Both Danny Alverez and Matthew Tanner were in your church camp this past summer."

"Really?"

"You didn't know?"

"We had over two hundred boys last summer. I wish I could get to know them all, but there just isn't time."

"Do you have pictures taken with all of them?"

"Excuse me?"

"My nephew, Timmy Hamilton, has a photo of about fifteen to twenty boys with you and Mr. Howard."

"Oh, yes." Father Keller raked his fingers through his thick hair, and only then did Nick realize it wasn't wet. "The canoe photos. Not all the boys qualified for the races, but, yes, we did take pictures with the ones who qualified. Mr. Howard is a volunteer counselor. I've tried to include Ray in as many church activities as possible ever since he left the seminary last year and came to work for us."

Howard had been in a seminary. Nick waited for more.

"So Timmy Hamilton is your nephew? He's a great kid."

"Yes, yes, he is." Did he dare ask more questions about Howard or was the distraction exactly what Father Keller wanted? There was no need to have mentioned Howard leaving the seminary.

"You started a similar church camp for boys at your previous parish, didn't you, Father Keller? In Maine." Nick pretended to look at his notepad, though it was blank. "Wood River, I believe it was." He watched for a reaction, but there was none.

"That's right."

"Why did you leave Wood River?"

"I was offered an associate pastor position here. You might say it was a promotion."

"Were you aware of a murder of a little boy in the Wood River area just before you left?"

"Vaguely. I'm not sure I understand your line of questioning, Sheriff. Are you accusing me of having some knowledge about these murders?"

Still, there was no alarm in his voice, no defensiveness, only concern.

"I'm just checking as many leads as possible." Suddenly, Nick felt ridiculous. How could Maggie ever have led him to believe that a Catholic priest was capable of murder? Then it hit him. "Father Keller, how did you know I served mass for Father Francis at the old St. Margaret's?"

"I'm not sure. Father Francis must have mentioned it to me." Again the priest avoided Nick's eyes. A sudden knock at the door interrupted them, and Father Keller quickly got up, almost too quickly, as if anxious to escape. "I'm certainly not dressed for company." He smiled at Nick as he tucked in the lapels of his robe and tightened its cinch.

Nick took the opportunity to escape the fire's heat. He got up and paced the large room. Huge built-in bookcases made up one wall, on the opposite were a bay window and window bench used for green plants. There were few decorations—a highly-polished, dark wooden crucifix with an unusual pointed end. It almost looked like a dagger. There were also several original paintings by an obscure artist. Quite nice, though Nick knew little about art. The swishes of bright color were hypnotic, swirling yellows and reds in a field of vibrant purple.

Then Nick saw them. Tucked away around the side of the brick fireplace that jutted out into the room was a pair of black rubber boots, still plastered with snow and sitting on an old welcome mat. Had Father Keller lied about being out this evening? Or perhaps the boots belonged to Ray Howard.

From the foyer Nick heard voices raised, a hint of frustration in Father Keller's and accusations from a woman's voice. Nick hurried to the entrance, where he saw Father Keller trying to remain calm and cool while Maggie O'Dell assaulted him with questions.

CHAPTER 56

At first Nick didn't recognize Maggie's voice. It was loud, shrill and belligerent—this from a woman who appeared to be the essence of control.

"I want to see Father Francis now," she said and pushed past Father Keller before he could explain. She almost ran into Nick. She backed away, startled. Her eyes met his. There was something wild and dark in hers—something a bit out of control to match her voice.

"Nick, what are you doing here?"

"I could ask you the same thing. Don't you have a flight to catch?"

She looked small in the oversize green jacket and blue jeans. Without makeup and with her windblown hair, she could have passed for a college coed.

"Flights are delayed."

"Excuse me," Father Keller interrupted.

"Maggie, you haven't met Father Michael Keller. Father Keller, this is Special Agent Maggie O'Dell."

"So you're Keller?" There was accusation in her voice. "What have you done with Father Francis?"

Again, the belligerence. Nick couldn't figure out this new approach. What happened to the cool, calm woman who usually made him look like the hothead?

"I tried to explain..." Father Keller tried again.

"Yes, you do have some explaining to do. Father Francis was supposed to meet me at the hospital this afternoon. He never showed up.'' She looked to Nick. "I've been calling here all afternoon and evening.''

"Maggie, why don't you come in and calm down?''

"I don't want to calm down. I want some answers. I want to know what the hell's going on here.''

"There was an accident this morning,'' Nick explained, since she wouldn't allow Father Keller to speak. "Father Francis fell down some basement steps. I'm afraid he's dead.''

She was quiet, her entire body suddenly still. "An accident?'' Then she looked up at Father Keller. "Nick, are you sure it was an accident?''

"Maggie.''

"How can you be sure he wasn't pushed? Has anyone examined the body? I'll do the autopsy myself if necessary.''

"An autopsy?'' Father Keller repeated.

"Maggie, he was old and frail.''

"Exactly. So why would he be going down basement steps?''

"Actually, it's our wine cellar,'' Father Keller tried to explain.

Maggie stared at him, and Nick noticed her hands clenched into fists. It wouldn't have surprised him if she took a swing at the priest. Nick couldn't figure out her angle. If she was playing bad cop, good cop, he wished she'd let him know.

"What exactly are you implying, Father Keller?'' she finally asked.

"Implying? I'm not implying anything.''

"Maggie, maybe we should go,'' Nick said, taking her gently by the arm. Immediately, she wrenched it from his hold and shot him a look that made him take a step backward. She stared at Father Keller again, then suddenly pushed past both of them and headed for the door.

Nick glanced at the priest, who looked as embarrassed and confused as Nick felt. Without saying a word, he followed Maggie out the front door. He caught up with her on the sidewalk. He reached for her arm to slow her down, but thought better of it and simply increased his pace to stay alongside her.

"What the hell was that about?'' he demanded.

"He's lying. I doubt that it was an accident.''

"Father Francis was an old man, Maggie.''

"He had something important to tell me. When we talked on the phone this morning, I could tell someone else was listening in. I'm guessing it was Keller. Don't you see, Nick?'' She came to a halt and turned to look at him. ''Whoever was listening decided to stop Father Francis before he had a chance to tell me whatever was so important. An autopsy may show whether or not he was pushed. I'll do it myself if—''

''Maggie, stop. There's not going to be an autopsy. Keller didn't push anybody, and I don't think he had anything to do with the murders. This is nuts. We need to start looking at some real suspects. We need to...''

She looked as though she would be sick. Her face went white, her shoulders slumped, and her eyes were watery.

''Maggie?''

She turned and hurried off the sidewalk into the snow, back behind the rectory and out of the bright streetlights. Shielded from the wind and clinging to a tree, she bent over and began retching. Nick grimaced and kept his distance. Now he understood the belligerence, the loud accusation, the uncharacteristic anger. Maggie O'Dell was drunk.

He waited until she finished, standing guard in the shadows, keeping his back to her in case she was now sober enough to be embarrassed.

''Nick.''

When he turned, she was walking away from him, behind the rectory toward a grove of trees that separated the church property from Cutty's Hill.

''Nick, look.'' She stopped and pointed, and he wondered if she was delusional. Then he saw it, and immediately he, too, felt sick to his stomach. Tucked back in the trees was an old blue pickup with wooden side racks.

CHAPTER 57

"**I**'ll get Judge Murphy to issue a search warrant first thing in the morning." Nick was still explaining when they got back to Maggie's hotel room. She wished that he would just shut up. Her head ached and her stomach hurt. Why in the world did she drink all that Scotch on an empty stomach?

She threw her laptop and jacket onto the bed and lay down next to them. She was lucky to get her room back with there being so many stranded motorists.

Nick stood in the doorway, looking uncomfortable, but making no effort to leave.

"I couldn't believe the way you were going at Keller. Jesus, I thought you were going to punch him."

She looked up at him without moving from her resting place. "I know you don't believe me, but Keller has something to do with all this. Either come in or leave, but don't stand in the open doorway. I have a reputation, after all."

He smiled and came in, closing the door. Once inside, he paced until he noticed her frowning at him. He pulled a chair to the edge of the bed where she could see him and not have to move.

"So what did you do, decide to have a little going-away party?"

"It seemed like a good idea at the time."

"Aren't you going to miss your flight?"

"I probably already have."

"What about your mother?"

"I'll call in the morning."

"So you came all the way back just for a piece of Keller?"

She pulled herself up on one elbow and dug through her jacket pockets. She handed him the small envelope and lay back down.

"What is it?"

"I was in the airport lounge when the bartender gave me that—said a guy at the bar asked him to deliver it to me. Only the guy was gone by the time I got it."

She watched him read it. There was confusion, and she remembered she hadn't told him about the first note.

"It's from the killer."

"How does he know where you live and your husband's name?"

"He's probing me, investigating me, digging into my background just like I'm doing to him."

"Jesus, Maggie."

"It comes with the territory. It's not that unusual." She closed her eyes and massaged the throbbing in her temples. "No one answered the phone at the rectory for hours. Plenty of time to make a trip to the airport and back."

When she opened her eyes, Nick was studying her. She sat up, suddenly feeling exposed under his concerned gaze. His chair was close to the bed. Their knees almost touched. The room started spinning, tipping to the right, setting everything off balance. She almost expected the furniture to start sliding.

"Maggie, are you okay?"

She looked into his blue eyes and felt the electrical current even before his fingers touched her face and his palm caressed her cheek. She leaned into it, closing her eyes again and allowing her body to absorb the spinning and the electricity. Suddenly, she vaulted from his touch, scrambling from the bed and from him. Her breathing was uneven, and she steadied herself with both hands, leaning against the dresser. She looked up and saw him in the mirror, behind her. Their eyes met in the reflection, and she held his gaze even though what she saw in his eyes made her stomach flutter. This time it wasn't because of the alcohol.

She watched as he came up behind her, so close she felt his breath on her neck even before he leaned down to kiss it. The Packers jersey had slipped off her shoulder, and she watched in the mirror as his soft, wet lips moved slowly, deliberately from her neck to her shoulder to her back. By the time they moved up her neck again, she had trouble breathing.

"Nick, what are you doing?" she gasped, surprised by her reaction and no longer able to control it.

"I've wanted to touch you for days."

His tongue flicked at her earlobe, and her knees went weak. She leaned back against him, afraid she'd fall.

"This isn't a good idea." It came out as a whisper, not the least bit convincing. And it certainly didn't stop his big, steady hands from coming around her waist, one palm flat against her stomach, sending a shiver down her back and the flutter from her stomach down between her legs.

"Nick." It was useless. She couldn't talk, couldn't breathe, and his gentle, urgent mouth was devouring her in soft, wet explorations while his hands made their way up her body. She noticed one had a bandage wrapped around the knuckles. She wanted to ask what had happened, but she couldn't concentrate on anything except her breathing.

She watched in the mirror as his hands moved over her breasts, swallowing them and beginning their circular caress, rendering her completely helpless. It was too much. It was sensory overload. She was already wet between her legs before one of his hands strayed and began to caress her there, the fingers gentle and expert. She was close to the edge when finally she found enough strength to twist herself around to face him, to push him away. But when her hands came up to his chest, they betrayed her, beginning their own exploration and unbuttoning his shirt, desperate to gain access to his skin.

He actually trembled when his mouth finally found hers. She hesitated, surprised by her own moans, her own urgency. His mouth urged her on with delicate but persistent nibbles until she couldn't stand it any longer and kissed him back with the same urgency. Again, her body seemed powerless, and she leaned against the dresser attempting to find relief from the magnetic force of his hot body. She was gasping for air when his mouth left hers and made its way to her neck and then down to her breasts, sucking at her nipples through the cotton of the jersey and sending a jolt so powerful she clung to the dresser top.

"Oh, God, Nick," she gasped. She needed to stop, couldn't stop. The room was spinning again. Her ears ringing. Her heart banging against her rib cage and her blood rushing from her head. That constant ringing. No, it wasn't her ears. It was the phone. The phone—reality—pulled her back from the edge.

"Nick...the phone," she managed.

He was kneeling in front of her. He stopped and looked up, his hands on her waist, his eyes filled with desire. How did she ever let it get this far? It was the Scotch. It was that damn fuzziness in her head. It was that delicious mouth and those strong hands. Damn it, she needed to gain control.

She pulled away from him and stumbled to the nightstand, knocking the phone and grabbing the receiver as the base crashed to the floor. She kept her back to Nick, avoiding his eyes, or she'd never be able to stop the trembling her body was experiencing.

"Yes," she said, trying her voice and disappointed that her breathing still came in gasps. "This is Maggie O'Dell."

"Maggie, oh, thank God, I got ahold of you. This is Christine Hamilton. I don't know what to do. I'm sorry I'm calling so late. I tried to get ahold of Nicky, but no one knows where he is."

"Calm down, Christine." She glanced back at Nick.

The mention of his sister's name brought him to attention. She watched his fingers fumble with his shirt buttons as though Christine had walked into the room and caught them. Maggie crossed her arms in an attempt to stop her breasts from tingling, the memory of his mouth on them still fresh, the front of her jersey still damp. She turned her back to Nick again, avoiding the distraction, and pushed her hair out of her face, tucking wild strands behind her ears.

"Christine, what's wrong?"

"It's Timmy. He wasn't here when I got home. I thought he just went home with one of his friends. But I've called. No one has seen him since this afternoon. They all went sledding on Cutty's Hill. The other kids said they saw him walking home, but he's not here. Oh, God, Maggie, he's not here. That was over five hours ago. I'm so scared. I don't know what to do."

Maggie cupped the mouthpiece and sat on the edge of the bed before her knees could give out.

"Timmy is missing," she said calmly, but felt the panic in the pit of her empty stomach. She watched Nick's eyes fill with his own panic.

"Jesus, no," he said, and they stared at each other, the electricity quickly replaced by the terrifying realization.

CHAPTER 58

Christine bit her nails, an old childhood habit absently resurrected as she watched her father pace her living room. At first, when she called Nick's and her father answered, she was surprised and relieved. But now there was no comfort in watching him stomp back and forth while he barked orders to the deputies who filled her house and yard. She felt even more helpless in his presence. Suddenly, she was that invisible little girl, incapable of doing anything.

"Why don't you go lie down, honey. Get some rest," her father said in one of his passes.

She only shook her head, unable to answer.

Not knowing what else to do, he simply ignored her.

When Nick and Maggie shoved their way into the crowded living room, Christine jumped up and almost ran to her brother. She stopped herself and teetered on weak knees, hovering close to the sofa. Even in her panic, throwing her arms around her brother seemed awkward. As if sensing all this, Nick made his way across the room. He hesitated in front of her, then gently pulled her to him and wrapped his strong arms around her without saying a word. Until now, she had held it together—her father's strong little soldier. Suddenly, the tears came in a choking rush that shook her entire body. She clung to Nick tightly, muffling her retching sobs into the stiff fabric of his jacket. Her entire body hurt, aching from her failed attempt at warding off the tremors.

Nick eased her back to the sofa, keeping an arm around her.

When she finally looked up, Maggie was in front of them and handed her a glass of water. It was an effort to drink without spilling water all over herself. She looked to find her father, not surprised to see he had disappeared. Of course, he wouldn't want to witness such a sniveling display of weakness.

"Are you sure there isn't some place or someone you haven't checked?" Nick asked.

"I've called everyone." Her plugged nose distorted her voice. It was difficult to breathe. Maggie handed her several tissues. "They all said the same thing—that he was headed for home after sledding."

"Could he have stopped somewhere on the way?" Maggie asked.

"I don't know. Other than the church, there's only houses between Cutty's Hill and here. I tried calling the rectory, but never got an answer." She saw them exchange a glance. "What? What is it?"

"Nothing," Nick said, but she knew it was something. "Maggie and I were at the rectory earlier. I'm going to check what Dad has my men doing. I'll be right back."

Maggie took off her jacket and sat next to her. The impeccable Agent O'Dell wore a faded, stretched-out football jersey and blue jeans. Her hair was tousled and her skin flushed.

"Did I get you out of bed?" Christine asked. She was surprised to see her question embarrassed Maggie.

"No, not at all." She ran her fingers through her tangled hair. Then she looked down, as if only now noticing her inappropriate attire. "Actually, I was on my way home…home to Virginia. My flight was delayed. I checked all my luggage." She glanced at her watch. "It's probably somewhere over Chicago about now."

"You can borrow something of mine, if you like."

Maggie hesitated. Christine was sure she would decline, when Maggie said, "Are you sure you don't mind?"

"Not at all. Come on."

Christine led Maggie to her bedroom, surprised that her body had any energy left and suddenly relieved to have something to do. She closed the bedroom door behind them, though the sounds of voices and trampling couldn't be stifled. She opened her closet and several drawers. She was taller than Maggie, but otherwise about the same size, except for her flat chest next to Maggie's full breasts.

"Please, help yourself." Christine sat on the edge of the bed while Maggie very apprehensively pulled a red turtleneck sweater from one of the drawers.

"I don't suppose you have a bra I could borrow?"

"Top, left dresser drawer, though mine may be too small. You might try one of the sports bras. They, at least, have some extra stretch."

She sensed Maggie's discomfort. It had been a long time since Christine had had any girlfriends close enough to share a dressing room. She thought about leaving the room, but before she stood up, Maggie peeled off the football jersey and struggled into a gray sports bra. It stretched tightly across her full breasts, and she tugged at it as though it were a straitjacket. Before Christine looked away, she noticed a scar across Maggie's abdomen. In the mirror, Maggie caught her.

"I'm sorry," Christine said, but didn't look away. "Excuse me for asking, but that doesn't look like a surgical scar."

"No, it's not." It wasn't embarrassment in her voice. Christine detected something a bit more haunting. Maggie ran her fingertips carefully over the red puckered skin. There was a red gash on her shoulder blade, too. "This was a gift," she said quietly, almost reverently. "A reminder from a murderer I helped track down."

"I can't even imagine some of the horrible situations you must have experienced."

"It comes with the job. Do you have a camisole or tank top I could use instead?"

"Bottom left. How do you keep it from affecting you?"

"I never said it didn't affect me." Maggie squirmed out of the sports bra and pulled on a cream-colored camisole. Satisfied with the fit, she tucked it into the waistband of her jeans. "I try not to think about it."

The red turtleneck sweater was also tight, but the camisole helped smooth out the results. She left it untucked.

"Thanks," she said, turning back to Christine.

"Danny's and Matthew's bodies were cut badly, weren't they?"

Before, Christine had probed for all the grisly details to enhance her articles. Now she needed to know for herself.

The straightforward Maggie O'Dell looked uncomfortable, even a bit flustered. "We'll find Timmy. In fact, Nick has already called Judge Murphy. We're getting a search warrant, and we have a suspect."

The reporter in her should have been asking questions. Who was the suspect? What was the warrant for? But the mother in her couldn't shake the image of her small, fragile little boy cringing in a dark corner somewhere all alone. Could they really find him before his soft, white skin puckered with red gashes?

"He bruises so easily."

Christine felt the tears welling up in her eyes again, the intense panic gnawing at her insides. Maggie watched from the other side of the room, respecting the distance, for which Christine was grateful. She wouldn't break down, not now, not in front of this woman who had endured a madman slicing up her body. This woman who apparently had drained all emotion from her life and replaced it with strength. Yes, that's what Christine needed to do. Crying certainly wouldn't help Timmy.

She swiped at the few tears that escaped down her cheek and stood up feeling a new energy, despite the violent gnawing in her gut.

"Tell me what I can do to help," she said to Maggie, ignoring the tremor in her voice.

CHAPTER 59

Thursday, October 30

Sunlight streaked in through the rotted slats, waking Timmy up. At first, he didn't remember where he was, then he smelled the kerosene and the musty walls. The metal chain clanked as he sat up. His body ached from being curled up into the plastic sled. Panic filled his empty stomach. He needed to stop it this time, before it started the convulsions again.

"Think of good things," he said out loud.

In the sunlight he noticed the posters that covered the cracked and peeling walls. They looked like ones he had in his room back home. There were several Nebraska Cornhuskers, a *Batman* and two different *Star Wars*. He listened for sounds of traffic and heard none. Only the wind whistled in through the cracks, rattling the broken glass.

If he could just reach the window, he was sure he could pull the boards off. The window was small, but he could fit through and maybe call for help. He tried to shove the bed, but the heavy metal frame wouldn't budge. And he was weak and light-headed from not eating.

He stuffed a few of the French fries into his mouth. They were cold, but salty. Under the crate he found two Snickers bars, a bag of Cheetos and an orange. His stomach felt a little sick, but he devoured the orange and candy bars and started on the Cheetos while he examined the chain that connected him to the bedpost. The links were metal with a paper-thin slit in each, but it was impossible to pull any of them apart, not even to slip just one through the slit. It was useless. He wasn't strong enough and, again, he hated how small and helpless he was.

He heard footsteps outside the door. He scrambled up into the bed, crawling beneath the covers as the locks whined and the door screeched open.

The man came in slowly. He was bundled in a thick ski jacket, the black rubber boots and a stocking cap over the rubber mask that covered his entire head.

"Good morning," he mumbled. He set down a brown paper sack, but this time didn't remove his coat or boots to stay. "I brought you some things." His voice was soft and friendly.

Timmy came to the edge of the bed, showing his interest and pretending not to be frightened.

The man handed him several comic books, old ones, but in good condition. In fact, Timmy thought they were brand new until he saw the twelve-cent and fifteen-cent prices. He also handed him a stack of baseball cards, secured with a rubber band. Then he started unpacking some groceries and filling the crate where Timmy had found the candy bars. He watched as the man pulled out Cap'n Crunch cereal, more Snickers bars, corn chips and several cans of SpaghettiOs.

"I tried to get some of your favorite food," he said, looking back at Timmy, obviously wanting to please him.

"Thanks," Timmy found himself saying out of habit. The man nodded, the eyes sparkling again as though he was smiling. "How did you know I love Cap'n Crunch?"

"I just remember things," he said softly. "I can't stay. Is there anything else I can get you?"

Timmy watched him extinguish the kerosene lamp and felt a twinge of panic.

"Will you be back before dark? I hate being in the dark."

"I'll try to come back." He started for the door then glanced back at Timmy. He sighed and then dug in his pockets, finally pulling out something shiny.

"I'll leave my lighter, just case I don't get back. But be careful, Timmy. You don't want to start a fire." He tossed the shiny metal lighter next to Timmy on the bed. Then he left.

The panic stirred again in Timmy's stomach. Maybe it was all the junk food he had eaten. He hated being trapped, but at least if the man didn't come back he couldn't hurt him. He had the entire day to plan his escape. He picked up the lighter and ran his fingers over the smooth finish. Timmy noticed the logo stamped on the side of it. He recognized the dark brown crest. He had seen it many times on the jackets and uniforms his grandfather and Uncle Nick wore. It was the symbol for the sheriff's department.

CHAPTER 60

The smell of coffee nauseated Maggie, though it seemed to be the only thing to combat the effects of the Scotch. She picked at the scrambled eggs and toast while she watched the door of the diner. Nick said it would take only ten to fifteen minutes. That was an hour ago. The small diner was beginning to fill with its breakfast rush, farmers in feed caps next to business men and women in suits.

Maggie had hated leaving Christine this morning, though she knew she wasn't much of a comfort. She had never been good at offering words of reassurance or doing the hand-holding routine. After all, her only experience had been as a twelve year old, a small, gangly child struggling with and dragging a drunken mother up a flight of stairs to their run-down apartment. No words or courtesies had been necessary when dealing with someone who was half-conscious. Even as an FBI agent, etiquette skills were unnecessary. Most of the people she dealt with were corpses or psychos. Questioning the victims' families didn't require anything more than polite condolences, or so she had convinced herself long ago.

Last night she'd simply felt paralyzed. She hardly knew Christine. One dinner surely didn't enforce any obligation of friendship. Yet, Timmy's small, freckled face remained etched in her mind. In her eight years of tracking killers, no one she had known personally had ever been a victim. However, every corpse stayed with her, their ghosts a permanent part of her mental scrapbook.

She couldn't imagine—didn't want to imagine—adding Timmy to that portfolio of tortured images.

Finally, Nick came into the diner. He spotted her immediately and waved, making his way to the booth but stopping several times to talk to customers. He was dressed in his usual uniform of jeans and cowboy boots, only this time under his unzipped jacket he wore a red Nebraska Cornhuskers sweatshirt. The swelling was gone from around his jaw, leaving a bruise. He looked exhausted. He hadn't bothered to comb his hair or shave after showering. He looked even more handsome than she remembered.

He slid into the booth opposite her and grabbed a menu from behind the napkin dispenser. "Judge Murphy is stalling on the search warrant for the rectory," he said quietly as he looked at the menu. "He didn't have a problem with the pickup, but he thinks—"

"Hi, Nick. What can I get for you?"

"Oh, hi, Angie."

Maggie watched the exchange between Nick and the pretty blond waitress and knew immediately the woman wasn't used to just taking his diner orders.

"How have you been?" she asked, trying to make it sound like casual conversation, though Maggie noticed she hadn't taken her eyes off Nick.

"Things have been pretty crazy. Could I just get some coffee and toast?" He avoided her eyes. His discomfort speeded up his speech.

"Wheat toast, right? And lots of cream with the coffee?"

"Yeah, thanks." He looked anxious for her to leave.

She smiled and left the table without even noticing Maggie, though before Nick's arrival she had been interested enough to fill Maggie's coffee cup three times.

"An old friend?" Maggie asked, knowing she had no right to, but enjoying his fidgeting.

"Who, Angie? Yeah, I guess you could say that." He dug Christine's cellular phone from his jacket pocket, set it on the table, then twisted out of the jacket. "I hate these things," he said, referring to the phone and desperately trying to change the subject.

"She seems very nice." Maggie wasn't ready to let him off the hook.

This time his eyes met hers, their intense blue looking deep inside her and reminding her once more of last night.

"She is nice, but she doesn't make my palms sweaty and my knees weak like you do," he said quietly, seriously, and managing to set that damn flutter going again in her stomach.

She looked away and concentrated on putting butter on her cold toast as though suddenly hungry.

"Look Nick, about last night..."

"I hope you don't think I was trying to take advantage of you. I mean, you did have a lot to drink."

She glanced at him. He leaned forward, his entire face serious. He was genuinely concerned. Had last night meant more to him than his ordinary trysts with women? Something made her want it to mean more, but she said, "I think it's best if we just forget last night ever happened."

He looked wounded, a slight grimace, then that same intensity.

"What if I don't want to forget? Maggie, I haven't felt like that in a long time. I can't—"

"Please, Nick, I'm not some naive waitress. You don't have to feed me some line or pretend—"

"It's not a line. Yesterday when I thought you were leaving and I'd never see you again, I felt as if someone had punched me in the gut. And then last night. Jesus, Maggie, you turn me inside out. I get all weak-kneed and tongue-tied. Believe me, that doesn't usually happen with me and women."

"We've been spending a lot of time together. We were both exhausted."

"I wasn't that exhausted. And neither were you."

She stared at him. Had it been that obvious how much she had wanted him? Or was it simply his ego?

"What did you expect to happen, Nick? Are you disappointed you're not able to add one more name to your list of conquests?" She glanced around them. No one seemed to notice her angry whispers.

"You know that's not what this is."

"Then maybe it's simply the thrill of being forbidden. I *am* married, Nick. It may not be the best marriage in the world, but it still means something. Please, let's just forget about last night.'' She stared at her coffee, feeling his eyes on her.

"Here's your toast and coffee,'' Angie interrupted, and Maggie found no relief in ending the subject. Maybe she didn't want to forget it, either.

Angie set the plate and cup in front of Nick, forcing him to sit back, though his eyes stayed on Maggie. She wondered if the pretty waitress could feel the tension.

"Can I get you anything else?'' she asked only Nick.

"Maggie, do you need anything?'' He purposely drew attention to Maggie, and Angie immediately looked embarrassed.

"No, thanks.''

"Okay,'' Angie said, now anxious to make an exit.

There was an awkward moment of silence.

"You said Judge Murphy is hedging on the rectory warrant. Why?'' Maggie tried to focus, still avoiding his eyes and pouring more sugar into her coffee. She waited out his silence, then finally she heard a sigh of resignation.

"Murphy and my dad come from a generation that believe you just don't mess with Catholic priests,'' he said, slathering his toast with quick, jerky swipes of butter.

"So is a warrant even possible?''

"I tried to convince him that it's Ray Howard we're after.''

"You still think it is Howard.''

"I don't know.'' He pushed the toast aside without taking a bite and scratched at his bristled jaw. She noticed the bandage again.

"What did you do to your hand?''

He stared at it for a moment as though he couldn't remember.

"It's no big deal. Look,'' he said, leaning toward her again, and she could smell the faint hint of his aftershave lotion though he obviously hadn't shaved. Behind the exhaustion in his eyes, Maggie could see the beginning panic he was so desperately trying to hide. Suddenly, she realized he was waiting for her attention.

"Sorry,'' she said, putting down the spoon, folding her arms and giving him her attention.

"Father Keller told me last night that Ray Howard left the seminary last year. While I was waiting on Murphy I did some checking. Howard was at a seminary in Silver Lake, New Hampshire. It's just across the border to Maine and less than five hundred miles from Wood River.''

Now he did have her attention. She sat up and stared at him.

"How long was he there?"

"The last three years."

"Well, that rules him out on the Wood River murder."

"Maybe, but isn't that just a little too strange of a coincidence? Three years in the seminary, he should know a little about administering last rites."

"Was he here during the first murders?"

"I'm having Hal check it out. But I did talk to the head guy at the seminary. Father Vincent wouldn't give me the details, but he did say Howard was asked to leave due to improper conduct." He said it as if it were some sort of proof.

"Improper conduct at a seminary could be anything from breaking a vow of silence to spitting on the sidewalk. I don't know, Nick. Howard just doesn't seem sharp enough to pull this off."

"Maybe that's what he wants everyone to believe."

Maggie watched Nick fold his paper napkin over and over again, his fingers revealing his internal turmoil. Underneath the table, she heard his foot nervously tapping.

"Both Howard and Keller would have had the opportunity to get rid of Father Francis."

"Jesus, Maggie. I thought you believed that only because you were drunk last night. You really don't think it was an accident?"

"Father Francis told me yesterday morning that he had something very important to tell me. I know someone was listening in on our conversation. I could hear the click."

"So maybe it's a coincidence."

"I learned a long time ago that there are few coincidences. An autopsy might show whether he was pushed or whether he simply fell."

"Without any evidence, we can't just order an autopsy." Nick fidgeted with the cellular phone, and Maggie could feel his restlessness.

"Maybe I can talk to Father Francis' family. Or the archdiocese."

"Thing is, Maggie, we don't have time to wait for permission or for autopsies or even search warrants. I'd like to just scare the living crap out of Howard.''

She couldn't believe he still thought it was Howard. Or was it simply his desperation, grabbing for easy answers. Instead of arguing, she said, ''Whether it's Howard or Keller, we need to be very careful. If he panics...''

She stopped herself, remembering this was Timmy, Nick's nephew, they were talking about and not an anonymous victim. She hadn't shared with Nick her discovery of the killer's acceleration. She glanced at him and saw the realization there in his eyes. Somehow he already knew.

''We don't have much time,'' he said as though reading her mind. He was getting good at it. ''He's speeding things up, isn't he?''

She nodded.

''Let's get out of here.'' He threw a wad of bills on the table without counting it out and wrestled back into his jacket, waiting while she did the same.

''Where are we going?''

''I need to impound a pickup, and you need to apologize to Father Keller for last night.''

CHAPTER 61

Father Keller looked quite official this time when he answered the rectory door, still dressed from morning mass. However, Nick immediately noticed the white Nikes peeking out from under the black floor-length cassock.

"Sheriff Morrelli, Agent O'Dell. I'm sorry, but this is a surprise."

"Can we come in for a few minutes, Father?" Nick rubbed his hands together to ward off the cold. Although the sun had made its first appearance in days, the piles of snow and sharp wind kept the temperature well below freezing. Even for Nebraska, this was unusual Halloween weather.

Father Keller hesitated. At first, Nick thought he'd protest as he glanced at Maggie, checking to see if it was safe to let her in. Then he smiled and moved away from the door, leading them into the living room where a fire blazed in the grand fireplace. Only this morning there was a faint scent of something scorched—something not meant to burn. Immediately, Nick wondered if Keller was trying to hide something.

"I'm not sure how I can be of help to the two of you. Last night—"

"Actually, Father Keller," Maggie interrupted, this morning back to her cool, calm self. "I wanted to apologize for last night." She glanced up at Nick, and he saw a spark of indignation in her eyes. "I had a bit too much to drink, and I'm afraid I get somewhat antagonistic. It was certainly nothing personal. I hope you understand and accept my apology."

"Of course, I understand. And I'm relieved to know it wasn't anything I did. After all, we hadn't even met."

Nick watched the priest's face. Maggie's apology relaxed him. Even his hands dropped to his sides, no longer wringing behind his back.

"I was just about to make myself some hot tea. Can I get some for the two of you?"

"We are here on official business, Father Keller," Nick said.

"Official business?"

Nick watched the young priest stuff his hands into the deep pockets of the cassock, suddenly uncomfortable, though his voice appeared remarkably calm. Nick couldn't help wondering if this, too, was something Father Keller had learned in the seminary. He pulled the warrant from his jacket pocket and began unfolding it, while he said, "Last night we noticed the old pickup you have out back."

"Pickup?" Father Keller sounded surprised. Was it possible he didn't know or, again, was this only a part of his schooling?

"The one in the trees. It matches the description a witness gave of a pickup she saw Danny Alverez get into the day he disappeared." Nick waited and watched. Maggie stood silently by his side, but he knew she would memorize every twitch and shift Father Keller made.

"I don't know if that old thing even runs. I think Ray uses it when he goes to chop wood out by the river."

Nick handed Father Keller the warrant. The priest held it by its corner and stared at it as though it were a foreign object, secreting slime.

"Like I told you last night," Nick said calmly, "I'm just trying to follow up on as many leads as possible. You probably know that the sheriff's department has come under considerable fire lately. I just want to make sure no one can say we didn't check. Do you have the keys, Father?"

"The keys?"

"To the pickup?"

"I can't imagine that it's locked. Let me put on a coat and some boots, and I'll go back with you."

"Thanks, Father. I appreciate it." Nick watched the priest go to the side of the fireplace and slip on the pair of rubber boots he had noticed last night. So, they were Keller's boots. Last night, he had told Nick that he hadn't left the rectory. But then Nick reminded himself that snow-covered boots could mean that Keller had only stepped out to get more wood.

The three of them started for the door. Suddenly, Maggie grabbed on to a small table and doubled over.

"Oh, God. I think I'm going to be sick again," she mumbled.

"Maggie, are you okay?" He glanced at Father Keller and whispered, "She's been like this all morning." Then to Maggie, "What in the world did you drink last night?"

"Could I use your rest room?"

"Oh, sure." Father Keller's eyes darted across the floor, his obvious concern directed at the pearl-white carpeting. "Down the hall, second door on the right," he said quickly, as if to hurry her along.

"Thanks. I'll catch up with you guys." She disappeared around the corner, holding her side.

"Will she be okay?" Father Keller seemed concerned.

"She'll be fine. Believe me, you don't want to be too close. Earlier she made a mess all over my boots."

The priest grimaced and glanced at Nick's boots, then followed him outside to the back of the rectory.

Drifts encased the pickup, forcing them to shovel a path and dig out the old metal heap. The door stuck then creaked, metal grinding against metal, as Nick jerked and pulled it open. A musty, pent-up smell hit Nick's nostrils. The cab looked as though it had been closed up and unused for years. Disappointment stabbed at Nick. He was tired of coming up with empty leads. Still, he crawled into the cab with the flashlight and absolutely no clue as to what he was even looking for. Perhaps he should leave the search to the experts, but they were running out of time.

He lay on the cracked, vinyl seat then stretched and twisted his arm, allowing his hand to blindly search under the seats. The cramped quarters made it difficult to maneuver his body. The steering wheel cut into his side and the gearshift stabbed him in the chest. It reminded him of when he was sixteen and had used his dad's old Chevy for making out with his dates. Only his body ached more now and certainly wasn't as flexible as it used to be.

"I can't imagine there being anything but rats in this old heap," Father Keller said, standing outside the door.

"Rats?" He hated rats.

Nick snatched his hand back, hitting the raw knuckles on an exposed spring. He closed his eyes against the pain and bit down on his lower lip to contain the obscenities. He punched the glove compartment open and blasted the dark hole with the flashlight.

Carefully, he poked through the sparse contents: a yellowed owner's manual, a rusted can of WD-40, several McDonald's napkins, a matchbook from some place called the Pink Lady, a folded schedule with addresses and codes he didn't recognize and a small screwdriver. He palmed the matchbook, feeling Father Keller's eyes on him. Before he closed the compartment he ran his fingers back behind the contents in the deep groove. He felt something small, smooth and round, pinched it out of the groove and palmed it with the matchbook. He slipped both items into his coat pocket after checking to make sure he was out of Father Keller's line of vision. As he started to close the compartment, he noticed handwritten notes scrawled on the folded schedule. Unable to read the writing, he grabbed the paper and tucked it up his sleeve. Then he slammed the compartment shut.

"Nothing here," he said, scooting himself up and slipping the paper down into his pocket. He slid across the vinyl seat, taking one last look around. It occurred to him that, although the cab smelled musty and shut-up, everything—dash, seat, carpet—looked remarkably clean.

"Sorry you wasted your time," Father Keller said as he turned toward the rectory and started up the path.

"Actually, I still have the bed to search."

The priest stopped, hesitated, then turned back. The wind swirled the long cassock, snapping it violently, sounding like the crack of a whip. This time Nick noticed a hint of frustration in Father Keller's blue eyes—frustration, impatience. If he wasn't a priest, Nick would have said Father Keller simply looked pissed. Whatever it was, there was definitely something more. Something that made Nick anxious and apprehensive about what he might find in the pickup's bed.

CHAPTER 62

Maggie checked the window again. Nick and Father Keller were still at the pickup. She continued her search down the long hall, stopping in front of each closed door, listening and carefully peeking into every unlocked room. Several were offices, one a supply room. Finally, she came across a bedroom.

The room was plain and small with wooden floors and white walls. A simple crucifix hung above the twin bed. In the corner sat a small table with two chairs. Another stand sat in the opposite corner with an old toaster and teapot. An ornate lamp sat on the nightstand, looking out of place. Other than the lamp, there was nothing to draw attention. No clutter, no drawers or boxes.

She turned to leave, and immediately, three framed prints on the wall next to the door caught her eye. They hung side by side and were prints of Renaissance paintings. Though Maggie didn't recognize any of them, she recognized the style—the perfectly rendered bodies, the motion and color. Each one depicted the bloody torture of a man. Upon closer inspection she read the small print beneath each.

The Martyrdom of Saint Sebastian, 1475, Antonio Del Pollai-volo, showed a bound Saint Sebastian tied to a pedestal with arrows being shot into his body. *The Martyrdom of Saint Eras-mus,* 1629, Nicolas Poussin, included winged cherubs hovering above a crowd of men who had one man stretched out and chained down while they pulled out his entrails.

Maggie wondered why anyone would want such artwork on their bedroom walls. She glanced at the last print. *The Martyrdom of Saint Hermione,* 1512, Matthias Anatello, showed a man tied to a tree while his accusers slashed at his body with knives and machetes. She started out the door when something made her look at the last print again. On the tortured man's chest were several bloody slashes, two perfect diagonals intersecting to create a jagged cross, or from Maggie's angle, a skewed X. Yes, of course. Now it made sense. The carving on each boy's chest wasn't an X at all. It was a cross. And the cross was part of his ritual, a mark, a symbol. Did he think he was making martyrs of the boys?

She heard footsteps. They were close and getting closer. She hurried into the hall just as Ray Howard turned the corner. She startled him, but he still noticed her hand on the doorknob.

"You're that FBI agent," he said in his accusatory tone.

"Yes, I'm here with Sheriff Morrelli."

"What were you doing in Father Keller's room?"

"Oh, is this Father Keller's room? Actually, I need to use the bathroom, and I can't seem to find it."

"That's because it's way down on the other end of the hall," he scolded, pointing and keeping his eyes on her as though he didn't trust her.

"Really? Thanks." She squeezed past him and made her way down the hall, stopping in front of the correct door and glancing back at him. "Is this it?"

"Yes."

"Thanks again." She went in and listened at the door for a few minutes. When she peeked out again, she saw Ray Howard disappear into Father Keller's bedroom.

CHAPTER 63

The bed of the pickup was filled with snow, but Nick crawled up over the tailgate.

"Could you hand me the shovel, Father?"

The priest stood paralyzed, staring at the drifts that swallowed Nick's legs. Keller's ungloved hands were at his chest, the long fingers intertwined as though he were in prayer. The wind whipped at his dark, wavy hair. His cheeks were red and his eyes watery blue.

"Father Keller, the shovel, please," Nick asked again, this time pointing when the priest finally looked up at him.

"Oh, sure." He made his way to the tree where they had left it. "I can't imagine there being anything of use to you."

"I guess we'll see."

Nick had to reach down to take the shovel, since Father Keller made no effort to lift it to him. The priest's behavior propelled Nick's adrenaline. There was something here. He could feel it. He started digging a bit frantically at first. He needed to slow down. How could he possibly find anything in all this snow? He scooped smaller shovelfuls for fear of tossing evidence over the side. The handmade wooden stockracks creaked and whined against the wind gusts. The cold sliced through Nick's jacket. It assaulted his eyes and pricked at his face, turning his ears into red pincushions. Yet, perspiration slid down his back. His palms were sweating inside the thick leather gloves he had found with the shovel in the storage shed.

Suddenly, the shovel struck something hard, encrusted beneath the snow. The dull sound alerted Father Keller who approached the tailgate, close enough to look down into the hole Nick had created.

Carefully, Nick dug around the object with small scoops and delicate plunges. Unable to contain his curiosity, he tossed the shovel aside and dropped to his knees. With his gloved hands he brushed and wiped and scooped at the snow, feeling the edges of the object, but still not able to determine what it was. Snow crusted around it in chunks of ice. Whatever the object was, it had been warm when it was tossed into the pile of snow.

Finally, Nick could see what looked like skin. His heart raced. His hands frantically pulled and chipped at the ice. A huge chunk broke away, and Nick jerked backward in surprise.

"Jesus," he said, feeling his stomach lurch.

He glanced at Father Keller, who grimaced and stepped backward. Encased in the snow tomb was a dead dog, its black fur peeled away, its skin carved and shredded, and its throat slashed.

CHAPTER 64

Nick and Father Keller stomped their way up the steps just as Maggie came out the front door of the rectory. Immediately, Nick checked her eyes, anxious to see if she had found anything. Her quick glance and a smile for Father Keller left him without a clue.

"Are you feeling any better?" Father Keller sounded genuinely concerned.

"Much. Thank you."

"It's a good thing you didn't come with us," Nick said, still feeling sick to his stomach. Who could do something like that to a defenseless dog? Then he felt ridiculous. It was obvious who had done it.

"Why? What did you find?" Maggie wanted to know.

"I'll tell you about it later."

"Would the two of you like some tea now?" Father Keller offered.

"No, thanks. We need—"

"Yes, actually," Maggie interrupted Nick. "Perhaps that might settle my stomach. That is, if it's not an inconvenience?"

"Of course not. Come in. I'll see if we have some sweet rolls or perhaps doughnuts."

They followed the priest in, and again Nick tried to catch a glimpse of Maggie's face, unsure of her sudden enthusiasm to spend more time with the priest she despised.

"Nice to see you supporting the local merchants." Father Keller smiled as he took her jacket.

She smiled back without an explanation and went into the living room. Nick brushed off his boots, staying on the welcome mat in the foyer. He glanced up to find Father Keller checking out Maggie's tight jeans. Keller's wasn't a simple glance, but a long, self-indulgent look. Suddenly, the priest looked back at Nick, and Nick bent over his jacket's zipper, pretending to struggle with it. Before the suspicion and anger crept into his mind, Nick reminded himself that even Father Keller was a man. And Maggie did look awfully good in jeans and that tight red sweater. Any man would have to be brain-dead not to notice.

Father Keller disappeared around the corner, and Nick joined Maggie in front of the fireplace.

"What's going on?" he whispered.

"Do you have Christine's cellular?"

"I think it's still in my jacket pocket."

"Could you please get it?"

He stared at her, waiting for some explanation, but instead she squatted in front of the fire to warm her hands. When he came back with the phone, she was poking through the ashes with an iron poker. He stood with his back to her, as though standing guard.

"What are you doing?" It was difficult to whisper through clenched teeth.

"I could smell something earlier. It smelled like burnt rubber."

"He'll be back any second."

"Whatever it was, it's ashes now."

"Cream, lemon, sugar?" Father Keller came around the corner with a full tray. By the time he set it on the bench in front of the window, Maggie was standing by Nick's side.

"Lemon, please," Maggie answered casually.

"Cream and sugar for me," Nick said, only now noticing that his foot was tapping nervously.

"If you two will excuse me, I need to make a phone call," Maggie said suddenly.

"There's a phone in the office down the hall." Father Keller pointed.

"Oh, no thanks. I'll just use Nick's cellular. May I?"

Nick handed her the phone, still looking for some sign as to what she was up to. She went back toward the foyer for privacy while Father Keller handed Nick a steaming cup of tea.

"Would you like a roll?" The priest offered a plate of assorted pastry.

"No, thanks." Nick tried to keep an eye on Maggie, but she was gone.

A phone began ringing, muffled but insistent. Father Keller looked puzzled, then headed quickly for the hallway.

"What on earth are you doing, Agent O'Dell?"

Nick slammed down his cup, spilling hot liquid on his hand and the polished table. He scrambled around the corner to see Maggie with the cellular phone to her ear as she walked down the hall, stopping and listening at each door. Father Keller followed close behind, questioning her and receiving no answers.

"What exactly are you doing, Agent O'Dell?" He tried to get in front of her, but she squeezed past.

Nick jogged down the hall, his nerves raw, the adrenaline pounding again.

"What's going on, Maggie?"

The muffled ringing of a phone continued, the sound getting closer and closer. Finally, Maggie pushed open the last door on the left, and the sound became crisp and clear.

"Whose room is this?" Maggie asked as she stood in the doorway.

Again, Father Keller seemed paralyzed. He looked confused, but also indignant.

"Father Keller, would you please get the phone," she asked politely, leaning against the doorjamb, careful not to enter. "It sounds as if it's in one of those drawers."

The priest still didn't move, staring into the room. The ringing grated on Nick's nerves. Then Nick realized that Maggie had called the number. He saw Christine's cellular phone in Maggie's hand, the buttons lit up and blinking with each ring of the hidden phone.

"Father Keller, please get the phone," she instructed again.

"This is Ray's room. I don't believe it's proper for me to go through his things."

"Just get the phone, please. It's a small, black flip-style."

He stared at her, then finally went into the room, slowly and hesitantly. Within seconds the ringing stopped. He came back

out and handed her the small black cellular phone. She tossed it
to Nick.

"Where is Mr. Howard, Father Keller? He needs to come
down to the sheriff's department with us to answer some questions."

"He's probably cleaning the church. I'll go get him."

Nick waited until Father Keller was out of sight.

"What's going on, Maggie? Why are you suddenly convinced
we need to question Howard? And what's with calling his cell
phone? How the hell did you even know his number?"

"I didn't dial his number, Nick. I dialed *my* cellular phone
number. That's not his phone. It's mine. It's the one I lost in the
river."

CHAPTER 65

Christine squirmed to get comfortable in the swivel chair, drawing groans from the redheaded woman with the palette of makeup. As if out of punishment, the woman swabbed even more blush on Christine's cheeks.

"We're on in ten minutes," said the tall man with the headset strapped to his bald head.

Christine thought he was talking to her and nodded, then realized he was talking into the mouthpiece of the headset. He bent over her to snap a tiny microphone onto her collar, and she couldn't help noticing the reflection on his shiny head. The bright lights blinded her, their heat stifling and adding to the cockroaches in her stomach. Her palms were sweaty. Certainly it was only a matter of time before her face began to melt into pools of plum-glow blush, soft-beige foundation and lush-black mascara.

A woman sat in the chair opposite her. She ignored Christine while she riffled through the papers just handed to her. She swatted away the bald man's hand and grabbed the microphone to pin it on herself.

"I hope you got that fucking TelePrompTer fixed, because I'm not using these." She threw the handful of papers across the stage, and a frantic stagehand scrambled around the floor, scooping them up.

"It's fixed," the man patiently reassured her.

"I need water. There's no water on the side stand."

The same stagehand scurried over with a disposable cup.

"A real glass." She almost knocked it out of the girl's hand.

"I need a real glass and a pitcher. For Christ's sake, how many times do I have to ask?"

Suddenly, Christine realized the woman was Darcy McManus, the evening anchor for the station. Perhaps she wasn't used to doing the morning news show. Perhaps she wasn't used to mornings. In the harsh lighting, McManus's skin looked weathered with crinkled lines at the eyes and mouth. Her usual shiny, black hair looked stiff and unnatural. The startling shade of red lipstick looked brash against her white skin until the redheaded makeup artist swabbed on a thick layer of artificial tan.

"One minute, people," the headset man called out.

McManus dismissed the makeup woman with a wave of her hand. She stood up, smoothed out her too-short skirt, straightened her jacket, checked her face in a pocket mirror, then sat back down. Just then, Christine realized she'd been staring at the woman the entire time. The countdown brought her back to reality, out of her trance. She wondered why in the world she had agreed to do this interview.

"Three, two, one..."

"Good morning," McManus said into the camera, her entire face transformed into a friendly smile. "We have a special guest with us today on *Good Morning Omaha*. Christine Hamilton is the reporter for the *Omaha Journal* who has been covering the Sarpy County serial killings. Good morning, Christine." McManus acknowledged Christine for the first time.

"Good morning." Suddenly, lights and cameras were real and all focused on her. Christine tried not to think about it. Ramsey had told her earlier that even ABC's network news would be broadcasting the segment live. That was, no doubt, why McManus was here instead of the show's regular host.

"I understand that this morning you're joining us not as a reporter, but now as a concerned mother. Can you tell us about that, Christine?"

She was intrigued by McManus, the convincing concern manufactured at a moment's notice. Christine remembered that McManus's career began as a Miss America, which spiraled her to broadcast news, skipping the field reporting and landing top anchor positions in medium-size markets like Omaha. Christine had to admit, the woman was good. Even as she appeared to be looking at Christine with that genuine, contrived concern, her eyes actually looked just over Christine's shoulder to the Tele-PrompTer. Suddenly, Christine realized McManus was waiting for her response, the impatience starting to reveal itself in the pursed lips.

"We think that my son, Timmy, may have been taken yesterday afternoon." Despite all the distractions, her lip quivered, and Christine resisted the urge to bite down and stop it.

"Oh, how awful." McManus leaned forward and patted Christine's folded hands, missing on the third pat and touching her knee instead. McManus snatched her hand back, and Christine wanted to turn to see if the TelePrompTer included gestures. "And the authorities think it's the same man who brutally murdered Danny Alverez and Matthew Tanner?"

"We don't know that for sure, but yes, there's a good possibility."

"You're divorced and raising Timmy all by yourself, aren't you, Christine?"

The question surprised her. "Yes, I am."

"Both Laura Alverez and Michelle Tanner were single mothers, as well, isn't that right?"

"Yes, I believe it is."

"Do you think perhaps the killer is trying to say something by choosing boys who are being raised by their mothers?"

Christine hesitated. "I have no idea."

"Is your husband involved in raising Timmy?"

"Not very much, no." She restricted the impatience to her hands wringing in her lap.

"Isn't it true that you and Timmy haven't seen your husband since he left you for another woman?"

"He didn't leave me. We got a divorce." The impatience bordered on anger. How would any of this help find Timmy?

"Is it possible your husband may have taken Timmy?"

"I don't think so."

"You don't think so, but there may be a possibility, isn't there?"

"It's unlikely." The lights seemed brighter, scorching hot. A trickle of perspiration ran down her back.

"Has the sheriff's department contacted your ex-husband?"

"Of course we would contact him if we knew how or where to... Look, don't you think I would much rather believe that

Timmy is with his father than with some madman who carves up little boys?''

"You're upset. Perhaps we should take a few minutes." McManus leaned forward again, her brow creased with concern, but this time her hands reached over and poured a glass of water. "We all understand how difficult this must be for you, Christine." She handed her the glass.

"No, you don't." Christine ignored the offer, and McManus became flustered.

"Excuse me?"

"You can't possibly understand. Even I didn't understand. I just wanted the story, like you."

McManus looked around for the stage director, trying to appear casual while frustration clouded her cool exterior. The thin painted lips were pursed tightly over white, even teeth.

"I'm sure you're under a lot of stress, Christine. And this must also be stressful. Let's take a commercial break and give you a chance to pull yourself together."

McManus kept the smile until the camera lights dimmed and the stage director motioned to her. Then the anger erupted on her face with a scowl that cut new lines in her makeup. But the anger was directed at the tall, bald man and not Christine. In fact, Christine became invisible again.

"Where the hell are we going with this? I need something I can work with."

"Do I have time to go to the rest room?" Christine asked the stage director, and he nodded. She unsnapped the microphone and laid it next to the rejected glass of water.

McManus looked up at her and manufactured a curt smile.

"Don't take too long, honey. This isn't like your newspaper. We can't just stop the presses. We're live." She reached for the glass and drank in delicate sips so as not to mess up her lipstick.

Christine wondered if McManus even knew Timmy's name without the help of the TelePrompTer. The high-priced anchor didn't care about Timmy or Danny or Matthew. Dear God, how close had she come to being just like Darcy McManus?

Christine made her way backstage, carefully avoiding and stepping over all the cables and cords. As soon as she was out of the bright lights, her body felt a rush of cool air. She could breathe again. She marched down the narrow hallway, dodging stagehands and finding her way past the dressing rooms, past the rest rooms and, finally, escaping out the gray metal door marked Exit.

CHAPTER 66

"**A**m I under arrest?" Ray Howard wanted to know while fidgeting in the hard-backed chair.

Maggie stared at him. His pasty complexion made his eyes bulge out—eyes a dull, watery gray with red veins telegraphing his exhaustion. She rubbed her own exhaustion from the back of her neck. A tight knot pinched the muscles between her shoulders. She tried to remember when she had slept last.

The small conference room hummed with the percolating of fresh coffee, filling the room with its aroma. A stream of orange sunset seeped in through the dusted blinds. She and Nick had been here for hours, asking the same questions and getting the same answers. Even though she'd insisted they bring Howard in for questioning, she still believed he wasn't the killer. Nothing had changed, but she hoped he might know something, anything, and break under pressure. Nick, however, persisted, convinced Howard was their man.

"No, Ray. You're not under arrest," Nick finally answered.

"You can only hold me here for a certain number of hours."

"And how do you know that, Ray?"

"Hey, I watch *Homicide* and *NYPD Blue*. I know my rights. And I have a friend who's a cop."

"Really? You have a friend?"

"Nick," Maggie cautioned.

Nick rolled his eyes and pushed up the sleeves of his shirt. She noticed his clenched fists, his impatience boiling close to the surface.

"Ray, would you like some of this fresh coffee?" she asked politely. The well-dressed janitor hesitated, then nodded.

"I use cream and two teaspoons of sugar. Real cream. If you have it. And I prefer not using those little sugar cubes."

"How about something to eat. I know we kept you over lunch, and it's almost dinnertime. Nick, perhaps you could order all of us something from Wanda's."

Nick scowled at her from across the room, but Howard sat up, delighted.

"I love Wanda's chicken-fried steak."

"Great. Nick, would you please order Mr. Howard a chicken-fried steak?"

"With mashed potatoes and brown gravy, not the white. And I like creamy Italian dressing for my salad. But on the side."

"Anything else?" Nick didn't bother to hide his impatience or his sarcasm. Howard shrunk back into the chair.

"No, nothing else."

"And what for you, Agent O'Dell?" He shot her a look of contempt clouded with frustration.

"A ham and cheese sandwich. I believe you know how I like it." She smiled at him, pleased when his dark bristled jaw relaxed and his eyes softened.

"Yes, I do." It was obvious the memory immediately replaced the sarcasm and frustration. "I'll be right back."

She set a steaming mug of coffee in front of Howard, then paced the length of the room, waiting for him to relax. She flipped on the overhead lights. The fluorescents flooded the room, making him blink. He reminded her of a lizard with slow deliberate blinks while he tested the hot coffee with a long pointed tongue. He was listening to the noises of the sheriff's department. Though the walls muffled the activity, it was easy to hear footsteps scurrying, phones ringing and an occasional voice raised above the hum.

Just when she knew he had forgotten her presence, she stood behind him and said, "You know where Timmy Hamilton is, don't you, Ray?"

He stopped slurping. His back straightened, ready to defend himself again.

"No, I don't. And I don't know how that phone got in my drawer. I've never seen it before."

She came around the table and sat down directly across from him. The blinking lizard eyes tried to avoid hers and finally settled on her chin. There was a glance to her breasts. Quickly he looked back up, but not quick enough to stop the red from crawling up his otherwise white neck.

"Sheriff Morrelli thinks you killed Danny Alverez and Matthew Tanner."

"I didn't kill nobody," he blurted.

"See, I believe you, Ray."

He looked surprised and checked her eyes to see if it was a trick. "You do?"

"I don't think you killed those boys."

"Good, 'cause I didn't."

"But I think you know more than you're telling us. I think you know where Timmy is."

He didn't protest, but his eyes darted around the room—the lizard looking for an escape. He held the hot mug with both hands, and Maggie noticed the short, stubby fingers with chewed-off nails, some down to the quick. They certainly didn't look like the hands of a man obsessed with cleanliness.

"If you tell us, we can help you, Ray. But if we find out you knew and didn't tell us, well, you could end up going to jail for a long time, even if you didn't kill those boys."

His head cocked to one side. He was listening again to the activity on the other side of the door, perhaps listening for Nick's return or maybe for someone to rescue him.

"Where's Timmy, Ray?"

He brought a hand in front of his face, inspected the fingers then began biting and peeling what was left of his fingernails.

"Ray?"

"I don't know where any kid is!" he yelled, holding the anger behind clenched, yellow teeth. "And just because I drive the pickup sometimes to cut wood doesn't mean nothing."

Maggie dragged her fingers through her hair. The lack of sleep and food made her light-headed. Had they just wasted an afternoon? Keller could easily have hidden the cellular phone in Howard's room. Yet, Maggie couldn't imagine anything happening at the rectory without Howard making it his business to know.

"Where do you go to cut wood, Ray?"

He stared at her, still sucking on his fingertips. He was trying to figure out why she wanted to know.

"I've seen the fireplace in the rectory," she continued. "It looks like it would take a ton of wood over the winter, especially starting this early."

"Yeah, it does. And Father Francis likes..." He stopped and looked down at the floor. "God rest his soul," he muttered to his feet, then looked up again. "He liked it really warm in that room."

"So where do you go?"

"Out by the river. The church still owns a piece of property. Out where the old St. Margaret's is. It was a beautiful little church. It's falling apart now. I get lots of dried-out elm and walnut. Some oak. There's tons of river maples. The walnut burns the best." He stopped and stared out the window.

Maggie followed his empty gaze. The sun sank behind the snow-covered horizon, blood-red against the white. Cutting wood had reminded him of something, but what?

Yes, Ray Howard knew much more than he was letting on, and neither the threat of jail nor the promise of Wanda's chicken-fried steak would get him to talk. They were going to have to let him go.

CHAPTER 67

Nick hung up the phone and sat back in his office chair, rubbing the sting of anger from his eyes. He realized that Maggie must have seen how badly he wanted to hit something, maybe even Ray Howard. How could she remain so cool and calm?

He couldn't stop thinking about Timmy. He felt as though a time bomb had been planted inside his ribs, the ticking getting faster and faster, drumming against his chest. The ache was unbearable. It didn't help matters that he couldn't erase the image of Danny Alverez. That small body lying in the grass. Those vacant eyes staring up at the stars. He had looked so peaceful. That is if you didn't notice the red-raw slash under his chin and gouges in his small, white chest.

They were running out of time.

Aaron Harper and Eric Paltrow had been murdered less than two weeks apart. Matthew Tanner was taken exactly a week after Danny Alverez. It was only several days since Matthew, and now Timmy. The timetable grew shorter. Something was making the killer explode, sending him over the edge. And if they didn't catch him, would he simply disappear again for six years? Or worse, would he melt into the woodwork of the community just as he had before? If it wasn't Howard or Keller, who the hell was it?

Nick grabbed the crumpled paper from his desktop. The obscure schedule he had found in the pickup's glove compartment had a strange grocery list scrawled on the back. He scanned the items one more time, trying to make sense of them: wool blanket, kerosene, matches, oranges, Snickers bars, SpaghettiOs, rat poison. Perhaps it was a simple camping-trip list, yet something told Nick it was more.

There was a knock on the door, and Hal came in without waiting for an invitation. The big shoulders slumped from exhaustion. His normally well-groomed hair stuck to his head from too many hours stuffed in his hat. His shirt collar was unbuttoned and his coffee-stained tie was twisted loose and at an odd angle.

"What do you have, Hal?"

He sank into the chair opposite Nick on the other side of the desk. "The empty glass vial you found in the pickup contained ether."

"Ether? Where in the world did it come from?"

"More than likely the hospital. I checked with the director, and he said they have similar vials down in the morgue. They use it as some sort of solvent, but it could be used to knock someone out. All it takes is a couple whiffs."

"Who would have access to the morgue?"

"Anyone, really. They don't lock the door."

"You're kidding?"

"Think about it, Nick. The morgue's hardly ever used, and when it is, who's gonna want to mess around down there?"

"When there's a criminal investigation, it should be locked, with only authorized personnel allowed in." Nick grabbed a pen and started tapping out his anger. The desire to hit something still raged inside him.

Hal didn't respond, and when Nick glanced up at him he wondered if even Hal thought he was losing it. "Were you able to get any prints off the vial?"

"Just yours."

"What about the matchbook?"

"Well, it's not a strip joint. Get this—the Pink Lady is a small bar and grill in downtown Omaha, about a block from the police station. Evidently a lot of police officers hang out there. Eddie says they serve the best burgers in town."

"Eddie?"

"Yeah, Gillick was with the OPD before he moved here. I thought you knew that. 'Course, it's been a while…six or seven years now."

"I don't trust him," Nick blurted out, then regretted it as soon as he saw Hal's face.

"Eddie? Why in the world wouldn't you trust Eddie?"

"I don't know. Forget I said anything."

Hal shook his head and pushed himself out of the chair. He started for the door then turned back as if he had forgotten something.

"You know, Nick, I don't want you to take this the wrong way, but there's a lot of people in this department who feel the same way about you."

"What way is that?" Nick sat up. The tapping stopped.

"You have to admit, the only reason you got this job is because of your dad. What experience do you have in law enforcement? Look, Nick, I'm your friend, and I'm with you every step of the way. But I have to tell you, some of the guys aren't too sure. They think you're letting O'Dell run the show."

There it was—the slap he had been expecting for days. He wiped a hand across his jaw as if to erase the sting.

"I guess I figured as much, especially since my dad seems to be running his own investigation."

"That's another thing. Did you know he has Eddie and Lloyd tracking down this Mark Rydell guy?"

"Rydell? Who the hell's Rydell?"

"I think he was a friend or partner of Jeffreys'."

"Jesus. Doesn't anybody get it? Jeffreys didn't kill all three—" He stopped when he saw Christine standing in the doorway.

"Relax, Nick. I'm not here as a reporter." She hesitated, then came in. Her hair was a tangled mess, her eyes red, her face tearstained, her trench coat unevenly buttoned. She looked like hell.

"I need to do something. You have to let me help."

"Can I get you some coffee, Christine?" Hal asked.

"Yes, thanks. That would be nice."

Hal glanced back at Nick as if looking to be excused, then left.

"Come, sit down," Nick said, resisting the urge to go to her and help her walk across the room. It unnerved him to see her this way. She was his big sister. He was the one always screwing up. She was the one who always held it together. Even when

Bruce left. Now she reminded him of Laura Alverez—that unsettling quiet.

"Corby gave me a temporary leave of absence with pay from the newspaper. Of course, that was only after he made sure *The Journal* would have the exclusive on whatever happens."

She struggled out of her coat, tossing it carelessly onto a chair in the corner and only staring at it when it slid to the floor. Then she paced in front of his desk, though she didn't seem to have the energy to even stand.

"Any luck tracking down Bruce?" She avoided his eyes, but he already knew it was a touchy subject that his sister had no clue as to where her ex-husband was.

"Not yet, but maybe he'll hear about Timmy on the news and get in touch with us."

She grimaced. "I need to do something, Nick. I can't just sit at home and wait. What are you doing with that?" She pointed at the grocery list of items, which he'd turned over so that the strange schedule with its bizarre codes faced up.

"You know what this is?"

"Sure, it's a bundle label."

"A what?"

"A bundle label. The carriers get one each day with their newspapers. See, it shows the route number, the carrier's code number, how many papers there are to deliver, what inserts—if any—and the starts and stops."

Nick jumped out of his chair and came around to her side of the desk.

"Can you tell whose it is and what day it's for?"

"It looks like it was for Sunday, October 19. The carrier's code is ALV0436. From the addresses listed on the starts and stops, it looks like…" The realization swept over her face. She looked up at Nick with wide eyes. "This is Danny Alverez's route. It's for the Sunday he disappeared. Where did you find this, Nick?"

CHAPTER 68

When darkness came, it came quickly. Despite Timmy's efforts to remain calm, the inevitable prospect of the long, dark night ahead destroyed his defenses.

He had spent the day trying to come up with an escape plan or at least a way to send a distress signal. It certainly wasn't as easy as they made it look in the movies. Still, that helped him stay focused. He thought of Batman and Luke Skywalker. And Han Solo, who was his favorite.

The stranger had brought him *Flash Gordon* and *Superman* comic books. Yet, even equipped with the knowledge and secrets of all those superheroes, Timmy still couldn't escape. After all, he was a small, skinny ten year old. But on the soccer field, he had learned to use his smallness to his advantage, sneaking under and through other players. Maybe strength wasn't what he needed.

It was too hard to think with the dark swallowing up corners of the room. He could see that the lantern had very little kerosene left, so he needed to hold off lighting it for as long as possible. But already the panic crawled over him in shivers.

He considered the kerosene heater. Perhaps he could drain kerosene from it for the lantern. Gusts of wind still knocked at the boarded window, rattling slats and sneaking through the cracks. Without the heater he might freeze before morning. No, as much as he hated to admit it, he needed the heater more than he needed the light.

He replayed scenes from *Star Wars* in his mind, repeating

dialogue out loud to keep himself occupied. He squeezed the lighter, reminding himself that he did have control over the darkness. Every once in a while he flicked it on and off, on and off. But the darkness wasn't the only enemy. The silence was almost as unsettling.

All day he forced himself to listen for voices, for barking dogs or car engines, for church bells or emergency sirens. Other than a distant train whistle and one jet overhead, he had heard nothing. Where in the world was he?

He had even tried yelling until his throat hurt, only to be answered by violent gusts of wind, scolding him. It was much too quiet. Wherever he was, he had the feeling it was far, far away from anyone who could help him.

Something skidded across the floor, a *click-click* of tiny nails on the wood. His heart pounded and the shivering took over. He flicked on the lighter, but couldn't see anything. Finally, he gave in. Without leaving the bed, he reached over to the crate and lit the lantern. Immediately its yellow glow filled the room. He should have felt relief. Instead, he curled up again into a tight ball, pulling the covers to his chin. And for the first time since his dad had left town, Timmy allowed himself to cry.

CHAPTER 69

She was smart, despite all the curves. Definitely a worthy adversary. But he wondered how much Special Agent Maggie O'Dell really knew and how much was just a game. It didn't matter. He enjoyed games. They took his mind off the throbbing.

No one noticed him as he walked down the sterile hallways. Those who did, nodded and scurried past. His presence was accepted here as easily as anywhere in the community. He fit in, though it was here—out in the open—that he wore another mask, one he couldn't just peel off like rubber.

He took the stairs. Today even the stairwells smelled of ammonia, immaculately scrubbed. It reminded him of his mother, down on her lovely hands and knees, quietly scrubbing the kitchen floor, often at two and three in the morning, while his stepfather had slept. Her delicate hands had turned red and raw from the pressure and harsh liquid. How many times had he silently watched without her knowing? Those stifled sobs and frantic swipes had been spent as though her secret early-morning ritual would somehow clean up the mess she had made of her life.

Now, here he was, so many years later, trying to clean up his own life, scrubbing out the visions of his past with his own secret rituals. How many more killings would be enough to wipe out the image of that sniveling, helpless boy from his childhood?

The door slammed shut behind him. He had been here before and found comfort in the familiar surroundings. Somewhere above, a fan wheezed. Otherwise there was silence, appropriate silence for this temporary tomb.

He snapped on the surgical gloves. Which will it be? Drawer number one, two or three? Perhaps four or five? He chose number three, pulling and wincing at the scrape of metal, but pleased to see he had been correct.

The black body bag looked so small on the long silver bed. He unzipped it carefully, reverently, tucking and folding it to the sides of the small gray body. The coroner's surgical wounds—precise slices and cuts—disgusted him, as did the puncture marks he, himself, had administered. Matthew's poor, little body resembled a road map. Matthew, however, was gone—to a much better place. Someplace free of pain and humiliation. Free of loneliness and abandonment. Yes, he had seen to it that Matthew's eternal rest would be peaceful. He could remain an innocent child forever.

He pulled on rubber gloves and unwrapped the fillet knife, setting it to the side. He needed to destroy the one piece of evidence that could link him to the murders. How careless he had been. How insanely stupid. Maybe it was even too late, but if that were true, Maggie O'Dell would now be reading him his rights.

He unzipped the body bag farther until he could examine Matthew's small legs. Yes, there it was on the thigh, the purple teeth marks. The result of the demon's rage inside him. Shame burned down into his stomach, liquid and hot. He moved the boy's leg and picked up the knife.

Somewhere outside the room and down the hall a door slammed. His hands stopped. He held his breath. He listened. Rubber-soled footsteps squeak-squawked, squeak-squawked—closer and closer, until they were right outside the door. They hesitated. He waited, the fillet knife clutched tightly in his gloved hand. How would he explain this? It could be awkward. It might be possible, but awkward.

Just as he was certain his lungs would burst, the squeak-squawk began again, passing the door. He waited for the footsteps to reach the end of the hall. He waited for the slam of the door, and then he drew in air, a generous gulp laced with enough ammonia to sting his nostrils. The powder inside the gloves caked to his sweaty palms, making them itch. A trickle of sweat slid down his back. He waited for it, anxious to feel it slither down into his underpants. Then ashamed when the thrill left him.

Yes, he was getting reckless. It was becoming harder and harder to clean up after himself, to stifle that hideous demon that sometimes got in the way of his mission. Even now, as he gripped the knife, he couldn't bring himself to cut. His hand shook. Sweat dripped from his forehead into his eyes. But soon it would be over.

Soon, Sheriff Nick Morrelli would have his prime suspect. He had already made sure of that, laying the groundwork and planting enough evidence, just enough clues. He was getting good at it. And it was so easy, exactly as it had been with Ronald Jeffreys. All it had taken with Jeffreys was an assortment of items in Jeffreys' trunk and an anonymous phone call to the super-sheriff, Antonio Morrelli. But he had been reckless even then, including Eric Paltrow's underpants in Jeffreys' treasure chest of incriminating items.

He had always taken each boy's underpants for his own souvenir, but with Eric, he had forgotten. It had been easy to retrieve them from the morgue. His mistake, however, had been including Eric's and not Aaron's underpants among the items he had planted in Jeffreys' trunk. Curiously, he had never known if his blunder had gone unnoticed or if the great and powerful Antonio Morrelli simply chose to ignore it. But he would not chance it this time. He would not be reckless. And soon, he would be able to put the throbbing to a stop, maybe for good. Just a few loose ends to tie up and one more lost boy to save. Then his demons could rest.

Yes, poor Timmy would finally be saved. So many bruises—he could only imagine what the boy had to endure at the hands of those who claimed to love him. And he did like the boy, but then, he had liked them all, chosen them carefully and saved each and every one of them. Delivered them from evil.

CHAPTER 70

Christine pushed the copier button and watched Timmy's toothy grin slide out into the tray. He'd hate that she was using last year's school photo. The one with his collar twisted and his cowlick sticking straight up. It was one of her favorites. Suddenly, it struck her how much younger he looked in the photo. Would anyone even recognize him? He had changed so much in one short year.

She set the counter and pushed the button again, watching a succession of the toothy grins slide one over another. Behind her, the sheriff's department rumbled and vibrated with mumbling voices, shuffling shoes and clicking machines. Despite her chore, she felt isolated, invisible. She wondered if the task simply kept her out of Nick's way. He insisted the more photos they got out to the news media and store owners, the better chance of triggering someone's memory. It was a far cry from the way he had treated the Danny Alverez case. But then, maybe they had all learned lessons, expensive lessons. Walking out of this morning's interview would cost her the high-priced TV job. But she didn't care. Right now, Christine couldn't care about anything but Timmy.

She felt him standing behind her. It came in a disturbing chill as if he had slipped an ice cube down her back. She turned slowly just as Eddie Gillick pressed in close against her, trapping her between the copy machine and his body. Sweat beads gathered on his lip above the thin mustache. He was breathing hard as

though he had just come in running. The smell of his aftershave
lotion assaulted her as his eyes traveled the length of her body.

"Excuse me, Christine. I just need to make a couple of copies
of these photos." He flashed them at her. When she only glanced,
he held them up to her, slowly shuffling them one after another.
Glossy eight-by-tens, the brilliant color emphasized the red
gashes. A close-up of skin peeled back. A throat slashed. And
Matthew Tanner's pale face, his glassy eyes staring out at her.

Christine squeezed past, scraping her shin on the copy machine's stand in order to escape Eddie Gillick. He watched, smiling at her as she bumped into a state trooper, smashed a knee
into a desk and finally made it across the room. Safe in the corner
next to the watercooler, she leaned against the wall and stared
out at the chaos. Were they all moving in slow motion or was it
just her imagination? Even the voices sounded slow, all melting
together into one low baritone. And that ringing, that constant
high-pitched ringing. Was it a phone? Maybe a siren or a fire
alarm? Shouldn't they be concerned? Couldn't someone stop the
noise? Couldn't they hear it?

"Christine?"

She heard her name being called from another dimension, far
away. She pressed her body against the wall, clinging to the
smooth cool texture while the room moved. A slight tip to one
side. No one else seemed to notice. Then a slight tip to the other
side.

"Christine, are you okay?"

Lucy Burton's face appeared in front of her, the heart-shaped
face oversize with wide eyes bulging like in one of those grocery-
store mirrors. Only there were no mirrors. Lucy was saying
something to her again. The brightly painted lips moved but emit-
ted no sound. Where was the remote control? She needed to turn
up Lucy Burton's volume.

The hands came at her from nowhere, clutching at her, grabbing for her. She batted them away, but they came again. She
couldn't breathe. She needed water. The watercooler was next to
her just to her left, several miles away, far in the distance. She
slapped at the hands again.

"No, I can't hear you, Lucy," she said, and realized her words
were confined to her thoughts.

She felt her body sliding down the wall. She couldn't catch it, had lost control of her own body as it, too, moved in slow motion. So many feet, scuffed shoes, red toenails, a pair of cowboy boots. Then someone shut off the lights.

CHAPTER 71

Nick came out of his office just in time to see a crowd gathered around the watercooler. He saw Christine slumped on the floor. Lucy fanned her with a file folder, while Hal held her up against his shoulder. Nick's father looked on with the rest, his hands deep in his pockets. Nick heard the irritation in his father's jingling pocket change. He recognized the taut jaw and rigid stance. Nick knew what he was thinking. How dare Christine show such weakness in front of his colleagues.

"What happened?" Nick asked Eddie Gillick at the copy machine.

"Don't know. Didn't see it happen," Eddie said as he pressed the copier's buttons, his back turned to the commotion.

It occurred to Nick that Eddie was the only one on this side of the room. He glanced down at the copies spitting out into the tray and watched pieces of Matthew Tanner cover Timmy's smiling face. Maybe asking Christine to make copies of her missing son's face was too much.

"You have the autopsy photos," he said, keeping his eyes on Christine.

"Yeah, just picked them up from the hospital morgue. I knew you'd be wanting copies."

"Great. Put the originals on my desk when you're finished."

At least Christine looked conscious now. Adam Preston handed her a paper cup, and she gulped water as if they had pulled her out of the desert. Nick watched from across the room, paralyzed, helpless. The ticking in his chest drummed harder than ever. He glanced at Eddie. Could he hear the ticking?

"Okay, everybody," his father announced. "Show's over. Let's get back to work."

Without hesitation they followed his orders. When he saw Nick, he waved him over. Nick stood firm, a last-ditch effort to gain back a shred of authority. His father signed something for Lloyd, then wandered over, completely oblivious to Nick's defiance.

"Lloyd's found Rydell. We're bringing him in for questioning."

"You have no authority to do that." Nick concentrated. He needed to sound calm, cool, in-charge.

His bushy eyebrows raised as he stared at Nick. "Excuse me?"

His father had heard perfectly well. It was part of his intimidation. It had always worked...in the past.

"You no longer have the authority to bring anyone in for questioning." He met his father's narrowed eyes.

"I'm trying to help you, boy, so you don't look like a fucking idiot to the whole goddamn community."

"Mark Rydell had nothing to do with any of this."

"Right. You're placing your money on some gimpy church janitor."

"I have evidence that implicates Ray Howard. What do you have on Rydell?"

By now the office had come to a standstill again. Only this time no one dared gather around them. Instead, they quietly watched from doorways and behind desks, pretending to go about their work.

"Rydell's a known fag. Has a rap sheet as long as my arm for beating up other fags. He was Jeffreys' fag for a while. I was never convinced that he wasn't in on the whole thing with Jeffreys. I'd bet the farm that he's your copycat killer. Only you can't see it 'cause you can't see beyond Agent Maggie's cute little ass."

The heat crawled up Nick's neck. His father turned away from him, finished, dismissing him in his usual manner. Nick glanced around at the eyes pretending to work. Then he saw Maggie in the doorway to the conference room. His eyes met hers. In an instant, he knew she had heard.

"This isn't a copycat killer," he said to his father's back.

"What the fuck are you talking about now?"

He only glanced at Nick over his shoulder. He took the set of autopsy photos from Eddie, who willingly handed over the originals without even looking in Nick's direction.

"Jeffreys was only responsible for Bobby Wilson's death." His father didn't look up from the photos. "He didn't kill all three boys. But then, you already knew that." Nick waited for the implication to sink in, for it to register as the accusation he meant it to be.

Finally, his father looked at him with the scowl usually powerful enough to transform him into a sniveling teenager. Nick stood straight, keeping his hands from hiding in his pockets. Instead, he crossed his arms over his chest. He was ready.

"What the fuck are you implying?"

"I've read Jeffreys' arrest file. I've seen all the autopsy reports. There's no way in hell Jeffrey committed all three murders. Even Jeffreys told you that, over and over again."

"Oh, so now you believe a goddamn murdering fag over your own father?"

"Your own reports prove Jeffreys didn't kill the other two boys. Only you were too blind. No, you wanted to be a hero. So you ignored the truth and let a killer get away. Or maybe you even helped plant the evidence. Now your own grandson's going to pay the price for your mistakes and your fucking pride."

The fist took Nick completely off guard. It slammed into his jaw and knocked him back into the copy machine. He caught his balance, but his vision was still blurred when the second fist slammed into his face. He looked up to see his father in the same place, same stance, photos still in his hands, a look of surprise on his face. Nick didn't even realize it wasn't his father's fists that had hit him until he saw Hal restraining Eddie Gillick.

CHAPTER 72

Maggie waited but wasn't surprised when Nick didn't come back to their makeshift interrogation room. Adam Preston delivered dinner from Wanda's. She told Ray Howard he was welcome to stay and eat his steak, then he was free to go. He eyed her suspiciously until Adam placed the steaming plate in front of him. Then all seemed to be forgotten.

She started to leave while Adam unpacked and laid out the rest of the food.

"Agent O'Dell, this is for you."

"I'm not very hungry." She turned to him, but it wasn't a sandwich he handed her. She stared at the small, white envelope from across the table. "Where did you get that?"

"It was in the order from Wanda's. It has your name on it." He held it out to her, his arm stretched over the table, but she made no attempt to take it. Even Howard looked up at her from his banquet.

"Agent O'Dell? What is it? Do you want me to open it?" Adam's green eyes were serious. His boyish face concerned.

"No, I'll take it." She slowly grabbed a corner, pretending—though it was too late—that it was no big deal. To prove it, she opened it without hesitation while Adam watched. Her fingers were amazingly steady though her stomach did acrobatic flips.

She read the note. It was simple, only one line: "I KNOW ABOUT STUCKY."

She glanced up at Adam.

"Is Nick around?" She needed to keep her breathing even and

steady. She needed to contain the crawly things invading her insides.

"No one's seen him since..."

"Since Eddie decked him," Howard finished for Adam. He smiled up at them over a forkful of mashed potatoes. "Eddie's my man," he said, then stuffed his mouth.

"What do you mean by that?" Maggie snapped at him, and Howard's look told her it was too much, too shrill. She needed to be careful, but it was too late. She had set him on edge again.

"Nothin'. He's just a friend."

"Deputy Gillick is a friend of yours?" She looked at Adam who simply shrugged.

"Yeah, he's a friend. There ain't no crime in that, is there? We do stuff together. It's no big deal."

"What kind of stuff?"

Howard looked from her to Adam. His hands had stopped cutting and scooping. His back straightened. When he looked back at Maggie, she saw the cold defiance.

"Sometimes he comes over to the rectory and plays cards with Father Keller and me. Sometimes just him and me go out for burgers."

"You and Deputy Gillick?"

"Didn't you say I was free to go?"

She stared him down. She was right. Those clever, reptilian eyes did know more, much more. Deep down, she knew he wasn't the killer, despite Nick's hunches. Howard may have been unfortunate enough to be in possession of her cellular phone, but Ray Howard was not the killer. His limp would never allow him to maneuver the steep woods along the river, let alone carry a sixty- to seventy-pound boy. And despite his smart remarks, he simply wasn't smart enough to carry off a series of killings.

"Yes, I did say you were free to leave," she finally answered without breaking his gaze. She wanted him to see the suspicion. She wanted him to slip up, sweat a little. Instead, he ignored her and went back to scraping great globs of food onto his fork, anchoring it with his knife and stuffing his mouth full before he started to chew.

She gestured to Adam, and he followed her out. Safely down the hall, she stopped and leaned against the wall, holding herself up from the exhaustion. Adam waited patiently with quick glances in both directions, although making sure no one saw him alone with her. He was too young to be a leftover of Antonio Morrelli's regime, though he, too, seemed anxious to please, anxious to be a part of the group. Still, his respect for authority extended to Maggie, and his tall, thin frame slouched, ready to listen.

"You grew up in Platte City, right?"

The question surprised him. Of course, it would. He nodded, anyway.

"What can you tell me about the old church, the one in the country?"

"We checked it out, if that's what you mean. Lloyd and I went out there before the snow and then again after. The place is boarded up. Didn't look like anyone's been in there for years. No footprints, no tire tracks."

"It's close to the river?"

"Yeah, just off Old Church Road—guess that's probably where it gets its name. The church is listed as an historical landmark. That's why no one's torn it down."

"How do you know all of that?" She pretended to be interested, though its location was really all she needed to know. If Howard went there to cut wood, perhaps he had seen something close by. She rubbed the knot in her neck, squeezing and applying pressure. Exhaustion clouded her thoughts. Or maybe she just didn't want to think anymore.

"My dad owns land close by," Adam continued. "He wanted to buy the church property, tear down the building. It's prime farmland. Father Keller told him it couldn't be torn down on account of it's registered as an historical landmark. I guess it was used as part of John Brown's Underground Railroad in the 1860s. Supposedly there's a tunnel from the church to the graveyard."

Maggie stood up, suddenly interested.

Adam seemed pleased.

"They hid runaway slaves in the church. At night they used the tunnel to sneak them to the river where a boat would take them upstream to the next hideout. There's an old church down by Nebraska City that was used, too. They've made that one into quite the tourist trap. This one's too deteriorated. They say the tunnel's all caved in—too close to the river. They don't even use the graveyard anymore. A few years ago when the river flooded, it uprooted some graves. Even sent a few coffins floating down the river once. That was kind of a creepy sight.''

Maggie imagined the deserted graveyard and the swift river current sucking corpses from their graves. Suddenly, it sounded like the perfect place for a killer obsessed with his victims' salvation.

CHAPTER 73

Maggie decided to leave Nick a note, though she had no clue what to say.

"Dear Nick, went off to find the killer in a graveyard." It sounded bizarre, but it would be more than what she had left before she ran off to find Albert Stucky. Except that night, she hadn't intended to really find Stucky. She had simply been checking a lead. Had hoped to find his hiding place. That he would be waiting for her, setting a trap for her, had never occurred to her until it was too late. Could that be what this killer was doing? Setting a trap and waiting for her to walk right into it?

"I think Nick's gone," Lucy announced from down the hall, catching Maggie with her hand on the knob of his office door.

"I know, I'm just leaving him a note."

Lucy didn't look satisfied, her hands planted firmly on her hips as if expecting more of an explanation. When Maggie didn't offer her one, she added, "There was a call for you earlier from the archdiocese's office."

"Any message?" Maggie had spoken to a Brother Jonathon, who assured her the church did not believe Father Francis' death to be anything criminal nor anything more than an unfortunate accident.

"Hold on." Lucy sighed and riffled through a stack of messages. "Here it is. Brother Jonathon said Father Francis has no living relatives. The church will be making all the burial arrangements."

"No mention of allowing us an autopsy?"

Lucy looked up at her, surprised. Maggie no longer cared.

"I took the message myself," Lucy said softly, now almost sympathetically, understanding what the need for an autopsy implied. "That's all he said."

"Okay, thanks." Maggie grabbed the doorknob to Nick's office again.

"I can take your message for Nick if you want."

The sympathy was gone, quickly replaced by mere curiosity.

"Thanks, but I'll just leave it on his desk."

Maggie went in, but she left the lights off, using the glow from the streetlights below to guide her. She bumped her shin into a chair leg.

"Damn it," she muttered, reaching down to catch the pain though it already shot up her thigh. While bent over and rubbing her leg, she noticed Nick sitting on the floor in the corner. In the dark, she saw him hugging his knees to his chest, staring out the window, apparently oblivious to her presence.

It would have been easy to pretend she hadn't seen him. She could write the note and be on her way. Without a word, she walked over to him and quietly, slowly took a place beside him on the floor. She followed his gaze out the window. From this angle only the black sky filled the frame. Out of the corner of her eye she saw the cracked lip, bruised and swollen. Dried blood stained that perfectly chiseled jaw. He still didn't move, still didn't acknowledge her presence.

"You know, Morrelli, for an ex-football player you fight like a girl."

She wanted to make him angry, to make him feel. She recognized that numbness, that emptiness, that could paralyze a person for a long, long time if not confronted. There was no response. She sat quietly by his side. Minutes passed. She should get up, leave. She couldn't afford to share his pain. She couldn't risk caring about him. Her own vulnerability was already a tremendous liability. She couldn't take on his.

Just as she stretched her legs to get up, he said, "My dad was wrong to say what he did about you."

She leaned back. "You mean I don't have a cute little ass?"

Finally, she caught a hint of a smile.

"Okay, only half-wrong."

"Don't worry about it, Morrelli. I've heard worse." Though the sting always surprised her.

"You know, when all this began, the only thing I cared about was how I'd look, whether people would think I was incompetent."

He kept his gaze out the window to avoid looking at her. Her eyes had adjusted to the dark now, and she studied him. Despite the disheveled look, he was remarkably handsome with all the classic features—strong, square jaw, dark hair against tanned skin, sensuous lips, even his earlobes were perfectly sculpted. Yet, those physical characteristics that she initially found so attractive now seemed minor. It was his smooth, steady voice she looked forward to. It was his warm, sky-blue eyes that made her weak in the knees. The way they held her, as if she was the most important person in the world. The way they searched deep inside her, as if hoping for a glimpse of her soul. Those eyes made her feel naked and alive. Now that he kept them from her, she felt robbed, removed from the intimate bond that had begun forming between them. At the same time, she knew it wasn't right to feel this close to a man she had met less than a week ago. She kept quiet and waited, half dreading that he would share some secret that would bring them even closer. At the same time, part of her hoped he would.

"I'm incompetent. I don't know the first thing about heading a murder investigation. Maybe if I had admitted that in the beginning...maybe Timmy wouldn't be missing."

His confession surprised her. This wasn't the same cocky, arrogant sheriff she had met several days ago. Yet, his admission wasn't self-pity. It wasn't even regret. Instead, Maggie sensed it was a relief for him to finally say it out loud.

"You've done everything possible, Nick. Believe me, if there was something I thought you should have done or should be doing differently, I certainly would have told you. If you haven't noticed yet, I'm not shy in that area."

Another smile. He leaned back against the wall and released his knees from his chest. He stretched those long, lean legs out in front of him. For a minute she thought it was over.

"Maggie, I am so...I keep imagining finding him. I keep seeing him...lying in the grass, that same vacant stare. I've never felt so..." The strong, steady voice hitched, caught on a lump in his throat. "I feel so fucking helpless." The knees came back to his chest, brushing his chin.

Her hand went up, then stopped in midair at the nape of his neck. She wanted to comfort him, caress him. She snapped back her hand, scooted farther away and leaned against the wall, trying to get comfortable, trying to dislodge the overpowering urge to touch him. Another glance. Moonlight crept into a corner of the window, framing his profile. What was it about Nick Morrelli that made her want to be whole again? That made her realize she wasn't whole?

"You know all my life I've done everything my dad told me... suggested I do." He kept his chin on his knees. "It wasn't even so much that I wanted to please him. It was just easier. His expectations always seemed to be lower than my own. Being sheriff of Platte City was supposed to be writing tickets and rescuing lost dogs, and breaking up a few bar fights now and then. Maybe an occasional traffic accident. But not murder. I'm not prepared for murder."

"I don't know if there's anything to prepare you for the murder of a child, no matter how many dead bodies you've seen."

"Timmy can't end up like Danny and Matthew. He can't. And yet...there's nothing I can do to stop it." The catch in his voice was back. She glanced over at him, and he turned his face away. "There's not a fucking thing I can do."

She heard the tears in his voice, though he tried his best to disguise them with anger. She reached out again, hesitated again, her hand hovering. Finally, she touched his shoulder. She expected him to bolt. Instead, he sat quietly. She stroked his shoulder blades and ran her hand over his back. When the comfort started turning too intimate for her, she pulled her hand away, but he reached up and caught it, gently trapping it in his large hand. He looked up at her and brought the palm of her hand to his face, rubbing it against his swollen jaw.

"I'm glad you're here." His eyes held hers. "Maggie...I think I—"

She snatched her hand back, suddenly uncomfortable with his attempted revelation. He was beyond flirting. She could see him testing, struggling with feelings she didn't want to know about.

"Whatever happens, it won't be your fault, Nick." She changed the subject while pretending to be on it. "You're doing everything possible. At some point you have to let yourself off the hook.''

He looked at her with that deep gaze, the one that made her feel as if he was searching her soul. ''Your nightmares,'' he said quietly. ''You haven't let yourself off the hook for something. What is it, Maggie? Is it Stucky?''

CHAPTER 74

"How do you know about Stucky?" Maggie sat up, trying to ward off the tension brought on by just the mention of his name.

"That night at my house, you yelled out his name several times. I thought you'd tell me about him. When you didn't...well, I figured maybe it wasn't any of my business. Maybe it's still none of my business."

"By now it's a matter of public record."

"Public record?"

"Albert Stucky is a serial killer I helped capture a little over a month ago. We nicknamed him The Collector. He'd kidnap two, three, sometimes four women at a time, keeping them, collecting them in some condemned building or abandoned warehouse. When he got tired of them, he killed them, slicing their bodies, bashing in their skulls, chewing off pieces of them."

"Jesus, I thought this guy we're chasing was screwed up."

"Stucky is certainly one of a kind. It was my profile that identified him. Over the course of two years, we tracked him. Every time we got close, he moved to another part of the country. Somewhere along the line, Stucky discovered that I was the profiler. That's when the game began."

The moonlight flooded the office now. She glanced at him, uncomfortable under his penetrating blue eyes that were filled with as much concern as interest. He must have bitten down on his lip. It was bleeding again. She shifted, dug in her jacket pocket and pulled out a tissue, handing it to him. "You're still bleeding."

He ignored the tissue and wiped a sleeve across his mouth. "What else is new? I fight like a girl." Then his expression went serious again. "Tell me about the game."

"Stucky probed my background. Somehow he found out about my family, my father's death, my mother's alcoholism. He knew everything, or so it seemed. About a year ago I started receiving notes. Actually, it's not that unusual, but Stucky's were. He always included a piece of his victims—a finger, sometimes just a piece of skin with a birthmark or tattoo, once a nipple."

Nick shook his head but didn't say anything.

"He started a sort of scavenger hunt with me," she continued. "He'd send clues as to where he was keeping the women. If I guessed right, he rewarded me with a new clue. If I guessed wrong, he punished me with a dead body. I was wrong a lot. Every time we found one of his victims in a Dumpster, I felt like it was my fault."

She closed her eyes, allowing herself to see the faces. All of them with that same horrified stare. She could remember them all, could recite their names, addresses, personal characteristics. It sounded like a litany of saints. She opened her eyes, avoided Nick's and continued.

"He would quit for a while but only to move to another part of the country. We finally tracked him down in Miami. After a few clues I was almost certain I knew he was using an abandoned warehouse by the river. I dreaded being wrong. I didn't think I could handle another dead woman on my conscience. So I didn't tell anyone. I decided to check it out myself. That way, if I was wrong, no one ended up dead. Only, I was right, and Stucky was waiting for me. He ambushed me before I even saw it coming."

Her breathing was uneven. Her heart raced. Even her palms were sweaty. It was over. Why did it still have such an effect on her?

"He tied me to a steel post, and then he made me watch. I watched while he tortured and mutilated two women. Actually, the second one was punishment because I closed my eyes while he was bashing in the skull of the first woman. He had warned me that he would just keep bringing out another if I closed my eyes. He seemed so oblivious to their pain, to their screams."

God, it was hard to breathe. When would she stop seeing those pleading eyes, hearing those unbearable screams? "I watched him beat and slice and rip apart two women and I felt so...so goddamn helpless.''

She stared out at the moon and stars. ''I was so close...'' She rubbed her shoulders. She could still feel it. ''I was so close I could feel their blood splatter me, along with pieces of their brains, chips of their bones.''

''But you did get him?''

''Yes. We got him. Only because an old fisherman heard the screams and called 911. We certainly didn't get him on my account.''

''Maggie, you're not responsible for those women.''

''Yes, I know that.'' Of course, she knew, but it didn't erase the guilt. She wiped at her eyes, disappointed to find her cheeks already wet. Then she stood, much too abruptly but gratefully closing the subject.

''That reminds me,'' she said, trying to resume normalcy. ''I got another note.'' She dug out the crumpled envelope and handed it to Nick.

He pulled out the card, read it, and leaned back against the wall. ''Jesus, Maggie. What do you suppose this means?''

''I don't know. Maybe nothing. Maybe he's just having some fun.''

Nick untangled his legs and stood without assistance of the wall or desk. ''So what do we do now?''

''How do you feel about raiding graveyards?''

CHAPTER 75

Timmy watched the lantern's flame dance. It was amazing how such a small slit of fire could light up the entire room. And it gave off heat, too. Not like the kerosene heater, but it did feel warm. It reminded him again of the camping trips he and his dad had taken. It seemed like such a long time ago now.

His dad hadn't been an experienced camper. It had taken them almost two hours to set up the tent. The only fish they had caught were tiny throw-backs they ended up keeping when they had gotten too hungry to wait for a bigger catch. Then his dad had melted his mom's favorite pot by leaving it in the fire too long. Still, Timmy hadn't minded the mistakes. It was an adventure he got to share with his dad.

He knew his mom and dad were mad at each other. But he didn't understand why his dad was mad at him. His mom had told him his dad still loved him. That he didn't want anybody to know where he was because he didn't want to pay them any money. That still didn't explain why his dad didn't want to see him.

Timmy stared at the flame and tried to remember what his dad looked like. His mom had put away all the pictures. She said she burned them, but Timmy had seen her looking through some of them a few weeks ago. It had been late at night, when she thought Timmy was asleep. She was up drinking wine, looking at pictures of the three of them and crying. If she missed him that bad, why didn't she just ask him to come home? Sometimes Timmy didn't understand grown-ups.

He brought his hands up to the lantern's glass to feel its glow. The chain attached to his ankle clinked against the metal bedpost. Suddenly, he stared at it, remembering the metal pot his dad had ruined on the campfire. The chain links weren't thick. How hot did metal need to get to bend? He didn't need to bend it that much—a quarter of an inch at the most.

His heart raced. He grabbed the glass, but snatched his hands back from the heat. He pulled off the pillowcase and wrapped his hands, then tried again, gently tugging the glass casing off without breaking it. The flame danced some more, reared up, then settled down. He put the pillowcase back on the pillow. Then he set the lantern on the floor in front of him and lifted his leg, grabbing a length of chain close to his ankle. He let several links swoop into the flame. He waited a few minutes, then started to pull. It wasn't working. It just took time. He needed to be patient. He needed to think of something else. He kept the links in the flame. What was that song his mom was singing the other morning in the bathroom? It was from a movie. Oh yeah, *The Little Mermaid*.

"Under the sea." He tried his voice. It shook a bit from the anticipation. Yeah, that was it, anticipation, not fear. He wouldn't think about being afraid. "Under the sea... Darling it's better, down where it's wetter." He pulled on the chain again. Still no movement. It surprised him how many of the words he remembered. He tried out his Jamaican accent. "Under the sea."

It moved. The metal was giving. Or was it his imagination? He strained, pulling as hard as he could. Yes, the slit between the two links grew little by little. Just a little more, and he could slip it through.

The footsteps outside the door sent his heart plunging. No, just a few more seconds. He pulled with all his might as the locks clanked and screeched open.

CHAPTER 76

Christine tried to remember the last time she had eaten. How long had Timmy been gone? Too long. Whatever it was, it was too long. She pulled herself up off the old couch where Lucy had left her, somewhere in a back office used to store files.

The couch smelled of stale cigarettes, though it looked clean. At least, there appeared to be no hideous stains. The rough-textured fabric left an imprint on her cheek. She could feel it tattooed into her skin.

Her eyes burned. Her hair was a tangled mess. She couldn't remember when she had combed it. Or brushed her teeth, though she was certain she had done all those things before her morning interview. God, that felt like days ago.

The door opened, its squeak startling her. Her father came in carrying more water. If she drank one more glass, she would vomit. She smiled and took it from him, taking only a sip.

"Feeling better?"

"Yes, thanks. I don't think I've eaten today. I'm sure that's why I got so light-headed."

"Yep. That'll do it."

Without the glass he seemed uncertain what to do with his hands and shoved them into his pockets, a trait Christine recognized in Nick.

"Why don't I order you up some soup," he said. "Maybe a sandwich."

"No, thanks. I really don't think I could eat."

"I called your mother. She's trying to catch a flight later this evening. Hopefully, she'll be here by morning."

"Thanks. It'll be nice to have her here," Christine lied. Her mother panicked at the mention of a crisis. How would she ever handle this? She wondered what her father had told her mother. How much had he watered down?

"Now, don't get upset, pumpkin, but I also called Bruce."

"Bruce?"

"He has a right to know. Timmy is his son."

"Yes, of course, and Nick and I have been trying to contact him. You know where he is?"

"No, but I have a phone number for emergencies."

"So you've known all along how to contact him?"

Her father looked stunned. How dare she direct such shrill anger toward him.

"And you knew that I've been trying to find him to make him pay child support for over eight months. Here, all this time, you've had his phone number?"

"For emergencies, Christine."

"Seeing that his son has food on the table isn't an emergency? How could you?"

"You're exaggerating, Christine. Your mom and I would never let you and Timmy struggle. Besides, Bruce said he left you with plenty in savings."

"That's what he said?" She laughed, and she didn't care that it sounded on the verge of hysteria.

"He left us with exactly $164.21 in our savings account and over five thousand dollars of credit card bills."

She knew her father hated confrontation. She had spent a lifetime tiptoeing around the great Tony Morrelli, letting his opinions be the only ones, his feelings more important than anyone else's. Her mother called it respect. Now Christine saw it for what it was—foolish.

He paced in front of her, his hands deep in his pockets, the change noisily keeping his fingers busy.

"That son of a bitch. That's not what he told me," he finally said. "But you threw the man out of his own house, Christine."

"He was fucking his receptionist."

His face grew scarlet with disapproval. A lady never used such language.

"Sometimes a man strays, Christine. A minor indiscretion. I'm not saying it's right, but it's not a reason to throw him out of his own house."

So there it was. She had suspected his disapproval, but until now neither of her parents had spoken it. Her father's world was fraught with double standards. She had always known that, had accepted it, kept quiet about it. But this was her life.

"I wonder, would you be this forgiving if I had been the one who had the affair?"

"What? Don't be ridiculous."

"No. I want to know. Would you have called it a minor indiscretion if I had fucked the UPS man?"

He winced again, and she wondered if it was her language or the image that disgusted him. After all, Tony Morrelli's little girl didn't fuck.

"Look, you're upset, Christine. Why don't I have one of the guys drive you home?"

She didn't answer, couldn't answer over the rage boiling inside. She only nodded, and he escaped.

After a few short minutes the door opened again, and Eddie Gillick came in.

"Your dad asked me to drive you home."

CHAPTER 77

What an idiot he was, Nick thought as he rammed the Jeep into gear, picking up speed and leaving Platte City behind. He glanced at Maggie sitting quietly next to him. He should have never allowed her to see the weakness, the absolute terror that had taken control of his insides. Despite her revelation about Stucky, she remained in control and composed, staring out at the dark countryside. How did she do it? How did she keep Albert Stucky and all the other horrors carefully tucked away? How did she keep herself from slamming a fist through a wall and shattering glass doors?

He couldn't think, could barely concentrate on the dark road. The drumming continued in his chest, a persistent pounding, a time bomb ticking off the seconds, each second maybe Timmy's last.

And through the panic, and maybe because of it, he had almost gone way over the line and told Maggie that he loved her. What an idiot—what a complete idiot he was. Maybe it wasn't just his virility and charm he was losing. Hell, maybe he was losing his mind, too.

Now sitting here in the quiet dark with Maggie beside him, he felt a sudden strength. He had to be strong for Timmy's sake, and maybe, just maybe, he could do that as long as he didn't have to do it alone. Jesus, that was a first—Nick Morrelli might actually need someone?

He could ignore the sick feeling in his gut. He would put the vision of Danny Alverez's vacant eyes out of his mind. Timmy had to be okay. It couldn't be too late. He stepped on the accelerator, zigzagging the Jeep over the black highway. Wisps of snow scampered across in spots, but the wind had died down considerably.

"Maybe you should fill me in," he said, managing to keep the panic from his voice. "Why are we going to a graveyard in the middle of the night?"

"I know your men checked the old church, but what about the tunnel?"

"The tunnel? I think that caved in years ago."

"Are you sure?"

"Well, no. Actually, I've never seen it. When I was a kid we thought it was just made up. You know, to scare us, to keep us from screwing around the church at night. There were stories about bodies rising from the dead, digging out of their graves and crawling through the tunnel. Finding their way back to the church to redeem their condemned souls."

"Sounds like the perfect place for a killer who believes in redemption."

"You think that's where he's keeping Timmy? In a hole in the ground?" He remembered Maggie's story about the father who buried his son in the backyard. Again, he slammed on the accelerator, drawing a concerned look from Maggie.

"It's only a hunch," she said, but her tone told him she thought it was more. "At this point, I don't think we have anything to lose by checking it out. Ray Howard mentioned going there to cut wood. He knows something. Maybe he's seen something."

"I can't believe you let him go."

"He's not the killer, Nick. But I think he might know who is."

"You still think it's Keller, don't you?" He shot her a look, but in the dark he saw only that her face was turned away from him, staring again into the black night.

"Keller could have easily planted my cell phone in Howard's room. He had access to the pickup. He keeps those strange paintings of tortured martyrs, martyrs with the sign of the cross sliced into their chests."

"The guy has bad taste in art, that doesn't make him a killer.

Besides, anyone could have seen Keller's paintings and gotten the idea.''

"Keller also knew all three boys.''

"Actually, all five boys,'' Nick interrupted. "Lucy and Max were able to dig up lists and applications. Eric Paltrow and Aaron Harper did attend church camp the summer before they were murdered. But that means Ray Howard knew all the boys, too.''

"It's more than that, Nick. Somehow, I think this killer believes he's making these boys martyrs, saving them from something. Most serial killers murder for pleasure, for sexual gratification or to fill some other egocentric need. It's like something clicks in this guy and sends him on a mission. Father Keller fits much of that profile. Who else would administer last rites to his victims but a priest? And who else would have the perfect opportunity to push Father Francis down a flight of stairs and get away with it?''

"Jesus, Maggie. You still won't let that go?''

"Looks like I may not have a choice. The archdiocese is in charge of Father Francis' remains, since there's no next of kin, and they see no reason for an autopsy.''

There was silence between them. If Father Francis had been shoved down those stairs, Nick could imagine Howard being more than capable of doing it. But now he wondered what it was Father Francis wanted to share with Maggie.

"Maybe we've got this wrong,'' Nick said, unraveling the thought as he spoke. "Maybe Keller is involved, but maybe he's protecting someone.''

"What do you mean?''

"Father Francis couldn't tell us about Jeffreys' confession. Suppose the killer confessed to Father Keller?''

Maggie sat quietly. She was obviously mulling over the idea. Perhaps it wasn't so far-fetched, Nick realized.

Suddenly, out of the darkness, Maggie said, "Did you know Ray Howard and Eddie Gillick are friends?''

CHAPTER 78

Christine knew it was the anger that had rendered her temporarily insane. Otherwise, why would she be climbing into Eddie Gillick's rusted Chevy? Even his apology about the state of the vehicle sounded half-sincere. Yet, here she was with her feet kicking empty McDonald's containers. A spring poked into her back, and crumb-filled stuffing grew out of the cushion next to her. It smelled of French fries, cigarettes and that annoying aftershave lotion. Something smelled like the back of her refrigerator.

Eddie slid into the driver's seat, tossing his hat into the back and stealing a long glance of himself in the rearview mirror. He stuck the key in the ignition, and the loose tailpipe sent the car vibrating.

Christine wished she had changed clothes after the interview. Despite her long trench coat, it felt as if something was crawling on her bare legs. She opened her coat to make sure there weren't black bugs skittering up her thighs. As she ran a hand over one leg, she noticed Eddie watching, smiling. She pulled her coat closed and decided bugs were better than Eddie's eyes.

He gunned the engine, slamming her back into the seat. She reached up for the seat belt and saw it had been cut out. He sped past the turn to her street and a fresh panic sent her hand to the door handle. It broke off with a snap, and Eddie frowned at her.

"Relax, Christine. Your dad said I should get you something to eat."

"I'm really not hungry," she blurted quickly, the panic slipping out. "Really, I'm just tired." That was better. She couldn't let it sound as if she didn't trust him.

"I can grill you up a steak that'll make your mouth water. Just happen to have a couple in my fridge."

Oh, God. Not his place.

"Maybe another time, Eddie." She made her voice as sweet as possible, despite the revulsion. "I really am tired. Could you please just take me home?"

She watched his face out of the corner of her eye. His mustache twitched, then a crooked smile. Another glance at himself in the rearview mirror.

"You came on to me pretty strong that evening out by the river," he said.

Big mistake. How could she be so stupid? Yet, other reporters did that sort of thing all the time, didn't they?"

"Look, I'm sorry about that, Eddie." Be sincere. Don't let him see you're scared. "It was my first big assignment. I guess I was nervous."

"It's okay, Christine. I know it's been over a year since your husband left. Hell, you don't have to play shy with me. I know women get horny, too."

Oh, dear God. This was not going well. She felt sick again as she watched houses pass by. A few more blocks and they'd leave streetlights behind. They were headed out of town. Her heart raced. She was beyond playing cool and calm. She shoved her weight against the door. It didn't move. Her shoulder throbbed. Eddie scowled at her, then the scowl grew into another twisted smile, telling her it didn't matter whether or not she played along.

His eyes were coal black to match his greased-back hair. She remembered he was about her height but muscular. After all, he had knocked Nick off his feet with two lousy punches. Of course, Nick hadn't seen it coming. Something told Christine that was how Eddie operated. Attacking when his victims least expected. Like a spider.

"Eddie, please." She was not above pleading. "My son's missing. I'm really in awful shape. Please just take me home."

"I know what you need, Christine. Take your mind off things for a while. Just relax."

Her eyes darted around the car. Anything...was there anything she could use as a weapon? Then in the glow of the panel lights she saw a long-necked beer bottle roll out from under the seat, as though answering her prayer.

He was driving awfully fast. She needed to wait. Wait until they stopped, or they'd end up in a snow-filled ditch, stranded in the middle of nowhere. Could she contain the panic until then? Could she keep the scream that clawed at her throat from escaping her lips?

"It wouldn't hurt you to be nice to me, Christine," he said slowly. "If you're nice, I might just tell you where Timmy is."

CHAPTER 79

Timmy hid his feet under the covers. He scooted into the corner while the stranger paced in front of the bed. Something was wrong. The stranger seemed upset. He hadn't said anything since he came into the room. Instead, he threw his ski jacket onto the bed and started pacing.

Timmy kept quiet and watched. Under the covers, he pulled and yanked the chain. The stranger forgot to close the door behind him, leaving it wide open. The smell of dirt and mold came in with a draft. It was black on the other side of the door.

"What happened to the lantern?" the stranger suddenly wanted to know. The glass casing still lay on the crate.

"I...I couldn't light it, so I had to take that thing off. Sorry, I forgot to put it back on."

The stranger took the glass and snapped it in place without looking at Timmy. When he bent over, Timmy saw black, curly hair sticking out from under his mask. Richard Nixon. That was the dead president the mask resembled. It had taken Timmy three attempts at naming the presidents before he remembered. But there was still something very familiar about Richard Nixon's blue eyes. Something in the way they stared at him, especially tonight. As if they were apologizing.

Suddenly, the stranger grabbed his jacket and wrestled into it.

"It's time to go."

"Where?" Timmy tried to control his excitement. Was it really possible that the stranger might take him home? Maybe he'd realized his mistake. Timmy crawled out of bed, keeping the chain behind his feet.

"Take off all your clothes, except your underpants."

Timmy's excitement shattered. "What?" he asked over the lump gathering in his throat. "It's awfully cold out."

"Don't ask questions."

"But I don't understand what—"

"Just do it, you little son of a bitch."

The unexpected anger felt like a slap in the face. Even Timmy's eyes stung, his vision suddenly blurred by the tears gathering. He shouldn't cry. He wasn't a baby anymore. But he was scared. So scared his fingers shook as he untied his shoes. He noticed the cracked sole on his tennis shoe as he kicked it off. It had leaked in snow when they were sledding, getting his feet cold and wet, but he couldn't imagine how cold it would be without shoes.

"I don't understand," he mumbled again. The lump obstructed his breathing now as well as his voice.

"You don't need to understand. Hurry up." The stranger paced, the huge rubber boots caked with snow and mud, a *thump-squash* sound with each step.

"I don't mind staying here," Timmy attempted again.

"Shut the fuck up, you little bastard, and hurry up."

Tears ran down Timmy's cheeks, and he didn't bother to wipe at them. His fingers were shaking something terrible as he undid his belt, remembered the chain on his ankle, then worked on his shirt buttons, instead. The stranger would need to unchain him. Would he notice the bent links? Would he get even more angry? Already Timmy felt a cold draft swirling around him. His stomach hurt. He wanted to throw up. Even his knees were shaking, and his vision blurred from the tears.

Suddenly, the stranger's pacing stopped. He stood perfectly still in the middle of the room, cocking his head to one side. At first Timmy thought the stranger was staring at him, but instead, he was listening. Timmy strained to hear over his thumping heart. He sniffed back tears and dragged a sleeve across his face. Then he heard it—a car engine in the distance, getting closer and slowing down.

"Fuck!" the stranger spat, grabbing the lantern and heading for the door.

"No, please don't take the light."

"Shut the fuck up, you little crybaby."

He wheeled back around, smashing the back of his hand across Timmy's face. Timmy scrambled into the bed, escaping into the corner. He hugged the pillow, but jerked away at the sight of the red blotch.

"You better be ready when I get back," the stranger hissed. "And stop bleeding all over the place."

The stranger ran out the door, slamming it and the locks back into place, leaving Timmy in a hole of solid black. He hurried out in such a rush that he didn't even notice Timmy's chain, broken and dangling over the edge of the bed.

CHAPTER 80

Christine didn't need to ask what Eddie was planning. She recognized the winding dirt road that climbed then plunged. It snaked through the towering maples and walnut trees that lined the riverbank. It was where all the kids went to make out, just off Old Church Road. It looked out over the river. It was deserted and quiet and black. This was where Jason Ashford and Amy Stykes were probably headed the night they were sidetracked. The night they stumbled over Danny Alverez's body.

Was it possible that Eddie knew where Timmy was? Christine remembered that a church janitor had been brought in for questioning. Could Eddie have overheard something? Yet, if Nick knew something, *anything,* wouldn't he have told her? No, of course not. He'd want to keep her out of the way, give her some menial task like photocopying pictures of her son.

Eddie disgusted her, but more importantly, he frightened her. He was reckless, a bit over the edge. She imagined him to be one of those cops who pulled you over for driving thirty-six in a thirty-five-mile-an-hour zone just because he could. But if he knew where Timmy was... Oh, God, if she could just have Timmy back, safe and sound. What price would she be willing to pay? What price would any mother—Laura Alverez, Michelle Tanner—what price would they pay to have their sons back? Christine had been willing to sell her soul for a lousy paycheck. What was she willing to do to save her son?

Nevertheless, when the car pulled off the road and slid into the clearing overlooking the river, the panic crawled through her, sending a shiver down her back. Her empty stomach churned. She felt light-headed again. No, she couldn't pass out. Something told her that if an unwilling woman couldn't stop Eddie, neither could an unconscious one.

Eddie cut the engine and extinguished the headlights. The dark engulfed them as though they hovered in it, looking down on black ruffled treetops, the glittering river below. Only the sliver of moon added a pathetic reassurance that the darkness couldn't swallow everything.

"Well, here we are," Eddie said, turning toward her expectantly, but staying behind the wheel.

Her foot found the beer bottle, and she kept it from sliding under the seat. Without the car's inside panel lights, it was too dark to see his face. She heard a wrapper crackle, followed by a slap. Then a match sizzled, the smell of sulfur attacking her nostrils as he lit a cigarette.

"Mind if I have one of those?"

In the light of his cigarette, she saw the twisted smile. He handed her one, lit another match and waited for her. The match burned down close to his fingers. By the time he lit hers, he ended up scorching his fingertips.

"Damn," he muttered and shook his hand. "I hate matches. Lost my lighter someplace."

"I didn't know you smoked." She inhaled, waiting, hoping the nicotine could calm her.

"I'm trying to quit."

"Me, too." She smiled at him. See, they did have something in common. She could do this, couldn't she? By now her eyes had adjusted to the dark, and she could see him. She wondered if it would have been easier if she hadn't been able to see him. He looked so cool and calm, his arm stretched out over the cracked seat. She needed to stay cool and calm, too. Maybe she could, at least, keep the situation from getting violent. "Do you really know where Timmy is?"

"Maybe," he answered in a puff of smoke. "What are you willing to do to find out?" He moved his arm across the seat until his stubby fingers brushed her hair, then wandered across her cheek, swooping down to her neck.

"How do I know this isn't just some trick?"

"You don't."

His fingers slid under her coat collar, unbuttoning and pulling the coat open until he could see her blouse and skirt. Her skin crawled under his touch. It was difficult not to grimace. Even the nicotine couldn't help.

"That's not really fair, Eddie. There has to be something in it for me."

He pretended to look hurt. "I would hope your incredible orgasm would be enough."

His fingertips brushed across her breasts. It was all she could do to stop from slamming her body against the side of the car, bolting from his reach. Instead, she sat perfectly still. Don't think, she told herself. Shut off. But she wanted to scream when his hand fondled her breast, squeezing her nipple, watching and smiling at it growing hard and erect under his touch.

He put out his cigarette and scooted closer so that his other hand could assault her thigh. The stubby fingers slithered up, and she watched as they disappeared under her skirt. She refused to part her thighs for him, and this time he laughed, his breath sour in her face.

"Come on, Christine, relax."

"I'm just nervous." Her voice quivered, and he seemed pleased. "Do you have protection?"

"Don't you use anything?" He shoved his hand between her thighs.

"I haven't..." It was hard to think with his rough gropes. She wanted to throw up. "I haven't been with anyone since Bruce."

"Really?" His fingers poked at her, pulling at her underwear to allow him access. "Well, I don't use condoms."

She couldn't breathe. "I'm afraid we can't do this if you don't."

He obviously mistook her breathlessness for excitement.

"That's okay," he said, running the fingertips of his other hand over her lips and pushing his thumb into her mouth. "There's other things we can do."

Her stomach lurched. Would she throw up? She couldn't...couldn't afford to make him angry. He reached down, unzipped his trousers and pulled out his erect penis. It snaked out of his pants, long and thick. He took her hand. She snatched it away. He smiled and took it again, wrapping her fingers around him and squeezing his hand over hers until she could feel the bulging vein throbbing alongside it. He groaned and leaned back.

She couldn't do this. There was no way she could put her mouth on him.

"Do you really know where Timmy is?" she asked one more time, trying to remind herself of her mission.

He closed his eyes and his breathing rasped. "Oh baby, squeeze and suck me real good, and I'll tell you anything you want to hear."

At least his hands were off her. Then she remembered the cigarette in her other hand, the long ash lingering at the end. She took another draw until the end glowed red-hot. She squeezed him, digging her nails into the hard thickness.

"What the fuck!"

His eyes flew open. He grabbed for her hand. She shoved the flaming cigarette into his face. He howled, reeling against the door and swatting at his scorched cheek. She reached around him, grabbing the door handle. His hands snapped around her wrists, immediately letting go when she slammed her knee up into his erect penis. He sucked in for air. She scooped up the beer bottle, and when he grabbed for her again, she cracked it across his head. Another howl, a high-pitched, inhuman screech. She scooted to her side of the seat, anchored her back against her impenetrable door. She brought her knees up, and with all the strength she could gather, slammed her high-heeled feet into his chest. Eddie flew out the door.

He sprawled in the snow and dirt, but was getting to his feet when she pulled his door shut, locking it and checking the other doors. He pounded on the glass as her fingers fumbled with the keys in the ignition. The Chevy sputtered to life with one try.

Eddie climbed onto the hood, screaming at her and kicking at the windshield. A small crack raced across, spreading into a spiderweb. She threw the car into reverse and slammed on the accelerator, sending the car careening backward, almost into the ditch. Eddie flew from the hood. He scrambled to his feet as she shifted into Drive and floored it, skidding recklessly from ditch to ditch, sending gravel spitting.

Then the car plunged down the winding road into a hole of black. The headlights. She grabbed at knobs, sending the wipers swishing and the radio blaring. She looked down for only a second, found the knob and lit up the road, just in time to see the sharp curve. Even with both hands twisting the steering wheel, it wasn't enough. Both her feet slammed on the brake, and the car screeched as it flew across the snow-filled ditch, through the barbed-wire fence and into a tree.

CHAPTER 81

Nick watched the dark church in the rearview mirror as the Jeep bounced over the deep tire tracks, the only things identifying the deserted road.

"You sure you didn't see a light?"

Maggie glanced over the back of the seat. "Maybe it was a reflection. There is a moon out tonight."

The wood-framed church looked dark and gray, disappearing from the rearview mirror as he took the sharp turn up into the graveyard. Now to his left, he stared at the church again. It was set in the middle of a snow-covered field with tall, brown grass stabbing through the white. The paint had peeled away years ago, leaving raw and rotting wood. All the stained-glass windows had been removed or broken and boarded up. Even the huge front door deteriorated behind thick boards that were haphazardly pounded in at odd diagonals.

"It looked like a light," Nick said. "In one of the basement windows."

"Why don't you check it out. I can wander around here for a while."

"I only have one flashlight." He leaned over, careful not to touch her, snapping open the glove compartment.

"That's okay, I have this." She shined the tiny penlight into his eyes.

"Oh, yeah. That should show you a lot."

She smiled, and suddenly he realized how close his hand was to her thigh. He grabbed the flashlight and made a hasty retreat.

"I can leave the headlights on." Though at this angle they shot into the trees, over the rows of headstones.

"No, that's okay. I'll be fine."

"I don't understand why they always build graveyards on hills," he said, switching off the headlights. They both sat still, neither making an effort to leave the Jeep. There was something more she was thinking about. He'd sensed it ever since they left his office. Was it Albert Stucky? Did this place—this dark—remind her of him?

"You okay?"

"I'm fine," she said too quickly, continuing to stare straight ahead. "Just waiting for my eyes to adjust to the dark."

A fence surrounded the graveyard, twisted wire held up by bent and leaning steel rods. The gate hung on one hinge, swinging and clicking back and forth though there was no wind. A chill slithered down Nick's back. He'd hated this place, ever since he was a kid and Jimmy Montgomery dared him to run up and touch the black angel.

It was impossible not to notice the angel, even in the black of night. At this angle, looking up the hill, the tall stone figure hovered above the other tombstones. Its chipped wings only made it more menacing. His memory was of Halloween, almost twenty-five years ago. Then suddenly, he remembered that tomorrow was Halloween. And, although it was silly, he swore he could hear the ghostly groans again. The pained, hollow moans rumored to seep from the tomb the angel guarded.

"Did you hear that?" His eyes darted over the rows. He flashed on the headlights, realized he was being ridiculous and snapped them off. "Sorry," he mumbled, avoiding Maggie's eyes, though he could feel them studying him now. Another bubbleheaded move like that and she'd be wondering why she'd invited him along. Thankfully, she said nothing.

As if reading each other's minds, they reached for the door handles at the same time. Again, hers clicked.

"Damn," he muttered. "I've got to get that fixed. Hold on."

He jumped out and hurried around to open the door for her. Then he stood silently by her side, mesmerized by the spot of moonlight caught on the angel's face, radiating a glow almost as if from within.

"Nick, are you okay?"

"Yeah, I'm fine." How could she not see that? He pulled his eyes away. "I'll just go... I'll check out the church."

"You're starting to spook me."

"Sorry. It's just...the angel." He waved a hand at it, streaking its surface with the light from his flashlight.

"It doesn't come to life at midnight, does it?"

She was making fun. He glanced at her. Her face was serious, only adding to the sarcasm. He started walking away, heading down the road to the church. Without looking over his shoulder, he said, "Just remember, tomorrow is Halloween."

"I thought we canceled that," she yelled back.

He didn't let her see his smile. Instead, he kept to his path, following the tunnel of light he created. Without the wind it was unbearably quiet. Somewhere in the distance a hoot owl tested its voice, receiving no reply.

Nick tried to stay focused, to ignore the blackness pressing against him, swallowing him with each step. It was ridiculous to let those old childhood fears creep into his gut. After all, he *had* crossed the dark cemetery that night. He had touched the angel while his friends watched, none of them attempting to follow. He had been reckless and stupid even back then, more afraid of what others would think than the consequences of his actions. Yet, if he remembered correctly, the earth hadn't opened up and swallowed him, though it had felt as if it would at the time. There had been that ghostly moan. And he wasn't the only one who had heard it.

On this side of the church, the side that faced the old pasture road, there were no footprints. Which meant Adam and Lloyd hadn't even bothered to get out of their vehicle. They simply had driven by, so they could honestly say they had checked. He wondered if they'd even stopped. He didn't blame Adam. The kid was young, wanted to make a good impression, be a part of the group. But Lloyd...damn it. Lloyd was just lazy.

Nick kicked at the snow and plodded through the unbroken drifts. He crouched at one of the basement windows and shined light through the rotted slats. There were crates stacked on crates. Movement in the corner. His light caught a huge rat escaping into a hole in the wall. Rats. Jesus, he hated rats.

He made his way to the next window and suddenly heard the crack of wood. It cut through the black silence. He shot light at the plugged windows ahead of him. He expected to see something or someone smashing through the rotted wood.

Another crack, then splintering of more wood and the tinkle of broken glass. It must be around the corner. He tried running. The snow slowed his feet. He extinguished the flashlight. His hand pulled at his gun—once, twice, three times—before he unsnapped the restraint. The noises continued. His heart drummed against his rib cage. He couldn't hear, couldn't see. He slowed as he approached the corner. Should he call out? He held his breath. Then he rushed the corner, pointing his gun into the blackness. Nothing. He snapped on the flashlight. Wood and glass lay scattered in the snow. The opening was no bigger than a foot wide and high.

Then he heard bursts of crunching snow. His light caught movement disappearing into the trees—a small, black figure and a flash of orange.

CHAPTER 82

Maggie concentrated on the ground, looking for any breaks in the snow or freshly dug holes. Timmy had disappeared after the snowfall. If he was here, the snow would be disturbed. If a tunnel existed, where in the world would the entrance be?

She glanced up at the black angel perched on what looked like an above-ground tomb. Weather had chipped at the facade, leaving white wounds. It stood high above everything else, four to five feet tall. The wings spread out, protecting the tomb beneath, an ominous creature exuding power simply with its presence.

Maggie's penlight searched the engraving: In memory of our beloved son, Nathan, 1906-1916. A child, of course, that was the reason for the guardian angel. Her fingers dug deep into her jeans pocket until she felt the chain and found the medallion at the end. Her own guardian angel, which she kept tucked out of sight. Did the same power exist for skeptics? Yet, how much of a skeptic was she if she still carried the thing?

A breeze swirled up out of the trees that lined the back of the graveyard. The huge maples were the beginnings of the thick woods that led down to the river. She tried to imagine frightened runaway slaves navigating the steep decline without the aid of flashlights or lanterns. Even with the sliver of moonlight and sprinkling of stars, the black overwhelmed.

A flapping sound came from behind her. Maggie spun around. Something moved. The tiny penlight picked out a black shadow sprawled on the ground at the end of the rows. Was it a body? She approached slowly. Her hand crawled inside her jacket and rested on the butt of her revolver. She recognized the black tarp, the kind used to cover freshly dug graves. She sighed, then remembered the graveyard hadn't been used in years. Wasn't that what Adam had told her? The adrenaline started pumping.

The tarp was down the hill, close to the tree line. Only a few headstones existed on this side. Here, she could no longer see the Jeep or the road, only a piece of the church roof in the distance.

The tarp looked new, no cracks or worn patches. Rocks and snow anchored the corners, but one corner flapped free, its rock set aside. Set aside, not blown aside, not by tonight's slight breeze.

She realized her hands were sweating, despite the cold. Her heartbeat pounded in her ears, too fast, too hard. She should wait for Nick, head back to the Jeep and wait. Instead, she pulled the loose corner and whipped the tarp aside. She didn't need extra light to see. Underneath was a door, narrow and long, thick wood rotting around the hinges and caving in slightly in the middle.

Again, she stopped and glanced up the hill. She should wait. Remember Stucky, she scolded herself. Then, suddenly, she remembered the note, "I know about Stucky." Was this another trap? No, the killer couldn't possibly know she'd come here.

She paced, staring at the door. Another quick glance. Her heart pounded too loudly for her to think. She needed to calm herself. She could do this.

She grabbed the edge of the door. There was no handle. She pulled and yanked until it gave way, but it was heavy, straining her muscles, splinters threatening her fingers. She dropped the door, got a better grip and tried again. This time she swung it open. The musty odor slapped her in the face. It was filled with decay, wet earth and mold.

She searched the black hole but couldn't see beyond the third step with her penlight. It would be ridiculous to go down with such poor lighting. The pounding of her heart continued. She pulled out her revolver and was annoyed by the tremor in her hand. She glanced back up the hill one more time. Silence. No sign of Nick. She descended slowly into the narrow, black hole.

CHAPTER 83

Timmy skidded down into a prickly bush. He had heard the stranger close behind, felt the flash of light on his back. He didn't dare stop or look back. He kept a hold of the sled, no matter how awkward. His breathing came in spastic gasps. Branches grabbed at him. Twigs slapped him in the face. He stumbled, did a little dance and kept from falling. He tried to keep quiet, but the snaps and cracks were explosions he couldn't prevent. He couldn't see his feet in the black. Even the sky had disappeared.

He stopped to catch his breath, leaned against a tree and realized in his rush he hadn't put on his coat. He couldn't breathe. His teeth chattered. His heart exploded against his chest. He wiped at his face and discovered more blood, as well as tears.

"Stop crying," he scolded himself. Han Solo never cried.

Then he heard it. In the black silence he heard branches snapping, snow crunching. The sounds came from behind him, close and getting closer. Could he hide, hope the stranger would pass right by? No, the stranger would surely hear the massive pounding of his heart.

He ran recklessly, tripping over stumps and smashing through the thicket. A twig swiped at his cheek and ripped at his ear. The sting brought fresh tears. Then suddenly he felt the ground slip out from under him. A steep decline forced him to grab on to a branch, a rock, anything to keep from sliding down. Below, he saw the glitter of water. He'd never make it. The woods were too thick, the ridge too steep. The cracking of branches was even closer now.

He noticed a clearing to his right. He climbed over the rocks that blocked his path, hanging on to tree roots with one hand while clutching his sled with the other.

It wasn't much of a clearing. Instead, it looked like an old horse trail, a path worn into the woods but now overgrown with spindly branches, alien arms with long, thin fingers waving to him. As far as Timmy could see, the path went all the way down to the river, with a few sharp turns. It looked like something from one of his video games, narrow and dangerous and clogged with heaps of snow. The snow made it impossible to climb without sliding. It was perfect. Of course, it was also reckless and crazy. His mom would have a fit.

A crack close behind made him jump. He crouched in the snow and grass. Even in the dark he saw the shadow crawling down, clinging to the ridge, his back to Timmy. He looked like a giant insect, tentacles outstretched gripping roots and jutted rocks.

Timmy laid his orange sled in the snow. He crawled in carefully, its angle steep—really steep. He allowed himself one more frantic glance over his shoulder. The shadow edged closer. Soon, the stranger would be at the rocks. Timmy pointed the sled into the horse trail and scooted his body down until he was almost lying. There was no other choice. This was it. He jerked, one quick shove, and the sled plunged downward.

CHAPTER 84

Nick stood at the edge of the woods, every nerve ending on alert. It was impossible to see with only a flashlight. Branches swayed in a fresh breeze. Night birds exchanged calls. The black figure was gone. Or hiding.

He remembered a road that snaked through the woods, not far from here. It went all the way to the river. He'd have a better chance with the Jeep. He hurried back toward the church. When he stuffed his gun into the shoulder holster, he realized the other bulge in his jacket was Christine's cellular phone. Great, he thought, pulling it out. At least he could avoid a flood of media hounds if he didn't use the Jeep's CB radio.

Lucy answered on the second ring.

"Lucy, it's Nick."

"Nick, where in the world are you? I've been so worried."

"I don't have time to explain. I'm going to need some men and searchlights. I think I just chased the killer into the woods, behind the old church. He's probably headed for the river again."

"Where do you want the guys to meet you?"

"Down by the river. There's an old gravel road that winds through the woods. It's just off Old Church Road past the state park, not far from where we found Matthew. You know the one?"

"Isn't that the one with Make-out Point?"

"Make-out Point?"

"Well, that's what the kids call it. There's a clearing overlooking the river. Kids go there to make out."

"Yeah, I'm sure that's the one. Lucy, tell Hal. Let him decide who to bring, okay?"

"Okay."

He slapped the phone shut. What if it was only a vagrant he'd seen, who had used the church to get in out of the cold? He'd look like a fool again. The hell with what he looked like. He didn't care, if they could just find Timmy.

He stopped at the window, kicked aside the wood and glass, then crouched to shine light into the hole. Sure enough, there was a bed, posters on the wall, a crate with food. Someone had been staying here. The light reflected off a glimpse of chain. Or someone had been imprisoned here. He saw the comic books, the scattered baseball cards and the small child's coat. Timmy's coat. The drumming started again, the rhythm an erratic war dance against his rib cage. He couldn't be sure it was Timmy's, he made a feeble attempt to convince himself. Yet, he knew this was it. This was where the boys had been kept. Maggie was right. Then he saw the bloody pillow.

CHAPTER 85

Maggie heard small creatures skitter across the ceiling above her. Dirt crumbled down into her hair, but she didn't dare look up. She swatted at cobwebs. Something ran across her foot. She didn't need light to tell her it was a rat. She could hear them in the corners, behind the dirt walls, escaping into their own little tunnels.

The space was small enough to take in with a few swipes of the penlight. She had counted eleven steps, carrying her deep into the ground where the damp air became heavier with each step. The hole resembled an old storm cellar, an odd comparison considering the graveyard's residents no longer needed shelter from any storm. Other than a thick wooden shelf and a large crate in the corner, the space was empty. Even the shelves were empty, coated with cobwebs and rat feces. Disappointingly, there were no signs of Timmy and no tunnel. How could she be so wrong? Had Stucky sabotaged her instincts, too?

Still, someone had cleared the snow from the door and attempted to hide it with the tarp. Was there something here, a clue, anything to help find Timmy? She surveyed the space again, stopping this time when the light hit the crate.

On closer inspection, the old wooden crate was actually in good shape with no signs of rot or beginning decay. It certainly had not spent much time in the wet dark hole. Very few crumbs of dirt covered its surface. Even the lid was attached with shiny new nails.

Maggie holstered her revolver. She pried at the lid, but her fingers weren't strong enough to loosen the nails. She found a broken steel rod in the corner and began using it to pry the lid. The nails screeched but held. Immediately, a rancid smell leaked out, quickly filling the small space. Maggie stopped and backed off just a few steps to examine the crate again. Was it big enough to hide a body? A child's body? She had seen body parts stuffed into smaller spaces. Like the pieces of Emma Jean Thomas, which Stucky had crammed into take-out containers and left in a Dumpster. Who would have guessed a pair of lungs could fit into a foam container the size of a sandwich?

She tried to lift the crate, hoping to drag it up into the fresh air. She could barely lift it a foot off the ground. She would never be able to drag it up eleven steps. She pried at the lid again. This time the smell made her gag. She spat out the penlight she had anchored between her teeth and let it lie on the ground. She held her breath and tried again.

Something scraped in the dirt. Maggie spun around. In the black there was movement. Something bigger than a rat. She dropped to her knees, grabbing for the penlight. She clutched the steel rod, holding it above her head, ready to strike. Then she held her breath again and listened. All sound, all movement had come to a halt. The narrow light whipped across the opposite wall. The wooden shelf leaned forward, shoved away from the wall. Maggie now saw a hole, large enough to be an entrance to the famed tunnel.

In the black silence, something stirred behind her. She was no longer alone. Someone stood behind her, blocking the steps. She felt his presence, heard the soft wisps of his breathing as though it was suctioned through a tube. The panic Stucky had left with her unleashed itself and raced through her veins, ice-cold and rapid. And just as her fingers snuck inside her jacket, a smooth knife blade slid under her chin.

CHAPTER 86

"Agent Maggie O'Dell, what a lovely surprise."

Maggie didn't recognize the muffled voice in her ear. The knife's razor-sharp point pressed into the softness of her neck. It pushed with a steady pressure, forcing her head back until her neck lay completely exposed, completely vulnerable. She felt a trickle of blood run down inside the collar of her jacket.

"Why a surprise? I thought you'd be expecting me. You seem to know so much about me." With every syllable she felt the knife dig deeper.

"Drop the steel rod." He pulled her against him, wrapping his free arm around the front of her, squeezing harder than necessary to emphasize his strength.

She dropped the rod while he dug inside her jacket. He carefully grabbed the butt of the gun, his hand jerking away when he accidentally grazed her breast. He tossed the gun into a dark corner where she heard it knock against the crate. Of course, she wasn't surprised he would be much more comfortable using the knife.

She tried to concentrate on his voice and the feel of him. He was strong and four to six inches taller than her. The rest of himself, he disguised. A brush of rubber against her ear and the muffled sound told her he wore a mask. Even his hands were camouflaged in plain black gloves. They were made of cheap-department store leather, sold by the hundreds.

"I wasn't expecting you. I thought perhaps you might have

gone back home to your safe condo and your lawyer husband and your sick mother. How is your mother, by the way?''

"Why don't you tell me?"

The blade pushed up. Maggie sucked in air and resisted the urge to swallow while another trickle of blood found its way down her neck, traveling between her breasts.

"That wasn't very nice," he scolded.

"Sorry," she said carefully, not moving her mouth or chin. She could do this. She could play his game. She needed to stay calm, level the playing field somehow. "The smell is getting to me. Maybe we could discuss this outside."

"No, sorry. You see that's a bit of a problem. I'm afraid you won't be leaving here at all. What do you think of your new home?'' He made her turn around to examine the area with her penlight while the knife scraped her flesh. "Or should I say your tomb?"

The ice shot through her veins again. Calm, she needed to remain calm. If only she could remove the image of Albert Stucky carving her abdomen. If only she could get this madman to ease the pressure. One small jerk and she'd be tasting the knife's metal in her mouth.

"It won't matter...getting rid of me." She talked slowly. "The entire sheriff's department knows who you are. About a dozen deputies will be here in a few minutes."

"Now, Agent O'Dell, you can't bluff me. I know you like to be on your own. That's what got you in trouble with Mr. Stucky, isn't it? And all you have on me is your little psychological profile. I bet I even know what it says. My mother abused me as a child, right? She turned me into a fag, so I murder little boys now.'' The attempt at laughter sounded like a manic cackle.

"Actually, I don't think your mother abused you." She tried frantically to remember what little family history she had found on Father Keller. Of course, his mother had been a single parent just like the victims' mothers. But she had died when Keller was young—a fatal accident. Why couldn't she remember the details? Why was it so hard to think? It was the smell, the pressure of the knife, the feel of her own blood.

"I think she loved you," Maggie continued when he remained silent. "And you loved her. But you *were* abused." A twitch told her she was right. "By a relative...perhaps a friend of your mother's...no, a stepfather," she remembered suddenly.

The knife slipped, only a quarter of an inch, but she could breathe again. He was quiet, waiting, listening. She had his attention. It was her move.

"No, you're not homosexual, but he made you doubt yourself, didn't he? He made you think that maybe you could be."

The arm around her waist loosened. She felt his breathing grow rapid, a steady movement against her back as his chest moved laboriously.

"You don't kill little boys for kicks. You try to save them because they remind you of that scared, vulnerable little boy from your past. They remind you of yourself. Do you think that by saving them, you might be able to save yourself?"

His silence continued. Had she gone too far? She tried to concentrate on his hand with the knife. If she jabbed her elbow into his chest, perhaps she could grab the knife before it cut her. She needed to keep him distracted.

She continued. "You deliver these poor boys from evil, is that it? By inflicting your own evil, you transform them into martyrs. You're quite a hero. You might even say yours is a perfect evil."

His arm squeezed tight and jerked her back against him. She had gone too far. The knife shot up to her throat, this time lengthwise so that the sharp blade pressed full against her skin. In one quick motion, he could slit her throat.

"That's a bunch of psychological bullshit. You don't know what you're talking about." The low guttural sound came from someplace deep inside him. "Albert Stucky should have gutted you when he had a chance. Now, I guess, I'll have to finish the job. We need more light." He dragged her to the tunnel's entrance and extracted a lantern. "Light it." He shoved her to her knees, keeping the knife at her throat and throwing a matchbook into the dirt. "Light it so that you can watch."

"I want you to watch," she heard Albert Stucky say, as if he stood in the dark corner, waiting. "I want you to see how I do it."

Her fingers felt as though they belonged to someone else. There was no feeling in them, but she lit the lantern on the first attempt. The yellow glow filled the small space. Her entire body felt numb. All the blood had drained from her veins. Her mind was paralyzed, preparing for the pain by disconnecting. She recognized all the familiar signs. It was Albert Stucky all over again. Her body responded to the overwhelming terror by simply shutting down.

It was hard to breathe the thick air, now filled with the smell of spoiled meat. Even her lungs refused to work. The knife blade continued to press against her throat. There was a slight tremble in his hand. Was it from anger or fear? Did it matter?

"Why aren't you crying or screaming?" It was anger.

She didn't answer, couldn't answer. Even her voice had abandoned her. She thought of her father, those warm brown eyes smiling at her while he put the chain with the medallion around her neck. "Wherever you go, it'll protect you. Don't ever take it off, okay, Mag-pie?" But it didn't protect you, Daddy, she wanted to tell him. And it didn't protect Danny Alverez.

The stranger grabbed her by the hair and yanked her back to her feet, the knife a permanent fixture at her throat. More blood trickled down between her breasts.

"Say something," he screamed at the back of her head. "Plead with me. Pray."

"Just do it," Maggie finally said, quietly and with much effort, having to coax her voice, her lips, her bruised and cut throat to cooperate just for those three simple words.

"What?" He sounded genuinely surprised.

"Just do it," she managed to repeat, this time louder, more forceful.

"Maggie?" Nick's voice sifted in from the top of the stairs.

The stranger spun around, startled and swinging Maggie along with him. As if watching from the corner, she saw her hand grab at the knife, snatching the stranger's wrist. She twisted out from his hold just as he jerked his hand away and slashed at her, the metal disappearing into her jacket, ripping fabric and flesh on the way out. He shoved her hard, sending her into the dirt wall with a loud thump.

Nick's stream of light came racing down the steps just as the black shadow grabbed the lantern and plunged into the hole. The wooden shelf teetered then crashed to the floor, almost hitting Nick.

"Maggie?" His light blinded her.

"In the tunnel." She pointed while struggling to her knees. A flash of pain set her back down again. "Don't let him get away."

Nick disappeared into the hole, leaving her in total darkness. She didn't need light to know she was bleeding. Her fingers easily found the sticky wound in her side. She dug deep in her pocket, pulled out the chain and medallion, rubbing her fingers over the smooth cross shape. In many ways the cool metal reminded her of the knife blade. Good and evil—was there really that fine a line between the two? Then she slipped the chain over her head and around her bleeding neck.

CHAPTER 87

Nick tried not to think. Especially now that the tunnel had started to curve and narrow, forcing him to crawl on his hands and knees. He could no longer see the masked shadow in front of him. The jerks of light from his flashlight revealed only more darkness ahead. Dirt and rock crumbled with every movement. Broken roots snaked out of the earth, sometimes dangling in front of him, sticking to his face like cobwebs. It was hard to breathe. The farther he went, the less air there was. What was left was stale and rancid, burning his lungs and adding to the ache already in his chest.

Fur brushed against his hand. He flung the flashlight, missing the rat and sending the batteries flying. The sudden darkness surprised him. Terror exploded inside him. Frantically, he groped for the flashlight, fistfuls of moldy dirt. One battery, two, finally three. Please let it work. He wasn't sure he could even turn around in the narrow, twisted space. Couldn't imagine backing all the way out.

He screwed the flashlight together. Nothing. He slapped it, tightened the clasp, slapped it again. Light, thank God. Only now he gasped for air. Had the darkness sucked out all the air?

He crawled faster. The tunnel narrowed even more, sending him to his stomach. He crawled using his elbows, propelling off his toes like a swimmer pushing against the current. He was an awful swimmer—a hot dog on the diving board, but lead in the water. And now he felt as if he was drowning, gulping for air and swallowing dirt from above.

How far had he come? How much farther could it possibly be? Other than the scratches of rat claws and the avalanche of dirt behind him, there was silence. Was he simply burying himself alive?

How could the shadow have disappeared so quickly? And if this was the killer, who had Nick seen disappear into the woods earlier?

This was nuts, absolutely crazy. He couldn't make it, couldn't breathe. Surely his lungs would explode any second. The dirt clung to him. Sandpaper scratched his eyes and throat. His mouth was dry with the taste of rot and death, gagging him. The walls narrowed still more, scraping against his body. He heard rips and tears—his clothing, sometimes his skin, catching on pieces of rock, wood, maybe even bones sticking out of the dirt walls.

How much farther? Was it a trap? Had he missed a turn somewhere back in the beginning where the tunnel seemed huge? Where he had walked crouched low, but still upright? Could he have missed another secret passage? That would explain why he couldn't see or hear the stranger up ahead. What if this tunnel led to a dead end, a wall of dirt?

Just as he felt certain he could go no farther, the flashlight caught a sliver of glittering white up ahead. Snow—it clogged the tunnel. In one last mad rush of panic, Nick clawed, pushed, tore and dug his way to the surface. Suddenly, he saw the black, starlit sky. And despite the miles he thought he had traveled, he realized he hadn't even left the cemetery. Instead, he rose from the ground like a corpse among the tombstones. Less than three feet away, the black angel hovered above him with a ghostly radiance that looked like a smile.

CHAPTER 88

Christine's neck ached like it usually did when she fell asleep on the sofa. She saw branches sticking through glass. Had the storm sent branches through her living-room window? She had heard a crash. And there was a hole in the ceiling. Yes, she could even see stars, thousands of them right there, sitting on top of her house.

Where was Grandma Morrelli's afghan? She needed something to stop the draft, to prevent the cold from swirling up around her. Timmy, turn up the furnace, please. Hot chocolate, maybe she could fix nice steaming mugs of hot chocolate for the two of them. If only she could push the furniture off her chest. And where were her arms when she needed them? She could see one of them lying next to her. Why couldn't she make it move? Had it fallen asleep like the rest of her?

Those annoying headlights made her eyes sting. If she could just find the plug, she could shut them off. They made the branches dance, a slow-motion rumba, bumping and grinding glass. It was too hard to keep her eyes open, anyway. Perhaps she could fall back to sleep if only that rasping sound would stop. It came from somewhere inside her coat, from somewhere inside her chest. Whatever it was, it was annoying and...and painful...yes, it was annoyingly painful.

What was President Nixon doing in the headlights? He waved at her. She tried to wave back, but her arm was still asleep. He came into her living room. He moved all the furniture off her chest. Then President Nixon carried her back to sleep.

CHAPTER 89

Timmy watched his sled drift downstream. The bright orange looked fluorescent in the moonlight. He crouched in the snow, hidden by the cattails along the river bank. All that catapulting practice on Cutty's Hill had paid off, though his mom would kill him if she ever found out.

He was feeling pretty confident. He only now realized he had lost a shoe in the jump. His ankle hurt. It looked funny, puffed up, almost twice the size of his other one. Then he saw the black shadow, spiderwebbing its way down the ridge, clinging to roots and vines, stretching and gripping rocks and branches. It moved quickly.

Timmy glanced back at the sled, now regretting that he hadn't stayed in it. The stranger came to the river's edge. He was watching the sled, too. It had drifted too far away for him to see inside. But maybe the stranger believed Timmy had stayed inside. He certainly didn't look as if he was in a rush anymore. In fact, the stranger just stood there, staring at the river. Maybe he was trying to decide whether to jump in after the sled.

Out here in the open the stranger looked smaller, and although it was too dark to see his face, Timmy could tell he wasn't wearing the dead president's mask anymore.

Timmy burrowed down farther into the snow. The breeze coming off the water brought a wet cold with it. His teeth started chattering and the shivers crawled over his body again. He hugged his knees to his chest and watched and waited. As soon as the stranger disappeared, Timmy decided he would follow the road. It looked all uphill, but it would be better than the woods again. Besides, it had to lead somewhere.

Finally, the stranger looked as if he was giving up. He fumbled through his pockets, found what he was looking for and lit a cigarette. Then he turned and started walking directly toward Timmy.

CHAPTER 90

Maggie clawed her way up the steps, annoyed that her knees wouldn't hold her. Her side burned, a fire blazing deeper and deeper, igniting her stomach and lungs. It felt as if the knife metal had broken off and was shooting through her insides. God, she should be getting good at this by now. Practice makes perfect. Yet, when she struggled up into the moonlight, the sight of her own blood made her light-headed and nauseated. It covered her side and soaked into her clothes, the red turtleneck black with dirt and blood.

She pushed her hair out of her face, away from her sweaty forehead, and realized her hand was filled with blood. She eased out of her jacket, pulled and ripped at the lining until she had a piece big enough to plug up her side. She wrapped chunks of snow inside the fabric, then applied it to the wound. Suddenly, the stars in the sky multiplied. She squeezed her eyes shut against the pain. When she opened them, a black shadow approached, staggering between the headstones like a drunkard. She reached for her gun, her fingers lingering at the empty holster. Of course, she remembered. Her gun lay somewhere below in a dark corner.

"Maggie?" the drunkard called out, and she recognized Nick's voice. Relief washed over her so completely she forgot about the pain for a second or two.

He was covered in mud and dirt, and when he knelt beside her, the smell of him made her gag. She leaned into him, anyway, and welcomed the feel of his arm around her.

"Jesus, Maggie. Are you okay?"

"I think it's just a flesh wound. Did you see him? Did you get him?"

She saw the answer in his eyes, only it wasn't just disappointment. There was something more.

"I think there must be a maze of tunnels down there," he said, out of breath. "And I took the wrong one."

"We need to stop him. He's probably at the church. Maybe that's where he has Timmy."

"Had."

"What?"

"I found the room where he kept them. Timmy's coat was left behind."

"Then we need to find him." She tried to get to her feet, but fell back into his arms.

"I think we're too late, Maggie." She heard the words struggle over a lump in his throat. "I also saw...there was a bloody pillow."

She leaned her head against his chest. Listened to the pounding, the uneven breathing. No, the uneven breathing belonged to her.

"Jesus, Maggie. You're bleeding awfully bad. I need to get you to the hospital. I sure as hell am not going to lose two people I love in the same night."

He propped her up while he crawled to his feet, still a bit wobbly. She held on to him and struggled to her knees. The pain came in fiery jabs, scorching and tearing, hot glass shards slicing farther and farther inside her. As she clung to his arm, she wondered if she had heard him correctly. Did he really just say that he loved her?

"Don't, Maggie. Let me carry you to the Jeep."

"I saw the way you were walking, Morrelli. I'll take my chances on my own two feet." She pulled herself up, gritting her teeth against the constant stab.

"Just hang on to me."

They were almost to the Jeep when she remembered the crate. "Nick, wait. We have to go back."

CHAPTER 91

Christine stared up at the stars. She easily found the Big Dipper. It was the only thing she could ever find in the night sky. On the soft bed of snow and under the wonderfully warm and scratchy wool blanket, she hardly noticed that she was lying on the side of the road. And if only she could breathe without choking up chunks of blood, maybe she could sleep.

Reality came in short bursts of pain and memories. Eddie fondling her breast. Smashed metal against her legs, crushing her chest. And Timmy, oh, God, Timmy. She tasted tears and bit down on her lip to stop them. She tried to sit up, but her body refused to listen, couldn't comprehend the commands. It hurt to breathe. Couldn't she just stop breathing, at least for a few minutes?

The headlights came out of nowhere, rounding the corner and barreling down on her. She heard the brakes screech. Gravel pelted metal. Tires skidded. The light blinded her. When two stretched shadows emerged from the vehicle and came toward her, she imagined aliens with bulbous heads and bulging insect eyes. Then she realized it was the hats that made their heads look oversize.

"Christine. Oh, my good Lord, it's Christine."

She smiled and closed her eyes. She had never heard that kind of fear and panic in her father's voice. How totally inappropriate for her to be pleased by it.

When her father and Lloyd Benjamin knelt beside her, the only thing she could think to say was, "Eddie knows where Timmy is."

CHAPTER 92

Nick tried to convince Maggie to stay in the Jeep. They had stopped the bleeding for now, but there was no telling how much blood she had already lost. She could barely stand on her own, had completely lost all color in her face. Perhaps she was delusional, too.

"You don't understand, Nick," she continued to argue with him.

He was ready to pick her up and throw her into the Jeep. It was bad enough that she wouldn't let him drive her to the hospital.

"I'll go check what's in the stupid crate," he said finally. "You wait here."

"Nick, wait." She dug her fingers into his arm, wincing with pain. "It may be Timmy."

"What?"

"Inside the crate."

The realization struck him like a fist. He leaned against the Jeep's hood, suddenly weak in the knees.

"Why would he do that?" he managed to say, though his throat strangled the words. He didn't want to imagine Timmy stuffed into a crate. Timmy, dead. Yet, hadn't he already thought that? "That's not his style."

"Whatever is in the crate might be for my benefit."

"I don't understand."

"Remember the last note? If he knows about Stucky, he may

have resorted to Stucky's habits. Nick, it could be Timmy inside that crate. And if it is, it isn't something you should see.''

He stared at her. Blood and dirt streaked her face. More dirt and cobwebs filled her hair. Those beautiful full lips held tight against the pain. Those soft, smooth shoulders slouched from the effort to hold herself up. And still, she wanted to protect him.

He turned on his heel and stomped back up the hill.

"Nick, wait."

He ignored her calls. Surely she wouldn't—couldn't—follow without his assistance.

He hesitated at the steps Maggie had uncovered. Then forced himself back down into the earth. The entire space reeked with the stifling smell. He found a steel rod and Maggie's revolver, which he slid into his jacket pocket. Then he tucked the rod and flashlight under his arm and hoisted the crate, lugging it slowly up the steps. His muscles screamed at him to put it down. He ignored them until he was out of the hellhole, until he could breathe fresh air again.

Maggie was there, waiting, leaning against a headstone. She was even more pale.

"Let me," she insisted, reaching for the rod.

"I can do this, Maggie." He shoved the rod under the lid and started pumping up and down. The nails screeched and echoed in the silent darkness. Even with the breeze and in the cold the smell of death overpowered all other senses. Once the lid snapped free, he hesitated again. Maggie came beside him, reached around him and pulled open the lid.

Both of them took a step backward, but it wasn't because of the odor. Tucked carefully inside and wrapped in a white cloth was the small, delicate body of Matthew Tanner.

CHAPTER 93

There was no place for Timmy to run. Nowhere to hide. He slipped down the riverbank, close to the water. Could he swim across, float downstream? He examined the black, churning river racing past him. It was too strong, too fast and much too cold.

The stranger had stopped to finish his cigarette, but his direction hadn't changed. In the silence, Timmy heard the stranger mumbling to himself, but he couldn't make out the words. Every once in a while he kicked rocks and dirt into the water. The splashes were now close enough to spray Timmy.

He'd have to make a run for it, back into the woods. At least there he could hide. He'd never make it in the water. His shivers from the cold were already close to convulsions. The water would only make it worse.

Timmy peeked over the riverbank. The stranger was lighting another cigarette. Now. He needed to go now. He scrambled up the bank, kicking rocks and dirt into the water—explosive splashes giving him away. He barely made it to the road when his ankle buckled under him. He slammed down on knees and elbows. He struggled to his feet, then suddenly flew up off the ground. He kicked at air and clawed at the arm around his waist. Another arm squeezed around his neck.

"Settle down, you little shit."

Timmy started screaming and shouting. The arm squeezed harder, cutting off his air, choking him.

When the car came squealing down the winding road, the stranger still kept his vise grip on Timmy. The car skidded to a stop in front of them, and still the stranger made no attempt to move or flee. The headlights blinded Timmy, but he recognized Deputy Hal. Why didn't the stranger release him? Timmy's neck hurt bad. He clawed at the arm again. Why didn't the stranger make a run for it?

"What's going on here?" Deputy Hal demanded. He and another deputy got out of the car and approached slowly.

Timmy didn't understand why they didn't draw their guns. Couldn't they tell what was going on? Couldn't they tell the stranger was hurting him?

"I found the kid hiding in the woods," the stranger told them, only he sounded excited and proud. "You might say I rescued him."

"I see that," said Deputy Hal.

No, it was a lie. Timmy wanted to tell them it was all a lie, but he couldn't breathe, couldn't speak with the arm squeezing his neck. Why were they looking as if they believed the stranger? He was the killer. Couldn't they see that?

"Why don't the two of you get in with us. Come on, Timmy. You're safe now."

Slowly the arm released from around Timmy's neck. His feet touched the ground. Timmy pulled free and ran to Deputy Hal, tripping on his swollen ankle.

Hal grabbed Timmy by the shoulders and gently shoved him behind him. Then Deputy Hal pulled out his gun and said to the stranger, "Come on, now. You've got a lot of explaining to do, Eddie."

CHAPTER 94

Friday, October 31

Christine awoke to a room full of flowers. Had she died, after all? Through a blur, she saw her mother sitting next to the bed, and Christine knew immediately that she was, in fact, still alive. Certainly the blue and pink jogging suit her mother wore would never be acceptable attire for heaven—or hell.

"How are you feeling, Christine?" Her mother smiled and reached for Christine's hand.

Her mother was finally letting her hair go gray. It looked good. Christine decided to tell her later when a compliment would come in handy to combat the inquisition.

"Where am I?" It was a stupid question, but after the hours of delusions, hallucinations—whatever they were—she needed to know.

"You're in the hospital, dear. Don't you remember? You just got out of surgery a little while ago."

Surgery? Only now did Christine notice all the tubes going in and out of her. In a moment of panic, she ripped off the covers.

"Christine!"

Her legs were still there. Yes, thank God. She could move them. There were bandages on one, but she didn't care as long as the leg moved.

"You don't need to catch pneumonia." Her mother tucked the covers back in around her.

Christine raised both arms, flexed the fingers and watched the fluids drip into her veins. The pieces all seemed there and working. That her chest and stomach felt like chunks of beaten and sliced chopped liver didn't matter. At least she was all in one piece.

"Your father and Bruce went for coffee. They'll be so pleased to find you awake."

"Oh, God, Bruce is here?" Then Christine remembered Timmy, and the panic began to suck all the air from the room.

"Give him a second chance, Christine," her mother said, completely oblivious to the lack of air in the room. "This ordeal has really changed him."

Ordeal? Was that the newest term they had given to the disappearance of her son?

Just then, Nick peeked into the room and relief swept over Christine. There was a new cut on Nick's forehead, but the bruises and swelling around his jaw were hardly noticeable. He was dressed in a crisp blue shirt, navy tie, blue jeans and navy sports jacket. God, how long had she been asleep? If she didn't know better, she'd think he looked dressed for a funeral. She remembered Timmy again. What exactly had her mother meant by ordeal? A new wave of pain and terror came crashing down, adding its weight to her chest.

"Hi, honey," their mother said as Nick leaned down to kiss her cheek.

Christine studied the two of them, watching for signs. Did she dare ask? Would they only lie to protect her? Did they think she was too fragile?

"I want the truth, Nicky," she blurted in a voice so shrill she hardly recognized it as her own. They both stared at her, startled, concerned. But she could see in Nick's eyes that he knew exactly what she was talking about.

"Okay. If that's the way you want it." He headed back for the door, and she wanted to yell at him to stop, to stay, to talk to her.

"Nicky, please," she said, not caring how pathetic she sounded.

He opened the door, and Timmy stood there like an apparition. Christine rubbed her eyes. Was she hallucinating again? Timmy hobbled toward her, and she could see the scratches and bruises, a cut on one cheek and a purple swollen lip. However, his face and hair were scrubbed clean, his clothes crisp and fresh. He even wore new tennis shoes. Had it all been a horrible, horrible nightmare?

"Hi, Mom," he said as though it were any other morning. He crawled into the chair his grandmother held out for him, kneeling and making himself tall enough to look over the bed. She allowed the tears, had no choice, really. Was he real? She touched his shoulder, smoothed down his cowlick and caressed his cheek.

"Aw, Mom. Everybody's watching," he said, and she knew he was real.

CHAPTER 95

Nick escaped before it got mushy, before his own eyes got blurry. It was all still a little hard to believe. He turned the corner and almost ran into his father, who stepped back, as though worried the coffee he carried would spill.

"Careful there, son. You're gonna miss quite a bit being in such a hurry."

Nick checked his father's eyes and immediately saw the sarcastic criticism. He was in too good of a mood to let his father spoil it. So he smiled and started to walk around him.

"It's not Eddie, you know," his father called after him.

"Yeah?" Nick stopped and turned. "Well, this time that'll be up to a court of law to decide and not Antonio Morrelli."

"What the hell is that supposed to mean?"

Nick took a step closer until he was standing eye to eye with his father.

"Did you help plant evidence against Jeffreys?"

"Watch your mouth, boy. I never planted a thing."

"Then how did you explain the discrepancies?"

"As far as I was concerned, there were no discrepancies. I did what was necessary to convict that son of a bitch."

"You ignored evidence."

"I knew Jeffreys killed that little Wilson boy. You didn't *see* that boy. You didn't see what he made that boy go through. Jeffreys deserved to die."

"Don't you dare make your horrors superior to mine," Nick said, hands clenched into fists but quiet and steady at his sides.

"I've seen enough this week to last me a lifetime. Maybe Jeffreys did deserve to die. But by pinning the other two murders on him, you let another murderer get away. You closed the investigation. You made a community feel safe again."

"I did what I thought was necessary."

"Don't tell me. Tell that to Laura Alverez and Michelle Tanner. Tell them how you did what was necessary."

Nick walked away, his knees feeling a bit spongy. There was little victory in telling Antonio Morrelli he had been wrong. Why had he expected there to be some feeling of celebration? But as his boot heels echoed down the quiet hall, he walked a bit taller.

He stopped by the nurses' station and was startled by the unit secretary dressed in a black cape and witch's hat. It took a minute before he noticed the orange and black crepe paper and pumpkin cutouts. Of course, today was Halloween. Even the sun had emerged, finally bright enough and warm enough to start melting some of the snow.

He waited patiently while the unit secretary recited ingredients of a recipe into the phone. Her eyes told him she'd only be a moment, but there was no urgency in her voice.

"Hi, Nick." Sandy Kennedy came up behind him, scooted back behind the secretary and grabbed a clipboard.

"Sandy, you finally made it to the day shift." He smiled at the shapely brunette, while thinking what a stupid thing to say. Why not "How are you" or "It's been a long time"? Then he wondered if there was anyplace in this city he could go without running into a former lover or one-night stand.

"Sounds like Christine is doing better," she said, ignoring his stupid comment.

He tried to remember why he had never pursued a relationship with Sandy. Just seeing her reminded him how bright and beautiful she was. But then, so were all the women he chose. However, not one of them could live up to Maggie O'Dell.

"Nick, are you okay? Can we do something for you?"

Both Sandy and the secretary stared at him.

"Can you tell me Agent O'Dell's room number?"

"It's 372," the secretary said without looking it up. "At the end of the hall and to the right. Although she may be gone."

"Gone? What do mean gone?"

"She checked out earlier and was just waiting for some

clothes. Hers were pretty trashed when she came in last night,''
she explained, but Nick already was halfway down the hall.

He burst through the door without knocking, startling Maggie,
who turned quickly from the window, then positioned her back—
and the open hospital gown—to the wall.

''Jesus, Morrelli, don't you knock?''

''Sorry.'' His heart settled down, almost to its regular rhythm.
She looked wonderful. The short, dark hair was smooth and shiny
again. Her creamy skin had some color. And her eyes—those
luscious brown eyes—actually sparkled. ''They said you might
be gone.''

''I'm waiting for some clothes. One of the hospital volunteers
offered to go shopping for me.'' She paced, carefully using the
wall to shield her back. ''That was about two hours ago. I just
hope she doesn't come back with something pink.''

''The doctor said it's okay for you to check out?'' He tried to
make it a simple question. Was there too much concern in his
voice?

''He's leaving it to my discretion.''

She caught him staring at her, and when their eyes met, he
held her gaze. He didn't care if she saw the concern. In fact, he
wanted her to see it.

''How's Christine?'' she asked, breaking the trance.

''Surgery went well.''

''What about her leg?''

''The doctor seems certain there won't be any permanent dam-
age. I just took Timmy in to see her.''

For a minute she stopped pacing. Her eyes softened, though
there was a faraway look in them.

''If I didn't know better, I'd almost believe in happy endings,''
she said.

Her eyes met his again, this time accompanied by a faint smile,
a slight tug at the corners of her lips. Jesus, she was beautiful
when she smiled. He wanted to tell her that. Opened his mouth,
in fact, to do just that, then thought better of it. Did she have
any idea how scared he was when he thought she'd left without
so much as a goodbye? Could she even tell what effect she had
on him? The hell with her husband, her marriage. He needed to
take the risk, let the chips fall where they may. He needed to tell
her he loved her.

Instead, he said, "We arrested Eddie Gillick this morning."

She sat on the edge of the bed and waited for more.

"We brought in Ray Howard again for questioning. This time he admitted that sometimes he loaned the old blue pickup to Eddie."

"The day Danny disappeared?"

"Howard conveniently couldn't remember. But there's more—lots more. Eddie came to work for the sheriff's department the summer before the first killings. The Omaha Police Department had given him a letter of recommendation, but there were three separate reprimands in his file, all for unnecessary force while making arrests. Two of the cases were juveniles. He even broke one kid's arm."

"What about the last rites?"

"Eddie's mom—a single mom, by the way—worked two jobs just to send him to Catholic school, all the way through high school."

"I don't know, Nick."

She didn't look convinced. It didn't surprise him. He went on with the rest.

"He would have had access to the evidence in Jeffreys' case and could easily have framed him. He's also had access to the morgue. In fact, he was there yesterday afternoon picking up the autopsy photos. He could have easily snatched Matthew's body when he realized the teeth marks in the photos might ID him. Plus, it would have been easy for him to make a few phone calls, use his badge number and get information on Albert Stucky."

There was the twitch, the slight grimace at just the mention of the bastard's name. He wondered if she was conscious of it.

"The morgue is never locked," Maggie countered. "Anyone could have had access. And much of what happened with Stucky was publicized in the newspapers and tabloids."

"There's still more." He'd left this for last. The most incriminating evidence was the most questionable. "We found some stuff in the trunk of his car." He let her see his skepticism. Was it Ronald Jeffreys all over again? They were both thinking the same thing.

"What kind of stuff?" Now she was interested.

"The Halloween mask, a pair of black gloves and some rope."

"Why would he have all that in the trunk of his abandoned

car if he knew we were hot on his trail? Especially if he was responsible for framing Jeffreys in the same manner? Also, how did he have time to do all this?''

It was exactly what Nick had wondered, but he wanted desperately for this to be all over.

"My dad just more or less admitted that he knew someone may have planted evidence."

"He admitted that?"

"Let's just say he admitted to ignoring the discrepancies."

"Does your father think Eddie could be the killer?"

"He said he's sure it's not Eddie."

"And that makes you even more convinced that it is?"

Jesus, she knew him well.

"Timmy has a lighter the guy gave him. It has the sheriff's department emblem on it. It's a reward type thing that my dad used. He never handed out that many of them. Eddie was one of about five."

"Lighters get lost," she said. She stood up and slowly made her way to the window.

This time her mind was clearly far away. She even forgot about the slit in the back of her hospital gown. Though from this angle he could only see a sliver of her back, part of her shoulder. The gown made her look small and vulnerable. He imagined wrapping his arms around her, wrapping his entire body around hers. Just lying with her for hours, touching her, running his hands along her smooth skin, his fingers through her hair. He simply wanted to get lost in her for a very long time.

Jesus, where in the world was this coming from? He dug his thumb and forefinger into his eyes, feigning exhaustion, when it was really that image he needed to dig out.

"You still think it's Keller?" he asked, but knew the answer.

"I don't know. Maybe it's just hard for me to realize I'm losing my touch."

Nick could certainly relate to that.

"Eddie doesn't fit your profile?"

"The man in that cellar wasn't some hothead who lost his temper and sliced up little boys. This was a mission for him, a well-thought-out and planned mission. Somehow, I really do think he believes he's saving these boys." She stared out the window and avoided looking at him.

He had never asked what had happened in the cellar before he got there. The notes, the game, the references to Albert Stucky— it all seemed so personal. Perhaps he could no longer count on Maggie to be objective.

"What does Timmy say?" She turned to him finally. "Can he identify Eddie?"

"He seemed certain last night, but that was after Eddie chased him down the ridge and grabbed him. Eddie claims he spotted Timmy in the woods and went after him to rescue him. This morning Timmy admitted he never saw the man's face. But, it can't all be just coincidence, can it?"

"No, it does sound like you have a case." She shrugged. "But do I have a killer?"

CHAPTER 96

He stuffed his few belongings into the old suitcase. His fingers traced over the suitcase's fabric, a cheap vinyl that cracked easily. He had lost the combination years ago. Now he simply avoided locking it. Even the handle was a mass of black tape, sticky in summer, hard and scratchy in winter. It was the only thing he had of his mother's.

He had stolen it out from under his stepfather's bed the night he ran away from home. Home—that was certainly a misnomer. It had never felt like his home, even less after his mother was gone. Without her, the two-story brick house had become a prison, and he had taken his punishment nightly for almost three weeks before he left.

Even the night of his escape, he had waited until after his stepfather had finished and then collapsed from exhaustion. He had stolen his mother's suitcase and packed while blood trickled down the insides of his legs. Unlike his mother, he had refused to grow accustomed to his stepfather's deep, violent thrusts, the fresh tears and old ones not allowed to heal. That night, he had barely been able to walk, but still he had managed somehow to make it the six miles to Our Lady of Lourdes Catholic Church where Father Daniel had offered refuge.

A similar price had been paid for his room and board, but at least Father Daniel had been kind and gentle and small. There had been no more rips and tears, only the humiliation, which he had accepted as part of his punishment. He was, after all, a murderer. That horrible look still haunted his sleep. That look of utter surprise in his mother's dead eyes as she lay sprawled on the basement floor, her body twisted and broken.

He slammed the suitcase shut, hoping to slam out the image.

His second murder had been much easier, a stray tomcat Father Daniel had taken in. Unlike himself, the cat had received room and board with no price to pay. Perhaps that alone had been reason enough to kill it. He remembered its warm blood had splattered his hands and face when he slashed its throat.

From then on, each murder had become a spiritual revelation, a sacrificial slaughter. It wasn't until his second year of seminary that he murdered his first boy, an unsuspecting delivery boy with sad eyes and freckles. The boy had reminded him of himself. So, of course, he needed to kill him, to get the boy out of his misery, to save him, to save himself.

He checked his watch and knew he had plenty of time. He carefully placed the old suitcase by the door, next to the gray and black duffel bag he had packed earlier. Then he glanced at the newspaper folded neatly on his bed, the headline garnering yet another smile: Sheriff's Deputy Suspected in Boys' Murders.

How wonderfully easy it had been. He knew the minute he had found Eddie Gillick's lighter on the floor of the old blue pickup that the slick and arrogant bully would make the perfect patsy. Almost as perfect as Jeffreys had been.

All those evenings of excruciating small talk, playing cards with the egomaniac, had finally paid off. He had pretended to be interested in Gillick's latest sexual conquest, only to offer forgiveness and absolution when the good deputy finally sobered up. He had pretended to be Gillick's friend when, in fact, the conceited know-it-all turned his stomach. Gillick's bragging had also revealed a short temper, mostly targeted at "punk kids" and "cock-teasing sluts" who, according to Gillick, "had it coming." In many ways, Eddie Gillick reminded him of his stepfather, which would make Gillick's conviction even sweeter.

And why wouldn't Gillick be convicted, with his self-destructive behavior and all that damning evidence tucked neatly inside the trunk of the deputy's very own smashed Chevy? What luck, stumbling across it in the woods like that, making it so easy to stash the fatal evidence. Just like Jeffreys.

He remembered how Ronald Jeffreys had come to him, confessing to Bobby Wilson's murder. When Jeffreys asked for forgiveness there hadn't been a shred of remorse in his voice. Jeffreys deserved what had happened to him. And it had been so simple, too. One anonymous phone call to the sheriff's department and some incriminating evidence was all it had taken.

Yes, Ronald Jeffreys had been the perfect patsy just like Daryl Clemmons. The young seminarian had shared his homosexual fears with him, unknowingly setting himself up for the murder of that poor, defenseless paperboy. That poor boy whose body was found near the river that ran along the seminary. Then there was Randy Maiser, an unfortunate transient, who had come to St. Mary's Catholic Church seeking refuge. The people of Wood River had been quick to convict the ragged stranger when one of their little boys ended up dead.

Ronald Jeffreys, Daryl Clemmons and Randy Maiser—all of them such perfect patsies. And now, Eddie Gillick could be added to that list.

He glanced at the newspaper again, and his eyes rested on Timmy's photo. Disappointment clouded his good mood. Though Timmy's escape had brought a surprising amount of relief, it was that very escape that required his own sudden exodus. How could he continue his day-to-day routine knowing he had failed the boy? And, eventually, Timmy would recognize his eyes, his walk, his guilt. Guilt because he hadn't been able to save Timmy Hamilton. Unless...

He grabbed the newspaper and flipped to the inside story of Timmy's escape and his mother, Christine's, accident. He scanned the article using his index finger until he noticed the ragged fingernail, bitten to the quick. He tucked his fingers into a fist, ashamed of their appearance. Then he found the paragraph, almost at the end. Yes, Timmy's estranged father, Bruce, was back in town.

He glanced at his watch again. Poor Timmy and all those bruises. Perhaps somehow, some way, Timmy deserved a second chance at salvation. Surely he could make time for something that important.

CHAPTER 97

Maggie wanted to tell Nick it was over. That no more little boys would disappear. But even as they went over the case against Eddie Gillick, she couldn't dislodge that gnawing doubt. Was it possible she was just being stubborn, refusing to believe that she could be so wrong?

She wished the hospital volunteer would be as punctual as she had been perky. How could anyone carry on a serious conversation in these paper-thin gowns? And would it be so much trouble to provide a robe, a sash, anything to prevent a full view of her unprotected backside?

She could see Nick's eyes exercising extreme caution, but all it took was a few unintentional slips to remind her of how naked she was under the loose garment. Worse yet was that damn tingle that spread over her skin every time his eyes were on her. And that stupid fluttering sensation that teased between her thighs. It was like radar. Her entire body reacted beyond her control to its own nakedness and Nick's presence.

"Okay, so it does look as though Eddie Gillick could be guilty," she admitted, trying to keep her mind off her reactions to him. She crossed her arms over her chest and found her way back to the window, carefully keeping her back against the wall.

Today the sky was so blue and large it looked artificial, not even a hint of a cloud. Most of the snow had melted off the sidewalks and lawns. Soon only the piles of black ice chunks along the streets would be left. Trees that hadn't lost their leaves now shimmered with wet glossy gold, red and orange. It was as if a spell had been broken, a curse lifted, and everything was back to normal. Everything except the slight tug in Maggie's gut, not from the stitches, but from her own nagging doubt.

"What was Christine doing with Eddie last night?"

"I haven't talked to her about it this morning. Last night she said Eddie was supposed to take her home, but he took a detour. He told her if she had sex with him, he'd tell her where Timmy was."

"He said he knew where Timmy was?"

"That's what Christine said. Of course, I think she was delusional. She also told me President Nixon carried her to the side of the road."

"The mask, of course. He carried Christine out of the car then stuffed his disguise into the trunk."

"Then hurried along to chase Timmy through the woods," Nick added. "This, of course, is after he tried to rape Christine, then attack you in the graveyard cellar. Busy guy."

They stared at each other. The obvious left unsaid, settling between them and stirring up the same disappointment and panic that had driven them to this point.

"Did he try anything with you?" Nick finally asked.

"What do you mean?"

"You know... Did he..."

"No," she said, cutting him off, rescuing him. "No, he didn't."

Maggie remembered the killer fishing her gun out from inside her coat, accidentally grazing her breast. He had snapped his hand back instead of letting it linger. When he whispered into her ear, he never once touched her skin. He wasn't interested in sex, not with men and certainly not with women. His mother was a saint, after all. She remembered the images of tortured saints on Father Keller's bedroom wall. The priesthood and its vow of celibacy would have been an excellent escape, an excellent hiding place.

"We need to question Keller one last time," she said.

"We have absolutely nothing on him, Maggie."

"So humor me."

"Ms. O'Dell?" A nurse peeked around the door. "You have a visitor."

"It's about time," Maggie said, expecting the perky, blond volunteer.

The nurse held open the door and smiled flirtatiously at the handsome, golden-haired man in the black Armani suit. He carried a cheap overnight case, and a matching garment bag was slung over his arm.

"Hi, Maggie," he said, walking into the room as if he owned it, throwing a look at Nick before smiling his expensive-lawyer smile at Maggie.

"Greg? What in the world are you doing here?"

CHAPTER 98

Timmy listened for the vending machine to swallow his quarters before he made his selection. He almost chose a Snickers, but his gut remembered, and he punched the Reese button, instead.

He tried not to think about the stranger or the little room. He needed to stay focused on his mom and help her get better. It scared him to see her in that huge, white hospital bed, hooked up to all those machines that gurgled, wheezed and clicked. She seemed to be okay, even seemed happy to see his dad after, of course, she had yelled at him. But this time his dad didn't yell back. He just kept saying he was sorry. When Timmy left the room, his dad was holding his mom's hand, and she actually let him. That had to be a good sign, didn't it?

Timmy sat in the plastic waiting-room chair. He unwrapped his candy bar and separated out the two pieces. Grandpa Morrelli was supposed to bring him a sandwich from Subway after the two of them had inspected the cafeteria's meat loaf. The Subway was only across the street, but Timmy hadn't had breakfast. He popped one whole peanut butter cup into his mouth and let it melt before he started chewing.

"I thought you were a Snickers guy."

Timmy spun around in the chair, startled. He hadn't even heard footsteps.

"Hi, Father Keller," he mumbled over a mouthful.

"How are you, Timmy?" The priest patted Timmy's shoulder, his hand lingering on Timmy's back.

"I'm okay." He swallowed the rest of the candy bar, clearing his mouth. "My mom had surgery this morning."

"I heard." Father Keller slid a duffel bag into the seat next to Timmy's then knelt down in front of him.

Timmy liked that about Father Keller, how he made him feel special. He was genuinely interested. Timmy could see that in his eyes, those soft, blue eyes, that sometimes looked so sad. Father Keller really did care. Those eyes... Timmy looked again and suddenly a knot twisted in his stomach. Today, there was something different about Father Keller's eyes. Timmy didn't know what it was. He squirmed in his seat, and Father Keller looked concerned.

"You okay, Timmy?"

"Fine...I'm fine. It's probably just all the sugar. I didn't eat breakfast. You going someplace?" Timmy asked, swinging a thumb at the duffel bag.

"I'm taking Father Francis to his burial place. In fact, that's why I'm here, to make sure the body is ready."

"He's here?" Timmy didn't mean to whisper, but that's how it came out.

"Down in the morgue. Would you like to come with me?"

"I don't know. I'm waiting for my grandpa."

"It'll only take a few minutes, and I think you'll enjoy seeing it. It looks like something out of *The X-Files*."

"Really?" Timmy remembered watching Special Agent Scully doing autopsies. He wondered if dead people really did look all stiff and gray. "You sure it's okay if I come along? Won't the hospital people get mad?"

"Nah, there's never anyone down there."

Father Keller stood up and grabbed the duffel bag. He waited while Timmy shoved the rest of the Reese's into his mouth, accidentally dropping the wrapper. When he knelt to pick it up, Timmy noticed Father Keller's Nikes, crisp and white, as usual. Only today there was...there was a knot in one of the shoestrings. A knot holding it together. The knot in Timmy's stomach tightened.

He stood up slowly, a bit dizzy. A sugar rush—that was all it was. He glanced up at Father Keller's smiling face, the priest's hand outstretched to him, waiting. One last quick glance at the shoe. Why did Father Keller have a knot in his shoestring?

CHAPTER 99

"How did you find out I was in the hospital?" Maggie asked when she and Greg were alone. She spread out the suits she had carefully packed days ago, pleased with their appearance despite two trips halfway across the country.

"Actually, I didn't know until I arrived at the sheriff's department earlier this morning. Some bimbo in a leather skirt told me about it."

"She's not a bimbo." Maggie couldn't believe she was defending Lucy Burton.

"This just reiterates my point, Maggie."

"Your point?"

"That this job is much too dangerous."

She dug through the overnight case he'd brought her, keeping her back to him and vowing to ignore the mounting anger. She concentrated on how good it felt to have her own things back. Perhaps it was ridiculous, but fingering her own underwear gave her an odd sense of control and security.

"Why won't you just admit it?" Greg insisted.

"Admit what?"

"That this job is too dangerous."

"For who, Greg? You? Because I don't have a problem with it. I've always known there would be risks."

She stayed calm, glanced over her shoulder at him. He was pacing, hands on his hips as if waiting for a verdict. "When I asked you to pick up my bags from the airport, I didn't mean for you to deliver them.'' She tried a smile, but he looked determined not to let her off so easily.

''Next year I'll make partner. We're on our way, Maggie.''

''On our way to what?'' She pulled out a matching bra and panties.

''You shouldn't have to do all this dangerous fieldwork. For God's sake, Maggie, you've got eight stinking years with the Bureau. You finally have the clout to be...I don't know, a supervisor, an instructor...something, anything else.''

''I enjoy what I do, Greg.'' She started to pull off the hideous gown, hesitated, then glanced over her shoulder. Greg threw his hands in the air and rolled his eyes.

''What? You want me to leave?'' His voice was filled with sarcasm, a hint of anger. ''Yes, maybe I should leave so you can invite your cowboy back.''

''He's not my cowboy.'' Maggie felt the anger color her cheeks.

''Is that why you haven't returned my calls? Is there something going on with you and Sheriff Hardbody?''

''Don't be ridiculous, Greg.'' She yanked off the gown and struggled into the panties. It hurt to bend, to lift her arms. She was grateful a bandage covered the unsightly stitches.

''Oh my God, Maggie.''

She spun around to find him staring at her wounded shoulder, a grimace contorting his handsome features. She couldn't help wondering whether it was disgust or concern. His eyes examined the rest of her body, finally resting on the scar below her breasts. Suddenly, she felt exposed and embarrassed, neither of which made sense. He was her husband, after all. Yet, she grabbed the gown and pressed it to her breasts.

''Not all of those are from last night,'' he said, the anger more prevalent than the concern. ''Why didn't you tell me?''

''Why didn't you notice?''

''So this is my fault?'' Again, the hands in the air. It was a gesture she recognized from when he practiced his summations. Perhaps it worked with jurors. To her, it was worthless melodrama, a simple technique to draw attention to himself. How dare he make her scars about him.

''It has nothing to do with you.''

''You're my wife. Your job leaves your body carved up. Why

shouldn't I be concerned?'' His fair complexion turned crimson with anger, large raspberry splotches that looked like a rash.

"You're not concerned. You're angry because I didn't tell you."

"Damn right I'm angry. Why didn't you tell me?"

She threw the gown aside, giving him a good look at the scar.

"This is from over a month ago, Greg," she said, tracing the scar that Stucky had left. "Most husbands would have noticed. But we don't even have sex anymore, so how could you notice? You haven't even noticed that I don't sleep next to you. That I spend most nights pacing. You don't care about me, Greg."

"This is ridiculous. How can you say I don't care about you? That's exactly why I want you to leave the Bureau."

"If you really cared, you'd understand how important my job is to me. No, you're more concerned about how I make you look. That's why you don't want me in the field. You want to be able to tell your friends and associates that I have some big FBI title, a huge office, a secretary to put you on hold. You want me to be able to wear sexy black cocktail dresses to your fancy attorney parties so you can show me off, and my hideous scars don't fit into that scenario. Well, this is me, Greg," she said with her hands on her hips, trying to ignore the chill on her naked body. "This is who I am. Maybe I just don't fit into your country-club life-style anymore."

He shook his head at her, like a father impatient with his errant child. She grabbed the crumpled gown again and smashed it against her breasts, suddenly feeling vulnerable, having exposed much more than her nakedness.

"Thank you for bringing my things," she said quietly, calmly. "Now, I want you to leave."

"Fine." He swung his arms into his trench coat. "Why don't we get together for lunch after you've cooled off."

"No, I want you to go back home."

He stared at her, his gray eyes going cold, his pursed lips stifling the angry words. She waited for his next onslaught, but he turned on his expensive, leather heels and stomped out.

Maggie collapsed onto the bed, the pain in her side only a minor contributor to her exhaustion. She barely heard the tap on the door but braced herself for the rest of Greg's fury. Instead, Nick came in, took one look at her and spun around.

"Sorry, I didn't realize you weren't dressed."

She glanced down, only now realizing she just wore under-pants and the thin gown carelessly pressed across her breasts, hardly covering anything. She looked up at him, checking to make sure his back was to her before she grabbed the bra and wrestled into it. The stabs in her side slowed her down.

"Actually, I should be the one to apologize," she said, adopting Greg's sarcasm. "It seems my scarred body repulses men."

She snatched a blouse from the pile and thrust her arms into it, then realized it was inside out. She whipped it off and tried again.

Nick glanced over his shoulder, but snapped back to his same position. "Jesus, Maggie, you should know by now that I'm the wrong one to say that to. I've been trying for days now to find one little thing about you that doesn't turn me on."

She heard the smile in his voice. Her fingers stopped at the buttons, a slight tremor making it difficult to continue as the heat crawled down her body. She stared at the back of him and won-dered how in the world Nick Morrelli could make her feel so sensuous, so alive without even looking at her.

"Anyway, I didn't mean to barge in on you," he said, "but there's a slight problem with bringing in Father Keller for ques-tioning."

"I know, I know. We don't have enough evidence."

"No, that's not it." Another glance to see if it was safe. Mag-gie had her trousers halfway up, but he turned again to the door. She smiled at his caution. After all, he had already seen her in much less. She remembered the football jersey and his soft, com-fortable robe.

"If it's not evidence, what's the problem?" she asked.

"I just called the rectory and talked to the cook. Father Keller is gone and so is Ray Howard."

CHAPTER 100

As soon as they got off the elevator Timmy noticed the sign that read Restricted Area—Hospital Personnel Only. Father Keller didn't seem to notice the sign. He walked down the hallway without even hesitating, as if he had been down here many times before.

Timmy tried to keep up, although his ankle still hurt. It almost hurt more after the doctor wrapped it in all that elastic stuff, so tight Timmy was sure it was adding more bruises.

Father Keller glanced down at him, only now noticing the limp.

"What happened to your leg?"

"I guess I sprained my ankle last night in the woods."

Timmy didn't want to think about it, didn't want to remember. Every time he remembered, that terrible knot returned inside his stomach. Without much prompting, he knew the shivers would start again.

"You've been through quite a lot, huh?" The priest stopped, patted Timmy on the head. "You want to talk about it?"

"No, not really," Timmy said without looking up. Instead, he stared at his own brand-new Nikes. Air Nikes, the cool expensive kind. Uncle Nick had given them to him this morning.

Father Keller didn't insist, didn't ask more questions like the rest of the adults. Timmy was getting tired of all the questions. Everybody—Deputy Hal, the reporters, the doctor, Uncle Nick, Grandpa—everybody wanted to know about the little room, the stranger, his escape. He just didn't want to think about it anymore.

Father Keller pushed open a door and flipped a light switch. The huge room grew bright as the lights flickered on, one at a time.

"Wow, this does look like on *The X-Files*," Timmy said, running his fingers over the spotless counters, stainless steel just like the table in the center of the room. His eyes jumped around the assortment of odd equipment and tools neatly placed on trays. Then he noticed the drawers, lined up side by side in the opposite wall. "Is that..." He pointed. "Is that where they keep the dead people?"

"Yes, it is," Father Keller said, but he seemed distracted. He carefully placed the duffel bag on the metal table.

"Is Father Francis in one of the drawers?" Timmy whispered, then felt stupid. After all, nobody could hear them.

"Yes, unless they have already picked up his body."

"Picked up?"

"The mortuary may have already picked up Father Francis and taken him to the airport."

"The airport?" Timmy was confused. He'd never heard of dead bodies traveling on planes.

"Yes, remember I told you I was taking Father Francis to his burial place?"

"Oh, okay." Timmy scanned the countertops again, this time paying more attention. He came in for a closer look, tempted to touch but keeping his hands at his sides. Some of the tools were sharp, some long and narrow with teeth. One of them looked like a miniature chain saw. He'd never seen such odd tools before. He tried to imagine what each one did.

"I heard your father is back in town," Father Keller said, standing stiff and still next to the table.

"Yeah, I'm hoping he'll stay," Timmy said with only half a glance at the priest. There were too many interesting vials, test tubes, even a microscope. Maybe he would ask for a microscope for his birthday.

"Really? You'd like your father to stay?"

"Yeah, I guess I would."

"Wasn't he mean to you?"

Timmy looked at Father Keller. The question surprised him,

and he wondered what Father Keller meant, but the priest unzipped the duffel bag and was immediately preoccupied by its contents.

"How do you mean?" Timmy finally asked.

"Didn't he hurt you?" Father Keller said without looking up. "Didn't he do unpleasant things to you?"

Timmy wasn't sure what unpleasant things were. He knew he wore that scrunched look on his face that automatically happened when he was confused. He could hear his mom saying, "Don't look at me like that, or your face will stick that way." He tried to wipe it away before Father Keller noticed, but the priest was busy digging in the bag.

"My dad was mostly nice to me. Sometimes I guess he yelled."

"What about your bruises?"

Timmy felt his face grow warm with embarrassment. But, thankfully, Father Keller still didn't look up. "I guess I just bruise easily. Most of 'em are from soccer." Soccer and Chad Calloway.

"Then why did your mom make him go away?" Father Keller's voice surprised Timmy. Suddenly, it was low with a hint of anger while his eyes stayed focused inside the bag.

Timmy didn't want to make Father Keller mad. He heard the clink of metal and wondered what kind of tools Father Keller had in the bag.

"I don't know for sure why my mom made him leave. I think it had something to do with a slutty, big-breasted receptionist," Timmy said, trying to use the exact words he had overheard his mom use.

This time Father Keller did look up at him, only the piercing blue eyes sent a shiver through Timmy. Usually, Father Keller's eyes were kind and warm. But now...those eyes...no, it couldn't be. Timmy's stomach churned. He felt sick, tasted the sourness backing up into his mouth. He resisted the urge to throw up. The shivers started in his fingertips. One slid down his back. He felt dizzy.

"Timmy, are you okay?" Father Keller asked, and suddenly his cold eyes warmed with concern. "I'm sorry if I upset you."

The panic settled, sliding back down Timmy's throat and resting like a lump in his stomach. He never left Father Keller's eyes, mesmerized by the drastic change in them. Or had he imagined it all?

"Timmy," Father Keller said softly. "Do you think your mom and dad will get back together? Do you think you can be a real family again?"

Timmy swallowed hard, making sure the icky taste and feeling were gone for good. His stomach still ached. Maybe it was eating the candy bar on an empty stomach.

"I hope so," he answered. "I miss my dad. We used to go camping sometimes. Just the two of us. He'd let me bait my own hook. We'd talk and stuff. It was pretty cool. Except my dad's an awful cook."

Father Keller smiled at him now as he zipped up the duffel bag without ever taking anything out.

"Here you two are," Grandpa Morrelli said, swinging open the door to the morgue and startling both Timmy and Father Keller. "Nurse Richards thought she saw the elevator go down here. What are you two up to?"

His grandpa smiled at them while bracing the door open and staying in the doorway. His hands were filled with bags, all with the yellow Subway logo. Timmy could smell pastrami, vinegar and onion despite the overwhelming smell of cleaning solution in the room.

"Father Keller was just picking up Father Francis for their trip." Timmy checked the priest's face and was pleased to see the smile still there. Then to his grandpa, he said, "Doesn't this look like something from *The X-Files*?"

CHAPTER 101

Nick slowed his pace when he noticed the tight, pale look on Maggie's face. Of course, she was hurting and, of course, she wouldn't complain.

The Friday crowds had descended upon Eppley Airport. Business men and women hurried to get home. Fall vacationers and those getting away for the weekend moved more slowly, dragging too many pieces of home to really get away.

Mrs. O'Malley, St. Margaret's cook, had told Nick that Father Keller's flight left at two forty-five, and that he was escorting Father Francis' body to its final resting place. When Nick had asked to speak with Ray Howard, she said Ray was gone, too.

"I haven't seen that one since breakfast," she had told Nick. "He's always sneaking off somewhere, saying it's for Father Keller, but I never know when to believe him." Then she added in a whisper, "He's sneaky."

Nick had tried to ignore her extra comments. He had been in a hurry and not interested in the seventy-two year old's paranoia. Instead, he had tried to keep her focused and on the facts.

"Where is Father Francis being buried?"

"A place somewhere in Venezuela."

"Venezuela! Jesus." Mrs. O'Malley must have never heard the "Jesus," or Nick was certain she would have lectured him on using the Lord's name in vain.

"Father Francis absolutely loved it there," she had offered, glad to be the expert, to have and hold Nick's attention. "It was his first assignment out of seminary. A small, poor farming parish. I don't remember the name. Yes, Father Francis always talked about all those beautiful, brown-skinned children, and how some day he hoped to return. Too bad it couldn't have been under different circumstances.''

"Do you remember what city it was close to?" Nick had interrupted.

"No, I can't say that I remember. All those places down there are so hard to remember, hard to pronounce. Father Keller will be back next week. Can't this wait until then?"

"No, I'm afraid it can't. What about the flight number or airline?"

"Oh my, I don't know if he said. Maybe TWA...no, United, I think. It leaves at two forty-five out of Eppley," she added, as if that should be all that was necessary.

Now Nick glanced at his watch. It was almost two-thirty. He and Maggie split up at the ticket counters, flashing credentials and badges to shove their way through the lines and hurry the desk clerks.

The tall woman at the TWA counter refused to be rushed by a county sheriff's badge. Nick wished he had Maggie's FBI influence. Instead, he used his smile and a little flattery. The woman's rigid expression slowly softened, though it was hard to see the change. Her hair was pulled back so tightly into a neat little bun that it made all her features look severe, stretched and pinned down. Perhaps that was also what made her lips so thin, barely moving when she talked.

"I'm sorry, Sheriff Morrelli. I cannot disclose our passenger list or information about any of our passengers. Please, you're holding up the line."

"Okay, okay. How about flights? Do you have a flight to anywhere in Venezuela, say in..." He glanced at his watch again. "In ten to fifteen minutes?"

She checked her computer screen, taking time despite the heavy sighs and shuffling coming from the line behind him.

"We have a flight to Miami that connects with an international flight to Caracas."

"Great! What gate?"

"Gate 11, but that flight left at two-fifteen."

"Are you sure?"

"Quite sure. The weather is excellent. All our flights are running on schedule.'' She looked around him at a short, gray-haired man, anxious to hand off his ticket.

"Can you check to see if a coffin was on that flight?'' Nick asked, refusing to budge despite an elbow in his back.

"I beg your pardon?''

"A coffin, as in a dead body.'' He could feel the eyes around him, now staring, now interested. "It would be considered cargo. I'm sure I wouldn't be infringing on its rights.'' He tried another smile. From behind him, someone giggled.

The ticket clerk wasn't pleased. The thin lips drew even tighter. "I still cannot divulge that information. Now, if you'll step aside.''

"You know I can get a court order and be back later this afternoon.'' No more Mr. Nice Guy. He was quickly losing his patience and time was slipping away.

"Perhaps that would be a good idea. Next, who was next, please?'' she said, stepping aside when Nick wouldn't, so she could help the elderly man behind him in line. The man shoved his way to the counter, shooting Nick a look filled with anger and impatience.

Nick moved over to stand near where Maggie talked to another ticket agent.

"Thanks, anyway,'' she told the desk clerk at the United counter, then followed him to a corner out of the traffic.

She looked drained, even more pale, if that was possible. He wanted to ask if she was okay, but had already gotten three or four "I'm fine's'' on the drive to the airport.

"TWA has a flight to Miami that connects to one that goes on to Caracas,'' Nick told her, watching her face.

"Let's go. What gate?'' But she didn't move, leaning against the wall as if to catch her breath.

"It left about twenty minutes ago.''

"We missed it? Was Keller on board?''

"The desk clerk wouldn't tell me. We may need a court order to find out. What do we do now? Is it worth going down there, trying to catch him before the connecting flight leaves? If he gets to South America we may never find him. Maggie?''

Was she even listening? It wasn't the pain that distracted her. Her eyes were focused over his shoulder.

"Maggie?" He tried again.

"I think I just found Ray Howard."

CHAPTER 102

Maggie recognized the confusion in Nick's face. She felt a bit of her own stuck somewhere down between her throat and chest. Confusion bordered on frustration, or perhaps frustration bordered on panic.

"Maybe he simply brought Father Keller to the airport," Nick said in a low, quiet voice, though Howard was clear across the ticket lobby, far from overhearing.

"I usually don't take along luggage when I drop people off at the airport," Maggie said.

The large gray and black duffel bag looked heavy, making Howard's limp more pronounced. He wore his usual uniform of well-pressed brown trousers, white shirt and tie. A navy blazer replaced the cardigan.

"Tell me again why he isn't a suspect?" Nick asked without taking his eyes off Howard.

Suddenly, Maggie couldn't remember any of her reasons. Finally, she said, "The limp. Remember the boys may have been carried into the woods. And Timmy was sure the guy didn't limp."

They watched Howard stop to examine the flight-schedule board, then head for the escalators.

"I don't know, Maggie. That duffel bag sure looks heavy."

"Yes, it does," she said, and hurried toward the escalators with Nick alongside.

Howard hesitated at the down escalator, waiting to get his footing right before stepping on.

"Mr. Howard," Maggie called out.

Howard looked over his shoulder, grabbed the railing and did a double take. This time a flash of panic appeared in his lizard eyes. He jumped onto the escalator and ran down the moving steps, clearing a path with the duffel bag, striking and pushing people out of the way.

"I'll take the stairs." Nick raced for the emergency exit.

Maggie followed Howard, ripping her revolver from its holster and holding it nose up.

"FBI!" she yelled, clearing her own path.

Howard's speed surprised her. He weaved through the crowd, zigzagging around luggage gurneys and leaping over an abandoned pet carrier. He shoved travelers aside, knocking down a small, blue-haired lady and smashing through a group of Japanese tourists. He kept looking back at Maggie, his mouth open to breathe, his forehead glistening with sweat.

She was closing in on him, though her own breathing disappointed her. The ragged gasps sounded as if they were coming from a ventilator, surely not her own chest. She ignored the flame in her side, burning her flesh once again.

Howard stopped suddenly, grabbed a luggage cart from a stunned flight attendant and shoved it at Maggie. The suitcases snapped free. One burst open, spewing cosmetics, shoes, clothes and assorted unmentionables across the floor. Maggie skidded on a pair of lace panties, lost her balance and fell into the mess, smashing a bottle of liquid makeup with her knee.

Howard headed for the parking garage, smiling over his shoulder. He was almost to the door, hugging the duffel bag, his gait finally staggered by the limp. He pushed open the door just as Nick grabbed his jacket collar and swung him around. Howard fell to his knees and covered his head with his arms as if expecting a blow. Nick's hands, however, never left Howard's collar.

Maggie struggled to her feet while the flight attendant scrambled for her belongings. Nick's eyes were filled with concern for Maggie, even as his hands clutched Howard's collar, rendering him immobile.

"I'm fine," Maggie said before he asked. But when she replaced her revolver, she felt the sticky wetness through her blouse. Her fingertips were smeared with blood when she brought her hand out from inside her jacket.

"Jesus, Maggie." Nick noticed immediately. Howard did, too, and he smiled. "What are you doing here, Ray?" Nick responded, tightening his grip and turning Howard's smile into a grimace.

"I brought Father Keller. He had a flight to catch. Why were you chasing me? I didn't do nothing wrong."

"Then why did you run?"

"Eddie told me to watch out for you two."

"Eddie did?"

"What's in the duffel bag?" Maggie interrupted the two of them.

"I don't know. Father Keller said he wouldn't be needing it anymore. He asked me to take it back for him."

"You mind if we take a peek?" She pried it out of his hands. His resisting arrest justified a search. The bag was heavy. She swung it up onto a nearby chair, stopped, then leaned against a pay phone until the faintness passed.

"You sure it's not your bag?" she said, grabbing the familiar brown cardigan and several well-pressed white shirts. Howard's face registered surprise.

A stack of art books accounted for the bag's weight. Maggie put them aside, more interested in the small, carved box tucked between several pairs of boxer shorts. The carved words on the lid were Latin, but she had no idea what they said. The contents didn't surprise her: a white linen cloth, a small crucifix, two candles and a small container of oil. She glanced up at Nick and watched his eyes examine the contents, his confusion replaced with frustration. Then Maggie reached underneath the pile of newspaper clippings to the bottom of the box. She pulled out a small pair of boy's underpants tightly wrapped around a shiny fillet knife.

CHAPTER 103

Sunday, November 2

Maggie punched another code into the computer and waited. Her laptop's modem was excruciatingly slow. She took another bite of her blueberry muffin, homemade, special delivery from— where else?—Wanda's. The computer screen still read "initializing modem." She sat down and looked around the hotel room, her foot tapping nervously, impatiently, but not making the computer work any faster.

Her bags were packed. She had showered and dressed hours ago, but her flight didn't leave until noon. She rubbed her stiff neck and still couldn't believe she had slept the entire night in the straight-backed chair. Even more surprised that she had slept through the night without visions of Albert Stucky dancing in her head.

Bored, she grabbed the huge Sunday edition of the *Omaha Journal*. The headlines only added to her frustration. However, she was glad to see Christine's byline back on the front page. Even from her hospital bed, Christine continued to crank out articles. At least she and Timmy were safe and sound.

Maggie scanned the article once again. Christine's writing now stuck to the facts, letting quotes from the experts draw the sensational conclusions. She found her own quote and read it for the third time.

Special Agent Maggie O'Dell, an FBI profiler assigned to the case, said it was "unlikely Gillick and Howard were partners. Serial killers," Agent O'Dell insisted, "are loners." However, the district attorney's office has filed murder charges against both former sheriff's deputy Eddie Gillick, and a church janitor, Raymond Howard, for the deaths of Aaron Harper, Eric Paltrow, Danny Alverez and Matthew Tanner. A separate charge has been entered for the kidnapping of Timmy Hamilton.

There was a tap at the door. Maggie tossed the paper aside and checked the computer screen again. "Redialing first number", flashed across the screen along with the low hum and a succession of beeps. It was Sunday morning. Why was it taking so long to make the connection?

On the way to the door, she checked her watch. He was early. They didn't need to leave for the airport for another thirty to forty minutes.

As soon as she opened the door, the uninvited flutter arrived. Nick stood smiling at her, the dimples in full force. Strands of hair fell across his forehead. His blue eyes sparkled at her as if there was a special secret his eyes shared with hers. He wore a red T-shirt and blue jeans, both tight enough to outline his athletic body, teasing her eyes and making her fingers ache to touch him. Why did he have this effect on her? she wondered as they exchanged hellos, and he came into the room. She caught herself checking out his backside, shook her head and silently chastised herself.

"It must be warm out," she heard herself say. Yes, resort to the weather. That seemed safe, considering the electrical current he had just brought into the room.

"It's hard to believe we had snow a few days ago. Nebraska weather." He shrugged. "Here, this is for you." He handed her a gift-wrapped box that had escaped her notice. "Sort of a thank-you, slash, goodbye present."

Her first inclination was to decline, to say it was inappropriate and leave it at that. But she took it and slowly unwrapped it, acutely aware of him watching her. She pulled out the red football jersey with a white number seventeen emblazoned on the back. She couldn't help but smile.

"It's perfect."

"I don't expect it to replace the Packers," he said with just a trace of embarrassment in his voice. "But I thought you should have a Nebraska Cornhuskers, too."

"Thanks. I love it."

"Seventeen was my number," he added.

Suddenly, the simple cotton jersey took on a greater significance. Her eyes met his, and without meaning it to, her smile disappeared as she combated the annoying flutter. However, he was the first to look away, and she saw a flicker of discomfort. It was times like this that he surprised her most, when the arrogant, self-assured bachelor showed just a hint of the irresistible, shy, sensitive man.

"Oh, and this is from Timmy."

She took the videotape, and as soon as she saw the cover, her smile returned. *"The X-Files."*

"He said that it has one of his favorite episodes—the one with the killer cockroaches, of course."

With no more gifts to keep his hands preoccupied, he shoved them into his pockets.

"I'll be sure to watch and...and I'll let Timmy know what I think," she said, surprised but pleased by the unfamiliar commitment to stay in touch.

They stood there staring at each other. Maggie didn't want to move, couldn't move. They had spent the last week together, almost around the clock, sharing pizza and brandy, exchanging opinions and views, wrestling madmen and holy men, dousing fears and expectations and grieving for small boys neither of whom they knew. She had allowed Nick Morrelli access to vulnerabilities she had shared with no one else, not even herself. Perhaps that was why she suddenly felt as if a major chunk of herself would be left behind. And, of all places, in a small Nebraska town she had never even heard of before. What had happened to the cool, aloof FBI agent who maintained her professionalism at whatever the cost?

"Maggie, I—"

"I'm sorry," she interrupted, not prepared for what might be a revelation of feelings. "I almost forgot. I'm trying to access some information.'' She escaped to the table in the corner. The computer connection had finally been made, and she punched several more keys, immediately annoyed by the unwarranted tremble in her fingers and the shortness of breath.

''You're still looking for him,'' he said without surprise or irritation, coming up behind her, too close to allow her normal breathing to resume.

''From Caracas, Father Francis' body was shipped by truck to a small community about a hundred miles to the south. Keller's airline ticket has him returning today. I'm trying to find out if he boarded the flight back to Miami or if he headed somewhere else.''

''It amazes me the information you can access.''

She felt him lean forward to examine the screen.

''At the airport,'' he continued, ''I remember thinking how nice it would be to have FBI credentials instead of my measly sheriff's badge. I was way out of my jurisdiction.''

''I certainly hope you aren't still worried about looking incompetent?''

''No. Actually, no, I'm not,'' he said, sounding like he definitely meant it.

Finally, the passenger list for TWA flight 1692 materialized on the screen. Maggie easily found Reverend Michael Keller's name, and it was on the list even after departure.

''Just because he's on the list doesn't mean he was on the plane.''

''I know that.'' She scooted out from between the computer and Nick before turning to face him.

''So what happens if he doesn't come back?''

''I'll find him,'' she said simply. ''What is that saying? He can run, but he can't hide.''

''Even if you find him, we don't have a shred of evidence to implicate him.''

''Do you honestly believe Eddie Gillick or Ray Howard killed those boys?''

He hesitated, glanced back at the computer, then around the room, stopping at her suitcases before returning to her.

''I'm not sure what part, if any, Eddie may have played in the murders. But you know I suspected Howard from the beginning.

Come on, Maggie. We found him at the airport with what could be the murder weapon.''

She frowned at him and shook her head. "He doesn't fit the profile.''

"Maybe not, but you know what? I don't want to spend my last hour with you talking about Eddie Gillick or Ray Howard or Father Keller or anything to do with this case.''

He approached slowly, cautiously. She nervously pushed her hair away from her face. Tucked a stubborn strand behind her ear. The look in his eyes made the tremble invade her fingers again, and the flutter raced from her stomach to between her thighs.

He touched her face gently, holding her eyes with an intensity that made her feel as though she was the only woman in the world—at least, for the moment. She could easily have stopped the kiss, had meant to when he first leaned down. But when his lips brushed hers, all her energy focused on keeping her knees from buckling. When she didn't protest, his mouth caught hers in a wet, soft kiss filled with so much urgency and emotion that she felt certain the room was spinning. Even after his mouth left hers, she kept her eyes closed, trying to steady her breathing, trying to stop the spinning.

"I love you, Maggie O'Dell.''

Her eyes flew open. His face was still close to hers, his eyes serious. She saw a bit of boyish apprehension and knew how hard those words had been to say. She pulled away, only now realizing that, other than his fingers on her face and his mouth on hers, he hadn't touched her anywhere else. Which made her retreat disappointingly easy.

"Nick, we barely know each other.'' It was still hard to breathe. How could one simple kiss take her breath so completely away?

"I've never felt this way before, Maggie. And it's not just because you're unavailable. It's something I can't even explain.''

"Nick...''

"Please, just let me finish.''

She waited, braced herself and leaned against the dresser. The same dresser she had clung to the night they had come so dangerously close to making love.

"I know it's only been a week, but I can assure you, I'm not impulsive when it comes to...well, sex, yes, but not this...not love. I've never felt this way before. And I've certainly never told a woman I loved her before.''

It sounded like a line, but she knew from his eyes that it was true. She opened her mouth to speak, but he raised a hand to stop her.

''I don't expect anything I say to compromise your marriage. But I didn't want you to leave without knowing, just in case it did make a difference. And I guess even if it doesn't, I still want you to know that I...that I am madly, deeply, hopelessly, head over heels in love with you, Maggie O'Dell.''

It was his turn to wait. She couldn't speak. Her fingers clawed at the dresser top, keeping her from going to him and wrapping her arms around him.

''I don't know what to say.''

''You don't have to say anything.'' His eyes told her he meant it.

''I obviously have feelings for you.'' She struggled with the words. She hated the thought of never seeing him again. But what did she know about being in love? Hadn't she been in love with Greg, once upon a time? Hadn't she vowed to love him forever?

''Things are really complicated right now,'' she heard herself say and wanted to kick herself. He had opened his heart to her, taken such a risk, and here she was being practical and rational.

''I know,'' he said. ''But maybe they won't always be complicated.''

''It does make a difference, Nick,'' she said, making a feeble attempt at correcting her ambiguity.

He seemed relieved by that simple revelation, as though it was more than he had ever hoped for.

''You know,'' he said, sounding more comfortable while her heart screamed at her to tell him how she felt. ''You've helped me see a lot of things about myself, about life. I've been following in these huge, deep footsteps my father keeps leaving behind and...and I don't want to do that anymore.''

''You're a good sheriff, Nick.'' She ignored the tug at her heart. Maybe it was better this way.

''Thanks, but it's not what I want,'' he continued. ''I admire how much your job means to you. Your dedication—your stubborn dedication, I might add. I never realized before how much I want something like that, something to believe in.''

"So what does Nick Morrelli want to be when he grows up?'' she asked, smiling at him when she really wanted to touch him.

"When I was in law school I worked at the Suffolk County district attorney's office in Boston. They always said I was welcome to come back. It's been a long time, but I think I might give them a call.''

Boston. So close, she couldn't help thinking.

"That sounds great,'' she said, already calculating the miles between Quantico and Boston.

"I'm going to miss you,'' he said simply.

His words caught her off guard, just when she thought she was safe. He must have seen the panic in her eyes, because he quickly checked his watch.

"I should get you to the airport.''

"Right.'' Their eyes met again. One last tug, one last chance to tell him. Or would there be plenty of chances?

She brushed past him and closed down the computer, unplugging cords, snapping the lid shut and shoving the computer into its case. He grabbed her suitcase. She grabbed her garment bag. They were at the door when the phone rang. At first, she thought about ignoring it and leaving. Suddenly, she hurried back and grabbed the receiver.

"Maggie O'Dell.''

"O'Dell, I'm glad I caught you.''

It was Director Cunningham. She hadn't talked to him in days. "I was just on my way out.''

"Good. Get back here as quickly as possible. I'm having Delaney and Turner meet you at the airport.''

"What's going on?'' She glanced at Nick, who came back into the room, his face filled with concern. "You make it sound like I need bodyguards,'' she joked, then tensed when his silence lasted too long.

"I wanted you to know before you hear it on the news.''

"Hear what?''

"Albert Stucky has escaped. They were transferring him from Miami to a maximum-security facility in North Florida. Stucky ended up biting the ear off one guard and stabbing the other with—get this—a wooden crucifix. Then he blew both their heads off with their own service revolvers. Seems the day before, a Catholic priest visited Stucky in his cell. He had to be the one who left the crucifix. I don't want you to worry, Maggie. We got the bastard before, we'll get him again.''

But the only thing Maggie heard was, ''Albert Stucky has escaped.''

EPILOGUE

One week later
Chíuchín, Chile

He couldn't believe how glorious the sun felt. His bare feet maneuvered the rocky shore. The minor cuts and scrapes were a small price to pay for the feel of the warm waves lapping at his feet. The Pacific Ocean stretched forever, its water rejuvenating, its power overwhelming.

Behind him, the mountains of Chile isolated this paradise, where poor, struggling farmers were as starved for attention as they were for salvation. The tiny parish included fewer than fifty families. It was perfect. Since he'd arrived, he hardly noticed the throbbing in his head. Perhaps it was gone for good this time.

A group of brown-skinned boys, clad only in shorts, chased a ball while they raced toward him. Two of them recognized him from the morning's mass. They waved and called out to him. He laughed at their mispronunciation of his name. When they gathered around him, he petted their black hair and smiled down at them. The one with the torn, blue shorts had such sad eyes, reminding him of himself.

"My name," he instructed, "is Father Keller. Not Father Killer."

A GREAT READ GUARANTEED

We are so confident that you will love this book that we are offering a 100% money-back guarantee!*

If you are not satisfied for whatever reason MIRA® Books** will refund the amount you have paid (as shown on receipt) in full. Simply fill in the form below and send us a **copy of your receipt**, along with a stamped, self-addressed envelope to*:

MIRA® Guaranteed Read,
PO Box 676, Richmond, Surrey TW9 1WU

A GREAT READ GUARANTEED   APE

Please send this form with a copy of your receipt and a stamped, self-addressed envelope to the address above. We will send you a cheque for the purchase price of the book within 4-6 weeks.

If you didn't enjoy this book, we'd really like to know why!

The book was not what I was expecting   ❏
The storyline did not hold my interest   ❏
I did not enjoy the characters   ❏
I did not think the book was good value for money   ❏

If you would like to give us more information, or if you have another reason, please let us know here:

_____
_____
_____

The fine line between good and evil is crossed in Alex Kava's

SPLIT SECOND

They dubbed him the Collector – so named for his ritual of collecting victims before disposing of them in the most heinous ways possible. Now Albert Stucky is on the loose again…

Criminal profiler Maggie O'Dell had been instrumental in putting this notorious killer away. Some say that, since then, she has lost her professional edge, tortured by nightmares and guilt for the ones she couldn't save.

But as the death toll increases, Maggie becomes the FBI's best hope to hunt this man down. Only she can see into the psychopath's twisted mind, only she can catch him. Albert Stucky wouldn't have it any other way.

A chilling, unflinching portrait of the human psyche pushed past its limits. A bold look at the nature of good and evil in all of us.

www.alexkava.co.uk

Maggie O'Dell confronts a new face of evil in Alex Kava's

THE SOUL CATCHER

A group of young men commit suicide in a secluded cabin. A senator's daughter is found strangled. Two seemingly unrelated cases. Both assigned to expert criminal profiler Maggie O'Dell.

As she delves deeper, it seems there is a connection – Reverend Joseph Everett, a charismatic leader of a religious sect who's attracted both rebellious teens and the lonely middle-aged into his fold.

Maggie's involvement becomes personal when she realises a member of her own family has been seduced by Everett's slick illusions. But the soul catcher wears many faces and the case is nowhere near as simple as it seems…

<u>www.alexkava.co.uk</u>

MIRA®

The new bestseller from

ALEX KAVA

AT THE
STROKE OF
MADNESS

A Maggie O'Dell novel

MIRA®

INTERNATIONAL BESTSELLING SENSATION

ALEX KAVA

NO TRESPASSING

Everything can be lost with . . .

ONE FALSE MOVE

MIRA®

M380

From the *New York Times* bestselling author
TESS GERRITSEN comes a plot that
will make you scream...

ISBN 1-55166-834-3

A ringing phone in the middle of the night shakes
newlywed Sarah Fontaine awake and brings the news that
her husband of two months has died in a hotel fire...in
Berlin. Convinced he is still alive, Sarah becomes
embroiled in the clandestine world of international espi-
onage, risking everything for answers that may prove fatal.

'Tess Gerritsen writes some of the smartest, most
compelling thrillers around' –*Bookreporter*

On sale 20th May 2005

New York Times **bestselling author
Diana Palmer introduces her most
mesmerising hero yet...**

ISBN 0–7783–0087–0

**It was in Paris she first saw him...
It was in Paris she fell in love.**

Obsessed with Brianne Martin since their first meeting,
her stepfather's corrupt business associate would stop at
nothing in his relentless pursuit of her, including master-
minding a marriage to merge their powerful families. All
seemed lost until tall, handsome and utterly dangerous
Pierce Hutton saved Brianne's life...as she'd once saved his.

On sale 20th May 2005

MIRA
An international collection of bestselling authors

EVER AFTER
by Fiona Hood-Stewart

"An enthralling page turner—
not to be missed." —*New York Times*
bestselling author Joan Johnston

**She belongs to a world of wealth,
politics and social climbing. But
now Elm must break away to find
happily ever after...**

Elm MacBride can no longer sit back and
watch her corrupt and deceitful husband's
ascent to power and his final betrayal sends her
fleeing to Switzerland where she meets
Irishman Johnny Graney. When her husband's
actions threaten to destroy her, Johnny must
save not only their love but Elm's life...

ISBN 07783 2078 2

Published 15th April 2005